Little,
Brown
Canada

BY THE SAME AUTHOR

WILLIAM TREVOR

TWO LIVES

READING TURGENEV
and
MY HOUSE IN UMBRIA

Little, Brown and Company (Canada) Limited

Boston • London • Toronto

For Jane

First Canadian Edition
Published in 1991 by Little, Brown and Company
(Canada) Limited
Second Printing 1995

PUBLISHER'S NOTE
This is a work of fiction. Names, characters, places, and incidents
either are the product of the author's imagination or are used
fictitiously, and any resemblance to actual persons, living or
dead, events, or locales is entirely coincidental.

Canadian Cataloguing in Publication Data
Trevor, William, 1928-
Two lives
1st Canadian ed.
ISBN 0-316-43384-5
I. Title.
PR6070.R4T8 1991   823'.914   C91-095564-6

Little, Brown and Company (Canada) Limited
148 Yorkville Ave
Toronto, Ontario
M5R 1C2

TWO LIVES

Two Lives

William Trevor is "one of the finest writers of fiction now at work in our language" (*The Boston Globe*). In *Two Lives* he has given us two books in one: two brilliant complementary full-length novels that illuminate the lives of two women, each irrevocably marked by the loss or absence of love.

The first of these narratives, *Reading Turgenev*, tells the story of Mary Louise Dallon, a country girl forced into a loveless marriage with a smug shopkeeper from the nearby small town. Desperately lonely, mistreated by her sisters-in-law and neglected by her husband, she suddenly finds her life transfigured by a bookish young man who reads her the novels of Turgenev during their trysts in a deserted country churchyard. But the transfiguration is fleeting—and tragedy lies ahead.

My House in Umbria is as intriguing and unsettling as *Reading Turgenev* is lyrical and tragic: a kind of psycho-autobiographical striptease performed by a mysterious and not entirely trustworthy former madam—Mrs. Emily Delahunty, a.k.a. Gloria Grey or Janine Ann Johns—who now runs a *pensione* in the Italian countryside. Here she muses on her past—her abused childhood in an English seaside town, her years in an African brothel—and writes romance novels; until one day the train she is riding is blown up by a terrorist bomb. Taken to a local hospital to recuperate, she befriends the other survivors—an elderly English general, an American child, and a German boy—and takes them all to convalesce at her villa, with surprising results.

Taken together, these two novels explore the twin faces of love and madness, loss and regeneration; and they illuminate the interplay of truth and fiction. But most important, they demonstrate unequivocally William Trevor's astonishing range as a writer—his humor, his subtlety, his knowing and compassionate grasp of the ways in which human beings evade and come back to themselves.

WILLIAM TREVOR was born in Ireland's County Cork in 1928. A graduate of Trinity College, Dublin, he has made his home for some years in England. He is the author of eighteen books, including *Fools of Fortune* and, most recently, the novel *The Silence in the Garden* and the short-story collection *Family Sins*. Among the awards he has received are the Whitbread Prize for Fiction (twice) and *The Hudson Review*'s Bennett Award.

READING TURGENEV

1

A woman, not yet fifty-seven, slight and seeming frail, eats carefully at a table in a corner. Her slices of buttered bread have been halved for her, her fried egg mashed, her bacon cut. 'Well, this is happiness!' she murmurs aloud, but none of the other women in the dining-room replies because none of them is near enough to hear. She's privileged, the others say, being permitted to occupy on her own the bare-topped table in the corner. She has her own salt and pepper.

'Hurry now.' Appearing from nowhere, Miss Foye curtly interrupts the woman's private thought. 'You have a visitor waiting.'

'Would be Peter Martyr.' Another woman, overhearing the news about a visitor, makes this suggestion, but at once there's a general objection. Why should the visitor be identified so since the lone woman wouldn't lift a hand to take the knife from his head, Peter Martyr not being of her religion?

'Heretic!' a voice calls out.

'Heathen,' another mutters.

The woman who eats alone pays no attention. They mean no harm; they are not against her; in their confusion they become carried away. But since she has been interrupted, she must make the best of things, she must consume the food: she will not be permitted into the visitor's presence until her plate is clean. She swallows a forkful of egg and bacon pieces without chewing. Grease, congealed, adheres to her tongue and the roof of her mouth. If she vomits she will not be permitted into the visitor's presence. She rinses her mouth with tea. With her fingers she presses more buttered bread between her teeth. The others will tell on her if she does not eat all the bread. They will shout out and she'll have to march back to the table. She softens the bread with more tea and washes it away. She passes among the women.

'Tell me about the graveyard.' A tiny woman, wizen-faced, rises and walks with her, whispering. 'Tell me, darling, about the graveyard.'

'Sit down, Sadie,' Miss Foye commands. 'Leave her be.'

'She took off every stitch,' another voice accuses and is immediately contradicted: Bríd Beamish it was who took off every stitch, who walked the streets for profit.

'It's not our business.' Stately in grey, Miss Foye is brisk. This is her manner. She stands no nonsense. 'Hurry now,' she urges.

In the hall there is a disappointment. The visitor is not a stranger. He stands by the window, and speaks when Miss Foye has gone away. He states the purpose of his visit, all he says a repetition. 'Nowadays it's what's being done,' he explains, the opposite of anything in the old days: for months Miss Foye and the medicals have been saying it too. Those who have somewhere to go are better off in the community, that has been established. In other countries the change came years ago, Italy, America, places like that. We're always a bit behindhand here.

'Well, you have somewhere to go,' the man reminds her. 'No doubt about that, dear.'

'I thought you might be Insarov. When I heard I had a visitor I said to myself it must be Insarov. To tell the truth, I was interrupted at my supper.'

She smiles and nods, then walks away.

'No, come back,' her husband begs. 'They've asked me to go into it with you.'

Obediently she returns. He means no harm.

2

Mary Louise Dallon retained in her features the look of a child. In an oval face her blue eyes had a child's wide innocence. Her fair brown hair was soft, and curled without inducement. Her temperament remained untouched by sophistication. Once in her life she was told she was beautiful, but laughed when the statement was made: she saw ordinariness in her bedroom looking-glass.

In the schoolroom next to the Protestant church Miss Mullover had once taught Mary Louise, and would have retained a memory only of a lively child had it not been for the same child's sudden interest, at ten, in Joan of Arc – or Jeanne d'Arc, as Miss Mullover insisted upon. The saint was a source of such unusual fascination that Miss Mullover wondered for a while if the child possessed depths she had overlooked: an imagination that would one day bear fruit. But Mary Louise left the schoolroom with no greater ambition than to work in the local chemist's shop, Dodd's Medical Hall, and in that she was frustrated. Circumstances obliged her to stay at home, helping in the farmhouse.

In a different generation Miss Mullover had taught Elmer Quarry, who left her schoolroom to board at the Tate School in Wexford, nearly sixty miles away. The three Quarry children – Elmer and his sisters – came of a family that for many decades had been important in the town. The Dallons – out at Culleen – had struggled for as long to keep their heads above water.

In later years Miss Mullover observed from a distance the vicissitudes and worries that governed the family life of the Dallons, and the changeless nature of the Quarrys' domestic and mercantile routine. She noted that money meant as much to Elmer Quarry in his middle age as it had to his forebears, that generally he was as cautious as his father and his grandfather had been, that he abundantly enhanced the Quarry reputation for good sense and a Protestant order of priorities. In each generation for more than a century the inheritor of Quarry's drapery had married late in life, establishing himself in the business before he turned his thoughts to the securing of the line: the old house above the shop in Bridge Street had seen more than its share of young wives made widows before their time. So it was that in 1955 Elmer Quarry was still a bachelor and the only well-to-do Protestant for miles around. All over the county wealth had passed into the hands of a new Catholic middle class, changing the nature of provincial life as it did so.

The Dallons' roadside farmhouse in the townland of Culleen had never been more than modest, and in 1955 even that modesty was considerably eroded: the whitewashed rendering was here and there fallen away, slates that had slipped out of place or cracked in half had not been replaced, a pane in an upstairs window was broken. Within the farmhouse, rooms were in need of redecoration; paint had chipped, damp loosened the tattered wallpaper of the stairway, the unused dining-room smelt of must and soot. Five Dallons lived in the farmhouse – Mary Louise and her sister Letty, her brother James, and her mother and father.

Standing on the edge of the farm's twenty-seven acres, the house was three miles from the town where Quarry's drapery had prospered for so long. On Sundays, driving into the town in their black, obsolete Hillman, the Dallons formed almost a quarter of the Protestant congregation; at Christmas and

Easter the numbers swelled to thirty-three or -four. Elmer
Quarry and his sisters were church-goers only on these festive
occasions, but for the Dallons – especially for Mary Louise
and Letty – the weekly occasion of worship provided a social
outing they enjoyed.

The town was small, its population just over two and a half
thousand. A turf-brickette factory had been opened seven years
ago, where once there'd been a tannery. There was a ruined
mill, a railway station that was no longer in use, green-stained
warehouses on either side of the town's single bridge over its
sluggish river. Shops, public houses, the post office, council
offices, two banks, and other businesses offered employment,
as did Hogan's Hotel, three builders, a creamery, an egg-
packing station and an agricultural machinery depot. The Electric Cinema was a going concern in 1955; the Dixie dancehall
continued to attract Friday-night crowds. The Catholic church
– on the town's northern outskirts – was dedicated to the
Virgin as Queen of Heaven; a convent – halfway up the town's
only hill – was of the order of the Sacred Heart. Boys were
educated behind the silver-painted railings of the Christian
Brothers' School in Conlon Street, and St Fintan's vocational
college offered opportunities to acquire further skills. Bridge
Street, where the pink-washed Hogan's Hotel and the principal
shops were, was narrow and brief, becoming South West Street
beyond the bridge. The gaunt, grey steeple of the Protestant
church rose from a boundary of yew trees that isolated it from
its surroundings. A pocket of lanes around the gasworks and
Brown's Yard comprised the slums. A signpost – black letters
on a yellow ground – partially obscured a statue of Daniel
O'Connell and gave directions to Clonmel and Cappoquin,
Cahir and Carrick-on-Suir. People who lived in the town knew
it backwards; those from the surrounding neighbourhoods
sometimes regarded it with wonder.

Elmer Quarry first noticed that Mary Louise Dallon was an

agreeable-looking girl in January of the year in question. He was thirty-five then, Mary Louise twenty-one. Paunchy – and as square-looking as the origins of his name suggested – he was attired invariably in a nondescript suit, mud-coloured, faintly striped. His receding hair, cut short, matched this shade; his features were small and regular, a neat configuration in the pale plumpness of his face. Elmer Quarry was not a tall man, but bulky none the less, an entrepreneurial presence, as his father and grandfather had been before him. He was assisted in the drapery by his sisters, Matilda and Rose, both of them his senior by a few years and possessing a handsomeness that had been denied him. Neither had married and both were displeased when Elmer's glances were cast in the direction of Mary Louise Dallon. Why should the status quo in the house above the shop, and in the shop itself, be disturbed? Quarry's would sustain the three of them during their lifetime, withering, then dying, with the Protestants of the neighbourhood. Neither Rose nor Matilda was the kind to avoid facing the facts: already Quarry's was a relic from another age. If the line came to an end the business would pass to distant cousins in Athy, who would probably sell it.

The present Quarrys remembered the time when there were five assistants behind the counters, and an overhead railway network that linked the shop to the accounting office, carrying money and returning change in hollow wooden spheres. There were just the three Quarrys in the shop now; the overhead system had years ago been dismantled and removed. But the red receipt books were as they'd always been, stacked every evening by the tills that had been fitted. Elmer's father had entered the accounting office every day only after the shop had closed its doors, when the clerk who returned the change in the wooden containers had gone home. But since there was no clerk now and since Matilda and Rose managed easily behind the counters, Elmer increasingly spent more time in the accounting office. Often he sat there staring down through the small-paned floor-to-ceiling window into the quiet shop below, at the rolls of material stacked on the shelves – nylon, chintz and silk, cotton and linen – at the spools of thread in their shallow glass case, and the dresses and suits on the window dummies. As still as these window dummies his sisters sometimes seemed, one behind either counter, waiting for another customer. Matilda liked to be smart; Rose dressed drearily. Matilda had more of a manner with customers, the best manner of the three, Elmer knew. Rose preferred housework and cooking. He himself belonged more naturally with the ledgers.

The courtship began on 11 January 1955, a Tuesday. Elmer invited Mary Louise to the pictures the following Friday evening. He had no idea what was showing at the Electric, but he considered that didn't matter. Now and again, perhaps once a year, he and his sisters went to see a film because it had been talked about in the shop. He liked the News best himself, but Rose and Matilda enjoyed something light and musical. He naturally had to tell them he'd invited Mary Louise Dallon. They continued to look displeased, but did not comment.

In the Dallon household the invitation came as a considerable surprise. Mr and Mrs Dallon – a thin, grey pair in their fifties whose appearance was so similar that they might have been twins – recognized all that it implied, and were well aware of the habit among the Quarry men of marrying younger wives. They talked about it in the privacy of their bedroom. Mrs Dallon made a special journey to the town, visited Quarry's drapery, bought a spool of white thread, and reminded herself of what Elmer looked like by glimpsing him through the panes of the accounting-office window. It might have been worse, she reported to her husband on her return, and later – in their bedroom – they went on talking about the development.

Mary Louise's older sister, Letty, and her brother James, who was older also, did not react as favourably. James – impetuous, known to be of uncertain temper, and remembered from his schooldays as being a little slow – declared the invitation to be an affront. Elmer Quarry was a man who never laughed and rarely smiled, born to be a draper. Letty – secretly annoyed that her sister had been preferred, not that she'd have set foot in the Electric with Elmer Quarry even if he'd gone down on his knees – warned Mary Louise about what might occur under cover of darkness and advised her to keep handy a safety-pin that could be opened at a moment's notice. Some of Elmer Quarry's teeth were false, she declared, a fact she claimed to have culled in the waiting-room of the town's more reliable dentist, Mr McGreevy.

Mary Louise herself was terrified. When the invitation had come, Elmer Quarry following her out on the street to issue it, she blushed and became so agitated in her speech that she began to stammer. On her bicycle, all the way back to the farmhouse, she kept seeing Elmer Quarry's square shape, and the balding dome of his head when he'd bent down to pick up the glove she'd dropped. Letty had gone out with a man or two, with Gargan from the Bank of Ireland two years ago, with Billie Lyndon of the radio and electrical shop. She had thought Gargan was going to propose, but unfortunately he got promotion and was moved to Carlow. Billie Lyndon married the younger Hayes girl. Letty had taken to saying she wouldn't be bothered with that kind of thing any more, but Mary Louise knew it wasn't true. If Gargan came back for her she'd take him like a shot, and if anyone else who was half possible appeared on the scene she'd start dressing herself up again.

'What's showing?' Letty asked.

'He didn't say.'

'Hmm,' Letty said.

Beggars couldn't be choosers, Mr Dallon reflected in the end. To marry either of the girls into the Quarrys would mean you'd breathe more easily, and you'd see the sort of future for the two who were left. Mrs Dallon reached similar conclusions: provided James didn't marry, the farm would sustain himself and Letty, he working the fields and seeing to the milking, she attending to the fowls. The place was right for two, comfortable enough. Three of them left behind would be noticeable, touched with failure, although no one was to blame; a family growing old together was never a good thing, never a stable thing.

The film was called *The Flame and the Flesh* and Elmer did not in the least enjoy it. But he bought a carton of Rose's in the confectioner's shop next to the Electric, and at least there was the consolation of the chocolates, for he had a sweet tooth. When he offered Mary Louise the carton for the fifth time she shook her head and murmured something, which he took to mean she didn't want any more. He knew that girls had to watch their figures so he ate the remainder of the chocolates himself, removing the wrappings as quietly as he could in order not to cause a disturbance. The film was all about a woman in Italy, with a number of men interested. 'Wasn't the picture great?' Mary Louise enthused when the lights went up, and he agreed it had been.

It was a cold night. Outside the cinema he belted his overcoat and drew on tan leather gloves; he didn't wear a hat. He noticed that his companion's cheeks were flushed from the warmth of the cinema and that she'd put on a blue and white woollen cap, which matched her gloves. She'd have bought the wool in the shop, and he thought he could even remember looking down from the accounting office and seeing her choosing it, last summer it would have been.

'I'll walk you out a bit towards Culleen,' he said.

'Oh, no need, Mr Quarry. Thanks though.'

In the lane that ran by the side of the Electric there was an ungainly chain and padlock on her bicycle, which she undid and dropped into the basket that was attached to the handle-bars. When she leaned down to do this lamplight from the street fell on the back of her legs, and for the first time Elmer experienced physical desire where Mary Louise was concerned. Between the hem of her shabby blue coat and the tops of her boots the silk of her stockings gleamed in a way he found disturbing. Once or twice during the film his attention had been held by Lana Turner's low-cut bodices.

'Give me the bike to wheel,' he urged, ignoring Mary Louise's protest that there was no need to walk through the streets with her.

The Quarrys did not possess a car. Living in the centre of the town, there had never been a need for one, just as in the past there had been no need for a horse-drawn vehicle of any kind. A bus carried you out of the town and another one brought you back again in the evening. Every December, before Christmas, the Quarry sisters took it to do any seasonal shopping there was. Elmer didn't bother with that. In winter he played billiards in the YMCA billiard-room, a big coal fire blazing in the grate between two glass-fronted bookcases that held a library of good books: Wild West stories and detective yarns, adventure novels by Sapper and Leslie Charteris, the *Encyclopaedia Britannica*. Elmer often had the place to himself since not many turned up in the YMCA billiard-room these days, but the caretaker always had the fire going in winter, and copies of the *Geographical Magazine* and the *Illustrated London News* were always to hand. In summer Elmer went for walks – Bridge Street, South West Street, Boys' Lane, Father Mathew Street, Upton Road, home by Kilkelly's Garage.

Intent upon entertaining Mary Louise, and since they happened to pass the YMCA billiard-room, he retailed some

of the detail of these two long-established habits. If he possessed a car, he added, he naturally would have called at the
farmhouse for her and would now be driving her home in it.
Kilkelly often told him he should have a car. 'A man in your
position, Elmer,' was how Kilkelly – who had the Ford fran-
chise – put it, but Elmer did not quote this statement since it
sounded like showing off. Instead, he asked Mary Louise if
she had learned to drive the Hillman he often saw the Dallons
in, and she replied that she had. This fact Elmer noted; he was
interested in things like that.

'Well, I'll leave you here,' he said when they reached the
last bungalow that could claim to belong to the town. A full
moon cast a light as bright as daylight. The road sparkled
where frost had settled in its crevices. Hedges and verges were
already whitening; ice had formed in patches.

'Your light's all right, is it?' Elmer solicitously inquired.

Mary Louise tried it. A beam hardly showed up in the
moonlight. 'Thanks for everything,' she said.

'Would next week interest you?'

'Interest?'

'Friday again.' Elmer had once heard in the shop that girls
liked to wash their hair on Saturdays, and certainly both Rose
and Matilda did, once a fortnight. Thoughtfulness never hurt
anyone, his mother used to say, which was why he'd mentioned Friday. His own preference would have been Saturday,
since the feeling of relaxation, to do with the weekend, began
then. With the shop closed until Monday morning, and the
streets more active than on other evenings, Elmer often experienced on a Saturday night an urge to mark in some way the
difference there was. Usually, though, he just slipped down to
the YMCA and played a solitary game of billiards.

'Friday?' Mary Louise said.

'Is Friday convenient? Would Saturday be better?'

'No, Friday's all right.'

'Will we say half-seven?'

Mary Louise nodded. She mounted her bicycle and rode off. The safety-pin Letty had insisted upon had not been opened. He hadn't tried to hold her hand. Come to that, she thought, they hadn't even said good-night to one another. There was a kind of intimacy about saying good-night to a person, and both of them had been shy of it. In the Electric, before the lights went down, she'd noticed people looking at them. By this time tomorrow it would be all round the town.

'Are you in one piece?' Letty asked when her sister walked into the kitchen with the bicycle lamp in her hand. Their mother and father had gone to bed, but Mary Louise knew they wouldn't be sleeping. They'd have lain there waiting for the sound of the bicycle wheels and the clatter of the barn door and her footsteps on the cobbles. They'd go on lying there, probably not communicating with one another, just wondering how she'd got on.

'What was the flick?' Letty asked.

'Lana Turner. *The Flame and the Flesh.*'

'Holy God!'

'Bonar Colleano was in it.'

'Did your man keep his hands to himself?'

'Of course he did,' Mary Louise retorted crossly, for the first time feeling a kinship with the man who'd taken her out. Letty had a tongue like a razor blade.

'Where's James?'

'He's over playing cards with the Edderys.'

'I'll go to bed so.'

'Is that the end of it, Mary Louise?'

'How d'you mean, the end of it?'

'Is he proposing anything further?'

'He asked me out Friday.'

'Don't go, Mary Louise.'

'I said I would.'

'He could nearly be your father. For God's sake, watch your step.'

Mary Louise did. She developed a cold during the week and gave Letty a note to take in to the shop. In the ordinary course of events a cold wouldn't have prevented her from going to the pictures, and she hoped Elmer Quarry would deduce that. She hoped he'd guess how she felt, not that she was all that certain how she felt herself. When she was alone, especially lying awake in bed, she didn't want ever again to have to walk up the stairs of the Electric Cinema with him. But when Letty started on with her advice, and when James put in a word or two also, she naturally tended to defy them. Neither her mother nor her father made a comment, beyond asking her what kind of a film it had been. But she knew what they were thinking, and that caused her mood to revert: once more she wished that she might never find herself repeating the experience of sitting in the Electric Cinema with the inheritor of the drapery. No reply to the note Letty delivered came, although Mary Louise expected there'd be something. She didn't know why it disappointed her that he hadn't managed to write a line or two.

At that time, from the town and from the land around it, young men were making their way to England or America, often having to falsify their personal details in order to gain a foothold in whatever city they reached. Families everywhere were affected by emigration, and the Protestant fraction of the population increasingly looked as if it would never recover. There was no fat on the bones of this shrinking community; there were no reserves of strength. Its very life was eroded by the bleak economy of the times.

In conversation, this subject cropped up often at the Dallons' table. From his card-playing evenings at the Edderys' James brought back tales of the search for local employment and the enforced exile that usually followed.

Returning with an unsold bullock from yet another cattle-fair, Mr Dallon reported the melancholy opinions of those he had conversed with. At the egg-packing station wages remained low. Talk of expansion at the brickette factory came to nothing.

The Dallons' kitchen, where all such conversations took place and all meals were taken, had whitewashed walls and an iron range. There was a dresser, painted green, that displayed the cups and saucers and plates in daily use. Around the scrubbed deal table were five green-painted chairs. The door to the yard was green also, and the woodwork of the two windows that looked into the yard. On one of the windowsills a stack of newspapers had accumulated, conserved because they were useful for wrapping eggs in. On the other was the radio that, ten years ago, had replaced a battery-operated model. James and Letty remembered the day the battery wireless had been brought to the farmhouse by Billie Lyndon's father, how an aerial had had to be attached to the chimney and a second wire connected to a spike that Mr Lyndon drove into the ground outside the window. 'That's Henry Hall,' Mr Lyndon said when a voice was heard announcing a dance tune. Mary Louise couldn't remember any of it.

'It's the way things are,' Mr Dallon was given to remarking in the kitchen, a general-purpose remark that might be taken to apply to any aspect of life. With a soft sigh, he had employed it often during the war, when the BBC news was gloomy; and after the war when starvation was reported in Europe. But in spite of the note of pessimism that accompanied the observation Mr Dallon was not without hope: he believed as much in things eventually getting better as he did in the probability that they would first become worse. There was a cycle in the human condition he might have reluctantly agreed if prompted, although the expression was not one he would voluntarily have employed.

Mrs Dallon valued her husband's instinctive assessments and the significance he attached to developments and events. She argued only about lesser matters, and then discreetly: she put her foot down when Mr Dallon set off for the town in clothes he had worn to clean a cowshed; she insisted, once every two months, that he had his hair cut; and in the privacy of their bedroom she argued about how best to handle James, who all too easily developed a resentful look if he felt he was being treated as a farm-hand. James would go, Mrs Dallon predicted, like all the others were going: if they took him for granted they'd wake up one morning to find he wasn't there any more. Push him too hard in the fields and he'd decide to do something ludicrous, like joining the British army.

In general conversation, these same subjects cropped up when the Protestant families in the neighbourhood greeted one another at St Giles's church on Sundays: the Goods, the Hayeses, the Kirkpatricks, the Fitzgeralds, the Lyndons, the Enrights, the Yateses, the Dallons. In 1955 they recognized that their survival lay in making themselves part of the scheme of things, as it was now well established. While they still believed in the Protestants they were, they hung together less than they had in the past.

'You'd need the patience of Job,' Mr Dallon had confided more than once after the Sunday service, referring to his efforts to teach his son to farm. It was James who mattered. It was he, not his sisters, who would continue to tease a living out of the twenty-seven indifferent acres, and to trade animals at the cattle-fairs: on his success depended the survival of all three of them. 'Pray to God he doesn't go marrying some flibbertigib-bet!' This worry of Mrs Dallon's was voiced, not in the church-yard, but to her husband when they were alone. James being James, any marriage he proposed would naturally be foolish, but if you hinted as much when the time came the chances were that he'd have the thing done in some out-of-the-way parish without anyone knowing. A flibbertigibbet could be the ruin of Culleen, and of Letty and Mary Louise with it – unless, of course, Mary Louise discovered in the meantime the advantages of marrying into the drapery. No word could be said in that direction either, no pressure applied. These days – more than ever before, Mrs Dallon considered – a family had to put its trust in God.

'Your cold cleared up,' she observed in the kitchen when she and Mary Louise were making bread a fortnight or so after the outing to the Electric Cinema. 'I thought we were in for 'flu.'

'Yes, the cold went off.'

Mary Louise sounded low, her mother noted, and said to herself that that wasn't a bad sign. It suggested that her pride had been disturbed because Elmer Quarry had failed to display his disappointment over the cancelled engagement. With a mother's instinct she guessed that Mary Louise was regretting her hastiness.

When Elmer entered the billiard-room the caretaker – Daly the church sexton – was sitting close to the fire that blazed between the glass-fronted bookcases. In a respectful manner he immediately stood up, pushed back the rexine-covered arm-chair and replaced on the magazine table the *Illustrated London News* he'd been perusing. He remarked on the continuing severe weather. He'd be back to lock up, he added, and indicated that there was plenty of coal in the scuttle.

It puzzled Elmer that hardly anyone but himself came in for a game of billiards or an exchange of views by the fire. He couldn't understand why others didn't find some attraction in the shadowy billiard-room with the powerful, shaded light over the table, the coal pleasantly hissing, the flames changing colour and causing the mahogany of the bookcases to glow. No refreshments were served in the billiard-room, but that didn't seem to Elmer to matter in the very least, since refreshment could be taken in your own dining-room, and if you cared to smoke – which he didn't himself – you could do so endlessly. Daly, a small, elderly man with a limp, was invariably ensconced with a magazine when Elmer arrived, but always rose and went away. It sometimes occurred to Elmer that the caretaker lit the fire and kept it up for his own comfort and convenience.

He chalked a cue and disposed the billiard-balls to his liking, preparatory to an hour's practice. The day had been a profitable one: seven yards of oilcloth, the tail-end of a roll that had been in the shop for fifteen years, were sold by Matilda to the Mother Superior at the Sacred Heart convent. A coat had been sold to a farmer's wife, and an overcoat to her husband, both purchases the fruits of a legacy apparently. The traveller from Fitzpatrick's had shown him a new line in carded elastic with a mark-up that was the most attractive he'd been offered for years. He had ordered a dozen boxes, and a hundred of Fitzpatrick's Nitelite nightdresses. Rose had sold ten yards of chiffon for Kate Glasheen's wedding-dress. You didn't often have a day like that.

Taking aim, Elmer closed one eye. He paused, then slid the cue smoothly forward. Ball struck ball, the resulting motion precisely as he'd planned. He would continue to wait, he reflected as he moved around the table: one day, sooner or later, she would walk into the shop and he would see what was what from the expression on her face. Rose and Matilda were pleased at the latest turn of events, but events that turned once could turn again. The glimpse of her stockinged calves in the light from the street lamp flashed into Elmer's consciousness, like a moment from the film they had seen. The Dallons weren't much of a family: she would walk into the shop.

Mary Louise did so twelve days later, and Elmer came down from the accounting office, solicitous about her cold. The

older of his two sisters – showing her a cardigan at the time –
was far from pleased when he approached them.

The cold had cleared up, Mary Louise said; it had been
heavy, but it had cleared up. The cardigan wasn't quite right,
she added. Attractive though it had seemed in the window,
under closer scrutiny the shade wasn't one that suited her.

'Wasn't that the powerful film?' he remarked while Rose
was returning the garment to the window.

'Yes, it was.'

'A grand evening.'

'Yes, it was.'

'Well, that unfortunate cold was a nuisance! In fairness to
yourself, I think I owe you another visit to the pictures.'

He smiled. His teeth were small, she saw, a fact that previ-
ously had escaped her.

'Oh,' she began.

'Would Friday interest you? Or Saturday? Would Saturday
be better?'

She chose Friday. They saw *Lilacs in the Spring*.

3

Arrangements are being explained to her: she doesn't listen. The words are no more than a gabble, a sound like a dog grieving in the distance or the wail of wind through branches. Jeanne d'Arc worked a plough like a man; she wasn't a mimsy thing like Possy Luke with her cracked spectacles. Miss Mullover said Jeanne d'Arc's courage was beyond all comprehension.

'Good of you to come over.' Miss Foye has returned. Her strict tone interrupts the visitor's drone, still going on about the way things are now being done. There is a smile on Miss Foye's plump face. Forty-two she is, a known fact. Courted by a road surveyor.

'We'll take it easy,' the man remarks, lowering his voice. 'We won't rush our fences.'

They glance at her, both of them. She introduces a vacancy into her eyes, staring over their heads, upwards, at the ceiling.

'It'll be a saving for you,' Miss Foye observes.

He shakes his head, implying that that isn't a consideration. 'All I want to do is the right thing. Will the house close down, Miss Foye?'

'We have fourteen to place elsewhere, fourteen that can't go back where they came from. The house'll put up its shutters then.'

'You'll be OK yourself?'

'To tell the truth I would be finishing with it anyway.'

Miss Foye looks coy. A month ago a ruby stone appeared on her engagement finger. Miss Foye is to become the wife of the road surveyor, an autumnal romance if ever there was one. 'There's juice in the old girl yet,' Dot Sterne remarked when the news spread. 'Isn't that one bold for her age?'

'Friday week.' He says it, Miss Foye nods. Friday week'll be grand. It'll give everyone time, only fair to an inmate to let her get used to the change in advance. 'D'you hear us, dear?' she asks, raising her tone. 'D'you follow what you've been told?'

The woman smiles, first at Miss Foye, then at her visitor. She shakes her head. She hasn't heard a thing, she says.

4

The wedding took place on Saturday, 10 September 1955. It was a quiet occasion, but even so Mary Louise had a traditional wedding-dress, and Letty a bridesmaid's dress in matching style. There was a celebration afterwards in the farmhouse. Everyone sat down in the dining-room, a room otherwise rarely used. Mrs Dallon had roasted three chickens, and there was spiced beef as well as bacon to go with them. Before the meal the health of the bride and groom was drunk in sherry or whiskey. The Reverend Harrington, who had conducted the ceremony, allowed himself a further homily.

Miss Mullover, now nearly seventy, small and slight, affected by arthritis, had a special place at the gathering as the one-time mentor of both bride and groom. She'd been surprised when she heard of Mary Louise's engagement to the draper, but only because of the difference of generation: nothing else about the present alliance caused her undue apprehension. Other girls had passed through her schoolroom, eventually to marry older men. Marie Yates, not yet thirty at the time of her marriage to Canon Moore at almost eighty, came most swiftly to mind: in all her life Miss Mullover had never witnessed such weeping as Marie's at the funeral of the old clergyman.

But this sanguine view was not unanimously to be found among the wedding guests. The continuing displeasure of Matilda and Rose was matched by Letty's, which took the form of a coldly distant manner and the firm rejection of any notion that the occasion was a festive one. When, in March, Mary Louise revealed that Elmer had proposed and that she had accepted him, Letty hadn't spoken to her for three weeks and when the silence was finally broken Letty was so changed that Mary Louise wondered if she would ever again know the old relationship she'd had with her sister.

'I'm the lucky man,' Elmer declared in a speech. 'There's no one for ten miles around wouldn't agree on that.'

That was enough, he considered, so he did not say any more. Last night Rose had actually dropped to her knees, tears streaming, begging him to reconsider at this eleventh hour. Matilda, grim-faced on the first-floor landing, had announced that he would regret this folly for the rest of his days. Mary Louise Dallon hadn't a brain in her head. She was marrying him for his money, since it was a known fact that the Dallons hadn't two coins in the house to rub together. There was flightiness in her eyes. She would lead him a dance, if not in one way then in another. She would drain him dry in ways he couldn't even imagine. She would upset him, and disturb him. His sisters didn't go to bed until half-past two, and even after he'd lain down, exhausted, Elmer could still hear their ranting, and Rose's weeping.

In a final passion of energy, the night before also, Letty had sought to dissuade her sister. In the warm darkness of the bedroom they shared Mary Louise listened to the persistent murmur, edged with bitterness one moment and scorn the next. A picture was painted of her future in the house above the shop, the two sisters critical of every move she made, the man she was to marry never taking her side. She'd be no more than a maid in the household and a counter girl in the shop. There would be smells and intimacies no girl would care for in the bedroom she'd have to share with the heavily-made draper; her reluctance to meet his demands would be overruled. The three Quarrys would beadily eye her at meal-times. Dried-up spinsters were always the worst.

But by midday on 10 September the pair were joined to-gether. The best man was one of Elmer's cousins from Athy, imported into the parish for the occasion, a man Mary Louise had never seen before. The Reverend Harrington – cherub-cheeked and rotund, not long married himself – had asked the necessary questions slowly and with care, his lingering tone designed to imbue the union with an extra degree of sanctity, or so it seemed. In the vestry while the register was signed Mr and Mrs Dallon stood awkwardly, and Rose and Matilda and Letty stood grimly. Sensing unease, the Reverend Harrington chatted about other weddings he had conducted and then recalled the details of his own.

'Phew!' Mary Louise's brother whispered to one of his Eddery cousins in the dining-room of the farmhouse. The exhalation was a reference, not to the nuptials of his sister, but to the agreeable effect of a second glass of whiskey. James could feel it spreading through his chest, a burning sensation that was new to him.

'I had two bob on a horse today,' the older Eddery brother revealed. 'Polly's Sweetheart.'

James, who spent all he earned in Kilmartin's the turf ac-countant's, was impressed. He hadn't gone for anything today, he said. He'd heard about Polly's Sweetheart.

Letty changed out of her bridesmaid's dress in order to help her mother in the kitchen. The chickens had roasted during the wedding service, the bacon and the spiced beef were cold, cooked the day before. Mrs Dallon's cheeks were flushed from the small glass of sherry she'd drunk and from the heat of the range. She strained potatoes and peas. Letty tipped them into warmed dishes and carried the dishes into the dining-room. Mr Dallon began to carve the meats while the guests were seating themselves.

'A great spread,' Elmer remarked. He was wearing a carnation in the lapel of a muddy-brown suit, his Sunday suit he called it, much less worn than his usual clothing. His short hair had been cut the day before, and the barber's application of brilliantine still kept it tidily in place. The back of his neck was a little red.

'Lovely,' a woman said. 'Lovely it all is, Mrs Dallon.'

Mrs Dallon, hurrying with two gravy boats, was too occupied to reply. She whispered to her husband and he paused in his carving to say:

'I'm told to say, start eating. Don't let the hot stuff get cold.'

Miss Mullover confided to the clergyman's wife that she loved a past pupil's wedding. It was surprising the emotions you felt. Mrs Harrington – who knew that at one stage her husband had had heart-searchings about this match – was relieved that Miss Mullover seemed pleased. He would have liked to say Grace, she thought, but unfortunately he'd had a call of nature.

James and the Eddery brothers poured more whiskey, finding the bottle behind a potted fern on a windowsill. The Eddery brothers were smoking cigarettes. They told Mrs Dallon they wanted to finish them before they sat down. They were in no hurry for the chicken and bacon, they said.

Letty, given the task of moving the vegetables about on the table in case anyone was missed out, thought about Gargan the exchange clerk at the Bank of Ireland who'd been promoted to Carlow. They'd gone out together for two years, to the pictures and on bicycle rides, twice to the Chamber of Commerce dance in Hogan's Hotel. When Gargan had gone to Carlow and enough time had passed to indicate that he wouldn't be coming back to see her, Billie Lyndon of the radio shop had suggested an evening at the Dixie dancehall and she'd gone there once with him, but had found it rough. It might have been herself and either of them, she thought as she

moved the vegetables about. In this moment she might be
sitting at the far end of the table, Mrs Gargan or Mrs Lyndon.
They'd both mentioned marriage, not exactly proposals but
the next best thing, sounding the notion out. In the Electric
they had acted similarly: putting an arm along the back of her
seat halfway through the big film and then, after another few
minutes, grasping her shoulder. With each of them, she'd felt
a knee pressing hers. Their fingers had caressed the side of her
face. On the way home there'd been the good-night kiss.

'You were lovely in that dress, Letty,' Angela Eddery, still a
schoolgirl, complimented while she spooned peas on to her
plate. 'Dead spit of Audrey Hepburn.'

Letty knew that wasn't true. Either Angela Eddery was
confusing Audrey Hepburn with someone else or was simply
telling a lie. She looked nothing like Audrey Hepburn; she was
a different type altogether.

'Did you make them yourselves?' Angela Eddery went on.
'God, I never saw dresses like them.'

'We made our dresses.'

When she offered the best man one of the potato dishes he
said they were in the same line of business today, bridesmaid
and best man. Mary Louise had said he was a bachelor,
manager of a creamery near Athy. Letty considered he was
familiar with her, calling her Letty straight off and talking the
way he did. He was taller than Elmer Quarry, but just as
paunchy, and balder.

Rose and Matilda, sitting together, didn't eat much. 'Oh, I
could never manage all that,' Rose said as soon as she received
her plate, staring at its contents as if making a judgement. The
chickens would have cost them nothing, Matilda reflected,
running about the yard they'd have been.

The Reverend Harrington spoke to Mr Dallon and again
Mr Dallon laid down his carving knife and fork. He said that
the clergyman had wanted to say Grace but had been out of

the room at the right moment. If nobody objected, he'd say it now, even though some people had started. That didn't matter at all, the Reverend Harrington added hastily. 'For what we're about to receive,' he added also, 'the Lord make us truly thankful.'

Mary Louise felt sleepy due to Letty's keeping her awake half the night with her haranguing. She had taken the plunge, she said to herself; she had made her own mind up and had done it; it was her own business, what she had done, it was her own life. She smiled at Miss Mullover, who was leaning across the table to speak to her.

'D'you remember,' the schoolteacher asked her, 'how you used to want to work in Dodd's Medical Hall?'

Mary Louise did. She'd wanted to serve in the chemist's because it was the nicest shop in the town. It had the nicest smell, and everything was clean. To serve there you had to wear a white coat. Everyone knew it was special.

'It'll be Quarry's now,' Miss Mullover went on, and Mary Louise wondered if the old schoolteacher was ga-ga, since it was apparent to everyone present that she had just married into the drapery. The truth was that the counters of Quarry's had always been her second choice. She'd clearly never said so to Miss Mullover or there'd have been a reference to it, but she'd said so at home. When she'd finished at school, a shop was the best that could be done for her; her father had said that, and she hadn't minded, thinking of Dodd's or Quarry's or even Foley's grocery and confectionery, two doors down from the drapery in Bridge Street. Word of her availability was put around the town on the next fair day, but it seemed that no assistance was required. Foley's was reserved for the Foley girls, Renehan the hardware merchant only had men behind the counters and didn't have to go outside the family either, with three sons. No daughter of his would go into a public house, Mr Dallon laid down, but that possibility did not arise either. For five years Mary Louise had remained at home, helping generally, waiting for a vacancy. That was what she had to weigh in her mind when Elmer Quarry displayed his interest – the long, slow days at Culleen, the kitchen, the yard, the fowl houses, for weeks on end not seeing anyone outside the family except at church or at the egg-packing station. All that was what Letty appeared to have forgotten.

'Algebra was Elmer's stumbling block. He could never get the hang of brackets.' Miss Mullover nodded repeatedly over her food, lending emphasis to the recollection. 'Twiddly brackets, square brackets, round brackets. He could never get the order right.'

'Fat lot of use they were.' Elmer laughed loudly, taking Mary Louise by surprise and causing her to jump. She tried to think if she'd ever heard him laugh before, and she remembered her brother saying he never did. His small teeth were all on display at once. The fat of his face was bunched up into little bags.

'*Algebra poor*,' Miss Mullover recalled. '*Arithmetic good*. I remember writing that. Nineteen thirty-one or thereabouts.'

Mary Louise imagined her husband at that distant time, a podgy boy, she imagined, with podgy knees. He'd have had long trousers at the boarding-school in Wexford.

'I saw a lot in the schoolroom,' Miss Mullover reminded Mr Dallon as he sat down at last, the carving complete.

'You did a great job in the schoolroom, Miss Mullover.'

Mr Dallon reached for salt and pepper. He remembered Mary Louise's birth, how he'd been worried because she was late arriving but hadn't said anything because that would only have made matters worse. Had she been a boy the names they had ready were William or possibly Nevil. She was called Louise after his mother; he couldn't remember how it was that they began to use both her names. He seemed to recall saying himself that the two names had a ring to them.

'Full of fun she was,' Miss Mullover was remembering now – meaning, he supposed, that Mary Louise's liveliness as a child had occasionally landed her in trouble. She'd thrown a stone once in the school yard and had been kept in; she and Tessa Enright had put worms in Possy Luke's desk and let down the tyres of bicycles. *Occasional boisterousness*, Miss Mullover had written on a report.

He supposed she was his favourite, although he didn't like having to admit, even to himself, that favourites came into it. But Mary Louise, born when they'd thought the family was complete, had acquired – possibly for no more reason than that – a special place in his heart. Solemn-eyed, she had listened when he reprimanded her for her misdemeanours at school. At hay-making or harvesting she had a way of staying close to him, telling him about the ailments that had befallen a little mechanical chicken. When you wound it up it pecked the ground. 'Pecker' she called it.

'You're happy for her, Mr Dallon?' Miss Mullover murmured.

He nodded. When she was older she'd wanted to be in the town, or any town. She began to go out with Elmer Quarry and this was how it had ended. It was a marriage of convenience: she knew that and he knew that and Elmer Quarry knew it. They were aware of it and they accepted it. 'You're certain, Mary Louise?' he'd pressed her, and not for a second had she hesitated with her reassurance. She had an innocent way with her: that had always been her over-riding quality. Innocent of the consequences, she had committed her small, childhood sins; innocently, she had always chattered on. You could silence her in an instant; you could snatch away her confidence, and feel guilty as soon as you did so. 'You won't tire of it?' he'd pressed her further. 'The town and all that?' Again there was the eager reassurance, leaving unsaid between them the fear he knew she suffered: of being obliged to remain in the farmhouse

for ever, with half a life to live. The pretty chemist's shop,
going to dances with some tweed-jacketed young man: that
had not happened, and she had concluded that time would not
hesitate long enough to allow it. Alone in their pews in the
church of St Giles were the Protestant spinsters of the parish,
there to be observed week after week, added to at Christmas
and Easter by Elmer Quarry's sisters and others besides.

'He's not a troublesome man,' Miss Mullover softly remarked, as if detecting what was passing through Mr Dallon's
mind. 'So often when a girl marries you can see some trouble
coming.'

Elmer Quarry was decent and reliable, Mr Dallon replied,
his voice kept low also. Mary Louise could do worse, he was
about to add, but changed his mind because it didn't sound
quite right. But Miss Mullover nodded all the same, silently
agreeing that his daughter could have done worse.

At three o'clock the car from Kilkelly's Garage arrived. Mary
Louise had changed into a pale green coat and skirt, and wore
a small black hat trimmed with a drawn-up veil. The night
before she had packed a suitcase.

The Eddery brothers tied an old creosote tin to the back
bumper, but Kilkelly's driver removed it. When the car drove
off James pedalled after it on Mary Louise's bicycle, and the
Eddery boys shouted. Everyone else waved, Letty and Elmer's
sisters half-heartedly.

'Did the thing go well?' The driver was the garage's chief
mechanic; he hadn't had time to change out of his overalls.

'Ah, it did,' Elmer replied. 'Smooth as velvet.'

'Well, that's great.'

The car stopped at the drapery. A notice in one of the
windows announced that it would re-open on Monday. Elmer
went in to collect his suitcase.

'Ye're off for the two days?' the driver chattily went on

while Mary Louise waited, and she explained that they'd be away, in fact, for eight days in all, nine if you counted the remainder of this one. When Elmer returned they were driven on to the railway junction, which was twelve miles away. They caught the five-to-four train, changed later to a bus, proceeding on their way to the seaside resort they had chosen for their honeymoon. Neither was at ease during the journey. Neither revealed that the night before there had been family opposition to the marriage. Instead they spoke of the wedding guests, and of the occasion at the farmhouse. In the months that had passed since their first visit to the Electric Cinema they had not come to know one another intimately. Each had become familiar with certain traits in the other, promoting a degree of ease that had not been there in the past; but the curiosity of affection was not present on either side. The Electric Cinema had been visited only twice after they'd seen *Lilacs in the Spring*: Elmer's courtship of Mary Louise had been conducted, for the main part, during Sunday afternoon strolls that had become customary. He would walk out from Bridge Street and she would cycle in from Culleen. They met on the town's outskirts, the bicycle was deposited in a gateway, and they walked slowly back the way Mary Louise had ridden. At a crossroads they turned to the right and proceeded along a meandering lane, down a hill, through woods and across a humped bridge. On one of these walks Elmer proposed marriage, and Mary Louise said she'd have to think about it. She spent a month doing so, and when she eventually agreed Elmer passed his tongue over his lips, dried them with a handkerchief and announced that he was going to kiss her, which he did. They were actually on the humped bridge at the time. His voice was hoarse; there was a trace of what Mary Louise imagined to be leeks on his breath. After Gargan and Billie Lyndon, she had argued to herself during the month, there had been no one else for Letty. Had there ever been anyone for his own sisters?

Elmer had never before embraced a girl. Years ago, when he was a boarder at the school in Wexford, he had experienced desire for the stout housekeeper. He had imagined what it would be like kissing her. In dreams he had removed her clothes.

'God, you're great,' he complimented Mary Louise when their lips parted, although in fact he had found the experience a little disappointing. She was blushing, he noticed on the hump-backed bridge. She wiped her mouth with the back of her hand, her eyes cast down.

They walked back to the town, her left arm where he had tucked it into his. He asked her what her mother would say when she heard the news. He said he'd have to speak to her father because that was a thing you had to do. While wondering how best to break it to them, he said his sisters would be delighted.

'Will you come out to Culleen?' Mary Louise suggested.

'Walk out now, d'you mean?'

'Have you a bicycle, Elmer?'

'I never had the need of one.'

'Could you walk out to the house next Sunday maybe? I won't say a word till then.'

'I'll come out of course.'

'I'll only say you're calling for me.'

They stopped on the road and embraced again. This time Mary Louise felt his teeth. One of his hands was pressed into the small of her back. She closed her eyes because she'd noticed in films that people always did. He kept his open.

On their honeymoon journey that particular Sunday was recalled by both of them. On subsequent Sundays there had been further embraces, and all the necessary plans for their wedding had been made on these afternoon walks. 'We're delighted,' Mary Louise remembered her mother saying. Her father had shaken Elmer's hand.

'The Strand Hotel it's called,' Elmer told her as they stepped from the bus in the seaside town. 'Excuse me,' he said to a man standing outside a sweetshop, 'where's the Strand Hotel?'

The man said to keep going. You couldn't miss it, he advised. When the road became sandy under your feet you were there but for another fifty yards. Four minutes at the outside it would take them.

'Thanks, sir.'

Elmer had a way, Mary Louise had noticed some time ago, of addressing men like that. He called her father sir, and the Reverend Harrington. It was because of the shop, she supposed, something that was natural to him.

They walked on with their suitcases, past a row of small shops, past two public houses and the Catholic church. The surface became sandy beneath their feet, and then they rounded the bend where the Strand Hotel was, the two words of its title painted across a bow-windowed façade.

'I wrote in for lodgings,' Elmer stated in the hallway. 'Quarry the name is.'

'Ah, you did surely, Mr Quarry.' A woman with a headscarf over her curling-pins greeted them. 'Mr and Mrs Quarry,' she added, glancing at Mary Louise, her eyes bright with a land-lady's interest. They passed swiftly from the little black hat that was still perched on the crown of Mary Louise's head, over her pale green coat and skirt. They rested on her wedding ring. 'Mr and Mrs Quarry,' she repeated, as though to reassure her visitors that since the scrutiny was complete all was now in order. She led the way up a narrow staircase.

It was a boarding-house rather than an hotel. Tea was in the dining-room sharp at six, the woman said, and it being well after that now would they come down quickly? She threw open a window in their room and stood back proudly. You could hear the sea, she said. If you woke in the night you could hear it.

'Grand,' Elmer said, and the woman went away.

Mary Louise stood by the bed. For the first time since she'd decided to accept Elmer Quarry's offer of marriage she experienced the weight of misgiving. Tendrils of doubt had now and again assailed her before; listening to Letty, she could hardly have escaped them. But there had never been a feeling that she had made a ludicrous, laughable mistake. Nor had she ever resolved that as soon as possible she must be released from her promise. During the month she had taken to consider the offer she had gone over the ground again and again, and, having reached a decision, she did not see much point in encouraging second thoughts. But in the bedroom of the Strand Hotel, with the lace curtains flapping on either side of the open window, Mary Louise wanted suddenly to be in the farmhouse, to be laying the places at the kitchen table or feeding the fowls with Letty. Somehow, later on, she was going to have to get her nightdress on to her and get into that bed with the bulky man whose wife she had agreed to be. Somehow she was going to have to accept the presence of his naked feet, the rest of him covered only in the brown and blue pyjamas he was lifting out of his suitcase.

'Comfortable enough,' he said. 'I'd say it was comfy, dear.'

Elmer's mother had sometimes employed that endearment, and it seemed to him to be equally appropriate between man and wife, now that they were alone in a room. It wasn't the kind of thing Rose or Matilda would say, but then the circumstances were different. He was glad he had remembered it.

'It's a lovely place,' Mary Louise said, still standing by the bed.

He agreed that it was. He'd been told about the Strand Hotel by Horton's traveller, now with Tyson's, who'd said it was second to none. Recalling in the train the dreams he'd had in his boyhood about the stout housekeeper at the boarding-school and later about Mrs Fahy and Mrs Bleddy, two shopkeepers' wives in the town, he had hoped his wife would change her clothes as soon as they arrived in the hotel. She was nothing like the size of the housekeeper or either of the shopkeepers' wives; definitely on the skinny side you'd have to call her, none of the sturdiness of her sister. The sister had come into the shop one day nearly a year ago and he'd looked down from the accounting office just as she was taking her purse out of her handbag. She wasn't bad-looking, he had considered, and he'd thought about the matter for a while, hoping she would return to the shop so that he could observe her again, in fact attending church one Sunday for that very purpose. But the trouble with the sister, which you had to set against the sturdiness of her, was that a few years ago she'd been seen about the place with Gargan from the bank and after that with young Lyndon. These facts stimulated unease in Elmer; that she was experienced in going out with men made him feel nervous, since it meant they wouldn't be in the same boat when it came to getting to know one another. Even so, if it hadn't been for noticing the sister with her purse that day he'd probably never have turned his attention to Mary Louise. That was the way things happened; chance played a part.

'Will we go down?' he suggested.

'All right.'

'You don't want to change your duds or anything?'

'She said to be quick. I'm OK the way I am.' Mary Louise took her hat off and placed it on the dressing-table. The fluted looking-glass in which it was reflected was cracked, a sharp black line jaggedly diagonal. There were cigarette burns on the dressing-table's surface.

'I'd say we'd be comfy all right,' he repeated.

In the dining-room other people were finishing their meal, spreading jam on slices of bread. The woman in the headscarf showed the newcomers to two places at a table where three men were already seated. Families occupied other tables.

'Wait till I get you a cup of tea,' the woman said. 'Is that tea still warm, Mr Mulholland?'

Mr Mulholland, a moustached man, smaller and older than Elmer Quarry, felt the metal of the teapot and said it was. The other men at the table were middle-aged also, one of them grey-haired, the other bald.

'Thanks, sir,' Elmer said when Mr Mulholland passed him the milk and sugar.

'Fine day,' the bald man said.

A plate of fried food was placed in front of Mary Louise and a similar one in front of her husband. Everything would be quiet at home, she thought. The wedding guests would have gone, all the clearing up would be complete. Her father would have changed back into his ordinary clothes, and so would James and her mother. Letty would probably be putting the food on the table.

Mr Mulholland was a traveller in various stationery lines. The grey-haired man was a bachelor, employed in the ESB, who came to the Strand Hotel for his tea every day of his life. The bald man lived in the Strand, a bachelor also.

These facts came out in dribs and drabs. Her husband, Mary Louise noticed, was very much at home with these three men, and appeared to be interested in the information they volunteered. He told them about the drapery. He was still wearing the carnation in his buttonhole, so they knew about the wedding even before he mentioned it.

'Well, I thought it was the case,' Mr Mulholland said. 'As soon as the pair of you walked into the room I said to myself that's a honeymoon.'

Mary Louise felt herself turning pink. The men were examining her, and she could guess what they were thinking. You could see it in their eyes that they were noticing she was a lot younger than Elmer, the same thought that had been in the eyes of the guard of the train and in the landlady's eyes.

'Would it be an occasion for a drink?' the bald man suggested. 'The three of us have a drink in McBirney's of an evening.'

'You'd have passed McBirney's on the way from the bus,' Mr Mulholland said.

'I think I saw it, sir,' Elmer agreed. 'We'll maybe see how things are after we've had a little stroll down by the sea.'

'We'll be in McBirney's till they close,' the grey-haired man said.

Soon after that the men went away, leaving Elmer and Mary Louise alone at the table. The families began to drift from the dining-room also, the children staring at Mary Louise as they passed.

'Wasn't that decent of them?' Elmer remarked. 'Wasn't it friendly?'

'Yes, it was.'

She didn't feel hungry. Her husband spread gooseberry jam on a slice of white bread and stirred sugar into his tea, and Mary Louise thought that what she'd like to do would be to walk on the seashore by herself. She'd only been to the sea once before, eleven years ago, when Miss Mullover had taken the whole school on the bus, starting off at eight o'clock in the morning. They'd all bathed except Mary Louise's delicate cousin and Miss Mullover herself, who'd taken off her stockings and paddled. Miss Mullover had forbidden them to let the sea come up further than their waists, but Berty Figgis had disobeyed and was later deprived of a slice of jam-roll.

'Eat up, dear,' Elmer said.

'I think I've had enough.'

'Your mother had a great tuck-in for us.'

'Yes, she did.'

'Everyone was pleased with it.'

She smiled. A cigarette-butt left behind by one of the men had been inadequately extinguished. It smouldered in the

ashtray, a curl of smoke giving off an acrid odour. Mary
Louise wanted to put it out properly but didn't feel like touching it with her fingers.

'Are you game for a walk, dear?' Elmer said. He was about
to add that it was the sea air they'd paid for, but somehow
that didn't sound appropriate. He said instead that he'd known
a Mulholland years ago, one of the clerks in the gasworks.
The jam he was eating was better than Rose's. It was thicker,
for a start. He liked thick jam.

'I'd love a breath of air,' she said.

So when he had finished his cup of tea and had another
slice of bread and jam they walked on the strand. The sea was
out. The damp sand was firm beneath their feet, smooth and
dark, the surface broken here and there by a tiny coiled hillock.
Sandworms, Elmer said. She wondered what sandworms were,
but didn't ask.

A dog barked at the distant edge of the sea, chasing seagulls.
Two children were collecting something in a bucket. She remembered shivering after the bathe the day Miss Mullover
had brought them, and how Miss Mullover had made them
run on the sand to warm themselves up. 'No, leave your shoes
and socks off, Berty,' Miss Mullover's voice came back to her,
cross with Berty Figgis again.

'Shellfish,' Elmer said, referring to what the children were
collecting in their bucket.

They went on walking, slowly as they always did on a
walk. Elmer had an unhurried gait; he liked to take things at a
pace that by now Mary Louise had become used to. The sun
was setting, streaking the surface of the sea with bronze high-
lights.

'Miss Mullover took us to the seaside.' She told him about
that day. He said that in his time in the schoolroom there
hadn't been such excursions. 'Algebra the whole time,' he
said, making a joke.

The sand ended. They clambered over shingle and rocks, but in a moment he suggested that the walking was uncomfortable so they turned back. They could still, very faintly, hear the dog barking at the seagulls.

'Would you like that, dear?' he suggested. 'Call in and have a drink with those men?'

Elmer was not, himself, a drinking man. He did not disapprove of the consumption of alcohol, only considered the practice unnecessarily expensive and a waste of time. But when the man had suggested a drink in McBirney's he had recalled immediately the glass of whiskey he'd drunk earlier in the day and had been aware of a desire to supplement it, putting this unusual urge down to the pressures of the occasion. He'd woken twice in the night with the abuse of his sisters still ringing in his consciousness, and he'd been apprehensive in the church in case one of them would make a show of herself by weeping, and at the occasion afterwards in case anything untoward was said. He'd been glad to get away in Kilkelly's car, but in the train another kind of nervousness had begun to afflict him. He couldn't quite put his finger on what it was or where precisely it came from, but none the less it was there, like very faint pins and needles, coming and going in waves.

'If you'd like to,' she said.

It surprised her that he suggested this. When the invitation had been issued she didn't think he meant it when he said they might look in at the public house. She'd thought he was being polite.

'Okey-doke,' he said.

They hardly said anything on the walk back. They passed by the hotel, eventually reaching McBirney's public house, which was a gaunt building, colour-washed in yellow. Two iron beer barrels were on the pavement outside, with bicycles propped against them. Inside, the three men were drinking pints of stout.

'Cherry brandy,' Mary Louise said when the bald man asked her what she'd like. A woman who'd damaged the Hillman a couple of years ago by backing into it in Bridge Street had given Mr Dallon a bottle of cherry brandy by way of compensation. For the last two Christmases a glass had been taken in the farmhouse.

'Whiskey,' Elmer requested. 'A small measure of whiskey, sir.'

A conversation began about scaffolding. A bricklayer in Leitrim, known to the bald man, had apparently fallen to his death because the scaffolding on a house had been inadequately bolted together. The grey-haired man said he preferred the older type of scaffolding, the timber poles and planks, with rope lashing. You knew where you were with it.

'The unfortunate thing is,' the bald man pointed out, 'the lashed scaffold is outmoded.'

The cherry brandy was sweet and pleasant. Mary Louise was glad she'd thought of asking for it. After a few sips she felt happier than she had on the strand or in the dining-room or the bedroom. Some boys of her own age were laughing and drinking in a corner of the bar. Two elderly men were sitting at a table, not speaking. Mary Louise was the only girl present.

'I was married myself,' Mr Mulholland confided to her while the others continued to discuss different kinds of scaffolding, 'in 1941. The day the *Bismarck* went down.'

She nodded and smiled. She wished she'd asked Elmer to take the carnation out of his lapel so that people wouldn't know they'd been married only a matter of hours. She'd seen the boys in the corner glancing at it a few times.

'The old ways can't always be improved, sir,' she heard Elmer saying, and then the grey-haired man said it was his round. He asked her if she'd like the same again, and she said she would.

'Excuse me a minute, Mrs Quarry,' the bald man said. 'I have to see a man about a dog.'

It was the first time anyone had addressed her directly as Mrs Quarry. When the landlady had used the term it hadn't been quite the same. Mary Louise Quarry, she said to herself.

'Paddy or JJ?' the grey-haired man asked Elmer, and Elmer said JJ without knowing why. She'd take off the little green jacket first, he supposed, and he wondered whether it would be the blouse or the skirt next. He looked at her. Her hair wasn't tidy after the walk they'd taken, and she'd gone a bit red in the face due to the stuff she was drinking. The sister wasn't as good-looking, no doubt about that.

'May the twenty-seventh,' Mr Mulholland said. 'Glasnevin, and the skies opened.'

Mary Louise had lost track of the conversation. She was puzzled for a moment, then realized Mr Mulholland was still talking about his wedding. The grey-haired man put a fresh glass of cherry brandy into her hand and took away the empty one.

'The wife's a Glasnevin woman,' Mr Mulholland said.

'Is that in Dublin?'

'We live there to this day. 21, St Patrick's Avenue.'

The conversation about scaffolding resumed, the bald man having returned. Then Mary Louise heard her husband talking about his shop, and a moment later she heard him saying, 'We're Protestants,' and heard the grey-haired man saying he'd guessed it.

'The same house she was married from,' Mr Mulholland said.

'I see.'

'We brought up seven there. When her father died she got the property, though the mother had a right to an upstairs room. They didn't get on, himself and the mother.'

'I don't know Dublin well.'

'You'd always be welcome in Glasnevin, Kitty.'

'Thanks very much.'

Mr Mulholland lowered his voice. His wife was having the change of life, he said. 'You'd understand that, Kitty? An upsetting period for her.'

'My name's not Kitty, actually.'

'I thought he called you Kitty.'

'My name's Mary Louise.'

'Welcome to the married state, Mary Louise.'

Mary Louise laughed. Mr Mulholland was funny, the way Letty's friend Gargan had been funny. Gargan did an imitation of a Chinaman, and told endless stories about the Englishman, the Irishman and the Scotsman. He also did imitations of Charlie Chaplin.

'There was a fellow opposite the shop one time,' Elmer was saying, 'dismantling a scaffold. He was up at the top of it throwing down the metal joints, and didn't one go through the roof of a van!'

'Some of those fellows are dangerous all right,' the grey-haired man agreed.

'A few years ago it was,' Elmer said. 'One of Joe Claddy's men.'

As she sipped more of her drink, Mary Louise felt glad they had come to the bar. Elmer was more loquacious than he'd been all day. It seemed to her now that she'd been silly to want him to take the carnation out of his buttonhole. If she'd asked him to he'd probably have said it would be a waste of a good carnation, and of course he'd have been right. Reminded of it by Elmer's recollection of the scaffolding joint going through the roof of a van, she told Mr Mulholland about the woman who'd given the family a bottle of cherry brandy because she'd backed into the Hillman.

'It's why I have a taste for it,' she said.

'The wife likes a medium sherry,' Mr Mulholland said.

The bald man recalled an occasion when he was driving

along the Cork road outside Mitchelstown and a ladder fell off the lorry in front of him. He described the damage to the car's radiator and one of the headlights.

'Tell them about the Hillman,' Mr Mulholland urged Mary Louise, and when she'd done so Elmer said he'd never heard that before.

'She got a taste for the brandy that time,' Mr Mulholland said.

They all laughed. Mr Mulholland put his arm around Mary Louise's waist and squeezed it. She had never been in a public house before and had often wondered what one was like. All she'd had were Letty's descriptions because Letty had often gone into MacDermott's or the lounge of Hogan's Hotel with Gargan. Letty used to smoke in those days. She used to come into the bedroom at night smelling of cigarettes and sometimes of drink. She never smoked in the farmhouse itself, though, it being purely a social thing with her.

'Excuse me a minute,' the bald man said, and again went away, repeating that he had to see a man about a dog.

Mary Louise told Mr Mulholland about the farm, answering questions he put to her. She heard Elmer saying it was difficult for a draper's shop to move with the times, that self-service wasn't always suitable.

'Oh, definitely,' the grey-haired man agreed.

She found herself telling Mr Mulholland about cycling from Culleen to school every day with Letty and James. She described Miss Mullover's schoolroom, with the map of Ireland that showed the rivers and the mountains and the other one that showed the counties in different colours. They would all crouch round the stove on a very cold day, permitted to leave their desks by Miss Mullover. Twelve or thirteen pupils there were, sometimes a few more, sometimes less, depending.

'What'll you have?'

The bald man had rejoined them. He had a Woolworth's

bladder, he said, and Mr Mulholland reprimanded him. Mr Mulholland put his arm round Mary Louise's waist again, as if to protect her from such observations. She said she'd like another cherry brandy.

One of the boys in the corner began to sing, softly beating time on the surface of the table with his fingers. Mary Louise could feel the palm of Mr Mulholland's hand massaging her hip-bone, but she knew he meant no harm. She remembered the safety-pin she'd brought to the Electric the first time she'd gone there with Elmer. She smiled. Ridiculous it seemed now; ridiculous of Letty to suggest it.

'Sorry about that reference I made,' the bald man apologized, handing her another drink. They'd find the place they were staying to their liking, he predicted. Family run. He hadn't made a complaint in twenty-two years.

'It seems nice,' Mary Louise agreed.

Mr Mulholland had moved away and was telling Elmer about the different kinds of stationery he travelled in: receipt books, account books, notepapers, occasion cards, mass cards, printed vouchers, printed invoices, envelopes of all descriptions. It wouldn't be as bad as she thought, having to share the big bed; the things Letty said were silly. Elmer had stopped saying sir to the men; he kept nodding and wagging his head while he listened to Mr Mulholland. 'Elmer Quarry's always polite to you,' her father had commented the Sunday evening after Elmer had told him he'd proposed marriage. A shopkeeper had to be, Letty had icily interjected. Politeness made money for shopkeepers.

'I keep the books in Traynor's,' the bald man said. He didn't reveal what Traynor's was, but from subsequent remarks Mary Louise was left with the impression that it had to do with animal foodstuffs.

'I see,' she said.

Listening to Mr Mulholland, Elmer privately reflected that he'd never drunk so much whiskey in a single day. No drink was kept in the house, and never had been, but sometimes at the funeral of a customer he felt he should accept what he was offered, and on Christmas Eve Renehan from the hardware next door always came in about half-past four and invited him to walk down the street to Hogan's lounge. He had a mineral then, while Renehan took gin and hot water. Renehan usually fell in with other men in Hogan's, and Elmer left them to it. Counting the glass of whiskey after the wedding ceremony, he'd had three already that day, and he wondered what Rose and Matilda would say if they could see him standing in a bar with his young wife and three strangers. Probably they'd be too astonished to say anything.

'I know what you mean,' he acknowledged Mr Mulholland's revelations concerning the necessity in any business for clearly printed up-market stationery. In a moment he'd buy a round himself, and then the grey-haired man would buy a round, and that would be that. Naturally you'd have a drink when you were on a holiday, naturally you wouldn't behave the way you would if you were still at home. Sixty-six pounds it would cost at the Strand.

Elmer turned to the bar to order the drinks. He remembered going by the Fahys' back-yard one time when the big double doors were open and seeing Mrs Fahy's clothes hanging on the line with her husband's. He'd stopped to look at them, fourteen or fifteen he'd been. Afterwards he'd thought about them, Mrs Fahy folding them after she'd taken them off, salmon-coloured some of the garments were. Remembering now, a jitter of excitement disturbed Elmer's stomach, like a breeze passing through it. He turned to glance down at the calves of Mary Louise's legs, but they were difficult to discern in the gloom. Sometimes he would glance out of the accounting-office window and see one of the counters spread over with suspender-belts and roll-ons, and some woman making up her mind, fingering the material or the elastic.

'You did right well with this one,' the bald man murmured out of the side of his mouth when Elmer gave him his drink. 'A lovely girl, Mr Quarry.'

Elmer didn't respond. He felt embarrassed by what had been said, although he wasn't sure why. Mr Mulholland raised his glass and proposed a toast to the happy couple.

'Was I out of turn?' The bald man's surreptitious murmur continued. 'I think I forgot myself there.'

Elmer realized a compliment was intended. He denied that offence had been given with a dismissive shake of his head.

'*What's the news, what's the news, O my bold chevalier?*' sang the boys at the corner table. '*With your long-barrelled gun of the sea . . .*'

While listening to details of the book-keeping conventions at Traynor's, it had occurred to Mary Louise that her husband might leave all the drink-buying to the men. Mean as an old crab, James had said he was. But if he had erred in that way, it would more likely have been because he didn't know about correct behaviour in a public house since she had never, herself, detected signs of meanness in him. And anyway there he was, handing out glasses just like the others had.

'Thanks, Elmer.' She smiled at him when he gave her hers.

He wondered what she was wearing under the two-piece. For all he knew, it was stuff she'd bought from Rose or Matilda in the shop. It was his sisters who said you must call it a two-piece these days, not a costume any more, which was what their mother had called it. The first day he served behind the counter a woman had come in and asked to see stockings, thirty denier. She'd run her hand down into one, and ever since he had enjoyed watching a woman doing that.

'I wouldn't like to offend your lord and master,' the bald man confided to Mary Louise. Bewildered, she frowned.

'I said to him you were a lovely girl. A bridegroom could take a remark the like of that the wrong way.'

Mary Louise laughed, and soon afterwards they all left the bar. Mr Mulholland and the grey-haired man went in one direction; Elmer, Mary Louise and the bald man returned to the Strand Hotel. The landlady had removed the headscarf and the curlers from her hair, which now – henna-shaded – displayed evidence of her earlier attentions. The bald man shook hands with Elmer and Mary Louise in the hall. He took cocoa at night, he confided, pursuing the landlady to the inner depths of the hotel.

When he'd stepped out into the fresh air Elmer had been aware of a sensation of floating in his head. The houses across the street, one pink, the other blue, were vivid in the gathering gloom. The pavement kept slanting away from him as he walked on it, first one way, then the other. In the Strand Hotel he held the banister-rail firmly as he climbed the stairs.

Mary Louise went in search of the bathroom and lavatory. She, too, was experiencing a degree of disturbance, a general muzziness she did not find unpleasant. When she returned to the bedroom she found her husband sitting on the edge of the bed with his jacket off and his tie loosened. His eyes kept closing.

Mary Louise put her nightdress over her petticoat and then slipped off the petticoat and the rest of her underclothes, and her stockings. She didn't like undressing even when it was only Letty in the room, unless the light was out or Letty averted her eyes. Letty was quite good about things like that. They both agreed without ever having talked about it.

Elmer tried to watch, but his efforts at concentration caused a visual confusion he had not experienced before. A second image of his bride floated out of the first, precisely the same outline, hands and head, the white nightdress picked up from the bed, the body bent, then turned away from him while some sort of groping took place, stockings in her hands. He wanted to tell her she was great, but when he tried to his voice wouldn't work properly. In the hall, when the man had begun about his cocoa, he'd attempted to compliment the landlady on her jam, but the same thing had occurred. He'd tried to say he liked thick jam, but he couldn't manage to get the words right.

'Will I help you?' she was saying, and he screwed his eyes up to see her properly. 'Will I put the light out?' she said, and a moment later she did so. He leaned back, turning himself round, finding a pillow for his head. At the Tate School the housekeeper could be seen putting on her vest, her reflection in the glass of the window that swung outwards. He shouldn't be falling asleep, Elmer said to himself, but nevertheless did so.

5

'Your Ovaltine, dear.'

Miss Foye places a tray containing a mug on the bedside table. The night-time tray is always the same one – made of tin, round and with a lip, blue flowers on a green ground. She asked about the flowers once and Miss Foye said she thought they were hydrangeas, a nice bunch of hydrangeas.

'Be a good girl now, don't let it get cold.'

'What's it all about, Miss Foye?'

In the dormitory the other women are obediently sipping their Ovaltine. Miss Foye always waits until all of them have finished, then collects the mugs on the tray and turns the light out. There are seven women in the dormitory: 'Miss Foye's best girls' she calls them because they are able to sleep together without disturbing one another. Each night the last one to receive her Ovaltine receives the tray as well. Fairness is important in the house.

'You know, dear, what it's all about. I saw you listening to him.'

'I didn't understand.'

'Drink up, love. Please now. Miss Foye is tired.'

'I don't want to leave the house.'

'It's not for us to say a thing like that. They know better.'

'Who knows?'

'The medicals, dear.'

'They don't know better where you'd want to be.'

'Drink your drink, dear. Please now.'

Miss Foye moves away. She collects the empty mugs from the other bedside tables, one between each bed. She bids the women good-night, and each replies. She calls them Miss Foye's best girls.

'I remember the day I came to the house,' the woman who is giving her trouble tonight remarks. 'A Thursday afternoon.'

'Good girl now. Finish up. Of course you do.'

'"You'll be happier here," you said.'

'You would say that in those days. Don't cry, dear. Miss Foye is tired.'

But the woman does cry. She finishes her drink and hands back the mug, and when Miss Foye has turned the light out she sobs beneath the bedclothes so that the others cannot hear her.

6

Mary Louise served in the shop, instructed by Matilda and Rose. They showed her where everything was, and how to make out a bill, and how to roll and unroll the bolts of material. She heard them muttering to one another about her, Rose saying she was slow to pick things up.

In the kitchen she was allocated certain tasks, specifically to lay the table in the dining-room before each meal and to carry in the plates and dishes when the food was ready, afterwards to wash them while Matilda dried. Rose liked using the vacuum cleaner on the stairs and in the dining-room and the front room, the bedrooms and landings. Matilda dusted and attended to the front-room fire in winter; all the cooking was done by Rose. Mary Louise made the bed she shared with her husband, Matilda and Rose each made her own.

When she'd been a member of the household for a few months Mary Louise explored a narrow staircase behind a door on the upper landing. There were two attics when she reached the top of it. The toys that had belonged to Elmer and his sisters were neatly arranged on the deep shelves of a cupboard, toys that by the look of them might have belonged to an earlier generation of Quarrys also. Framed pictures were stacked against a wall, books piled against another. Outmoded display dummies stood like statues, some of them shrouded with sheets. An old sewing-machine, replaced by the one Matilda used in the dining-room, had been kept. So had sofas and chairs in need of re-upholstering, and a rocking-horse. A tea-chest contained unidentified objects wrapped in yellowing newspaper – china, Mary Louise presumed. In the steeply pitched roof there was a single window in each of the two rooms. There was a stillness up there and the fusty airlessness was somehow comforting. With the door at the bottom of the staircase closed behind her, Mary Louise sensed the only real privacy she was offered, and on occasions when she knew where everyone was she took to quietly slipping up the steep uncarpeted stairs, taking her shoes off so that her footsteps wouldn't echo through the house. She sat in an armchair, sinking down into its depths. She closed her eyes and thought about things, about how she missed the farmhouse and the fields at Culleen, and riding her bicycle along the familiar roads. She enjoyed serving in the shop, and she knew Rose was wrong to say she was slow. She was quicker than either of the sisters at grasping a customer's needs. She could already gauge precisely the amount of brown paper required to wrap whatever had been purchased, and her parcels were tidier than theirs, the string looped so that they might easily be carried. When discount was mentioned by a customer she knew better than to quote a figure without consulting Elmer first, but she also knew that soon the day would come when she'd be able to anticipate his wishes down to the last ha'penny. As second-best to Dodd's Medical Hall, the drapery was interesting enough. It was when the shop closed that melancholy set in.

In the past, in the days when Mary Louise had been a modest customer herself, Matilda and Rose had always been agreeable. She remembered buying hooks and eyes and other necessities in Quarry's, and groceries in Foley's during her years at Miss Mullover's schoolroom. She remembered a time when she could only just see over the counter in Quarry's, being in the shop with her mother and being lifted on to a round-bottomed chair that was still there. Matilda had once asked her what age she was. Rose had run into the back and returned with a sweet oatcake. Now they were like two other people.

Her mother, in whom she confided during one of her Sunday visits to Culleen, said it maybe wasn't easy for them, having a newcomer about the place, their long-established routine shaken up. It wasn't easy for her either, Mary Louise began to reply, but her mother just shook her head. 'You're looking well,' she observed in the silence that developed, implying that that, too, was important.

There were other matters, which Mary Louise did not discuss with her mother, nor with anyone. She would have with Tessa Enright, but Tessa Enright had gone to Dublin to train as a physiotherapist and only returned to the town at Christmas. No correspondence had developed between the two girls, except that Mary Louise had found out her friend's address and had written to invite her to the wedding. She hadn't been able to come.

There were other girls, still in the neighbourhood, whom Mary Louise had known well at school, but none had been as close as Tessa Enright, and certainly none would have been a candidate for the confidences Mary Louise felt she couldn't share with her mother. Nor could she have shared them with Letty, and when she thought about it she wondered about Tessa Enright: even if she had never gone away and their friendship had continued to thrive, this particular subject might have been easier to raise with a girl who was married herself.

So Mary Louise kept to herself an awkwardness that had arisen in the bedroom she shared with her husband. But as the year came to an end, and the spring and summer of the following year passed by, she was increasingly aware of the interest taken in her person by people who came into the shop. As soon as they'd requested whatever it was they needed,

women would glance down her body, the movement of their
eyes briefly halting when it reached her stomach, then swiftly
retracted. She knew what was in their minds. On Sundays she
was also aware of it in her mother's mind, and in Letty's.
'You're looking well': the repeated observation of her mother's
acquired an edgy significance, seeming now to be a question
almost. In the bedroom the matter was not discussed, either:
Elmer said nothing, and never had. He watched her brushing
her hair, seated in front of the dressing-table mirror, and she
could see him also, already in his pyjamas, a vagueness in his
eyes that had not been there in the past. At first she smiled
into the mirror at him, but she stopped because he didn't seem
to notice.

'No need to bang that door, Mary Louise,' Rose reprimanded her one morning when she closed the dining-room
door because there was a draught. She had pushed at it with
her shoulder because her hands were carrying a tray that
contained four plates of porridge. It wasn't her fault that the
door caught in the draught and banged. 'Close the door after
you, Mary Louise,' Rose had commanded a week before.

'Sorry,' she said, passing round the plates of porridge. Any
one of the three of them might have risen and closed the door,
since it was clear that it had been difficult for her to do so.
'Sorry,' she had said on the earlier occasion, not voicing her
thoughts then either.

She didn't like Rose's food, the fatty chops, the bits of steak
fried too hard and too long, the swedes and watery cabbage.
Rose only enjoyed making cakes and sweet things and was
more successful with them. There was always a cake on the
table at the meal they sat down to at six o'clock in the
evening, but the brown bread and soda bread were heavy and
seemed to Mary Louise not to be baked all the way through.
She offended Rose by buying a loaf now and again, and by
making toast for breakfast. 'Her Ladyship,' she heard Rose

saying to her sister, and it occurred to Mary Louise that whenever one of them said something she was apparently not meant to hear it was always said when she was just within ear-shot.

In the autumn of 1956, when the marriage was just over a year old, Mary Louise awoke one morning in the bleak hour before dawn to find tears on her cheeks. She hadn't been dreaming; for no specific reason the tears continued to slip out, soundlessly, without sobbing. What she had imagined before her marriage had not come about. Being looked up to in the town, with money to spare for the clothes she wanted, pleasantly going from shop to shop without having to hesitate over the cost, as her mother did: all this had not replaced the long days at Culleen, with nothing to do when the kitchen work was over except to wash the eggs. Vaguely, she had imagined that as Elmer's wife the house would be hers and that in time she would be deferred to in the shop. On Sunday mornings, since Elmer didn't accompany her to church, she sat with her family, as if the marriage hadn't taken place, then stopped going altogether. On Sunday afternoons she continued to cycle out to the farmhouse – a weekly routine that took the place of the Sunday walk she and Elmer had become ac-customed to. It was when she found herself so eagerly looking forward to those visits that she realized she missed both the farmhouse and the companionship of her family more than she could ever have believed.

Waking in the very early morning and finding herself melan-choly became, after the first time, a familiar repetition. She lay beside her sleeping husband, dwelling on her own stupidity and what she recognized now as her simplicity, her stub-bornness in not perceiving a reality that was apparent. Before her marriage the Reverend Harrington had made her call to see him at the rectory. It was a joke among the Protestants of the neighbourhood that he always gave a parishioner raspberry

cordial with hot water in it when he wished to be serious, and
this he duly did, offering biscuits as well. 'Do you love Elmer?'
he asked bluntly, a month before the marriage. 'Please don't
be shy with me, Mary Louise.' She wasn't shy; no one ever
was with the Reverend Harrington. It was easy to tell him a
lie, easy to smile and say she did love Elmer Quarry, since she
didn't want to have a conversation like the ones she had with
Letty. When she was fourteen she'd thought she was in love
with her delicate cousin, and later with James Stewart. But all
that was silly when she looked back on it. It was far more
real, going for walks with Elmer Quarry and having him
tucking her arm into his. It was far more real to think of
herself in the shop on a winter's evening, when the lights were
lit and the radiators were warm, and to see herself the mistress
of the house above it. There would be card parties in the huge
front room, with its marble fireplace and grey flowered wallpaper. There would be music and even dancing, and a great
spread on the dining table, the doors between the two rooms
spread wide. 'I'm glad we've had this chat,' the Reverend
Harrington had said.

All those memories and imaginings came back to Mary
Louise in her sleepless hours. She had cut photographs of
James Stewart out of Letty's *Picturegoer* and framed them
with *passe-partout*. The cousin she'd thought she'd been in
love with hadn't been healthy enough in the end to continue
coming to the schoolroom every day. Grown up now but still
thin and weak-looking, suffering from something that couldn't
be cured, he'd been in the church on the wedding day but not
at the farmhouse afterwards. While she lay there in the mornings Mary Louise recalled the benign countenance of the clergyman, his good-natured smile, the glass of pink cordial held out
to her, the Everyday biscuits. Why had no one told her that it
was a terrible thing she was doing? Only Letty had done that
and Letty had rampaged and raved like a mad girl so that you

couldn't listen. Her mother had not said a word, her father only asking her if she was sure. Miss Mullover had congratulated her in a most profuse way. Would Tessa Enright have protested, Tessa who wasn't easily taken in? If she would, why hadn't she written a letter? Why hadn't she sent a wire, or come down on the bus, as any friend might? What was the use of the clergyman only asking if you loved him, nothing more? If his sisters didn't like her why hadn't they come up to her and said so? Why hadn't they warned her of their unpleasant intentions? Why hadn't she herself noticed how tedious it was when he told her yet again that a draper's shop couldn't move with the times? On their Sunday walks he had explained that certain haberdashery lines were being carried these days by the supermarkets and that this would increase. Why had she so foolishly listened instead of walking away?

On their walks she had heard about the shop in the past, about the time the overcoats had been sent to Mrs O'Keefe on approval, when a puppy had torn the fur off four of them. She had heard about bad debts, and the rules there were about the acceptance of cheques from strangers, and how some elderly woman came in from the hills every August and bought an outfit of clothes for a son who'd gone to England in 1941 and hadn't been back since. She had heard of her fiancé's astonishment that the YMCA billiard-room was not more frequented. She had apparently listened without it ever occurring to her that the repetition of these conversational subjects would one day grate on her nerves. Letty hadn't warned her about that; if only Letty knew that what she'd kept on about was the least of anyone's worries.

'There's something dried on to this plate,' Rose complained one evening in the dining-room. 'Cabbage it looks like.'

Rose had just eaten sausages and bacon from the plate. About to run a piece of bread over it in order to soak up the tasty fat that remained, she noticed that a shred of cabbage leaf had remained since the last time it was used.

'It's greens all right,' Rose said. She passed the plate to her sister, who scrutinized it in turn. It was definitely the remains of greens, Matilda said.

Elmer took no notice. Often at mealtimes he was lost in the depths of mathematical calculations that had originated in the accounting office.

'Take a look at that,' Matilda invited, and handed Mary Louise the plate, on which the well-peppered grease that Rose had been about to consume was now congealing. The offending piece of cabbage was stuck to the rim, its presence made more permanent by the heating of the plate in the oven. Probably it was cabbage, Mary Louise agreed, since cabbage had been the vegetable at the midday meal.

'I always took the mop to them when I washed the plates,' Matilda said. 'I used always to hold them up to see if there was anything like that left.'

'I could have eaten it,' Rose said.

'You would have shifted it wiping with the bread,' her sister agreed. 'You'd have eaten it then definitely.'

'Someone else's leavings.'

Mary Louise rose from the table and began to clear the supper dishes away. It could happen to anyone that a speck would be left behind on a plate. It wasn't as though it were poisonous.

'I wonder you didn't see it when you were drying,' she said to Matilda.

'When you're drying you take everything to be clean. You take it for granted.'

'Use a mop in future.' Rose's tone was peremptory, and Matilda glanced at Elmer, wondering if he'd heard. It was clear from the excitement in Matilda's face that she considered Rose had been more than a little daring to issue so direct an order, as to a child or a servant.

Mary Louise left the dining-room without replying but a

few minutes later, when she returned from the kitchen with a tray, she heard raised voices before she opened the door.

'No more than a pigsty,' Rose was saying.

Elmer mumbled something. Matilda said:

'The cheek of the creature, saying you'd see it when you were drying.'

'Knee-deep in manure that yard was! With people attending a wedding reception!'

Again there was a mumble from Elmer, interrupted by sudden shrillness from Rose.

'What the sister got up to with Gargan was the talk of the town. It's a wonder you didn't marry a tinker and have done with it.'

'Now look here,' Elmer protested, and Mary Louise heard his chair being pushed back. His voice, too, had become loud.

'Look nowhere,' shrieked Rose. 'We have her under our feet morning, noon and night.'

'Your own sister could have eaten the dirt on that plate,' Matilda reminded him. 'We could be killed dead as we sit here.'

'Arrah, don't be talking nonsense,' Elmer exclaimed crossly. 'What harm would a bit of cabbage do anyone?'

'Washed in soap it could do you harm,' Matilda insisted. 'And God knows what you'd find on your plate the next time.'

'The brother's a half-wit,' Rose said.

Elmer didn't reply to that. Matilda said that you might make a rice pudding in a dish that wallpaper paste had been mixed in. If the dish wasn't washed properly you'd be eating wallpaper paste. She suggested that Elmer should make inquiries as to whether or not wallpaper paste could kill you dead.

'She sucks up to the customers,' Rose said. 'Palavering all over them. D'you want a slice of cake, Elmer?'

There was a rattle of cups on saucers, and the sound of tea being poured.

'Is it cherry?' Elmer said.

'It is.'

'I'll take a slice so.'

There was silence then: the interlude was over. Mary Louise did not enter the dining-room, but returned to the kitchen. She was at the sink when the sisters came in ten minutes later with more of the suppertime dishes. They were quite nice to her, not mentioning the shred of cabbage. Rose offered her a slice of cherry cake but Mary Louise shook her head, not turning round from the sink because she didn't want them to see she'd been crying.

Elmer went out to the YMCA billiard-room that evening and when he returned Mary Louise was already in bed, with the light out, pretending to be asleep. They'd known she'd be coming back to the dining-room just at that moment. They'd known she'd pause outside the door, arrested by the cross voices. Her tears oozed from the corners of her eyes and ran into her hair, damping her ears and her neck. It hurt her most that they had called her brother a half-wit.

The following afternoon, when Rose and Matilda were engaged in the shop and Elmer was in the accounting office, Mary Louise ascended the bare stairs to the attics. There it was possible to weep noisily, sobbing and panting. She clenched her hands and beat the sides of her thighs with them, punishing her foolishness.

7

She dreams they are eight again, she and Tessa Enright. 'Once a month you have it,' Tessa Enright says on a road near Culleen, both of them sent out to look for a ewe that has strayed. 'You stop it with rags.'

It's the bane of a girl's life, Letty says. In the kitchen her mother says to be careful, picking the wedding date. The day she arrives in Miss Foye's house she has it. 'Don't leave me, please,' she begs that day, but he says he has to.

When they find the sheep it is dead beside a stone. She walks alone out of a wood and there Miss Foye's house is. 'You'll be well off there,' he says, and she puts her arms around his neck because he is right. He has never been unkind to her.

8

On Christmas Eve 1956 Elmer accompanied Renehan, the hardware merchant from the premises next door, to Hogan's Hotel. It was half-past four in the afternoon, as it always was when the two made their way along Bridge Street on Christmas Eve. A street musician who only appeared in the town at this time of year was playing a melodeon. The pavements were lively with people from the poor part of the town who left what shopping they could afford to the last couple of hours on Christmas Eve, hoping for bargains. A drunken man lurched in the street, talking to anyone who would listen.

'A poor year,' Renehan remarked as they turned into the side entrance that led to the hotel's bar. It was what the two men talked about on this Christmas occasion: the fluctuations of business during the previous twelve months, difficulties with suppliers in their two different fields of trade, profit and loss. Renehan was an older man, thin and trimly dressed, with a well-kept moustache and a reputation for personal vanity.

'Shocking,' Elmer agreed.

The hotel bar was crowded, as festive as the street outside. People like Elmer, not normally seen there, were standing in groups, talking loudly. Paper decorations were strung diagonally across the ceiling.

'You'll take the usual intoxicant, Elmer?' Renehan was known for his ornate, and in this case inaccurate, way of putting things. In his business life he cultivated a joky manner, believing that it attracted customers.

'As a matter of fact,' Elmer said, 'I'll take a small one.'

Renehan glanced amusedly at his companion. In all the years of this rendezvous the draper had never requested whiskey, not even the year he'd had a cold that should have kept him in bed. Renehan raised his eyebrows the way he'd once seen an actor doing all through a film.

'That's married life for you!' he suggested and gently touched Elmer's chest with his elbow.

Elmer didn't reply; you didn't have to with Renehan. He remained at the back of the bar while the hardware merchant pushed his way through the crowd. He hadn't drunk whiskey since the night of his honeymoon; last Christmas he'd had a mineral as usual. It might indeed be married life, he reflected as he stood there. Maybe there was more to Renehan's facetiousness than the man realized.

Noticing his presence, other men saluted Elmer across the bar, other shopkeepers for the most part, a couple of bank officials, Hanlon the solicitor. He wondered what they thought, or if they thought anything at all. Fifteen months he'd been married.

'Compliments of the season!' Renehan raised his glass and Elmer slightly raised his. The last thing he remembered of that Saturday night was the barman insisting that he wanted to close. The walk back to the Strand Hotel, the hall and the stairs, any parting words: none of that had remained with him. The next thing he could recollect after the barman said he had a home to go to himself was waking up with his clothes still on him.

Renehan offered him a cigarette, as if presuming that since Elmer was drinking whiskey he would have taken up tobacco as well. Elmer shook his head. He'd never smoked a cigarette in his life, he said, and didn't intend to.

'The better for it.' Renehan's thin brown fingers were illuminated by the flare of a match as he lit his own. He inhaled,
and blew a smoke-ring. He mentioned a farmer to whom he
had refused credit during the year.

'The same with myself,' Elmer said.

They hadn't revisited McBirney's bar during their remaining
days at the Strand Hotel because he considered that going
there in the first place had been a mistake. On their last night
one of the men who shared their table in the dining-room was
persistent with an invitation, and Mary Louise apparently
wished to return to the public house, indeed seemed to have
agreed that they would do so. But he'd stuck to his guns. For
one thing, the episode had cost a fortune.

Renehan spoke of other customers, of possible bad debts in
the months to come. He mentioned farmers on whom an eye
needed to be kept, whose fortunes were on the wane. As well
as the three sons who worked with him in the shop, Renehan
had a daughter who attended to the accounts. In the bar of
Hogan's Hotel the two men had many a time agreed that it
made a substantial difference, not having to employ anyone.

'Is it gin?' Elmer asked.

'With a drop of hot water.'

He made his way to the bar. The manageress of the hotel
was assisting the barman with the Christmas custom. She was
an unmarried woman of Elmer's age, on the stout side, with
plucked eyebrows and hair that reminded Elmer of the landlady's hair at the Strand Hotel, being the same reddish shade.
He had remarked on the similarity at the time, but Mary
Louise said she didn't think she'd ever laid eyes on the manageress of Hogan's. Bridget her name was.

'What'll I get you, Mr Quarry?' She smiled at him, her
hands held out for the glasses. She was wearing a black dress,
and a necklace that glittered on the flesh that was exposed
where the dress ended. One of her teeth was marked with

lipstick. 'Oh God, I'm sorry! I didn't say Happy Christmas, Mr Quarry.'

'Happy Christmas, Bridget. A small one for myself. A gin with hot water in it for Mr Renehan.'

Years ago he had wondered about marrying a Catholic. When the time came, he'd thought he might have to if there wasn't anyone else about. He'd looked down from the accounting office one day and seen the hotel manageress – assistant manageress she'd been then – holding a summer dress up against her. For a couple of weeks he'd considered making an approach, but then he'd decided there was no hurry. Would the whole thing be a different story now, he wondered, if he'd reached a different decision? Mixed marriages were two a penny these days.

'How's everything with you, Mr Quarry?' she asked, taking his money and quickly returning the change.

'Tumbling along, Bridget, tumbling along.'

'Well, that's great.' She turned, as she spoke, to serve someone else. He didn't know why she hadn't married.

'Good luck,' Renehan said, raising his glass again.

In previous years Elmer had drunk his second glass of lemonade quickly, gulping it and then putting the glass down on a nearby surface. He'd usually been back in the shop by ten to five. Now he sipped his whiskey slowly, actually savouring the harsh taste. He found it pleasant in the bar, pleasanter in a way than the empty YMCA billiard-room.

'Isn't it an extraordinary thing,' he said, 'that Bridget never married?'

Renehan told him a long story about Bridget being in love with a young curate when she was young herself, how it had been the passion of her life.

'Father Curtin. Whippersnapper with sideburns.'

'I remember the man well.'

'Changes were made when the p.p. got a whiff of it.'

'Ah, they would be all right.'

'There was talk at the time of Father Curtin leaving the priesthood. Anyway, he didn't and poor Bridget was left high and dry.'

'Well, I never heard that one.'

'It was kept under wraps. There's not many in this town that knows it to this day.'

'Only Bridget.'

'Well, Bridget naturally.'

Other scandals from the past, known to both men, were recalled. Renehan bought two more drinks, and then Elmer did.

'I'd best be getting back,' he said, realizing that it was almost six o'clock. Renehan moved away to talk to someone else. Elmer returned to the shop.

Something began that Christmas Eve, although Elmer at the time was not aware of it. Halfway through January, instead of looking in at the YMCA billiard-room, he found himself turning into the side entrance that led to Hogan's bar. It was much emptier on this occasion, but even so there were a couple of regular drinkers there. Knowing them by sight, Elmer nodded in their direction and ordered himself a glass of whiskey from the barman, Gerry, who also acted as the hotel's porter. He sat on a high stool at the bar, talking to Gerry about the weather.

A few weeks later this visit was repeated. Elmer left the house above the shop with every intention of playing a lone game of billiards for an hour or two, but found himself again turning into the side entrance. On both occasions he made no reference to this change of plan when he later returned home. The whiskey deadened an ache that oppressed him. It lifted a weight from his spirits, if only for an hour or so. Too much, as on his wedding night, would bring a fog of darkness, but often in the accounting room, watching his sisters and his wife in the shop below, such darkness seemed like a balm.

By the spring of that year Elmer's visits to the billiard-room had dwindled further, but since they had always fallen off when the days lengthened this passed unnoticed by Daly the caretaker. The difference was that with the advent of autumn they were not resumed. During the intervening months Elmer had had no excuse to leave the house in the evenings, for if he stated – as once or twice he did – that he intended to go for a walk Mary Louise prepared herself to accompany him. So instead he took to calling in briefly at Hogan's bar in the afternoon, and was glad when September came so that he could spend longer there under the pretext of playing billiards. By the end of the year people in the town had begun to notice that Elmer Quarry was often, these days, in Hogan's.

Nothing was missed by Rose and Matilda; nothing ever had been. They'd been sharp of eye and ear as children, and the tendency had developed in their spinsterhood. In Matilda's life – as in Letty's and Bridget the hotel manageress's – there had, once upon a time, been romance. Matilda's fiancé had joined the RAF on the outbreak of the war, and been killed in 1945, months before hostilities ceased. He had not gone down in action, for fighting was mostly over for aircraft gunners then, but had died as a result of an accident at an aerodrome in Leicestershire: a devil-may-care pilot, in attempting to fly through an open hangar, had caused a tragic disaster. Rose had never been proposed to, and the spinsterhood of the sisters had developed like two strengthening growths from the same root. The root was the family – generations of Quarrys, of small-town Protestants made special through not being of the mass. Matilda and Rose were steadfast, not in their beliefs or in their faith, but in what they believed themselves to be: a little superior.

The sisters could not help themselves, and long ago had become lost in assuming they could not: now they did not try. Why should they? And why should they put themselves out by the slightest iota for a penniless creature whom their brother might have bought at a fun-fair if they'd all been living a hundred years ago? He'd married her to breed with. He'd married her because of his sentimental notion that the name should continue above the shop. That kind of compulsion belonged to another age also – and had made sense then, neither would deny that. Now it was only slop.

On Christmas Eve when Elmer had returned to the house with the smell of drink on his breath they both noticed it at once. But they didn't comment on the fact to one another. They knew their brother always went to Hogan's on Christmas Eve with Renehan; they'd never thought about what he had to drink there. The whiff of spirits he brought back with him didn't seem significant, more something to be expected when you returned from a bar. But one evening in January the telltale whiff was there again. Neither of them asked him if he hadn't been at the YMCA; he said nothing himself; and then – not long afterwards – they smelt it on his breath on another occasion. Still they did not remark on this to one another.

Where the marriage was concerned, the sisters knew that nothing could be changed. Before he'd made the mistake they had pointed it out to him. They had done their best, as sometimes they'd had to as children, being older sisters. The mistake was what all of them had to live with now.

'He's drinking on the quiet,' Rose said at last.

'Yes.'

They were waiting for him one night on the first-floor landing. His eyes were bleary, both noticed. He kept opening and closing his lips in a way that was unusual for him: they knew his personal habits, the quirks and twitches that were part of him. They did not speak on the landing, nor did he. He passed them by, and went on upstairs. In the front room his wife, Her Ladyship, turned on the wireless. A few minutes later they heard her going upstairs too.

A veterinary surgeon began to take Letty out. He came to the farm to examine an ailing heifer, and when he'd finished he sat for a long time over a cup of tea in the kitchen. A fortnight later he called in with his account and invited Letty to the Electric Cinema. He was a good-looking man, red-haired, a few years older than she was, a Catholic called Dennehy. 'It's the way things are,' Mr Dallon remarked to his wife in the privacy of their bedroom. Both of them hoped that nothing would come of the relationship.

The schoolroom next to the church, in which Miss Mullover had taught from 1906 until 1950, closed on her retirement. Arrangements had since been made for the Protestant children of the town and the neighbourhood, either to be driven to a school fifteen miles away or to attend the convent or the Christian Brothers'. Miss Mullover had seen that coming, and even took a little pride in being the last Protestant teacher to have a school in the town: a successor – some flighty thing from the Church of Ireland Training College – might have irritated her more.

'You've settled down?' she prompted Mary Louise, meeting her one day in South West Street when enough time had passed to permit the question. She'd said the same thing often before, to pupils who had married. Settling was necessary, which was why, ages ago, she'd chosen that particular word. No girl, of whatever age – no man either, when it came to it – could expect to find the first year or so of marriage free of the hazards of personal adjustment. That stood to reason, yet was not always taken into consideration in advance.

'Oh, yes,' Mary Louise responded, but a quality in her tone of voice caused Miss Mullover to doubt her. Conversing with her on later occasions, she was confirmed in this opinion, and came to realize – to her great disappointment – that her optimism at the time of the wedding had been misplaced.

9

Memory is sometimes perfect, clear as a light. First thing when she wakes she wallows in it, assisted by the dusky tranquillity of dawn. The morning after the visit she wallows in the favourite year of all her life, the year the Russians put a dog into space, the year of Bill Haley, the year De Valera proclaimed a state of emergency. A nun in the Sacred Heart convent, expected to live to be a hundred, died at ninety-nine. A sewage problem occurred in Conlon Street, necessitating pneumatic drilling, new pipes and re-surfacing. A fawn-coloured tomcat, property of the gasworks manager, attacked a neighbour's birdcage, detaching it from its hook and provoking threats of legal action. Tyrell's the vegetable shop closed. Humphrey Bogart, Letty's favourite – plastered all over the bedroom at Culleen – died. 1957 it was.

'Mary Louise,' she whispers in the dawn that comes after the upset of her visitor. 'Mary Louise Dallon. Mrs Quarry as is.' He is old now, the sisters older still. He could live for a dozen more years, fourteen or fifteen even, the sisters endlessly. He pays for her keep in Miss Foye's house, and always has. Years ago the sisters tried to make her father pay but of course there was nothing to spare for that at Culleen. 'Your husband's good,' Miss Foye says often, because not everyone here is paid for. The bigger dormitories are bare; the unpaid-for have enamel mugs and plates. He's a decent man, driven to drink. It isn't his fault that they're closing down the houses.

They'll bundle the obstreperous together, somewhere else will be found for them. She's never been obstreperous herself.

A figure emerges from the gloom and sits on her bed with a blanket around her: Mrs Leavy from Youghal come over to tell her dreams.

She listens and then she tells her own.

10

On Sundays, having exchanged what news there was over a cup of tea at Culleen, Mary Louise usually began her journey back to the town at about a quarter to five, her spirits drooping as the journey progressed. But one March afternoon in 1957 she turned off the road that led to the town and cycled aimlessly, exploring a neighbourhood she did not know well. She chose a different direction the following week and when, eventually, all the ways became familiar to her she returned repeatedly to a favourite one. She was ironically reminded of the Sunday walks of her courtship, the bicycle left in a gateway, the crossroads where she and Elmer turned to the right, the woods they passed through, the humped bridge. It seemed like a lifetime ago, as deep in the past as the first day she attended Miss Mullover's schoolroom. Whenever she crossed the humped bridge on her bicycle she reflected again, each time with greater bitterness, that someone might have warned her. Why had it been only Letty? And why had Letty made her concern sound like envy?

One Sunday, having ridden further than usual, she found herself at the head of a grassy avenue. Rusty iron gates, set in a spacious curve of railings that long ago had lost all signs of paint, seemed as though they had been flung back with a gesture in some other generation, remaining so to support a jungle of brambles, and ivy branches as thick as an arm. From the road Mary Louise could see the stark white house to which the avenue led, the modest property of her Aunt Emmeline. Only once before had she been here, when she and Letty were entrusted with a gift: a pound of the butter their mother used to make. The butter was later sent to the house regularly, but after that single occasion the task of delivering it became James's because his sisters had complained so about a mile-long hill up which they'd had to push their bicycles. As she stared down the avenue, Mary Louise found herself recalling that her Aunt Emmeline's only child – the cousin with whom, for a while at school, she had imagined she was in love – had been able to attend the wedding service in spite of his invalid state. If his condition had worsened she'd probably have heard. Robert his name was.

Mary Louise turned away, pedalling back the way she'd come, but had hardly gone more than a few yards when a car, thick with dust, rounded the bend she was approaching. The horn was sounded, her Aunt Emmeline waved, and then the car drew up. Feeling stupid and caught out, cross because she should have avoided this neighbourhood, Mary Louise dismounted. She knew she'd gone red in the face, and hoped it would be assumed that she was simply out of breath.

'Heavens above!' her aunt exclaimed, winding down the car window. 'Are you visiting us, Mary Louise?'

She shook her head. She tried to think of an excuse, but none would come. There was no reason in the world why she should be here on a Sunday evening. She said the first thing that came into her head.

'I wondered how Robert was.'

'You've been to see him?'

'No, no. I just wondered – '

'Robert's not bad at all these days. Come on down, dear. He'd love to see you.'

The head – shaggy-haired, the skin of the forehead reddened by exposure to the weather, as the cheeks below it were – was withdrawn. The car moved forward, hesitated, then turned in wildly to the entrance, and advanced at speed on the avenue. Mary Louise rode after it.

Robert – a wiry, gangling child with mischievous eyes – was now a pale young man, and the mischief in his eyes had turned into what seemed like amusement. He wore glasses, which he had not in the past; but his spare, bony frame reminded Mary Louise of the child he'd been. A shock of dark hair kept falling over his forehead; an adult's smile hovered on his lips.

'Heavens above!' he exclaimed, exactly as his mother had. 'Mary Louise!'

He sat by a fire in a large untidy room. Tables and armchairs were covered with drawings of winter trees, and papers with scribbles in green ink on them, and books. In a window alcove battalions of toy soldiers were engaged in warfare. Fishing-rods and nets were a muddle in a corner. Glass doors led to a conservatory where a vine grew.

The time Mary Louise and Letty had cycled over with the butter they had not been invited to penetrate further into this house than the kitchen: all she saw now was strange to her. But she had often heard the house talked about, usually in the same breath as her Aunt Emmeline's husband, who had died before she was born. Her mother's sister had married money, it was said, a statement invariably followed by the reminder that the money hadn't lasted because the man she married was a gambler. 'Charm to burn,' Mr Dallon used to say, and – unlike the money – the charm had lasted to the end. Mary Louise never knew what it was her uncle had died of, and had sometimes wondered if it was the same affliction that Robert suffered from.

'I was out looking for primroses,' she lied to her cousin in the untidy room, having noticed a few by the side of the avenue. She always went to Culleen on a Sunday, she added, but today she'd ridden about a bit, thinking to pick spring flowers.

Becoming fuller as he listened, her cousin's smile straightened the line of his lips, which otherwise were on a slant. He didn't seem interested in the reasons for her presence.

'I met Aunt Emmeline,' she doggedly added.

'Does marriage suit you, Mary Louise?'

She replied that she was used to it by now. The words came scuttling out: she hadn't meant to answer the question quite like that, and realized he knew she was being evasive.

'Well, I suppose you would be used to it. What a silly question!'

He took his spectacles off and wiped them on a handkerchief. He was wearing brown corduroy trousers and a tweed jacket, and brown brogue shoes. A watch-chain hung from the buttonhole of his left lapel and disappeared into the pocket beneath it. The family rumour was that this watch had been returned from a soft-hearted pawnbroker when he heard that Robert's father had died without leaving much behind.

'D'you serve in that shop?'

'Part of the day I serve there.'

'I often wondered.'

Her Aunt Emmeline brought in tea. She placed a tray on a small table which she cleared of books and papers, and pulled the table closer to the fire. A dog had followed her, a Kerry Blue.

'We don't often have a visitor,' her aunt said, and Mary Louise could see that she was pleased, delighted even. She eked out a living selling apples and grapes, and the vegetables she grew. The pair of them wouldn't have survived, Mary Louise had heard her father say, were it not for the apples and the grapes.

'D'you remember you and Tessa Enright putting worms in that girl's desk?' Robert said. 'Who was that girl?'

'Possy Luke.'

'She screeched like she'd been bitten.'

'Poor Possy! She was afraid of worms.'

Their schooldays were talked about, and her aunt asked after Mary Louise's family. She'd heard about Letty going out with the vet. She knew him; she said he was likeable.

'How's James getting on?' Robert asked.

'James is fine.'

This appeared to be true. Her brother didn't complain as much as he used to; he didn't fly off the handle so easily. For the first time in his life he seemed to be aware that he was the farm's inheritor, that the work he did was for himself. This transformation had come about since Mary Louise's marriage, and had intensified since Letty had begun to go out with the vet.

'And how are the Quarrys?' her aunt inquired.

They, too, were fine, Mary Louise replied.

'Well, that's good.'

'I mustn't stay long.'

'Oh, don't be in a hurry, dear. We don't see much of you.'

Robert laughed. 'We don't see her at all.'

She told them how the bicycle ride, and the long hill, had years ago been too much for Letty and herself, how it had jaded them, which was why James had been given the task of delivering the weekly gift of butter. She thought she'd better say that, in case offence had ever been taken.

'That's why we know James better,' her aunt said.

'He used to play bagatelle with me,' Robert said. 'He loved bagatelle.'

'He plays cards with the Edderys now.'

They laughed. But she wondered if she should have mentioned cards in view of the stories about the gambling that had left her aunt and her cousin penurious. Again she felt warmth creeping into her cheeks, and hoped they wouldn't notice.

'Stay and talk to Robert for a little,' her aunt begged. The soft plea in her tone had an edge of anxiety to it. She rose as she spoke and poured them each another cup of tea. Then she went away, the Kerry Blue ambling sleepily after her.

'She thinks I don't see people,' Robert said when the door closed behind her. 'Which of course is true.'

'What do you do all day, Robert?'

'I come downstairs to this room. I'm very fond of this room. I light the fire when it's chilly. We have breakfast together in the kitchen. The rest of the day depends on all sorts of things.'

She remembered his being driven to school by his mother when everyone else either walked or cycled. She had always associated him with his mother, that weather-chapped face behind the steering-wheel. She never saw her aunt in the town these days, and she wondered where the shopping was done. She had passed a general store and a petrol pump a couple of miles back. It would be there, she guessed.

'A quiet life,' her cousin said.

'Yes.'

The crooked smile expanded and straightened. He was watching her: all the time he was talking she could feel him watching her.

'I don't think I'd have been much good at anything noisier.'

She smiled in turn, not knowing whether to deny that, deciding not to. He said:

'I used to want to be an auctioneer when I was at Miss Mullover's. I fancied myself shouting the odds. Can you believe it? I really did.'

'I can't see you an auctioneer, Robert.'

'Useless I'd have been.'

'I wanted to work in Dodd's. It seemed like paradise.'

'You got the next best thing.'

'I thought of Quarry's too.'

'And is it paradise, Mary Louise?'

'Oh, all that was just a childish thing.'

He laughed, still watching her. His eyes were brown, but very dark, nearly black when they lost their luminosity. His glasses, tortoiseshell-rimmed, perfectly round, suited him.

'Come and look at another childish thing,' he said.

He pushed himself out of his armchair and led her to the table in the window where the soldiers were displayed. It was the double battle of the Aisne and Champagne, he said.

'General Nivelle's plan was to break through the German line between Vailly and Reims. This cluster of German armies was under the command of the Crown Prince himself.'

He pointed to where the German line had held, between Vendresse and La Ville aux Bois. Elsewhere it had been pushed firmly back. Mary Louise wondered which war was being fought, and for what purpose.

'The Germans mustered a good counter-attack, but even so the French pressed on, breaking through the Chemin des Dames.'

Arrows with neatly printed names indicated all that. Some of the soldiers were lying down. These were the dead, he said.

She plucked up courage. 'Which war was this?'

'The one before last. The double battle took place in the spring of 1917.'

She followed him back to the fire. She began to say again that she must go, but already he was explaining that if the Russians hadn't been preoccupied with their revolution it would have been a different story. She wanted to tell him that in Miss Mullover's history lessons she'd been fascinated by Jeanne d'Arc. Shyness held her back again.

'In the end it was the Germans who emerged victorious from the Aisne and Champagne encounter. I'm sorry: this is boring.'

'No. No, it isn't.'

'I was explaining how I spend the day because you asked. I play with soldiers. And read. I read a very great deal.'

Mary Louise was not much of a one for reading herself. As well as *Picturegoer*, Letty bought *Model Housekeeping*, and there used to be the *Girl's Friend* years ago, when she and Letty were younger. In the farmhouse there was a bookcase on the landing. Mary Louise had read *The Garden of Allah* and *Greenery Street*; at school they'd read *Lorna Doone*. She had never even looked at the titles of the books in the attics of the Quarrys' house.

'When it isn't winter,' her cousin said, 'I do things in the vegetable beds. Sometimes I wander down to the stream. There's a heron on that stream.'

'I've never seen a heron.'

'You could see one here, Mary Louise.'

He smiled again, and all of a sudden she wanted him to know that once she'd thought herself to be in love with him. She didn't know why she had that urge, and of course it couldn't be realized. But she thought it would be nice if he knew that being an invalid didn't make him pathetic. He probably did know, she thought then: he seemed extraordinarily happy with the limited life he led.

'It's been nice seeing you again,' was what she said, and before she left the room she promised to return.

'It would be good of you,' his mother said in the kitchen. 'You've no idea how much your visit delighted him.'

Mary Louise wanted it to be a secret. She didn't want it known at Culleen, and certainly not in the Quarrys' house, that she had spent an hour with her invalid cousin. She almost asked her aunt if they might keep this afternoon as something among the three of them, but she could not find the words. Then it occurred to her that her mother and her aunt were nowadays not often in touch; sometimes a whole year went by. And since her aunt no longer shopped in the town there seemed little likelihood of anything slipping out in conversation there.

As she rode swiftly on the grassy avenue, she tried to remember what being in love with her cousin had felt like. Had it really been much the same, less potent even, than her feelings for the cinema images of James Stewart? For almost twelve years, since she was twelve herself, she had not devoted more than an ordinary, passing thought to the boy who'd been unable to go on attending school, even though he'd been driven in a car. Unfortunate, she had considered him, leaving it at that.

That Sunday evening it was easier in the dining-room when Mary Louise took her usual place between her husband and Matilda. Elmer helped himself to the egg salad Rose had prepared, asking questions about the farm, and vaguely responding to the answers.

'I hear your sister's chummed up with Dennehy,' Matilda said.

'I think so.'

'Funny, that.'

The silence that usually followed this favourite comment of Matilda's did so again. Elmer said eventually:

'Is that the vet from Ennistane crossroads?'

Rose affirmed this. Dennehy's father was the publican at Ennistane, she added.

'Does your mother mind?' Matilda asked.

'Mind?'

'A person like Dennehy.'

'She didn't say she minded.'

'RC of course?' Elmer always cut lettuce and tomato up very fine, and mashed a hard-boiled egg. Having done so now, he reached out for salad cream.

'Oh, yes,' Rose said.

'They're not without means, the Dennehys.' Matilda nodded

more than once, to lend significance to this. 'Perhaps there's that.'

She spoke lightly, as if she sought to rid her statement of its implication, or to suggest that if the words were examined carefully it would be found that, in spite of the emphasis of her nodding, nothing much was being suggested. Carefully, she scraped butter on to a slice of soda bread. Tidily, she cut the slice in half and then in half again.

'Even so,' Rose took up the theme, 'I'd have thought Mrs Dallon would be concerned.'

Mary Louise looked away. She half-closed her eyes and saw the soldiers on the table, the little printed arrows, the line of cannon. The uniforms were exactly as they'd been in reality, her cousin had explained, every detail right. She wondered where they'd come from. In a poverty-stricken household the wealth of colour seemed quite out of place.

'Rough,' Rose said, the word appearing to be thrown out at random, attached to nothing.

Matilda nodded, and again there was a silence. Elmer passed his cup for more tea. Rose poured it. Matilda added milk.

She would go again next Sunday. She would spend no more than ten minutes at Culleen and then ride quickly on. This time she'd find the courage to ask her aunt if it could be a secret. She'd give a reason, she'd think of something during the week.

'We need to order gimp,' Elmer was saying. 'And ticking.'

On Sundays he went through the stock. He had a method, he'd told Mary Louise on one of their pre-marriage walks. Every Sunday morning he took a different line and checked the supply in stock: haberdashery one week, velvets and velveteens the next, chintzes, satins and silks, then hats and dresses, then overcoats, suits, all menswear, socks and braces. On Sunday evenings he went through the books, minutely comparing the entries with last week's. It wasn't necessary, any more than it was necessary to keep a record of the particular garments that were repeatedly rejected when sent out on approval. But all this kind of thing interested him. All this was part of trading.

'I bet a shilling he'll be in this week,' Matilda said, referring to the traveller from whom gimp and ticking were ordered. 'He's due since February.'

Mary Louise wondered if there'd be a different battle on the table the next time. Would there be two different sides, the uniforms different, the words on the arrows printed in a different language? She imagined her cousin in the vegetable garden that kept his mother and him going. She saw him bent over a bed in the sunshine, weeding between rows of lettuce. How strange his solitary life must be! And how strange for her aunt to have married money that was not there! Was what they implied about Letty true? Was she going out with the vet in the same way as she herself had gone out with Elmer Quarry? Would Letty marry him and sometimes in the night reach out for him, seeking his physical warmth? Or would all that be a different kind of thing for Letty?

'There's a couple of those travellers getting slack,' Elmer said.

She and her cousin had nothing in common; pushed away into a corner, this realization had remained there ever since he'd talked about the battle in France. Reading was what he liked; sometimes when he said something she didn't understand it. He'd be bored if she kept turning up on Sundays; you could see he liked to be alone in spite of what his mother said.

'Surprising your mother could accept Dennehy's roughness,' Rose said. 'Surprising, that.'

11

In time all those who can understand realize that nowadays things are being ordered differently. The three doctors who regularly visit the house talk in turn to those whom they believe would be better off in what they make a point of calling 'the community'. Where there is no family, or if a family does not wish to cooperate, places will be found in sheltered accommodation.

'Is it community singing?' Belle D inquires. 'Is that what they mean?' Her name is Belle Dymock, but for reasons of her own she has forbidden her surname's use, while insisting also that her first name should not be employed on its own.

'The community's where you came from,' the Spanish wife replies. Her surname, too, has caused difficulties, not because she dislikes it but because no one can pronounce it. She is not, in fact, Spanish herself, but has acquired her sobriquet through marrying a Spaniard who deserted her in Gibraltar.

'Did you ever hear the like?' another woman asks, a faded woman who speaks only when a subject catches her imagination.

'It's the tablets,' Mrs Leavy explains. 'Medication works wonders.'

They all say that. They say it and repeat it: the new drugs of the 1980s make the miracle possible. The doctor who cares for Belle D has told her she could easily work in the carpet factory again. Pretty Bríd Beamish – no fault of her own she took a wrong turning – will be adorned in wedding finery yet, no reason in the world why she shouldn't be. All that must be ensured is that the medication is taken, daily and precisely as prescribed. The assistance of family members will be required, assurances insisted upon. 'Isn't it the best leave-taking you could have?' jovially remarks the doctor who has a beard, smiling at the faces of the unsmiling. Father Malley sits with each departing inmate, recalling Our Lady and her mercy.

'Mary Louise! Come here, Mary Louise!' Small Sadie beckons, and questions when she is obeyed: 'Will you go back to the graveyard, Mary Louise? Will you get up to your tricks?' Laughter cackles from the tiny woman's throat. In the house she is often likened to a hen because of that noise she makes.

'What tricks are those, Sadie?'

But Sadie only shakes her head. At night she is locked away alone. She broke a gardener's arm one time. She's in the house because too often she believes she has to break things and tear off wallpaper. A week ago she was told she would remain in care for a while yet.

'Sadie's the lucky one!' she cries in the same shrill way. 'Poor old eejits, what good is it to you? What good the Holy Apostolic Church? What good the dogs in the traps? Dog eats dog, Thundering Joe and Flashby. Tinned with rabbit.'

'Oh, hold your damn noise,' a woman snaps.

12

He brought binoculars in case the heron was about. The soldiers had been his father's, he said. There were just those she'd seen, French and German: the battles he could reconstruct were limited.

'You've heard about the watch?' He lifted it from his jacket pocket. They were standing on the shallow bank of the stream he'd spoken of. If Mary Louise kept watching she'd see tiny trout swimming by.

'It's a pretty watch.' She had admired it without saying anything when she'd first noticed him snapping it open. It was slender, golden, its case engraved, the chain finer than was usual.

'My father, you know.' He laughed. 'You have heard, haven't you?'

'People tell a story.'

'It's true. If he had remembered the soldiers were still in the house he'd have tried to sell them too. I wish I'd known him.'

He explained that at the time when he'd ceased to come to school it hadn't been because he was weaker than usual, but because his mother couldn't any longer spare the time to drive there and back twice a day. She couldn't afford help in the vegetable garden they made their living from: every hour was precious.

'She taught me in the evenings. Not that I know much.'

'Actually, you seem to know a lot.'

'Certain subjects we didn't bother with at all. I can hardly count, for instance.' He lifted the binoculars from around his neck and handed them to her. She focused them and searched the undergrowth, upstream and down. He took them from her, then shook his head.

'We're out of luck today.'

But at least they saw the trout going by, a couple at a time. You could catch them with a net, he said.

'Poor little things. I wouldn't want to.'

He laughed. He pushed the shock of hair back from his forehead, which was his most familiar gesture. The smaller the trout were, he said, the better they tasted. Then he said:

'They're an intimidating pair, aren't they, your husband's sisters?'

'A bit, I suppose.'

'You live in the same house as them?'

'Oh, yes. Above the shop.'

'I'm not so sure I'd entirely care for that.'

They walked back the way they'd come. He said:

'At your wedding my mother and I were in the second pew. I kept wondering what you'd look like. You passed up the aisle with your father but I only saw your back.'

'I turned round when the whole thing was over.'

'You were Mrs Quarry then.'

'Yes, I was.'

'I hadn't seen you before that for ages.' He paused. 'Actually, you were beautiful that day. If you want to know, that's what I thought.'

The flush came into her face. She looked away.

'To tell you the truth, I've always thought you were a beauty.'

'A beauty! Oh, go away with you, Robert!'

'I always thought that,' he repeated evenly.

He didn't look at her; he wasn't watching her, as he had on the previous Sunday. He stooped to pick a dandelion.

'But I'm not in the least – '

'You are, Mary Louise.'

She wanted him to go on, to say it again, to go into detail. But about to speak, he hesitated and then was silent.

'I'm not beautiful in the least.'

'Doesn't Elmer Quarry think you are?'

'I don't know.'

'Ask him and he'll tell you. Of course he does.'

They were not walking in the direction of the house any more. He had veered off to the left, crossing the slope of a field.

'Do you ever read Russian novels?' he suddenly asked, disappointing her with this change of subject.

She shook her head.

'I have a favourite Russian novelist,' he said.

He continued on the subject as they walked. He spoke of people with difficult Russian names. He described a man with a long thin face and a tapering, flat-topped nose.

'Where're we going?'

'There's a graveyard. A most peculiar place.'

He related the plot of a story, so meticulously describing a hero and a heroine that they formed in her mind, their features like features seen on the screen of the Electric, a little more shadowy at first, but then acquiring clarity.

'I used to think once,' he confessed, 'that I might try to write stuff like that.'

'And did you try?'

'I wasn't any good at it.'

'Oh, I'm sure – '

'No, I wasn't any good at it.'

They reached the graveyard, by the side of a lane that appeared to be no longer used. Its small iron gate could not be moved, he said, but the wall was not difficult to clamber over. He took her hand to help her.

'I'd love to be buried here,' he said. 'It isn't full but no one bothers with it now.'

It was hot among the headstones. The grass was long between the graves, like hay waiting to be cut even though it was spring.

'A secret place,' he said.

'Yes, it is.'

Stunted thorn trees bounded it within its stone wall. If ever there had been paths they were no longer to be discerned. Some headstones lurched crookedly; those flat upon the graves had mostly sunk at one end.

'I love it here,' he said.

They sat down on the long grass, leaning against a headstone that recorded a death in the Attridge family. Other Attridges were all around them, other branches of the family, other generations. *James Attridge, born 1742, died September 1803, Safe Now in Heavenly Love. Percival Attridge, 1769–1828. Charlotte Jane Attridge, died 1840, aged one year. Susan Emily, wife of Charles. Safe Now in Heaven's Arms. Peace, Perfect Peace.*

'It's funny there isn't a church,' Mary Louise said.

'It's half a mile away. Derelict now.'

'They're Protestants buried here, aren't they?'

'Yes, they're Protestants.'

'A pity about the church.'

'There's a rosebush growing all over it. In and out of the windows. June's the time to see that little church.'

'I'd like to see it.'

'I'll show you some time. And the heron's really there too, you know. I didn't make the heron up.'

'I didn't think you made the heron up. Why would you do that?'

'To make you come back.'

She wanted to say she'd thought her ignorance about the

things he liked would bore him, but she couldn't find the courage. She traced a pattern on her pale green skirt with the tip of a forefinger. Her legs were tucked beneath her. The stone was warm on her back.

'I'd have come back anyway.'

'When I had to be taken away from Miss Mullover's because there wasn't time to drive me I wanted to try cycling. I did one day, but it didn't work.' He smiled. He was wearing the same corduroy trousers and the same tweed jacket he'd been wearing last week. His tie was tweed also, quite colourful, greens and reds. 'I tried to arrange to go in with the milk lorry, but that didn't work either because it went some roundabout way, and I wouldn't have been able to get home again.'

'You see buses for country children these days.'

'D'you know why I wanted to continue at school so much?'

'No, I don't.'

'D'you mind if I tell you?'

'Why should I mind?'

'It might embarrass you.'

'Tessa Enright used to say everything embarrasses me. Miss Embarrassment she called me.'

'I was fond of you, Mary Louise.'

She closed her eyes. She felt a flush, hot as a red-hot poker, creeping over her neck, into her cheeks, over her forehead, down into her shoulders even. It was so intense it made her skin feel tight. She'd never had one as bad as this, she thought.

'I *have* embarrassed you,' he said, and added hastily: 'It all belongs to that time. It has nothing to do with now. It was awful not being able to turn my head to look at you, like having part of me cut away. I can't tell you what it was like. And yet what good would any of it have been?'

'When you're that age – '

'Oh, I know, I know.'

She felt the colour draining away from her face and neck. A

drop of perspiration itched on her chin, but she didn't lift a hand, not wishing to draw attention to it, nor to distract him.

'I've always wanted to tell you,' he said.

She nodded, not knowing how to respond in any other way. She might have said she had thought herself to be in love with him: it was the natural thing to do, yet she could not. Did she know of his glances in Miss Mullover's schoolroom without quite realizing it? What connection had there been? Something had been there, between them, something real – even if only for a week or two, before she transferred her affections to James Stewart. Yet a week or two was surely enough: that seemed so now.

'You'll still come back, Mary Louise? We're cousins, after all. And anyway, you're married now.'

'Of course I'll come back.'

'People should know when they've been admired. That's what I feel.'

'It's nice of you to tell me, Robert.'

The conversation ended there. Soon afterwards they walked back to the house, where the binoculars were hung on a hook in the passage outside the kitchen, and then there was tea beside the fire, as there had been the Sunday before. 'Let me read you this,' he said, taking a book from one of the piles around him.

It was time for her to go, but instead she watched him, opening the book, smiling, turning a page or two, raising his eyebrows before murmuring something about the length of the introduction, and then beginning:

'*A gentleman in the early forties, wearing check trousers and a dusty overcoat, came out on to the low porch of the coaching-inn . . .*'

She believed she had never listened to a voice as beautiful. Delight caressed each word he uttered, gentleness or vigour matched phrase and sentence. If all he'd read was a timetable she would have been entranced.

'The date was the twentieth of May in the year 1859 . . .'

It was later than it had been last week by more than two hours when Mary Louise left. On the outskirts of the town she dismounted and unscrewed the valve of her bicycle's back tyre. She'd had a puncture, she said when she arrived in the dining-room. The meal was over, and had been for some time.

The vet, Dennehy, was attentive. He and Letty saw *His Kind of Woman*, brought back for a second showing at the Electric, and *The Harder They Fall*, and *Cast a Dark Shadow*. Dennehy liked dancing and when he suggested the Dixie dancehall Letty did not demur, as she had in the past. It wasn't too bad, she even agreed after they'd been there a couple of times.

Dennehy always collected her in his car. He would arrive at the farmhouse, drive into the yard and blow his horn twice, then smoke a cigarette while he waited. If Mr Dallon passed through the yard Dennehy got out and passed the time talking to him, usually about livestock prices. Sometimes Dennehy took Letty to a restaurant that had opened in a town nineteen miles away, the Rainbow Café; sometimes, when it wasn't a night that the Dixie dancehall was open, or they'd seen the film at the Electric, they spent the evening in MacDermott's bar. On the way home from wherever they'd been Dennehy invariably made a detour, driving to an unoccupied farm and parking in the yard. The headlights passingly illuminated tattered curtains hanging in the windows of the house, a blue halldoor in a discoloured cement façade. 'An old fellow died there,' Dennehy revealed. 'You'd get a bargain with that place.' In the yard he turned the headlights off and drew Letty into an embrace. He took liberties she had not permitted Gargan or Billie Lyndon to take. In time she laid her head back against the car seat and gave herself up to them.

*

Miss Mullover heard that Elmer Quarry had taken to drinking. She recalled the rather heavy, squarely-made child he'd been, solemn-featured, slow when he wrote down his conclusions – liking to do things properly – but swift of thought, except where algebra was concerned. In her small bungalow, regularly visited by ex-pupils of all ages, she reflected that drinking was not a Quarry weakness and that there'd been no talk of it before the marriage. Did they not get on? Did they quarrel? Was it all too much, the sisters being there too? Time was when Matilda and Rose Quarry had been the belles of Protestant whist drives for miles around, lovely-looking girls.

Once, years ago, Miss Mullover had been asked by an ex-pupil to 'talk to' her husband because drink was threatening to destroy the marriage. This man, who had never lost either his respect or his affection for his teacher, rode up to her bungalow on a motor-cycle. Awkward and unhappy, he sat down with his crash helmet on the floor by his feet. It wasn't drink, he insisted, that had done the damage. 'The trouble is,' he said, 'I don't like her.'

Tannon, the accountant at the brickette factory, drove forty miles every Thursday afternoon to visit the wife of a bank manager in another town. That had been going on for twenty-six years, and had resulted in Tannon's never marrying. In the emergency period of the war, when petrol was unavailable to private motorists, he had arranged a lift in one of the brickette-factory lorries, his bicycle stowed away in the back so that he could make the return journey. The gossip went that when he arrived at his destination he parked his car in a side street and entered the bank house by a wicket gate in the double doors of the yard. Miss Mullover often wondered what the bank manager's wife looked like, what age she was and if she had children. A woman with plump lips came to mind, a slack-faced woman, powdered and scented, expensively dressed. She imagined Tannon making his way into the back of the house, dodging the office windows. She imagined all the bank business going on beneath the erring couple, loans being arranged, cash given out, the bank manager on the phone to his head office. A skinny boy Tannon had been, with rabbit teeth and very short trousers above fragile, bony knees.

In the town other such unconventional relationships were talked about. It was said that ever since they'd quarrelled about their daughter's mixed marriage, a certain elderly couple addressed one another only by way of their dog. One of the post office clerks, the mildest of men when he served you across the counter, gently tearing along the perforated edge of the stamps, was said to be violent in the home. A young wife's weekly presence in the Dixie dancehall was not known to her husband, who worked through the night at the electricity plant. One of the town's bread deliverers went off with a tinker girl and then returned, saying it was all a mistake. None of these people had passed through Miss Mullover's schoolroom, but she'd known all of them, at least to see, as children.

It was dispiriting news that Elmer Quarry had taken up drink.

'It's Hogan's he goes to,' Rose reported, having followed her brother in Bridge Street. She whispered, halfway up the stairs. Matilda was waiting on the first-floor landing.

'I thought it would be Hogan's. It was always Hogan's with Renehan.'

'It was different with Renehan.'

'I'm not saying it wasn't.'

Rose ascended the remaining steps of the stairs. Matilda led the way to the dining-room. Rose closed the door behind them.

'I didn't think he'd go into a public house,' Matilda said. 'The bar of a hotel's different.'

'I wouldn't be too sure what he'd get up to. If you could have seen the cut of him, nearly running on the street. Like he was chased by the bats of hell.'

'I don't know what to say.'

'I'll say it for you, Matilda. She's driven the man to drink.'

The sisters continued to discuss the matter. They began at what they saw as the beginning – the earliest attention paid to Mary Louise by their brother. They went through the events of the subsequent months; they dwelt upon their own protestations. Their opinion of the mental stability of James Dallon was aired, and related to that of his sister. They considered a step they might take: arranging to be driven out to the Dallons' farmhouse in Kilkelly's hired car and asking the Dallons to take their daughter back before further damage was done. They reached no decision about that. Eventually they heard Elmer's footfall on the stairs and heard him entering the front room, where Her Ladyship was listening to the wireless. They heard his voice raised cheerfully, calling her dear.

The Dallons, reconciled by now to the relationship that had advanced between Letty and Dennehy and pleased that their son was displaying signs of maturity, began to worry about their younger daughter. She stayed hardly any time when she visited them on Sundays, and increasingly did not come at all. As the year advanced – a warm spring giving way to a fine summer – they wondered more often why they were not yet grandparents. They did not say as much to one another, but a bewilderment that was fleeting at first lingered longer during the months that drifted by. Often, of course, such delays occurred: they had to remember that and be patient. Something in the manner of their younger daughter, and the impatient brevity of her Sunday visits, with no effort made to offer an explanation when she did not arrive at the farmhouse at all, concerned them more. Her manner was abstracted. Questions asked about the shop were summarily disposed of, and for the most part went unanswered. Gossip from the town was no longer conveyed to the farmhouse kitchen. The pleasure there had been at first in advising the shop's customers when colours had to be matched, or on the fit of a dress or the suitability of a hat, appeared to have evaporated. The wit of the drapery travellers was not repeated.

'You can't put your finger on it,' Mrs Dallon remarked before settling to sleep one night.

'She doesn't seem discontented, though.'

'No, she doesn't seem discontented.'

She'd gather herself together when a family began, both simultaneously thought. One of these Sundays she'd have a bit of news for them, and after that she'd be herself again.

In the quiet of the graveyard he read to her. She lay on her back, watching small white clouds drifting slowly across the curve of the sky. The difficult Russian names weren't easy to keep track of at first but then, with repetition, became familiar. 'Are you asleep?' he sometimes interrupted himself to ask, but she never was. She was seeing in her mind's eye Pavel Petrovich's study, its green velvet and walnut furniture, its vivid tapestry. Her cousin's voice curtly issued Arkady's orders; distressfully it conveyed to her Mitya's convulsions. *Madame will see you in half an hour,* a butler said. Swallows flew high, bees hummed in the lilac. A peasant with a patch on his shoulder trotted a white pony through an evening's shadows. Sprigs of fuchsia decorated the hair of a woman in black.

It was a coolness creeping into the graveyard that caused him, every week, to close whichever book he'd brought. 'We have stayed too long again,' he always said, amusing both of them with that most inappropriate remark.

For want of something else to say, Mary Louise pointed out to her husband that he had not, in the past, played billiards in the summer.

'Summer or winter, dear, it's relaxing to read the magazines.'

'I didn't know they had drink there.'

'What drink's that, dear?'

'I didn't know they had drink in the YMCA.'

'There's no refreshments of any kind, as a matter of fact.'

In their bedroom he stood with his trousers off, knowing what she meant and pretending not to. The conversation they were having was ridiculous. He'd categorically told her, ages ago, before they were even married, that he never bothered going to the YMCA billiard-room in the summer because what was attractive there was the winter cosiness of the fire, and the curtains drawn. He had described the curtains, heavy brown brocade purchased in Quarry's in his father's time.

'You sometimes have a smell of drink on you,' she said.

He wagged his head. This was a way of his when he was at a loss, a response that could have meant anything. He whistled soundlessly.

Mary Louise sighed. It didn't matter; she didn't care. She had no interest in his spending time in the billiard-room or spending it elsewhere. But something had to be said occasionally, else there would be only silence between them. The smell of drink was a smell like any other; all she was doing was making a comment.

He yawned, drawing his pyjamas on. There were good things about him, she reflected, even more good things than she'd been aware of when she married him. He was a little mean in some ways but not in others. She'd seen him taking a lump of coal off the fire, but she could have what she wanted from the shop, and he gave her money for other necessities – a little stack of notes and coins on the first day of every month: he never forgot. If she'd complained about the rudeness of his sisters he might even have spoken to them.

'Good-night, dear,' he said, and she reached to turn the light off, as she did every night, because the switch was closer to her.

'Good-night, Elmer.'

Almost at once he slept. His breathing, soft at first, became deeper, then stertorous. She moved her limbs towards his. Her hands lay lightly on his sleeping body.

13

The women talk of different times. For the years they have known one another they have marked out in their conversations certain periods they favour. Just as Mary Louise claims 1957, so Mrs Leavy of Youghal returns regularly to her infancy in 1921 and '22, Dot Sterne to 1984, Belle D to the advent of the Beatles, the Spanish wife to destitution in Gibraltar, 1986. Others have more precisely held to themselves days or moments or occasions, the hour of a tragedy or an act of violence.

People are claimed also, special and belonging, the personal baggage of the house's inmates. To a conversation that is endlessly renewed Mary Louise contributes the people of Culleen and of the town, her cousin and her aunt, her husband and his sisters. In turn she hears about people she does not know. Every day the house is thronged, the crowds impenetrable sometimes.

'God knows, it's nothing new,' the faded woman who is usually silent alleges in a quieter conversation. It's nothing new, reflection has revealed to her, that mad women should walk the roads and streets of Ireland. Once upon a time they did, in the old times, before the great brick asylums were built, before each town possessed a barracks for hiding the insane in.

'What's she talking about?' Bríd Beamish, wearing lipstick, asks.

'Loonies on the loose is what.' Dot Sterne has rolled her stockings down, hoping Miss Foye will notice and not put her back where she came from.

'Oh, of course,' Mrs Leavy agrees. 'We all knew the brick-work asylums. Many's the time me and Elsie looked over the wall.'

'I'm saying the time before the asylums were in existence,' the faded woman corrects her. 'I'm saying long ago.'

'Loonies on the loose,' Belle D repeats.

'Crazies,' a woman who was a priest's housekeeper adds. 'The brain in tatters.'

'It's a different kettle of fish now,' Mrs Leavy reminds them. 'The days of the old crazies is over. We don't use them expressions no more. This day and age, the nurse told me.'

'Swallow your medication.' Small Sadie's laughter cackles. 'Right eejits if you don't swallow the medication.'

'There's some would never have set foot in this place if the drugs had been to hand. A bottle of medicine would have kept them well.' Mrs Leavy has taken the lead. She has placed herself at the head of the inmates who are soon to be released. She is stating their case. She is offering the medical evidence as she had it personally from Miss Foye and a doctor, the bald one, not the one with the beard.

'Mary Louise should never be setting a foot out of it,' Small Sadie snaps back. 'Heathen bloody strumpet.'

She cries as soon as she has spoken, putting her arms around Mary Louise and saying she's sorry.

14

It seemed natural that her cousin should become Mary Louise's confidant. In September 1957, two years after her wedding, she told him the details of the courtship there'd been, of the proposal on the humped bridge, of her request for time to think it over, of the engagement and the journey on the wedding day by train and bus, and the arrival at the Strand Hotel.

They had seen, in June, the rose blooming wildly through the tiny derelict church. They had returned repeatedly to the stream, in search of the heron. But Mary Louise's confidences were offered in the graveyard, among the Attridge headstones.

'And what were you *thinking*?' Robert, fascinated, would interrupt, leading her back to some point that interested him particularly. What had her thoughts been when she sat beside Elmer Quarry for the very first time, during *The Flame and the Flesh*? Or when she stood in front of the altar? Or when the red-cheeked Reverend Harrington pronounced them man and wife?

She shared with him her emotions during the first few moments in the Strand Hotel, when she experienced misgivings that had not been there before, when her husband said that the place seemed comfortable enough. She described how, in the dining-room, the landlady had indicated a table where three men were already eating. She took him on the walk by the sea, the children collecting shellfish, the dog chasing the seagulls. She led him to McBirney's bar, told about the cherry brandies she'd drunk, about how Mr Mulholland had called her Kitty, how the bald man had said he had a Woolworth's bladder.

She'd been drunk in the end, she confessed, and Elmer had been too drunk to take his clothes off. When they'd woken up in the morning they'd both felt terrible. They'd gone for another walk along the strand, during which Elmer said they didn't feel so hot because they weren't used to drink. She recalled the remainder of the honeymoon, the same kind of conversations in the dining-room as there'd been in McBirney's bar on their wedding night. Mr Mulholland said goodbye on the Sunday morning, announcing that it was his due to kiss the bride. After breakfast every day Elmer sat outside the hotel and read the *Irish Times* from cover to cover while she accompanied to the strand one of the families who were staying at the hotel. She played with the children, helping them to make sandcastles. She bought a bathing-dress and bathed. On the Wednesday the bald man showed them round the animal-foodstuffs place where he worked. On Thursday they watched swing-boats being erected. On Friday they came back.

'Why did you get married, Mary Louise?'

'No one knows a thing like that.'

He shook his head. He said that, looking back, people knew.

'I thought it would be all right. I thought no one else would marry me. I wanted to be in the town.'

'My God!'

He reached for her hand and held it. He raised it to his cheek. She shouldn't have told him, she thought, yet in the same moment she knew it didn't matter. It didn't matter being here, or letting him take her hand. How could it matter?

'Tell me anything you want to,' he urged, and listened, her hand still held.

He heard about a marriage that was unconsummated, about the shock there'd been for husband and wife in the Strand

Hotel, about the state they had lived in since. Her voice was a toneless mutter, flattened and dead. Miss Embarrassment her friend had called her; but Mary Louise, who blushed so easily, was pale when she lay bare her confidences. Was it because he was an invalid that she told him? Robert wondered. Was it because he didn't count, because he seemed to her to be beyond the realm of ordinary humanity, as impotent as her husband?

'He has begun to drink,' she said. 'And I deceive him after only two years by coming here on Sundays.'

'But I'm your cousin, Mary Louise. Doesn't he know you come here?'

'Nobody knows.'

He imagined her in the house, the spinster sisters resenting her presence, hating her even, Elmer Quarry trudging upstairs at mealtimes, drinking his shame away. She told him about the attics, about the toys the Quarry children had played with, all carefully kept in a cupboard. And then she said:

'I used to think I was in love with you, Robert.'

'With *me*?'

'It might have been the time when you were fond of me. We might both have been in love with one another.'

He remembered again the pain of not being allowed to go to school, his anger with his mother, his refusal to understand. They would starve if things went on like this, his mother had said. No matter how early she rose in the mornings there weren't enough hours of daylight, especially in wintertime. She hadn't understood either; he couldn't tell her.

'When James came here with the butter every week I used to bring the conversation round to you. I often thought of giving a note to James.'

'I think I'd turned my attentions to Mr Stewart by then.'

Laughter relieved a constriction. Then he said:

'I'm in love with you still, to tell the truth. I wait for every Sunday with just the same feelings as I had then.'

In turn, for Robert, it didn't matter either. Telling more of the truth didn't matter because she would not come back in any case. After the intimacies she'd shared with him she would find it hard to cycle out next Sunday and the Sunday after, as if nothing different had occurred. She didn't know this, but it would be so.

'I couldn't face the wedding party,' he said.

'I thought you weren't up to it.'

'No. We were going to go. We intended to. "I'll wait in the car," I said. But my mother wouldn't have that.'

'You couldn't love me, Robert.'

'It's not a choice that people have.'

Did she mean, he wondered, that she couldn't love him? Did she mean that even before her marriage there couldn't have been love between them because he was only half a person? It was different for children was no doubt what she meant also: children didn't always notice.

But Mary Louise contradicted these thoughts almost as they occurred. She wasn't worth anyone's love, she said. She had married a man for gain. She had married out of impatience and boredom, and had been handed both back with interest added. She had calculated; she had coldly examined the pros and cons.

Robert laughed. He took her hand again, and again she permitted him to do so. Anyone would do as she had, he said.

'I wouldn't have if there'd been our friendship, Robert.'

'Then *I'd* have been insisting I was the guilty one.'

He felt the pressure of her fingers on his palm. Was this a sign, a statement she could not bring herself otherwise to make? Now and again, since the time they had been together in Miss Mullover's schoolroom, he had glimpsed her in the town when by chance they visited it on the same day, not often. Every autumn his mother drove to the Dallons' farmhouse with grapes and apples. He might have accompanied her but he'd never wished to, fearful of the renewal of emotions. The wedding had been impossible, entirely, to avoid.

'I'm sorry I said all that, Robert.'

'It means everything to me that you did.'

On his side, there were facts he might have added to what she'd said: his gloom and wretchedness while his mother chattered in the car, driving back after the wedding; the pain he experienced because he'd selfishly deprived her of an occasion she would have enjoyed; the greater pain of imagining the radiant happiness of the bride. While Mary Louise drank cherry brandy in McBirney's she had still been in his thoughts, still in her wedding-dress, as last he'd seen her. He had tortured himself while Mary Louise, in the presence of her already unconscious husband, undressed and crept woozily into her marriage bed. While she slept, virginal and alone, he had descended to the bitterest depths of melancholy.

'What an irony it is!' was all he observed in this respect, speaking softly in the graveyard.

'You are the only person in the world I could have told.'

He kissed her gently, their lips just touching. Then he pushed himself to his feet and held his hands out to her. They walked back towards the house, not saying anything else. Both were possessed by a warmth that delighted them, the warmth of secrets at last shared while still remaining secrets, the intimacy of a private truth.

Crossing the sloping field beyond which the house and garden lay, Robert said:

'Look! There he is.'

They had not, that day, brought the binoculars. But Mary Louise could see, at the very place where they often watched the fish going by, the grey, angular form of the heron they had hoped for so long to catch a glimpse of. Neck extended, it dipped its long beak into the water, no doubt fishing for the trout, although the distance was too great to allow them to observe how successful these efforts were. It stuttered closer to the water on its ungainly legs, then turned, spread out its wings and flew away.

'Clever creature,' Robert said.

In the house he read to Mary Louise from a reference book. It was a common heron they'd seen, not a Great White or a Purple: *Ardea cinerea*. The common heron wasn't rare, but even so was not often seen. Anglers had been known to persecute it.

He put the book away and hunted among some others. There were many stories by his favourite Russian novelist, he said, but he possessed only three. He spread these volumes out for her, each open at the title page, as if it was important for her to see them.

'Why did you do that, Robert?'

'In case you do not come back.'

'Of course I'll come back.'

'No one can be certain.'

The three volumes were left as he had opened them, on one of the tables that contained stacks of other books. If not because of what had been confided, he thought, then because of what had occurred: she would not return.

'You've been so good to me, Robert. I can't tell you what it means to have been able to talk to you.'

'May I kiss you in this room, Mary Louise? Just once?'

'Yes, you may.' She spoke quickly, without the slightest hesitation.

This time he put his arms around her and pressed her lips a little closer, then held her hand for a moment after they had parted. He said again that she was beautiful.

'But I'm not in the least,' she began, as she had before.

'Actually you are,' he repeated too.

They had tea in the kitchen, and when Mary Louise had

gone Robert carried a cup out to his mother, who was picking raspberries. Was it enough, he wondered, that they had talked so? Would all they had shared make up for her not returning? As he helped to pick the fruit, it seemed to Robert that his cousin's abrupt incursion into his life had from the very beginning been part of a pattern that their conversation today completed, with the telling of the truth. It seemed as if, outside their wills, their declaration of affection had been ordained. That his own love had persisted while hers had dwindled was just a circumstance; at least they'd honoured what there had been. But could he, he wondered, live off the moments of an afternoon?

As she cycled on the empty road, Mary Louise felt at first that she was riding away from a fantasy. It wasn't in the least like reality that Robert had taken her hand, that she had told him so much, that twice they had kissed. And yet all that had happened. What had occurred was the next thing to adultery; she was a sinful wife.

But she experienced neither regret nor the shadow of guilt. All afternoon the glow of her sinning had possessed her, and now she didn't want it to fade. She wanted to sense for ever the imprint of his lips, the coolness of his hand in hers. She wanted to hear him say again, as clearly, that she was beautiful and that he loved her.

In the hedges the summer's cow parsley was withered, only its brittle stalks remaining. Sloes and haws had already formed among the thorns. Somewhere, near where she rode, a bird-scare went off, and then again, becoming fainter as she cycled on. A woman, trimming the fuchsia hedge outside her cottage, waved and said it was a lovely day.

'Oh, lovely,' Mary Louise called back, reminded of the fuchsia in the blackly-dressed woman's hair. 'Lovely.'

*

That night, a few minutes before midnight, Robert dreamed that it was he who accompanied his cousin on her honeymoon to the seaside. The three men described to him were standing on a road, and on a wide, endless strand a flock of seagulls swooped down to the edge of the sea. Miss Mullover said he was not permitted to bathe, not even to paddle. 'You are a *disgraceful* child!' Miss Mullover reprimanded Berty Figgis. As soon as the birds touched the sand they were seen to be herons.

He put his arm around his cousin's waist and as they walked on the strand they talked about his father. In that moment Robert died.

15

She walks in the garden. She likes it best in the garden and always has, ever since she came to the house. She knows the name of every flower, she has a flowerbed of her own.

No one knows what will become of the place, and maybe it doesn't matter. Maybe a place changing its purpose, maybe a house falling into ruins, is of no possible importance, a grain of sand turning over on a shore, nothing more. Even so, it is sad that her flowerbed may perhaps become choked with weeds.

She does not take the medication and does not intend to; not once does she intend to take it. 'You're naughty, you know,' Miss Foye said once, but she didn't say it about the medication even though she suspects. Miss Foye likes the paid-for inmates, she likes the cheques coming in. Generally naughty was what Miss Foye meant, a tendency that way. The nurses watch her swallowing it down, but Miss Foye knows there's more to swallowing than meets the eye. Cute as a fox, Miss Foye is, over a thing like that.

16

James Dallon was inflating a tractor tyre in the yard when a
man he didn't know got out of a blue van and asked if this
was the Dallons' house. The man said something about having
called in for the raspberries and the last of the peas at James's
aunt's house, but James didn't know what he was talking
about. Then the man said he had a message. He didn't smile.
He didn't seem happy. James brought him into the kitchen.

Later that morning Mrs Dallon drove over to comfort her
sister. They sat together in the kitchen for most of the day,
Mrs Dallon making tea and toast in the afternoon, and poach-
ing an egg for each of them. She wanted to spend the night,
but her sister wouldn't permit that. They talked about the
time when they were girls together, before their marriages;
about when the men they'd married first came into their lives,
and the different lives they'd had because of that. They talked
about the birth of their children, how Robert had only just
survived. They talked about the existence he had had.

A reference to Mary Louise's Sunday visits did not fall
naturally into the conversation, except that her aunt said,
'Mary Louise was good to him.' Mrs Dallon took this to mean
in the past, when they were children in Miss Mullover's schoolroom. The small misunderstanding was neither here nor there.

In the room where her nephew had spent most of his time
she was shown his books, and the soldiers in the window
alcove. 'Take some grapes back with you,' her sister offered at

the end of the day, for she had come to terms by now with a death that she had always known would be like this, swift and out of the blue.

'Oh no, dear, please,' Mrs Dallon protested, but the grapes were cut none the less.

The Reverend Harrington came to the house, and later the same undertaker who, years ago, had laid out Robert's father. Robert's attachment to a graveyard that wasn't used any more was not known since he had kept that a secret, shared only with his cousin. A grave was to be dug beside his father's in the graveyard of the country church regularly attended by the household, where the Reverend Harrington offered holy communion once a month and officiated every Sunday at half-past six evensong.

There had been great happiness in Robert's life, the clergyman comforted in the kitchen. Robert had been amused by all sorts of things, given to laughter and to fun. All that was better than a longer lifetime – sixty or seventy years – passed in grumbling bitterness. The mother who was now alone found it hard to take consolation from this, but did not let it show.

'You'll take a bunch or two of grapes, Mr Harrington?' she offered, and the Reverend Harrington, too, drove off with grapes in his car.

Mrs Dallon considered it odd of her younger daughter to faint when she was told of her cousin's death since she had hardly known him, except years ago at school. Quite without pain, he'd died in his sleep, Mrs Dallon had been saying, having come into the shop to break the news and to pass on the funeral details. Mary Louise went as white as paper. The next moment her legs gave way and she collapsed in a heap behind the counter.

Elmer came hurrying from the accounting office and he and

Mr Renehan – hastily summoned from next door – between them carried Mary Louise upstairs. She came to on the way and struggled to her feet on the first-floor landing. She wept, in front of them at first, before turning her back on everyone and hurrying up the second flight of stairs. Mrs Dallon wanted to be with her and after a consultation with Elmer and his sisters she mounted, in turn, the second flight of stairs. But the door of the room they'd said was Mary Louise's and Elmer's bedroom was open and Mary Louise wasn't in it. In case in her flurry she had misunderstood what she'd been told Mrs Dallon tried the other doors, but again found only empty rooms and a narrow, uncarpeted stairway.

Tea in the meantime had been made, and Dr Cormican sent for. Mary Louise's sisters-in-law made Mrs Dallon sit down in the big front room, Elmer returned to take charge of the shop and to keep an eye out for the doctor, Mr Renehan offered Mrs Dallon sympathy on the family loss. When she was still explaining to the sisters that her nephew had never been strong and had not, in fact, led a normal life, Mary Louise's footsteps were heard upstairs.

'Was she in the lav?' Rose suggested, and Matilda said something about the time of the month.

But when she'd opened the door to the attic stairway Mrs Dallon had thought, but could not be certain, that she heard the sound of distant sobbing above her. Certainly her daughter had not been in the lavatory, the door of which she'd also opened. It puzzled her that as well as fainting so dramatically Mary Louise had apparently run away to an attic. At the time she hadn't felt she should ascend the poorly-lit attic stairs, but now wished she had.

'She doesn't know I'm here,' she said when footsteps crossed the landing and continued to descend. 'Mary Louise!' she called, hurrying from the room. 'Mary Louise!'

Mary Louise had reached the hall. She looked up, her face

still tear-stained and pale. She'd put a cardigan on over her blue-flowered dress.

'I'm all right,' she said. 'Don't worry about me.'

'The doctor's coming.'

'I don't need the doctor.'

She moved away. A door banged somewhere at the back of the hall. A moment later Rose called out from the front room that Mary Louise had ridden away from the house on her bicycle. She still held the edge of a curtain between her fingers, and Mrs Dallon approached the window to see for herself. But Mary Louise had already disappeared.

The weather had not changed. The early autumn sky, empty of clouds, had been as pale when they had walked, two days before, through the fields. The sun had abandoned not a jot more of its August vigour, the night-time dews stayed not an instant longer.

The brittle stalks of the cow parsley were as they'd been, the same bird-scare sounded in a field of corn. The woman who'd been clipping her fuchsia hedge was not outside her cottage, but the withered clippings were still strewn on the road. The same dog ran after Mary Louise's bicycle, a brindle-haired terrier with snappy eyes. On the roads there were the same potholes to avoid.

Yet everything was different. Vitality had drained away from all she passed through, leaving it dull. They had found four mushrooms in the sloping field, and in the kitchen he had laid them in a line on the wooden draining-board: vividly she saw them there.

She went to the graveyard and sat as they had sat, among the Attridge stones. Was this a punishment for their sinning? If so, it seemed unfair, since her living was a greater ordeal than his death. She didn't want ever to ride away, but to die as well, here in their place.

'I love you, Robert,' she whispered, knowing what she had not known in the last hours of his lifetime. 'I love you,' she said again.

Her tears came then, fresh tears that flowed more freely than before. And when eventually she wiped them away she thought: might there be some error? Had she stupidly misheard what her mother had said? Was he only ill? Was it her Aunt Emmeline who had died? If there had been some error, if she rode down the grassy avenue now and found him mourning his mother in the kitchen, she would not ever leave his side. She would remain in the house with him and care for him as no human being had ever before been cared for. She would make up for everything, none of it a sacrifice, for all she wanted was to be with him, each of them part of the other.

But Robert was dead. Her mother had clearly stated that. You do not make mistakes when informing about death, and she had not misheard. Robert was dead, and had not suffered. Robert was cold as ice already, his body stiff and useless, the amusement gone for ever from his expression.

Mary Louise remained in the graveyard when dusk came. Shivering, and longing for death herself, she stayed when darkness came too. She thought she might never leave the graveyard, and did not do so until the light of dawn.

17

Her flowerbed has always been for him. Being in the house has permitted that, no questions asked, the slow establishment of the chosen plants, the trial and error of their cultivation, buds breaking into colour, the clustering of petals.

'Oh, I expect it'll disappear,' the gardener grumpily replies when she asks about the flowerbed's fate. He's not the man whose arm was broken by Sadie swinging a pickaxe. Youngish, unsuited to the place in any case, that one went at once. This man is old; he has been here all her time; no wonder he's aggrieved. He says the house will become a hotel.

'My flowerbed is in memory. I hope they'll keep the garden.'

'I hear it said they'll have it up for a car park.'

Slowly she walks about, imagining the cars drawn up in rows, the different colours. Tessa Enright visited her once, Tessa Hospel as she became, mother of four children, wife of an oyster merchant. They strolled these same paths in the heat of an afternoon and suddenly her friend said: 'I am in love.' She had not told another soul and never would. 'No one except for you.' She wept into a lacy lilac handkerchief. She said she was ashamed that Mary Louise had been in the house for sixteen years before she visited her. She was in love with an Englishman whom she'd met when she and her husband, with all their children, were on holiday by the sea in France. Her husband was rich; there was a girl for the children. The

Englishman had said he could not live without her. 'Imagine that! To say that so soon! He hardly knew me.' Tessa Enright hadn't changed. As thin as fuse-wire, high cheekbones, hair like sun-bleached silk. Her eyes had always had a startled look, her lips still lazily pouted. She would never have visited the house if she hadn't been desperate for a confidante: here, of all places, her secret would be safe.

Alone in the garden fifteen years later, Mary Louise recalls precisely the shade of lilac of the handkerchief. It was lighter than that of the outfit that accompanied it, the blouse that buttoned to the neck, the very short skirt, the chic little shoes. She recalls being told that the oyster merchant had been met at a party. The Englishman was a person who had to do with boats, who delivered them from one harbour to another, acting for other people. Mary Louise imagines this man, as once she imagined Jeanne d'Arc and later her cousin's father, and later still the people in the novels her cousin read. She sees the children of her friend controlled by a calm nursemaid; she sees the husband. She places the family in a hotel dining-room, among waiters calling out to one another in French and expertly pouring wine. The Englishman approaches, flannels and a blazer with an emblem on it, brown as a nut, a smile lazing through his features. At some later time, when they are private, her friend puts her arms around him, slipping her hands beneath the blazer with the emblem on it, her fingers touching the muscles in his back.

Mary Louise stoops and lifts a rose petal from where it has fallen. Under no circumstances is it permitted to pick the flowers. Bríd Beamish did so once and was not allowed to enter the garden for seven months, seven being the number of flowers she filched. The petal has no scent, but in the palm of Mary Louise's hand it seems as beautiful as anything she has ever touched, crimson streaked with white. Roses mostly are what she has planted in her flowerbed, with a border of lily of the valley. She's glad it was not she who married the oyster merchant and had four children. She's glad she never had to turn with her intimacies to a childhood companion who is safely locked away and would not, anyway, be believed.

18

The mists of autumn came, clinging to the houses of Bridge Street, smudging the shop windows with drips and rivulets. The smell of the town was of turf smoke mainly, acrid in the damp air. The shortening days were caught between the seasons until November arrived, claiming them for winter.

By the middle of that month, for Mary Louise, the funeral seemed an age ago. She had stood in the small church with her family, in the front pew, across the aisle from the solitary presence of her aunt. There were all sorts of people there – neighbours mainly, a few from the town, Miss Mullover, the Edderys, relations from the other side of the family whom the Dallons had never seen before. In the churchyard the coffin was lowered; the Reverend Harrington intoned; a handful of clay was thrown on the brightly varnished surface. Afterwards nobody knew what to do: the occasion was sad, people felt, so brief a life, too sad for a funeral spread. Yet in the end some of the mourners returned to her aunt's house.

Ever since the death of her cousin the first thought that entered Mary Louise's waking consciousness every morning was that the death was a fact. Robert, thin and wiry in the classroom, was no longer there. Robert, smiling in the untidy room he was so fond of, was now a figment in her mind. A shadow pointed at the heron and bent to pick the mushrooms. A shadow kissed her twice. The fading images were not as good as photographs would have been, but she had no photograph of her cousin.

It was because of that that Mary Louise, on a Sunday afternoon in mid-November, cycled again to her aunt's house. She didn't quite know what she would say when she arrived, nor what she'd find there. She wondered if she'd be particularly welcome.

In fact she was. Her aunt was in the garden, rooting out her finished runner beans. She wore gum boots and an old mackintosh coat. A fire was smouldering near where she worked.

'Mary Louise!'

'Am I interrupting you?'

'No, no, you're not. I'm on the last row.'

She pulled out what remained of the row and threw the stalks on to the bonfire. A job she hated, she said, leading the way to the back of the house.

'I've wondered,' Mary Louise began in the kitchen.

'Oh, I'm managing all right.'

In the kitchen Mary Louise made tea while her aunt pulled off her boots and hung her mackintosh above the Esse to dry.

'It's good of you to come over, Mary Louise.'

'I was never able to offer you my sympathy.' She paused, pouring the boiling water into the pot. 'I needed it all for myself.'

'Nothing in the world is a greater consolation than that you and Robert were friends those last few months.'

'I was very fond of Robert, Aunt Emmeline.'

Her aunt had moved to the sink to wash her hands. She ran the taps, scouring her palms and fingers with a brush. Mary Louise poured their two cups of tea.

'Robert was fond of you too, Mary Louise.'

That was all that was said. The depth of the relationship had clearly not been guessed by her aunt. Nothing about it had worried her in her son's lifetime. She had seen no reason why a harmless affection should not be permitted in a life that was emotionally deprived.

'There's a cake your mother sent over. Your mother has been nice to me.'

An uncut fruitcake was placed on a plate. Mary Louise had hoped she could confide her feelings, that her aunt would understand and listen. But instead she cut slices of the fruit-cake, and Mary Louise sensed that the subject should not be pursued. That she and Robert had been fond of each other was one thing; condoning love was quite another.

'Whenever you feel like it,' her aunt said, 'come over and see me.'

The invitation softened what might have seemed like harsh-ness, but being in the house again was painful and Mary Louise knew she would not easily return. The abandoned graveyard and the ruined church through which the rose rambled in high summer were easier places. They were without distractions or voices that did not belong; they did not demand politeness.

'Might I have a drawing of Robert's, d'you think?'

'Oh, of course. Let's go and see.'

The three books were open on the table, as he had placed them. The French and German battalions were engaged in a conflict he must have arranged after she'd left. The room had been tidied a bit, but not much.

'I'm getting round to it,' her aunt said, her tone betraying her failure to find the heart for the task. 'I don't come in here much.'

Mary Louise wouldn't have changed the position of a single thing, not a book or a scribble or a drawing. She wouldn't have moved by an inch his armchair by the fire. In winter she'd have lit the fire again and kept it going every day.

'It's nice you want one,' her aunt said when a drawing of winter trees had been chosen. 'Have anything else you'd like.'

Mary Louise looked about her, and the urge not to disturb returned.

'Maybe these,' she reluctantly suggested, indicating the three books.

'Of course you must have them.'

They left the room and in the kitchen had another cup of tea. For a moment they did not speak. Then her aunt said:

'Your mother said I could live at Culleen. What would you think of that, Mary Louise?'

Her Sunday visits to this house would become known was what Mary Louise thought: daily contact would see to that. But what had mattered in his lifetime didn't matter now. Even if her revelation of today led in time to the dawning of suspicion in her aunt's mind, it wouldn't matter. She only wished she had known, that last Sunday, that she loved her cousin with the passion death had made apparent.

'It's lonely for you here, Aunt Emmeline.'

'Well, that's what they believe. And yes, it is. Just now it is, though perhaps I'll get used to it.'

'It's sensible.'

'Yes, it's sensible. If Letty marries Dennehy there'll be that bedroom.'

The Bank of Ireland owned more of the house than she did, she added. Getting rid of it would be a weight off her mind. The west side of the roof leaked, gutters needed to be replaced, lead was perforated.

'I'm fond of James,' she said. 'It would be nice to see something of a young person again.'

Mary Louise could discern what was in her aunt's mind, and in her parents'. The notion there had been – accepted almost as fact in the farmhouse – that Letty and James would see their way into old age together, now that Mary Louise had married, no longer appeared to be valid. More likely, now, it seemed that Letty would marry the vet and James would one day marry also. With a bedroom to spare, in such circumstances it was the natural thing to offer a home to a lone aunt.

'But I'm not sure, Mary Louise. I'm not sure I wouldn't be an intrusion.'

Mary Louise shook her head. That was the last thing her aunt would be, she reassured her. If the idea had been put to her the whole family would have discussed it. Her father would have agreed, and so would James. Letty must have made up her mind about Dennehy.

'Privately between us, I believe she has,' her aunt said.

'I didn't know.'

'It's always kept quiet for a while, news of a mixed marriage. Dennehy's priest will be having a go at Letty.'

'Letty would never turn.'

'The priest'll want the children though.'

Mary Louise felt that none of it concerned her. In the past Letty would have ages ago told her everything. They would have lain awake in the bedroom that soon was to be empty and Letty would have gone through every development in her romance, the nature and circumstances of the proposal, and the persuasion of the parish priest. When Gargan had been taking her out she'd come back to the bedroom at night with all sorts of information, often waking Mary Louise up to tell her: what Gargan had tried on, what he'd confided to her about his boyhood desires, revelations made about the customers at the bank, who was solvent and who was not. Now, apparently, her sister was going to marry a man Mary Louise had only spoken to once or twice and about whom Letty had told her nothing whatsoever. After the wedding everything in the farmhouse would be different – Aunt Emmeline would occupy the bedroom that had been theirs, James might marry the Eddery girl or someone like her. None of it was any longer Mary Louise's world. Her world was the drapery and the house above it, her sisters-in-law, her husband, the attic rooms, the memory of her cousin's love. The town she had so longed to live in was hers, its air odorous with turf smoke, its people interested in her seemingly barren state.

'The priests always have a go for the children,' her aunt said. 'Well, understandably, I dare say.'

'I must get back.' She hesitated. 'I don't suppose there's a photograph to spare of Robert?'

For the first time her aunt appeared surprised. Then she went away and returned with an album in which a dozen or so photographs were loosely caught between the pages. None was pasted in. 'The ones of Robert are precious to me,' she said. 'There's none of him grown up.'

Mary Louise looked at one after another: Robert as a baby, Robert at three or four, Robert in an overcoat and cap, much as she remembered him from their childhood. She handed them back.

'We didn't go in much for the camera,' her aunt said.

There were other photographs and she was shown them – of the house and of people she didn't know, of her aunt when she was a girl, and Robert's father, with a moustache.

'Thanks for showing me, Aunt Emmeline.'

Soon after she turned out of the avenue she heard an echo of her cousin's voice.

'*One hot summer day in 1853 two young men lay in the shade of a tall lime tree by the River Moskva, not far from Kountsovo . . .*'

Mary Louise was correct in imagining that the townspeople were interested in her childlessness. As well, it was considered that she was becoming strange, and often a connection was made. Women coming into the shop noticed what they agreed were oddities, and remarked upon them to one another. They said so in the other shops – in Renehan's next door, in Foley's, and elsewhere. They said so chattily, inquisitively, forebodingly, depending on who they were. The young wife was abstracted, they said; you addressed her and often she didn't hear you. You asked for Silko and she turned round and reached down the silk samples. She wasn't as friendly as she'd been; sometimes she hardly smiled at you, and then remembered and smiled effusively.

One day Letty came to the shop to tell her sister that she was engaged to Dennehy. She was immediately struck by what she afterwards described to her mother as 'Mary Louise's peculiar manner'. She had asked if they could go upstairs for a few minutes and Mary Louise led her to the big front room, a room Letty had never been in before. They sat on either side of the empty fire grate. Dennehy had bought the farmhouse and the yard of outbuildings to which so often they'd driven in search of privacy. Letty tried to remember the rooms, measuring them in her mind to establish if any was as large as this one. She extolled her fiancé's virtues, and his devotion, and all they had planned for the future. She turned her head away when she said she was head over heels with him, and had been from the first time he took her out. He was anxious to know Mary Louise better, she passed on.

'She didn't speak a word,' Letty reported later. 'She sat there hardly changing her expression.'

There was some exaggeration in this, but the statements none the less conveyed an accurate reflection of the truth since they also took into account Letty's own considerable surprise.

'Is she sick?' Mrs Dallon asked.

Letty shook her head. Her sister wasn't sick. It was nothing like that.

'Oh, I've noticed something,' Mrs Dallon said, recalling her visit to the Quarrys at the time of her nephew's death. Thinking that over afterwards, she had reached the conclusion that Mary Louise's behaviour had to do with not yet being pregnant. Increasingly, her younger daughter's moodiness – despondency transformed into elation, and then the grim mournfulness of the last couple of months – had appeared to Mrs Dallon to be an outcome of this fact. Neither she nor her husband had ever found it necessary to discuss, or even to mention, the known fact that for generations the Quarrys had taken the marriage step as a necessity rather than a desire. Mary Louise had wanted to be in the town, she had chosen to go out with Elmer Quarry. The Dallons, in the privacy of their bedroom or alone in the kitchen when James was out playing cards and Letty was out with Dennehy, did not openly progress from these facts to wonder aloud about Mary Louise's subsequent happiness. They had not used that word to one another before the marriage; they did not after it. It was not a word that naturally belonged in their vocabulary. They would have felt easier if Elmer Quarry had been younger, or even been someone else altogether and more of a companion for the girl. But other factors had to be taken into consideration. It was pure ill fortune that, as yet, there was no pregnancy.

'She didn't say she was glad or anything,' Letty went on. 'All she did was nod. I told her about the house and she didn't even ask where it is.'

'Was she maybe disappointed you didn't ask her to be your bridesmaid?'

'You can't have a married woman a bridesmaid. I told her, but afterwards I wondered did she hear.'

'She should see Dr Cormican. You can get tests these days.'

'I don't think it's that.'

'What else then?'

'He's drinking.'

'Who is?'

'Elmer.'

'Have sense, Letty. The man doesn't touch a drop. The Quarrys never have.'

'He's taken to it. It's all over town.'

Had Letty known it, she might have added that the unexpected resort to whiskey on Elmer Quarry's part was assumed in the town to be related to the childless marriage, which his sisters now openly implied he regarded as a mistake.

'Hogan's bar,' Letty said. 'I've seen him there myself.'

'My God!'

'You'd want to shake her when she's sitting there saying nothing. But the next minute you'd be sorry for her.'

Mrs Dallon later repeated the whole conversation, word for word, to her husband. He, too, was ignorant of the fact that Elmer Quarry had taken to spending time in Hogan's bar. It had never been mentioned to him by anyone at the cattle-fairs, but Mrs Dallon pointed out that it probably wouldn't be, the subject being delicate.

'Once a family's started it'll all settle down,' Mr Dallon said.

'Please God it will.'

But Mrs Dallon could not sleep that night. She lay there remembering the details of Mary Louise's own birth, so very late the baby had been, and then the easy time she'd had compared with Letty, and James. Growing up, Mary Louise had been a wide-eyed little girl, not sharp like Letty, nor rushy like James. Sometimes her dreaminess would irritate you, sometimes she forgot to do things and you'd think she'd forgotten deliberately but she never had. There'd been the day she'd fallen through the outhouse trap-door, when she'd lain on the straw for ages before the barking of the sheepdogs attracted their attention. There'd been the time Miss Mullover had written on her end-of-term letter that she was paying attention at last. Dr Cormican had thought she might have a grumbling appendix and they'd worried about the hospital charges, but it turned out to be nothing at all. She'd never looked more radiant than she did in her wedding-dress, with the Limerick veil borrowed from Emmeline.

Towards dawn Mrs Dallon slept. She dreamed, but afterwards remembered nothing, aware only vaguely that Mary Louise, as a baby and a child and a bride, had passed from her waking consciousness into a muddle of fantasy.

*

On Christmas Day Mary Louise sat with her husband and her sisters-in-law in church and afterwards they gave one another presents, as the Quarrys by tradition always did at that particular time, before the turkey was carved. Bitter weather came in January, and Mary Louise imagined the stream with the trout in it frozen over, and wondered if herons went away in winter.

Rose and her sister passed on to certain of their customers their belief that their sister-in-law was not in her right mind. There was something queer in that family, they said, James Dallon far from the full shilling and the cousin who'd died a peculiarity by all accounts. Increasingly in the new year the daily thoughts of the sisters were influenced by their observation of their sister-in-law and the disintegration, as they saw it, which she had brought about in their brother. They did not, in their gossiping with certain of their customers, ever touch upon this latter subject, feeling it to be one that shamed the family.

'What harm'll it do?' Matilda said early in February after they had yet again discussed – but more seriously now – the notion of visiting the Dallons' farmhouse and expressing their concern. They talked about this for a further week, and on the twentieth of the month arranged with Kilkelly at the garage to be driven to Culleen the following day.

Mary Louise no longer went secretly to the attic rooms but openly ascended the flight of stairs, even leaving the door at the bottom open. There'd been comment of course. Elmer had asked her if she was looking for something up there, and when Rose raised the matter in the dining-room Mary Louise replied that she went to the attics for privacy. She had taken to locking the door of the one she preferred and once Matilda rattled the handle, but she ignored the sound. 'Are you all right in there, Mary Louise?' her sister-in-law called out, and she didn't reply. She had moved everything out into the room next door except the armchair she sat in. When they said there was something they wanted she was able to tell them that.

It was often cold in her attic but that never mattered. She tucked her legs under her in the armchair and thought of her cousin in his grave, the bones revealed in his face, flesh putrefying. She blamed God for that; in her attic she made an enemy of God because all she had left was the echo of her cousin's voice – the way he had of pronouncing certain words, the timbre of his intonations, the images his voice conveyed.

'*I dreamed I was sad and sometimes cried. But through the tears and the melancholy, inspired by the music of the verse or the beauty of the evening, there always rose upwards, like the grasses of early spring, shoots of happy feeling . . .*'

Again and again his voice repeated it. Hers now joined in. For these were words they must learn by heart, he'd said.

19

She packs her things, empty of emotion. How many women have come and gone in thirty-one years? Some of them have died, others been moved because they had to be. The food has been indifferent for thirty-one years, often worse than that. In winter they have felt cold from time to time, due to economies.

'You'll be all right,' Miss Foye reassures. 'You'll be OK outside.'

'I thought I'd die here.'

'Oh, now, now.'

Miss Foye smiles it all away. It occurs to her that this one has been longer in the house than any of the others. She might say so in a sentimental way, but decides against it. A thought like that can be upsetting.

20

'We would not have come,' Rose said, 'in normal circumstances.'

'We didn't want to come,' Matilda emphasized.

'No, we didn't want to come at all. We held back – oh, for how long, Matilda? Would you say a year?'

'A good year.'

The panic that the first utterances of the sisters had stirred in Mrs Dallon did not quieten. Even before they stepped into the house, while Kilkelly's man was turning the car in the yard and bringing it to a halt to wait for them, they had offered an explanation for their unannounced presence, repeating in a different way what Letty had reported: there was something the matter with Mary Louise.

'She hasn't been herself, certainly.' Mr Dallon's narrow grey face was enlivened by a reflection of his wife's anxiety.

'Well, of course we don't know what being herself is,' Rose said. 'Strictly speaking. What I mean, Mr Dallon, is we only know the person Elmer brought into the household. To be candid with you, she was strange from the first.'

'Though of course, Mr Dallon, not as unusual as she is now. Not of course by a long chalk.'

Distractedly Mrs Dallon poured the tea she'd made, and even asked if the man waiting in the car would like a cup. The sisters said not to bother, but Mr Dallon felt the man should be offered something, and carried a cup out. Certainly Mary

Louise had become quieter, he reflected on this journey. Letty had been on about it again last evening: anyone would be quieter, she'd said, married to Quarry. But the marriage had taken place ages ago, she added, and every time she saw her Mary Louise was quieter still. When he returned to the kitchen Rose was saying:

'We sit in the front room of an evening. There's the wireless to listen to. Elmer buys the magazines when the YMCA has finished with them, hardly anything they cost him. They're there in the front room, she could look at them if she wanted to.'

Mr Dallon noticed that his wife's eyes had a distended look. They bulged and goggled. Never in all the years he'd known her did he remember seeing her eyes like that. Turning to him, she said:

'Mary Louise is always in that attic. I told you she went up there, the day I called. Apparently she locks herself in.'

'There's that and other things, Mr Dallon.' Rose's tone was brisk in confirmation. 'As we've been saying.'

'You'd ask her a question, Mr Dallon, and she'd not reply.'

'Why does she go up to an attic?'

'We've asked her that, Mr Dallon, Elmer has asked her repeatedly. She doesn't deign to reply.'

'Another thing is, there are certain tasks I have myself and certain that Matilda has, and a small number that are Mary Louise's. We reached that agreement, but to tell you the truth the entire house could be a rubbish dump for all she'd care.'

'A rubbish dump?'

'Filthy dirty,' Rose explained. 'If she has a mood on she won't lift a finger. She puts the plates on the table unwashed from the last time. There's grime and filth on the plates and she doesn't so much as blink.'

'Then again, in the shop, Mr Dallon. A person will come in looking for oilcloth and she'll say we don't stock it. When the fact of the matter is we have oilcloth in three different weights and more than a dozen patterns.'

'To tell the truth, we can't get rid of it.' Rose allowed herself a deviation, though her lips remained tightened in a knot even as she spoke. 'Nobody goes much for oilcloth these days, but Elmer says don't throw it out so we don't.'

'Yesterday, for instance, we heard her saying to a person that oilcloth might be obtained next door, in Renehan's.'

'Perhaps Mary Louise wasn't aware – '

'There is no commodity in the shop we haven't pointed out to her.'

'She locks the attic door on herself, Mr Dallon. There's a lot of property that she's moved from one attic to the next. It wasn't hers to touch, as a matter of fact, but never mind that. You rap on the door and ask her if she's sick. She doesn't say a word.'

'Not a word,' Matilda confirmed.

'We thought ourselves,' Mrs Dallon brought herself to say, 'that Mary Louise was perhaps disappointed because a family hasn't been started.'

'Wouldn't you say it's a godsend it hasn't, Mrs Dallon?'

'I'll give you an example,' Matilda offered. 'I was closing the shop a week or so back and I said to her, "Wait a minute, Mary Louise, I want to try on a few of the skirts that came in this morning." All I intended was that she'd give me an opinion – sometimes someone else is better than yourself. Well, she stood as still as a statue at the bottom of the stairs that goes up to the office, like she'd been put into the corner at school. "How's that?" I said when I'd slipped on the first one, a blue and mauve dog's tooth it was. D'you know the reply I received?'

Together, the Dallons indicated they didn't.

'She said I looked ridiculous in that skirt. Then she walked away. Ridiculous. No reason given.'

'Another thing.' Once more, Rose took up the catalogue of shortcomings. 'There's a little porcelain egg-cup our mother had. Now, no one uses that egg-cup except myself. "Rose can have my egg-cup," my mother said a week before she died. I walked into the kitchen one day and there she was, eating an egg out of it.'

'These days she sometimes takes her food in the kitchen,' Matilda explained. 'She won't enter the dining-room if she has a mood on.'

'"That's a special egg-cup, Mary Louise," I said, not cross, just gently. I said it even though I'd told her before. "I'd rather you didn't use it, Mary Louise," I said.'

Mrs Dallon was about to say that anyone can forget a request like that, or confuse one egg-cup with another. She began to speak, but Rose shook her head before she'd said more than half a dozen words.

'A week later I found it chipped on the rim. You couldn't have it on the table now.'

'It's going up to the attic I'd worry about more,' Mrs Dallon confessed. 'And eating her food in the kitchen. Why does she do that?'

'That's the difficulty we have,' Matilda said. 'You wouldn't know why she'd do anything. That's why we're sitting here.'

Mr Dallon asked how Elmer felt.

'Elmer's tormented by it,' Rose replied. 'You have only to look at the unfortunate man.'

Not here, any more than in the town, did they intend to mention that their brother had been driven to drink. With the girl gone from the house he'd be back to normal within a day, neither had the slightest doubt about that. He'd come and go as he had before the unfortunate entanglement, without bringing the odour of a distillery into the house every time he returned to it. A veil would be spread over the period of unpleasantness.

'But what on earth d'you think is the matter with Mary Louise?' Mrs Dallon agitatedly exclaimed. 'What's troubling her?'

'That's why we're sitting here, Mrs Dallon,' Matilda repeated. 'In order to gain your assistance. We were wondering could it be mental?'

'Mental?'

'If you were in the house ten minutes with her the word would come into your head. Is it a normal thing for any person to spend three-quarters of the day in an attic?'

'I thought it was just the evenings.'

'The evenings is the main time. But sometimes you look round in the shop and she's not to be seen. Well, you saw for yourself.'

'Sundays too,' Matilda put in. 'An entire Sunday morning. Many's the time.'

'Another thing, she'll go out on her bicycle on a Sunday after dinner and you'd worry in case she's ridden into a bog or something. Nine and ten o'clock she's not back.'

'She comes over here on a Sunday, but she's never as late as that.'

'Nine or ten, isn't it, Matilda?'

'Oh, easily. With the long evenings she's out till all hours.'

'There was one night she didn't come in at all.'

'What?' Just for an instant Mrs Dallon sounded hysterical. Her husband raised a hand, as though to calm her. 'What?' she said again, whispering now.

'The day you called in she walked out of the house and didn't come in till six o'clock the next morning.'

'But where on earth was she?'

'Matilda and I were all for going to the Guards. "She's gone over to Culleen," Elmer said.'

'She wasn't here.'

'Well, there you are then. To tell you the truth, Mrs Dallon,

we're worried the entire time. The state she's in she could end
up anywhere on that cycle. You hear terrible things these
days.'

'We didn't know any of this.' Mr Dallon slowly shook his
head, the skin of his face puckered with concern.

'She's riding wildly about the country, God knows where
she goes. There was another time we had to make Elmer go
out looking for her.'

Matilda didn't add that they had watched Elmer going
straight to Hogan's, that he hadn't returned until after ten, an
hour after Mary Louise had returned herself. Neither sister
revealed that Elmer had argued that it was up to his wife to
decide if she wanted to go for a bicycle ride, and how long she
should remain away. Rose said:

'"I wouldn't have it," she said to Mrs Riordan in the shop
a week ago. "The wide lapels don't suit you." The woman
had her money on the counter. You can't run a shop like that.
If Elmer knew the half of it he'd jump out of his skin.'

It was then that Matilda mentioned a place they'd heard of,
an asylum for women who were mentally distressed. They
hadn't made inquiries; a person had mentioned it to them,
which told a tale in itself.

'Very well looked after,' Rose said. 'A garden to go into.
The food's second to none.'

'My God!' Aghast, Mrs Dallon stared at her visitors. The
suggestion was horrible; the thought of it made her feel sick in
the stomach. No matter how oddly Mary Louise was behaving,
why should she be committed to an asylum?

'Mary Louise is not mad,' Mr Dallon protested. 'That
doesn't come into it.'

'It wasn't me who thought of that place,' Rose reminded
him. 'Another person was trying to help.'

'She should definitely see Dr Cormican.' He turned to his
wife. 'We'll drive in and have a word with Cormican.'

The sisters, feeling themselves dismissed by this decision, rose immediately. But before they left Rose said:

'Naturally, no one would want the poor girl confined in some place when she could be looked after by her own. We don't want to leave without saying that.'

'Her own?'

'Her family we were thinking.' Rose looked around the kitchen. 'Where things are familiar to her.'

Apart from words of leave-taking, nothing further was said. Kilkelly's car carried the sisters back to the town. The Dallons prepared themselves for an immediate visit to Dr Cormican.

More than most people, Bridget, the manageress of Hogan's Hotel, knew everything that happened in the town. She had noted with interest during the last eighteen months the intensifying of Elmer Quarry's addiction. It was a curious phenomenon, a considerable surprise that a Quarry should have come to err in this way, since the family was known for its longstanding tradition of sobriety. Bridget was also struck by a related habit Elmer Quarry had developed, that of leaving the bar by the door that led to the hall of the hotel and pausing there for a few minutes. She had observed him watching her through the glass partition of the reception desk, while pretending to admire the antlers on the wall at the bottom of the stairs or to consult the *Irish Field* calendar of the year's events. If through curiosity she emerged, he remarked on the weather and asked her how she was. Then he said good-night and went away.

Well used in her professional capacity to the attentions of men, surreptitious or otherwise, Bridget knew she was not mistaken in her surmises about all this. The direct way out of the bar to the street was by the other door: there was no call for any drinker to make his way into the hotel. And there was a quality in Elmer Quarry's mildly inebriated gaze that precluded any further doubt: when he was boozed up he wanted to take a gander at her. Bridget didn't mind – if you minded stuff like that you might as well change into another business. But she wondered about the girl Elmer Quarry had married, a kid whom no time ago she remembered seeing on the streets with a school satchel. She'd heard it said it couldn't be easy for the girl with two harridans breathing down her neck; even worse when Quarry had taken to the bottle and wasn't averse to eyeing other women.

'What d'you make of Quarry?' She put the question to the barman one evening, joining him in the bar when he'd closed it for the night. She usually looked in at this time and had a medium sherry while Gerry finished the glass of stout that had lasted all evening.

'He's the better for it with a couple inside him.' Experienced in such matters, Gerry was firm.

'It came on him suddenly though. Time was he only took a mineral.'

'You'd notice it in the older type of bachelor.' Gerry paused. He savoured another mouthful of stout, then slowly wiped a residue of foam from his upper lip. 'The Quarrys marry to get a baby,' he said.

'I know they do.'

'She saw what was there before she took the step herself. Isn't it evens Stephens if she can't oblige the man?'

'I wouldn't mind being a fly on the wall in that house.'

'I'll tell you this. In a twelvemonth he'll be well away.'

Later that night, as she undressed in her small room at the top of the hotel, Bridget was still thinking about Elmer Quarry and the girl who had married him. In particular she'd have liked to be a fly on the wall of their bedroom. She'd have liked to be a fly inside Elmer Quarry's head, able to see what he was thinking as he lay down beside his young wife, and to know why it was he loitered in the hall of the hotel. But in

bed, when she'd turned the light out, she forgot about the
Quarrys and thought about the curate she'd been in love with
when she was a girl herself, who'd been sent away to another
parish. 'I'll give it up for you,' he'd whispered, before Canon
Maguire stepped in.

'We just thought we'd see how you were getting on,' Mrs
Dallon said in the shop. 'We had to drive in anyway.'

'We haven't seen you for a while,' Mary Louise's father added.

From behind the counter their daughter acknowledged their
explanation. She asked them if they'd like to come upstairs
and then led the way. The sisters greeted them with nods of approval.

'You could swing a cat or two here,' Mr Dallon said in the
big front room.

Mary Louise made tea and brought it to them. Her mother
said:

'We've been a bit worried about you, Mary Louise.'

'Worried? Why worried?'

Neither replied, neither knowing quite how to. Dr Cormican
had explained to them that unless Mary Louise complained of
being ill and came to see him he could not help. There could
be a dozen reasons, he said, why she should choose to spend
so much time in a locked room. People got up to greater
eccentricities than that. 'Why don't you chat with her yourselves?' he'd suggested.

'Are you all right, Mary Louise?' Mr Dallon asked. 'Is
everything OK with you?'

'Why wouldn't it be?'

'Now, Mary Louise,' her mother began, then checked herself. 'What we mean is, maybe it's lonesome for you. Maybe
you miss the family and the farm.'

'I've been married two and a half years.'

'Even so, pet.'

'Has somebody said something?'

'The odd person has noticed you have a lonesome look.'

'You don't come out to see us on Sundays any more. We miss the visits, Mary Louise.'

'James misses seeing you. Letty was saying the same the other day.'

'Letty'll soon be married herself.'

'Yes, she will.'

'If there's anything troubling you, Mary Louise – '

'There's nothing.'

They talked of other matters, of Letty's wedding and of Mary Louise's Aunt Emmeline coming to live at Culleen, of the way James bossed them about these days and how pleased they were that he continued to display initiative. Driving back to the farm, Mr Dallon was silent. The visit had changed his mood. He felt foolish. He should have foreseen that a marriage with such an age difference would not be plain sailing: he should have been against it. But he hadn't been and that was that. He'd wasted a lot of time listening to the Quarry sisters and then waiting until Dr Cormican was ready for them, and then sitting down over a cup of tea in the middle of the morning. He resented, above all things, wasted time.

'They're troublemakers, those women,' he said.

Mrs Dallon nodded, and agreed that they were. But even as she spoke she shared, without knowing that she did, the Quarrys' view that Mary Louise's marriage of convenience had turned out to be a grievous mistake. Mrs Dallon was never to alter that opinion.

Mary Louise did not change her ways. She had come to terms with Elmer and his sisters; she no longer feared the wrath of the two women's tongues, and long ago she had ceased to wish to please her husband. She opened their bedroom window wider now, for his whiskey breath was so potent in the early part of the night that once or twice she felt light-headed through inhaling it.

Although her mother had hinted at the gossip that had begun, Mary Louise remained unaware of it. Nor did she know that her mother constantly worried, distressfully imagining a solitary figure in a locked room, nor that her father was angry with himself for permitting a marriage involving such an age difference. More and more she kept to the kitchen during mealtimes, in spite of Elmer's protests that in doing so she was upsetting his sisters. Why should she not? she thought. She didn't like them.

'*Bersenev took a droshky going back to Moscow and went in search of Insarov. But it took him a long time to find the Bulgarian because Insarov had moved to new lodgings . . .*'

His search dulled the ornaments in the Quarrys' dining-room, the grim dumb waiter, the sideboard, the double curtains of lace and chintz. Mary Louise hated the dining-room. She hated its Turkey carpet and its brown pictures and the salt and pepper in the left-hand sideboard drawer, and the smell of old food. But when she listened now, eating alone in the kitchen, she often heard the sound of Bersenev's droshky. Without closing her eyes, there was the brick façade of the house where Insarov lodged.

Yelena Nikolayevna loved Insarov and didn't know it. Yelena was a tall girl, olive-skinned and grey-eyed, with a complicated nature. She had been fond of her father, then cooled towards him, attaching herself to her mother instead. In the end she had distanced herself from both. Mary Louise tried to imagine that. Nothing even vaguely like it had occurred in her own childhood. Her first memory was of being with Letty, sitting beside Letty's doll on stubble and Letty saying she must be still because dolls always were. Letty pretended to give her things to eat, as she did with her doll. The sun was warm on her face and head. Not far away a tiny bird was

rooting in the stubble, and Letty tried to entice it towards
Mary Louise and the doll so that all three could be fed, but
the bird flew away. The first time she went to Miss Mullover's
schoolroom it was in the trap, James and Letty taking it in
turn to hold the reins. They tied the pony up in the yard of
Hogan's Hotel and then her brother and sister each took one
of Mary Louise's hands. 'A for Apple,' Miss Mullover said,
the tip of her cane on the rosy apple of her chart, then moving
on. 'B for Boot.' Miss Mullover gave her letters to copy.
'*Mary Louise,*' she said; and pointed out each letter, saying
that was what her name looked like. After the first time they
didn't go to school in the trap any more. Mary Louise sat on
the crossbar of James's bicycle, and he was made to promise
that he wouldn't ride fast. In time Mary Louise learned to ride
Letty's bicycle and Letty inherited her mother's. On Fridays
Miss Mullover always set more homework than she did on
other days and James and Letty complained all the way back
to the farmhouse. Two verses of poetry, ten spellings, three
sums, a composition, history or geography, tables. On
Mondays Miss Mullover was always cross, sarcastically reading out a composition if it was very bad, rapping knuckles
with her cane. 'You'll stay in, James,' she nearly always
snapped on Mondays. 'Until you know those verses perfectly
you'll not leave this room today.' When Mary Louise first
heard the story of Joan of Arc she imagined the peasant girl
kneeling on the ploughed earth, hearing the voices. She
imagined her waiting, tied to the stake, watching the building
of the fire that was to burn her. Sometimes the boys from the
Christian Brothers' shouted abuse when the three Dallon children rode by, calling them heretics, reminding them that they
would burn in hell. James always replied in kind, but Letty
took no notice. 'Why'll we burn in hell?' Mary Louise asked,
and Letty said they wouldn't.

Because Robert never came to Culleen when Aunt Emmeline

visited the farmhouse, Mary Louise hadn't known of his existence until she went to school. 'I'm your cousin,' he said one
day in the school yard, and that was the first memory she had
of him. After that she noticed he always finished his transcription before the others, and was best at spelling and tables. Her
mother explained what it meant, being a cousin. 'Aunt Emmeline's one child,' her mother said. She was twelve when she
fell in love with him.

In the locked attic, or crouched among the Attridge graves,
Mary Louise delighted in the intimacies death could not touch,
any more than it could touch the love story of Yelena and
Insarov. A legacy came to Robert from some distant relative
of his father's: he was no longer poor. On the day after Elmer
first invited her to the Electric Cinema Robert arrived at the
farmhouse. 'No,' she said when Elmer asked her to accompany
him again, and went instead in search of the heron with her
cousin. When they married they travelled in Italy and France.
They sat outside a café by the sea, watching the people stroll-
ing by, Robert in a pale suit and a hat that matched it. He
leaned across the table to kiss her, as he had the first time in
the graveyard. Light as a butterfly, his kisses danced up and
down her arm, from the tips of her fingers to her shoulders.
The café orchestra began. They drank white wine.

Without closing her eyes, Mary Louise could see the flare of
the gas-jets and snowy carriages drawing up. Tall Russians
conversed in rooms with polished floors; walls were lined
with mirrors, small oval tables covered with velvet and gold-
fringed cloths. There was a haziness, in which her cousin's
voice spoke, in which her own voice repeated the difficult
Russian names, and then through which they themselves
passed back and forth like softly coloured shadows.

21

Bríd Beamish is the first to go. Bríd Beamish received messages from U2. She was told U2 were in trouble. She kept contacting the Garda, saying the IRA were after them. Dave Lee Travis spoke personally to her, sending her messages through his disc-jockey chatter. When her father said he wouldn't have Dave Lee Travis' name repeated in the house she lit a cigarette and dropped it into the petrol tank of his Ford Cortina. She travelled to Lincolnshire in search of café life and was missing for a month. Afterwards she said she'd been on the game, an expression that confused her family until someone in a bar told her father what it meant. Schizophrenia was the diagnosis. And mild erotomania.

Bríd Beamish waves at the congregated women. She stands by the open back door of the car her father had to buy when she destroyed his Ford Cortina. Right as rain she'll be, provided she doesn't fall down on the medication: presentable is what they mean, and looking at her the women agree she's a lot more presentable now than she was the day she arrived, no reason not to believe she'll walk up the aisle. 'Cheers, dear!' the Spanish wife calls out, and old Sister Hannah, who developed a great affection for Bríd Beamish, who was her confidante, is tearful.

The car door bangs, tyres crunch on the gravel.

'Back to prostitution,' Small Sadie predicts in her shrill screech.

22

Letty's wedding party was very different from Mary Louise's. It was held in the public house referred to by Rose when the news of Letty's romance was first mentioned in the dining-room above the shop. As Rose had stated, the public house in question was at a crossroads, a long single-storey building advertised in blue and yellow neon letters as Dennehy's Lounge. In grey pebble-dash, it stood back from the intersection of roads, with a wide parking space in front of it. Dennehy's was known for miles around, its regular clientele consisting entirely of country people. Harp Lager had supplied the neon sign, and in return was advertised prominently as well.

After the wedding ceremony a lift was arranged for Mary Louise and Elmer with Bleheen of the artificial-insemination unit, a ferrety man of the same age as Elmer, who was still pursuing his search for a suitable wife. The conversation in the car reminded Mary Louise of the conversation with the three diners at the Strand Hotel on the evening of her own wedding. She sat in the back and didn't contribute to it.

'Ah, it's great you came on out,' Letty greeted her when they entered the lounge bar. Still in her wedding-dress, Letty was smoking a cigarette.

'No trouble at all,' Elmer said.

For some weeks there had been unpleasantness in the house because Rose and Matilda had not been included in the wedding invitation. They were indignant, pointing out that since they were family relations the oversight was hurtful. When he asked Mary Louise if she'd have a word with her sister, all she'd done was to shake her head at him.

'You'll take a glass, Mr Quarry?' the bridegroom's father offered from behind the bar. 'What'll I pour you?'

Elmer replied that he'd like some whiskey. 'An occasion and a half, sir,' he added agreeably. 'Wouldn't we be correct to call it that?'

'Oh, we would, Mr Quarry. He's the lucky man for himself.'

'He is of course.'

There the exchange of views terminated. Elmer returned to Mary Louise's side. He shook hands with her father and with her mother. He remarked again upon the importance of the occasion.

'Once in a lifetime, Elmer,' Mr Dallon said.

'That's true enough, sir.'

Mrs Dennehy came up and reminded them that all drinks were on the house. She wore a lot of lipstick, Elmer noticed, for a woman of her age. Into the bargain her fingernails were scarlet. A huge woman she was, with a brassy voice.

'What'll I get you all?' Mrs Dennehy arched her eyebrows, glancing hospitably from face to face. When a choice was made she turned away to fetch the drinks. Elmer wanted to take a look at her back but thought he'd better not. He said:

'Wasn't it great we could let Letty have the dress material at cost, Mr Dallon?'

'It was good of you, Elmer.'

'Any time we could oblige you in a matter like that, sir, just walk into the shop.'

The least he could do, Rose had said, was to mention the way they'd been treated to his in-laws. She'd come into the accounting office when he was up to his eyes and started on about it again. She'd wanted to know what Mary Louise had said when he'd put the thing to her, and he'd had to make up an excuse. 'No more manners to them than tinkers,' his sister snapped at him in the end. 'What good did getting in with them do you?'

The good it did was that they had an extra pair of hands in the shop and in the house. He put it like that to her because that was the type of talk she understood. They should be glad of an extra pair of hands, he said, but Rose ignored that completely. She mentioned drink. It was the talk of the town, she said.

He took a drink now and again. He went out to get company, the way any man might. What company was there in the snapping and offence-taking that occurred three times a day in the dining-room? You could spend two hours playing billiards down in the YMCA with no cause to open your mouth except to issue a greeting to an elderly caretaker. 'You're drinking like a fish,' Rose said.

Mrs Dennehy returned with a tray of glasses for Mary Louise and her mother and father. There was one for herself also, but nothing for him.

'To the pair of them,' Mrs Dennehy began, and Elmer interrupted. He pointed out that he would be unable to join in the toast, on account of having an empty glass. He began to move towards the bar, but Mrs Dennehy said she wouldn't hear of it at a private function. She seized his glass, giving him her own to look after.

'Let everyone hold on a minute!' she commanded in her rumbustious way. 'No one touch a drop till Mr Quarry is replenished!'

He couldn't recall her ever coming into the shop. He'd have noticed her all right, the lipstick and the fingernails. He suddenly remembered walking into the front room when he was no more than fifteen, to find a similar build of woman trying on petticoats.

'A drop of the hard stuff!' She handed him his glass, and he noticed that there was more than a small one in it. They all joined in the toast except Mary Louise, who took it into her head to walk away. It embarrassed Elmer that she did so, in the company of her mother and father and Mrs Dennehy.

'We're pleased about it, Mrs Dennehy,' Mr Dallon said, but Elmer doubted it: poor Protestants for donkey's years, why would they be pleased to see their grandchildren brought up holy Romans?

'I'm right pleased myself. Right pleased!' Mrs Dennehy exclaimed. Her teeth were in proportion to the rest of her. When she addressed anyone she opened her mouth very wide, which might have contributed to the loudness of her voice. You could see all the way back to her molars.

'It was a great spread you laid on for our own wedding,' Elmer confided quietly to his mother-in-law, who seemed to be a bit out of things. 'You did wonders that day, Mrs Dallon.'

He listened while Mrs Dallon told him that this wedding party, too, should be taking place at Culleen. But Mrs Dennehy had come over a month ago and put it to her that since such large numbers were expected, and since the Dennehys had such spacious premises and were in the business professionally, it might be in order to reverse the usual procedure. Letty had been in favour of that also, and reluctantly Mrs Dallon had given in.

'Ah, you would of course. And wouldn't you save a bit while you were at it?'

A familiar euphoria had begun to flow softly through Elmer. He'd taken to keeping a little John Jameson in the wall-safe in the accounting office, for any man would require a drink in certain circumstances. There was an expression Matilda had used one time: trapped like a squirrel she'd said he was. She was thinking of a time when they were children and a man had come into the shop with three squirrels in a cage, trying to sell them in some ignorant kind of way, beautiful soft fur, he kept saying. Their father had called Elmer and the girls downstairs so that they could get a close look at the creatures, and then had sent the man packing. In Elmer's view being trapped wasn't a bad description of his own predicament, but he had no intention of giving Matilda the satisfaction of knowing that he agreed with her. Ridiculous, he'd said when she made her observation. Another thing was that when you'd had a drink or two you got a predicament like that into proportion – which naturally he couldn't have said to Matilda either.

'Bullocks are fetching well,' he remarked to his father-in-law. 'What's that I heard a hundredweight?'

'Thirty-five last week.'

'You'd not turn up your nose at that, sir.'

Mrs Dallon had watched Elmer finishing the first drink he'd been given quicker than anyone else. He was three-quarters of the way through the second and his neck and forehead had begun to glow. She glanced across the bar to where the bridegroom was standing with Letty and some people she didn't know. To her relief, Dennehy appeared to be drinking some kind of fruit juice.

'I haven't a bullock to sell,' Mrs Dallon heard her husband saying. 'Unfortunately.'

She returned her attention to her younger daughter's husband. His conversation wasn't sensible. He was rambling in his speech, going on about what some bullock or other had fetched at a fair ten years ago. When Mrs Dennehy had been standing there he'd kept staring into her mouth. At one point he'd stood back in order to get a general view of her.

'The biggest price ever paid in the town,' he was saying now.

Dennehy, with his arm round Letty's waist, was thinking she

had a bit of style. She could hold her own on the family premises, calm as a cucumber. The dress suited her beautifully, greenish with shiny stuff run through it, threads that caught the light when she shifted. Underneath it, pinned to her straps, she was wearing the good-luck brooch he'd given her. The emerald engagement ring was still in place, with the gold band beside it.

'Hullo,' someone said, half behind him so that he had to turn his head. He dropped his arm from Letty's waist and smiled at Mary Louise. 'She's all over the place,' Letty had said earlier, asking him to be nice to her.

'Hullo, Mary Louise, how are you?'

'I'm fine. Are you OK yourself?'

'Never better. Have you something in that glass?'

'Oh yes, thanks.'

He heard Letty saying the honeymoon was a secret. When they'd still been undecided she'd mentioned places he'd never heard of before. Tramore he'd thrown in himself, and Tramore they'd agreed on.

'I hope it's all right with you, Mary Louise? The wedding?'

She nodded, a very slight movement of her head, her expression solemn. She looked as though she had weighed the matter up, as if she had actually wondered if it was all right or not. Dennehy felt reassured, but even so he wished his future sister-in-law was a little more forthcoming. She had committed an act of madness when she'd married Elmer Quarry, Letty said, and in her company Dennehy couldn't help agreeing. Protestant girl or not, surely she could have done better than a draper nearly twice her age?

'You heard I bought a house at Rathtrim?' he said.

'Letty told me that.'

'We've had the builders in.'

'It'll be like she wants in that case.'

'Oh, it's not bad at all.' He drank some of his pineapple

juice. There was a small measure of gin in it, which gave it an edge. 'They've only a few small things left to do. They'll do them while we're away.'

'I'm sure they'll have it ready for you.'

'They'll hear me a mile or two if they haven't.'

The lounge-bar filled up. Mrs Dallon was joined by her sister Emmeline, who said she didn't know anyone except the Edderys and Miss Mullover. Letty had invited other people she'd know, Mrs Dallon said, but they hadn't arrived yet. Apparently they were sharing a car. 'Would you say Elmer's sober?' she whispered, and both women observed him for a moment. He was still talking about livestock prices. They moved closer, still listening.

'Are your sisters keeping well?' Mrs Dallon interrupted when he'd gone on a little longer. It was typical of them not to attend Letty's wedding, she had already observed to her sister. Typical to be snooty.

Elmer said his sisters were fine. Neither of those girls had ever had a day's sickness in her life, he said. When they were small they'd maybe had the measles, he couldn't remember was it measles or chicken-pox, but they never caught a cold. They could be in the shop all day with the stove going and germs coming in with the customers, but never a cold between them. The same with indigestion, nothing like it at all. Which was more than he could say for himself.

Mrs Dallon glanced at her sister and then at her husband. She'd never heard Elmer Quarry talking like that before, in the shop or out of it. After his own wedding he'd been propriety itself.

'Will I get you another?' he suggested, reaching out for their three glasses. Mrs Dallon put her hand over the top of hers. Winter's Tale sherry it was, but a glass was enough.

'Well, it's good of you, Elmer,' Mr Dallon said. 'Will he get you something, Emmeline?'

'Ah, no, no, I'm all right.'

'He's footless,' Mrs Dallon said when Elmer had gone off.

'He's had a few certainly,' her sister agreed.

Mr Dallon hadn't noticed anything amiss, but on hearing this he realized that the draper was more easy-going than usual. He'd taken it with a pinch of salt when Letty had said her brother-in-law was drinking.

'Stotious,' Mrs Dallon pronounced.

While he was waiting for the drinks to be poured Elmer considered that there was no reason why he shouldn't refer to the unpleasantness back in the house, since Rose and Matilda were under discussion and the conversation had to be kept going. He'd been asked how they were and there was no reason why the thing couldn't be hinted at. He could hint at it when he gave out their drinks to them, best to get it out of the way, best not to have it hanging there.

'Who weren't invited?' Mrs Dallon said.

'Weren't we talking about my sisters?'

'Your sisters were invited, Elmer. I wrote the invitation out myself.'

He shook his head. The pair of them were fit to be tied, he said.

'You didn't get a written card yourself, Elmer. You and Mary Louise were taken for granted. But all the others on our side I wrote out.'

'They heard about that all right. Only nothing came to the house for themselves.'

She had given the invitation to Mary Louise. One Sunday in March, having not been at the farmhouse since before Christmas, Mary Louise had arrived, as she used to in the past. Mrs Dallon had actually been writing out the invitations at the time and she'd given her the one for Matilda and Rose. Mary Louise had said they wouldn't attend a Catholic wedding, but then had picked up the envelope, promising to pass it on to them anyway.

'I'm sorry, Elmer. Please tell your sisters I'm very sorry. The invitation . . . ' Mrs Dallon paused and then began her sentence again. 'The invitation must somehow have gone astray. That's most upsetting.'

'I wouldn't have mentioned it only they took it hard.'

Listening to all this, Mr Dallon remembered Rose suggesting that Mary Louise should return to Culleen, to be looked after in the farmhouse. Suddenly he wished that that could be so, that she could be rescued from Elmer's sisters. Clearly she'd been unable to bring herself to deliver the invitation to them. God alone knew what kind of a life she was leading.

'Did you mind me remarking on it?' Elmer's bulk swayed a little, the top half of his body seeming to bow repeatedly. 'Only they have me demented on that subject.'

At the other end of the long lounge-bar Baney Neligan was going through the words of a song, and Dennehy was doing his best to prevent him from singing them. Letty had specifically requested that there shouldn't be singing. Her parents would hate it, she'd said.

'Are you married yourself?' he heard someone ask Mary Louise.

'Yes, I am actually.'

'You're blind, Ger!' someone else exclaimed. 'This woman has a ring on her finger.'

Apologies were offered, and then the people moved away. Dennehy kept introducing Mary Louise to the wedding guests, but she didn't seem much inclined to converse. Out of the corner of his eye he could see that she was on her own again, but to his relief he noticed her brother and the Eddery boys approaching her.

'The hard man!' Father Mannion, who had conducted the

wedding service, struck him on the shoulder. Baney Neligan
began to sing.

'*Is Mr Insarov young?' asked Zoya.*
  '*He's a hundred and forty-four,' Shubin snapped.*
'What are you laughing at, Mary Louise?' James asked her,
and she said she was only smiling.
'How're you doing, Mary Louise?' one of the Eddery boys
asked.
Her brother and the Eddery boys were smoking. They were
drinking from pint glasses, holding them nonchalantly as if
they were well used to glasses of that size.
'I'm OK,' she said.
'God, I'll never forget that.' One of the Eddery boys recalled
how he and his brother had tied the empty creosote tin to the
bumper of Kilkelly's car on Mary Louise's wedding day.
The three of them laughed. The younger of the Eddery boys
asked her if she liked it in the town. He wouldn't be able to
stand a town himself, he'd feel closed in.
'D'you feel closed in?' the older brother asked.
'You get used to it.'
'Din Lafferty came back from Birmingham.'
Mary Louise said she didn't think she'd like Birmingham.
'Lafferty couldn't take it at all.'
When she and Elmer returned from their honeymoon his
sisters welcomed them on the first-floor landing, Rose saying
she'd wet the tea immediately because they must be parched.
But first Elmer took her to the bedroom that had been his
parents' bedroom, which would now be theirs. The air was
fusty there, the windows tightly closed, the wide double bed
not made up. 'They'll tell you where the sheets are,' he said,
and in the dining-room he reminded his sisters that he would
be moving out of his old room, that in future it could maybe
be used to store stuff in.

'D'you know Din Lafferty?' the older Eddery brother asked her, and she said she'd seen him a few times in the past.

'A right gawk,' James said.

She moved away.

'Come to see an old fellow?' Her father smiled at her. Her mother and her aunt had been taken upstairs by Mrs Dennehy to admire the wedding presents. Elmer was at the bar with Bleheen.

'Has Aunt Emmeline moved in yet?' she asked her father.

'Any day now.'

'She's lonely with Robert dead.'

'Ah, it's an awful old house for her. Sad old memories.'

'What was he like, that man she married?'

'Useless.'

'In what way useless?' Mary Louise asked.

'He led that poor woman a dance. He'd have seen her starve before he'd step off a racecourse.'

She reminded her father that once he'd said the man they spoke of had charm to burn, but she didn't receive a direct comment on that now.

'I wouldn't give you tuppence for him, Mary Louise. An awful streel of a fellow.'

'Robert wouldn't have been Robert if it hadn't been for him.'

'Well, no, that's true, I suppose.'

There was surprise in her father's voice, and for a moment Mary Louise almost told him that she and Robert had loved one another, first as children, and then when she was a married woman. Her father would keep it to himself, not wishing to cause anxiety: that was the way he was. She might have told him that Elmer came drunk to bed. She might have given the reason for their childless marriage. Her father would not have passed that on either. And would it matter that he knew all this, that the truth had been shared? It mightn't matter at all, but at the same time it would distress him.

'Father Mannion,' a voice said, and a priest held out a hand for her father to shake. 'How're you doing, Mr Dallon?'

The priest was smiling, a big, pink, boyish face on a middle-aged man, a pink neck and forehead. He held his hand out to Mary Louise also, and she laid hers in it. 'How are you, Mrs Quarry?' he said.

She hated being called that. Ever since the funeral she had hated it. She didn't listen when the priest and her father discussed some matter in businesslike tones, her father regularly nodding, the priest reaching out to press his arm every now and again. Gazing at the black cloth of Father Mannion's sleeve, Mary Louise recalled the bottom sheet spread out on the bed that first evening in the Quarrys' house, her own hands smoothing it. She walked round the bed itself to tuck it in, then spread the second sheet and smoothed away the wrinkles in that also. She remembered now the coldness of those sheets when later they slept together in his parents' bed, he on the left side, she to the right.

'*Zinaida drank iced water all day,*' her cousin said, and Mary Louise turned away to smile. The old princess complained that so much iced water could not be good for a girl with a weak chest. As for herself, she had a toothache . . .

'You have to be unmarried to be a bridesmaid,' Letty said. 'I told you, didn't I, Mary Louise?'

'Yes, you did.'

'Is it that that upset you?'

Mary Louise said she hadn't thought twice about the matter. Angela Eddery, in the same greenish shade as Letty, was the bridesmaid because the Edderys were distant relations.

'I'm not upset,' Mary Louise again assured her sister.

'You're different than you used to be.'

'I'll come out and see you when you're settled down in the house.'

'Yes, do,' Letty urged, placing a hand on Mary Louise's arm. 'Anytime come out.'

Other voices had joined Baney Neligan's now. A piano was being played; two girls had begun to dance. Men were crowded along the bar, talking and laughing. A uniformed garda, with his bicycle-clips still in place, searched through them to shake hands with Mr Dennehy. Two tinker children tried to enter the lounge-bar and were summarily ejected. Men she didn't know put their arms round Letty's waist or kissed her, saying it was their due. Mrs Dennehy went round the guests, announcing that there was a table laid out in the dining-room, down the passage next to the Ladies.

'I remember him at the Christian Brothers',' Father Mannion informed Mr Dallon, referring to the bridegroom. 'I used come in to give them a jaw. Your man sat at the end of a row.' Mr Dallon said that was interesting, and Father Mannion added that those were great old days. 'I better make the rounds,' he said. 'I have hands to shake myself.'

In an upstairs bedroom Mrs Dallon and her sister examined the wedding presents that were laid out on the candlewick cover of a bed and on the room's dressing-table and on a larger table. There were plates and sheets, tablecloths, ashtrays, vases, cups and a teapot, an electric kettle, an electric iron, table-mats, more plates, cutlery, a salt and pepper set, a special kind of rolling-pin, a corkscrew, various kitchen implements, saucepans, a doormat, basins, bowls, jugs, baking dishes and a framed picture of the Virgin Mary, incorporating the Sacred Heart. This last offended Mrs Dallon. It had come from someone who was unaware of Letty's religion, or else from someone who considered the reproduction a necessity in the household that was being set up. Letty wouldn't hang it up, she'd surely put it behind something.

'Ah, yes,' Mrs Dennehy said hastily, noticing that Mrs Dallon's attention had been caught by the picture. 'That's difficult certainly.'

'Some lovely stuff here.' Mrs Dallon was determined not to

reveal her displeasure. There were bound to be awkward-
nesses. There were areas that had to settle down in any mixed
marriage, no good pretending.

'Well, aren't people generous, Mrs Dallon? When you come
to the crunch of it you'll find they're generous.'

Other women entered the bedroom, Mrs Dallon and her
sister left it. On a corner shelf on the landing there was a
statue of a saint and downstairs there was a picture like the
one Letty had been given, with a red light flickering below it.
All of a sudden Mrs Dallon found herself wondering whom
James would marry.

'Doesn't the green suit Letty?' Angela Eddery came close to
Mary Louise to voice her admiration. She had a way of doing
that, of speaking in hushed, reverential tones with her packed,
pressed-out teeth a few inches from the face of the person she
addressed. Her breath was warm.

'Does it suit myself, Mary Louise? It suits Letty all right,
but I wondered about myself?'

'Mary Louise,' another voice said, upbraiding her. 'You didn't
give that invitation to Rose and Matilda. Why didn't you, pet?'

She did her best to explain. Her mother said if there ever
was anything that upset her she should bring the worry out to
Culleen. That was what home was for.

'Of course it is, pet,' her mother pressed, even though Mary
Louise hadn't sought to deny this opinion. Somewhere in the
crowd, a little earlier, she had glimpsed the wrinkled features
of Miss Mullover. The old schoolteacher was someone she
could tell, someone who wouldn't be upset, as her father
would have been.

'I haven't seen you for ages, Mary Louise.' Her aunt's
weather-chapped face was there also. Whatever she'd chosen to
drink had caused it to redden even further. 'Are you keeping
well these days?'

'Yes, I am. What'll become of the soldiers when you sell the house? And the books and things?'

There was a pause. Then her aunt said:

'There'll be an auction. Your father thought an auction was best.'

Mary Louise wondered about Robert's clothes. A dead person's clothes were sometimes given to charity, unless they were sold because money was short. You wouldn't auction clothes; she'd never heard of that.

'What'll happen to his watch?'

'I'll keep his watch, dear.'

Her aunt smiled at Mary Louise as she spoke. When would the auction be? Mary Louise asked, and her aunt said the second of May, all being well.

'Will you give away his clothes?'

The question appeared to cause consternation. Her mother asked Mary Louise to repeat it, which she did.

'There's a family in need,' her aunt said eventually, 'due to the father being out of work.'

Pressed further by Mary Louise, she added:

'That dingy blue-washed cottage on the Clonmel road.'

Responding to Mrs Dennehy's invitation, some of the guests had visited the dining-room and were now sitting at the tables in the bar, eating from cardboard plates. Miss Mullover, with modest portions of tongue and salad, saw Mary Louise on her own and waved across the room at her. The rumours about Elmer Quarry were true, she'd been thinking only a moment before. She'd seen for herself this afternoon: his eyes bleary, the lids inclined to droop. Like a sack of something, she'd thought, slouched against the counter of the bar.

'Hullo, Mary Louise.'

Every time she met her, the girl seemed more reticent. You had to prise responses out of her now. 'This tongue's good,'

she said, but the recommendation elicited no comment whatsoever. Then, as if reading those thoughts, Mary Louise
answered a polite query about her husband's well-being by
suddenly becoming garrulous. Elmer was a harmless man, she
said; he meant no ill-will. He had never struck anyone in his
life; he never got into a rage; he never shouted; in all sorts of
ways he didn't bother her.

'D'you remember, Miss Mullover, how my cousin always
finished his transcription first? He used to scribble on the
inside of his jotter cover. My cousin Robert?'

Miss Mullover, surprised, failed to remember that.

'We were in love you know, my cousin Robert and I. In
your schoolroom we were in love. We still were when he died.
We've always belonged to one another.'

Elmer and Bleheen were interrupted at the bar. Mary Louise
was suggesting they should go home.

'Home's where the heart is,' Elmer said, remembering the
expression suddenly, something his mother used to say. He lowered his voice. He'd had the whole thing explained, he said: an
invitation had been issued but it had never reached the house. He
was to carry her mother's apologies back to Rose and Matilda.

'Can we go now, Elmer?'

'We'll take a quick one for the road in that case,' Bleheen
said, raising his empty glass for attention.

'Five minutes, dear,' Elmer put in, 'while Mr Bleheen charges
his batteries.'

The remark was not made humorously but even so the
artificial-inseminator laughed. 'The three of us'll charge our
batteries,' he declared. 'What'll you take yourself, dear?'

'No, I'm all right, Mr Bleheen.'

Mrs Dennehy appeared at her side, reminding her about the
display of wedding presents upstairs. 'Your mother's been up,
along with your aunt. Wouldn't you slip up yourself?'

'Go up and enjoy yourself dear,' Elmer urged; but Mary Louise said they'd better be getting back. She'd ask her mother to describe the wedding presents when she saw her next.

'Well, wasn't it a great send-off for your sister?' Bleheen said in the car. 'Not a ha'penny spared.'

Elmer, beside him in the front, agreed. The time by the dashboard clock was five past five. As soon as they heard the key in the lock they'd be out on the landing, waiting, the way they'd taken to doing. They'd start in at once about the house smelling like a distillery, as though any normal person could go out to a party and not return bringing traces of festivity with him. Mary Louise would walk past them, different from the way she used to be, not timid in their presence any more. What he'd do would be to stay where he was for a few minutes in the hall, and then walk into the accounting office. After ten minutes or so he'd slip down to Hogan's.

'All right, are you, dear?' He half turned his head to address his wife, but she didn't appear to hear him.

23

Miss Foye kisses her. He carries her two suitcases. The Quarrys are decent people, she hears Mrs Leavy say, they have that reputation. While she was waiting in the hall Mrs Leavy told further stories about the old days in the asylums, relating the frightening scenes she and her friend Elsie witnessed when they looked over the brick wall.

The women wave, as they waved at Bríd Beamish. The asylums were built as charitable institutions, the fashion in mercy then, as the drugs are now. She waves back, and winds the window of the car down and waves again.

She has left the house before, on two occasions: for the funeral of her father, and a year and a half later for that of her mother. At both she'd been reminded of the death of her cousin, not that reminding was necessary; but the words of farewell were the same, the repetition causing her to reflect that the dead become nothing when you weary of doing their living for them. You pick and choose among the dead; the living are thrust upon you.

'Are they still alive?' she asks, the silence suddenly broken, the question emerging naturally from her thoughts.

'Who's that?'

'Your sisters.'

The car responds to the shock he experiences, juddering in its motion. He halts it to adjust himself, steering it into the gateway of a field. He turns to look at her.

'Why shouldn't my sisters be alive?'

'We all die some time.'

'Of course they haven't died.'

'I was not to know.'

'You'd have been told, dear.'

She doesn't say she might have been told and not been interested. She doesn't say anything, but listens while he warns her there'll be changes she'll notice, in the town and in his daily life.

'Do you remember what I told you about the shop?'

She considers for a moment, then admits she doesn't.

'I sold it out to the Renehans nine years ago. They joined the two premises together.'

'Yes, I remember that.'

The television tells you what the world is like, old Sister Hannah used to say, the changes that have come. If you can be bothered to pay attention, the television will tell you all you want to know.

'Over the shop's the same,' he says.

'Yes, I'm sure it is.'

Sister Hannah's the wise one. A person's life isn't orderly, Sister Hannah maintains; it runs about all over the place, in and out through time. The present's hardly there; the future doesn't exist. Only love matters in the bits and pieces of a person's life.

24

On the day of the auction at her aunt's house Mary Louise
cycled out of the town just before eight o'clock. The streets
were quiet. Mrs Renehan was out with her cocker spaniel.
The bell of the Church of Our Lady was chiming. A lorry
with barrels on it was drawn up at the bottom of the town,
waiting to make deliveries, its driver and his companion reading newspapers in the cab. Bakers' shops and paper-shops
were open. In the window of Foley's the elderly assistant was
laying out rows of rashers. Two nuns made their way to the
new convent classrooms on the Clonmel road.

Mary Louise wondered if he knew. If you believed in heaven
there was no reason to suppose that he wouldn't. She imagined
him with his half smile watching her, knowing what she was
up to. When she was seven or eight her mother had taken
Letty and herself to the auction there'd been when old Colonel
Esdaile died, three weeks after his wife had gone. She remembered a white marble statue in the garden, a draped
woman. 'Not another like it in Ireland,' the auctioneer had
bellowed. 'Every detail in place, down to the toenails.' And he
was right: the toenails were delicately incised, she and Letty
had gone to look. Mrs Dallon had hoped to bid for a job lot
that consisted of a clothes line, scrubbing brushes and a bucket,
but unfortunately the auctioneer, running out of time, placed
it beyond her reach by throwing it in with two other selections
of household items.

The morning was mild and sunny. Primroses still bloomed on the verges. Buds dotted the hedges, catkins were heavy on the new season's shoots. Still softly green, cow parsley and elder bided their time.

There was a car ahead of Mary Louise on the green avenue. It moved slowly, as if wary of an unfamiliar surface. She watched it draw away from her and finally turn on to the grass before it reached the house. She could just see figures moving away from it. When she was closer a cardboard sign read *Park Here*.

'The sale won't start till two, miss,' a man in the kitchen said. He was sitting at the table with another man and a boy. There was a blue Thermos flask on the table, and three cups without saucers. The boy was eating a doughnut he'd taken from a torn-open paper bag beside the flask.

'I just want to look around,' Mary Louise said.

The two men seemed doubtful, the boy wasn't interested. The man who'd spoken said that viewing would commence at ten. Ten was what was advertised, he added.

'I'm a member of the family,' Mary Louise explained, and the two men appeared to be relieved.

'Go ahead for yourself in that case,' the second man said, and Mary Louise passed through the kitchen.

Her aunt had declared she would herself find the auction too painful to attend, and in the circumstances Mary Louise guessed her mother would not drive over either. Other people she knew would arrive, but that didn't matter, provided they didn't bother her with their inquisitiveness. She mounted the stairs and opened the door of the first room she came to. Clearly it had been her aunt's. The mattress was rolled up on the bed, tied with string. Each piece of furniture had a number stuck on it.

In her cousin's room there were further numbers, black figures on a small blue rectangle. Framed in badly chipped

gilt, a picture on the wall facing the bed was 91: farm workers
in old-fashioned dress crowding round one of the wheels of a
hay-cart, which had broken beneath the strain; near by, a dog
was chasing a rat through the stubble. The mattress on this
bed also was rolled up and tied. A china water jug, and the
basin it stood in, were numbered 97, the wash-stand 96. There
was a sun-bleached wardrobe and a dressing-table without a
looking-glass, brown linoleum on the floor. The room's single
window had a view of the distant stream, and Mary Louise
remembered her cousin telling her that he'd first seen the
heron from his bedroom. On the mantelpiece, seeming as if he
might have left them there himself, were his binoculars. A
corner press, built into the two walls that formed it, was
empty. So was the wardrobe. The dressing-table had a single
drawer, lined with old newspaper. It, too, was empty, except
for a collar-stud and a bottle of green Stephens' ink, both of
which she took.

Downstairs, in the room he had been so fond of, the scat-
tered papers had been cleared. Books were tied into bundles.
The French and German soldiers, still battling as he had left
them, were numbered 39. She pulled out drawers and searched
in the mahogany cupboards on either side of the door, but her
cousin's papers, his drawings and his scribbles, were not there.
She had hoped to find them tied up in a bundle like the books
– not an item in the auction but simply tidied away. Her Aunt
Emmeline might have kept them by her, she decided; she
might have packed them into the luggage she had taken to
Culleen. One day, if her aunt didn't want them any more,
she'd ask if she could have them.

To pass the time, Mary Louise walked down to the stream,
but today no fish were to be seen. Cars appeared on the
avenue, one or two at first, then several at a time. She sat
down on the grassy bank and watched them turning at the
parking sign, and people getting out of them. The sound of

doors banging, and of voices, drifted down to her. She began the walk back to the house.

Some time during her first few weeks in the house above the shop Elmer had thought to amuse her by instructing her in the ingenuity of the wall-safe in the accounting office. It had no key, he began by explaining, but operated by what was known as a combination. Single digits were registered, following one another in rotation to form a given number. A lever was turned, then a second lever, and the door of the safe opened. 'Have a go,' Elmer had invited, as if they were two children playing. The combination of numbers had remained in her memory, often recurring to her, as if unconsciously she knew that one day she would need to make use of it.

The evening before, when Elmer was in Hogan's and her sisters-in-law already in bed, she discovered that a whole week's takings were there, and, in a strong-box at the back of the safe, hiding the Jameson bottle and a glass, a bundle of five-pound notes with a rubber band around it. She took everything except the coins: £403 she counted afterwards. Anything she didn't spend she intended to return.

'Toy soldiers!' The auctioneer's tone was wearily impatient, dismissive almost. 'Colourful set of soldiers! Who'll start me with a pound?'

No one did. Mary Louise bought the soldiers for ten shillings.

When Elmer opened the wall-safe he couldn't believe his eyes. He'd sustained one shock already that day – Rose's announcement that his wife had gone off cycling without her breakfast inside her. When he entered the dining-room at one o'clock he was immediately told she hadn't returned. Now, it seemed, he'd been robbed as well.

With the door of the safe hanging open, he sat down at his desk and endeavoured to think the matter out. Had he put the takings somewhere else? Had he moved the notes from the strong-box, taken them out and then omitted to return them? Sometimes, before setting out for Hogan's, it was necessary to open the safe and slip out a few pounds to keep him going. Sometimes, during the day, he opened the safe because he was feeling tired and needed a pick-me-up. Could he possibly, in his haste, have forgotten to lock it again? Had someone managed to get into the accounting office, noticed the safe door ajar, helped himself, and banged the door after him? But there was no sign of a break-in, unless someone had climbed in through a window of the house and made his way down-stairs on the chance that there'd be something lying about.

Sometimes if he felt a bit tired when he returned from Hogan's he sat at the desk and had a doze. When he woke up ten minutes later he often felt befuddled, the way anyone would after a nap. He'd go up to bed then, but when he entered the accounting room in the morning he'd notice that a few things were out of place, as if he'd picked them up and in his drowsiness forgotten where they should be returned to. He kept the bottle and the glass in the safe because of privacy. He'd bought the glass in Renehan's, knowing that if he took one out of the kitchen it would be missed.

He could have had a small one last night after he'd come in. When he'd had a doze he could have opened the safe and forgotten to close it again. He could even have taken the cash out to count it, which from time to time he did. He could have walked away and left the whole shooting-match spread out on the desk.

But the bottle and the glass were at the back of the safe, where they always were: feeling the need to, Elmer took advantage of their presence. His hands were shaking. If there had been a mirror in the office he'd have noticed that his face had acquired a grey tinge where the blood had drained from it.

He searched the office. He looked in the filing-cabinets and behind them. Glancing down into the shop to confirm that his sisters were there and occupied, he left the office with an eye still fixed on them. He passed soundlessly through the storeroom at the back of the shop and mounted the stairs to the house. He examined the first-floor windows, but could find no evidence of breaking and entering. In the bedroom he shared he searched the drawers of the wardrobe, even looked under the bed in case he had secreted money there due to an error caused by drowsiness. He searched the pockets of his suits.

In the shop – under the pretext that the lock was becoming worn – he examined the entrance doors for any tell-tale signs. In the storeroom he looked everywhere he could think of – behind bales of cloth, at the back of shelves, in the remnant baskets. Sometimes when he was taking a pick-me-up he put the glass down on a surface in the office and later couldn't quite remember where he'd placed it. He sometimes wandered down to the storeroom to cut off a pattern for re-ordering, and did the same thing. He'd end up having to put the main lights on in order to search for it.

Elmer returned to his office and sat down again at his desk. He tried to remember his movements the night before. He tried to remember if he had or had not poured himself a small one when he returned. No one could have made an entry through the storeroom window because it was barred. He'd had a look at the halldoor on his way from the house: it had not been tampered with.

'Did you go into the safe?' he demanded in the shop three-quarters of an hour later. He'd waited until a woman buying knitting wool had gone. He'd had a couple more drinks. 'Did you open the safe?'

He knew it was most unlikely. One or other of them always put the day's takings on the desk. He couldn't remember if they even knew the combination.

'What?' Rose demanded, sharpness already in her voice.

'There's money gone from the safe.'

Mary Louise spoke to two men with a lorry who were offering to deliver furniture that had been purchased. She gave them the numbers of what she'd bought – the soldiers and the bedroom furniture. The men promised to arrive with the goods the following day.

She rode away, pleased that she had succeeded in securing what she had: she'd been nervous about bidding, but no one else had wanted the soldiers, and the furniture was cheaper than she'd thought it would be. On the outskirts of the town she dismounted at the blue-washed cottage her aunt had mentioned at Letty's wedding party. She said who she was to a wan-faced woman with a child in her arms.

'I think my aunt gave you clothes.'

'God bless her, she did.'

'Would you rather have the money?'

'Money? What money's that?'

'If I bought the clothes back from you I'd pay for them like they were new.'

The woman, alarmed by this, called her husband. He was a big man, who had to bow his head in order to pass beneath the lintel of the door. Even before he learned the nature of Mary Louise's request, his wife's suspicion infected him.

'The clothing was given to us,' he said.

'I know it was. I'm saying I'm willing to buy some of it back. Anything you mightn't want.'

'It's for the boys growing up.' The woman's incomprehension made her sound stupid. She lifted the child from one arm to the other when it began to cry.

'It's only I thought the money might be useful. It was my cousin that died. I only want a few mementoes.'

The man nodded slowly. An agreement could be reached,

he said. He stood to one side, at the same time muttering to his wife. Mary Louise entered the cottage and selected some garments, which the woman wrapped up in newspaper for her. The parcel was tied with the length of string that had made a bundle of the clothes when they were delivered in the first place. The cottage smelt of poverty. Older children stared at Mary Louise from corners and from behind chairs. She left behind more money than had been agreed.

'You'll never manage that on the bike,' the woman warned, and further string was fetched. The parcel was folded in two and tied by the man on to the carrier of the bicycle. It would be secure, he said, if she rode carefully and didn't let the extra weight sway her.

'Were you mad?' Rose's tone was harsh, disguising excitement.

He didn't reply. When they got going with their questions they could draw the teeth out of your head. If he hadn't been so upset he wouldn't have told them that during the first few weeks of his marriage he'd instructed his bride in the ingenuity of the wall-safe, thinking to amuse her.

'There she is now,' Matilda said.

It was twenty to seven; the shop had been closed since six. It stood to reason, Rose and Matilda had declared, not once but several times. She'd gone for ever, they'd said, one of them agreeing with the other. They'd hurried upstairs to see if she'd packed her things and then reported, in disappointment, that apparently she hadn't. But even so they continued to insist that this time their brother's unsatisfactory wife had run away.

They stood in the accounting office, Rose and Matilda on either side of the desk, Elmer by the open safe. When they heard the sound in the house all three of them knew that Mary Louise had put away her bicycle in the yard and had

entered by the back door. They could tell it was her footfall.
Rose called her.

'I have this to return,' Mary Louise said when she entered
the accounting office. She held out most of the notes that had
been in the strong-box. The rest of the money she'd used, she
explained.

'Used?' Rose repeated. '*Used?*'

When he spoke Elmer's voice was hoarse. He asked his wife
where she'd been all day. They'd been beside themselves with
worry, he said.

'I was at my aunt's auction. I bought a few things.'

Elmer reached out and picked up the notes she had placed
on the desk. The rubber band was still around them. Only
two of them were missing.

'You stole money out of the safe,' Rose said.

Elmer began to protest but the words became a jumble,
running into one another incomprehensibly. Mary Louise said:

'I wouldn't say stole, Rose.'

'You stole money out of the safe to go to an auction.'

'Why didn't you ask me?' Elmer's question was a whisper,
just audible in the office.

'I did, only you were drunk.'

'My God!' Rose cried. 'My God, will you listen to this!'

'That's a disgraceful thing to say,' Matilda interjected. 'I
don't believe for an instant you asked him.'

'As a matter of fact, I asked him twice. I asked him the
night before last and I asked him last night.'

'You asked him when you knew – maybe when he was asleep.'

'I'm not a fool, Matilda. I don't go round talking to people
when they're asleep.'

'You go round doing all sorts of things. You go round
trying to get people to eat the food left behind on an unwashed
plate. You go round locking doors and interfering with property that isn't yours.'

'If I were you,' Rose said to her brother, 'I'd put the matter in the hands of the Guards. Stealing's stealing.'

'The furniture I bought will be coming tomorrow,' Mary Louise said. 'It won't be in anyone's way.'

With that she left the office. Her footsteps were heard on the stairs a moment later and then in the kitchen, which was partly above the accounting office.

'Listen, Elmer.' Rose spoke slowly and emphatically, isolating each word in a deliberate manner. 'That girl's worse than the brother. She's not the full shilling, Elmer.'

'She has caused disruption in this family,' Matilda threw in. 'Rose is right in what she says, Elmer.'

He did not speak. It could be true that she had asked him about the money. She might have said it and, due to evening drowsiness, he mightn't have heard her. He'd given her the combination ages ago. Since he hadn't been able to hear her, she might just have used it. God knows why he'd ever given her the thing.

'The family and the household,' Matilda reiterated. 'There isn't a day you can draw a breath in peace.'

'Look at the state she's put you in,' Rose said. 'You have a bottle and a glass in that safe, the way there never was in the past. She has you so's you can't think straight.'

'What's she want furniture for? Is the furniture we have not good enough for her?'

'She won't eat with us, Elmer. She won't sit down in a room upstairs with us. It's a wonder she'll lie in a bed with you.'

There was a silence after Rose said that. It continued for a minute and then for another. It went on after that.

'What d'you want me to do?' Elmer asked at last.

The next morning Rose saw the furniture lorry drawing up and snapped at the two men when they appeared in the shop.

No one wanted furniture, she said. 'Take it back where it came from,' she ordered.

But Mary Louise stepped round the counter and directed the men to the back door of the house. Rose's protests were ignored, as were the additional ones of Matilda: it was Mary Louise the men had bargained with concerning the expenses agreed upon.

'I'm afraid it's up at the top of the house,' she apologized.

The men were obliging. Upstairs or downstairs, it was all in the day's work. 'What's troubling them in the shop?' one of them asked.

Mary Louise explained it was a misunderstanding. Her sisters-in-law hadn't known the furniture had been bought. Her sisters-in-law were abrupt in their manner.

'That's the final straw,' Rose said, red in the face, glaring in the accounting office. 'She's filling our attics with rubbish.'

'I spoke to her last night, Rose. I said you were upset.'

'And what good did it do? What good's speaking to her? We told you what to do.'

'I can't go doing wild things like that, Rose.'

'It's an hour's drive in Kilkelly's car. There's a garden to walk in. She'll be with her kind.'

Over the years Elmer had become used to what he considered to be the outrageous side of both his sisters. It was nourished by a harsh matter-of-factness and fed on the confidence of their double presence in the household. When Rose, a few years ago, laid down that they should not pay Hickey the builder the full amount of his bill because he had been four months late in attending to the work and had thereby succeeded in making the job a bigger one, Matilda had unswervingly supported her. When Matilda insisted that Miss O'Rourke from the technical school should be obliged to accept a cardigan that had been singed by her cigarette, Rose didn't hesitate either, even though the cardigan was of a colour that in no way suited Miss O'Rourke, and had quite by accident come into contact with the cigarette Miss O'Rourke had momentarily placed on the counter. There had been many similar instances, all of them revolving round the fact that when Elmer's sisters felt themselves to be right they experienced no embarrassment in demanding excessive amends. They had little patience with the courtesies of moderation or compromise; pussyfooting was not in their nature.

'One of those men's carried in a box full of toys,' Matilda reported, leaving the shop unattended in her excitement.

'There you are, Elmer. Your wife's gone into her childhood.'

'A big cardboard box,' Matilda said. 'Filled up to the brim.'

The bell on the shop door jangled and both sisters hurried back to their duties. During the last twenty-four hours the excitement that possessed them had reached a fresh climax. It was an excitement that had begun when they first realized their brother's wife made regular journeys to the attic rooms, had intensified when they discovered she'd moved most of the furniture from one attic to the other and had taken to locking the door, had intensified further with each subsequent deviation from what the sisters regarded as normal behaviour. Mary Louise's disappearance the day before had been delight enough: not in their wildest hopes had they anticipated the ecstasy of money purloined in order to buy toys at an auction. For a single moment Matilda wondered if her sister-in-law could possibly have given birth to an infant which, for peculiar reasons, she chose to keep hidden in an attic room and for whom she was now making purchases. As well as the box of brightly-coloured soldiers, Matilda had watched a dismantled bed and a mattress, as well as other bedroom articles, being carried from the lorry. But a baby's cries would have been heard, especially at night, and the girl could not possibly have disguised her figure: the theory was abandoned almost as soon as it was born. Crazier, really, Matilda reflected, to have obtained toys in order to play with them yourself, at twenty-five years of age.

Elmer's footfall was heavy on the attic stairs. His knuckles rapped on the panels of the door. He tried the handle. Several times he spoke her name. Then he went away, heavily descending.

She would get the chimney-sweep in so that she could have a fire in the tiny grate. She wouldn't mind carrying sticks and coal up, or cleaning out the ashes. A fire would take the chill off the air.

She untied the string around the mattress and settled the mattress on the bed, which the men had erected for her. For all of his twenty-four years he had lain on it. For all of his twenty-four years he had woken every day to the scene of the hay-cart, and the dog chasing a rat in the stubble. Every day he had opened and closed the wardrobe's pale doors.

She placed his collar-stud on the dressing-table where she could readily see it. She arranged the soldiers on the floor, remembering as best she could how they had been. She hung his clothes up.

wow! what a scene!

25

She walks about the town. After thirty-one years she is a stranger and the town has changed, as her husband warned her. There is more of a bustle to it, more vehicles about, people hurry more. The goods in the shop windows look more interesting, French cheese and wines you'd never see in the old days, new kinds of sweets. The bill-posters are different, the old Electric's gone.

Glances, sometimes a stare, are cast in her direction. No one knows her well enough to address her; a few remember; hearsay attaches her to the town. She doesn't mind, one way or the other, and concerns herself instead with the place she has left behind. The last of the cars would have arrived by now; those permitted to go would have gone. It was said that the obstreperous were to be moved to a house near Mullingar. She wonders about that: if the remaining inmates have been taken away, if all chatter and arguing have ceased, if the hammering and whistling of workmen have begun. Soon, people who do not suffer from dementia paralytica or morbid impulses or melancholia will sleep in the rooms, men who have spent the day shooting or fishing, women dreaming beside them in chiffon nightdresses. Motor-cars will take up their positions on the smooth tarmac of the car park, a different one from time to time parked on top of his flowerbed.

That's why she has come back: she nods to herself in Father Mathew Street, reminding herself of her reason. That's why

she didn't make a fuss or run the risk of being taken to
Mullingar with the obstreperous: tomorrow she'll walk out to
the graveyard.

'It wasn't because I went there,' she told them – Sister
Hannah and Mrs Leavy, Belle D and all the others. 'It wasn't
because I went there that I had to leave the town. There was
another reason, a worse reason by a long way.'

26

'Rats?' Mr Renehan said.

'We have them in the attics.'

'Rats are most unpleasant. Is it a trap you're thinking of?'

'Or maybe poison. D'you keep poison, Mr Renehan?'

'I do of course. Rodenkil. Or Ridemquik. Something like that would do the trick.'

Bleheen the inseminator was in the shop, buying nails from one of the Renehan boys. He smiled blandly at Mary Louise, and she remembered how his car had kept swerving all over the road on the evening of Letty's wedding party. He asked her how she was keeping and she said all right. In the days when she had gone to the Electric Cinema Bleheen was often there also, either alone or with one of the widows whose company he was investigating in his search for a suitable wife. For reasons of his own he limited himself to widows.

'And a little yoke for coring apples,' he said when the Renehan boy had weighed out the nails. 'I have a weakness for stewed apples,' he informed Mary Louise, 'with a drop of Bird's custard.'

She nodded. A woman buying press-studs in the drapery one day had told her Bleheen would never marry. He could take every widow in Ireland to the pictures but in the end he'd remain the way he was, set in his ways and cautious.

'I had that little yoke,' he said, 'only I threw it out with the apple peelings by mistake.'

Mary Louise imagined him cooking his own meals, peeling apples and potatoes the way a man would. He went on talking to her about domestic matters. She didn't listen. '*The whole party gathered in the drawing-room. Arkady picked up the latest number of some journal. Anna Sergeyevna rose, and it was then that he glanced at Katya . . .*'

It was better for Bleheen not to marry if he didn't love anyone. He was right to be choosy, even if choosiness meant he'd be a bachelor till he died. Suddenly Mary Louise wondered if her mother and father loved one another. Never in her life had she thought about that before. Never before had it been in the scheme of things that love should enter into any consideration of her parents.

'I'd say the Rodenkil,' Mr Renehan advised. 'We sell a lot of Rodenkil.'

Letty became pregnant soon after her marriage. Dennehy bought her a second-hand Morris Minor; she loved the house they had settled in. All her life she'd had to look after hens, feeding them and finding their eggs: as long as she lived, she said, she didn't intend to lift a finger again for a hen, even though there were poultry runs in the yard. Her husband planned to keep a cow or two as well, but they agreed between them that he would see to the needs of all such animals himself. Letty made curtains and chair-covers on the sewing-machine her parents had given her as a wedding present; carpets were bought, the last of the decorating completed. 'You could grow something there,' her Aunt Emmeline suggested, pointing at two forgotten whitewashed tubs on either side of the front door. A week later her aunt arrived at the house and spent a few minutes turning over the soil and adding manure. She found an overgrown patch behind the house where vegetables had once been cultivated. This, too, she proceeded to reclaim.

Letty's concern about her sister was the only real agitation in the euphoria of her marriage. It came and went, nagging for a little longer each time she heard something new on the waves of gossip that spread from the town. She had known, since the time of the event itself, the details of the sisters' visit to Culleen; she had known of her parents' fruitless consultation with Dr Cormican, and their subsequent conversation with Mary Louise. She had since heard about the purchases made at the auction, and had heard also that Mary Louise was rarely to be found serving in the shop any more. All of it bewildered Letty. As an older sister, she had shared with her brother the task of keeping an eye on Mary Louise when all three were children. She still remembered the feel of a clammy, small hand in hers and her insistence that it should remain there. She had comforted away tears; she had been cross when necessary. More unhappily she remembered her opposition to Mary Louise's engagement to Elmer Quarry. She'd felt sick when she heard he had invited her sister to the Electric Cinema. On the wedding night – reflecting, without knowing it, the thoughts of her cousin – she couldn't keep her mind away from what Mary Louise was enduring. With his small teeth and his small eyes, Elmer Quarry reminded her of a pig. Alone in the bedroom she had shared all her life with Mary Louise, she had miserably wept that night.

The telephone in Letty's house – a necessity for her husband in his professional life – was something of a novelty for her. There wasn't one at Culleen, and rarely in the past had she had occasion to use one. But there the instrument was, on a shelf at the back of the hall, with a pencil and notebook hanging from a hook above it, and the directory on a shelf beneath. One morning, bored with sewing, she telephoned Quarry's drapery, to remind Mary Louise that she had not yet visited her as she'd promised.

'Yes?' Rose said.

'Could I speak to Mary Louise, please?'

'Who's that?'

'It's her sister.'

Letty heard Rose's breathing, and faintly in the background the sound of the bell at the shop door.

'It's Letty,' Letty said.

'Oh, yes.' It annoyed Rose that she'd had to climb the stairs to the accounting office because Elmer wasn't there, only to discover that she'd been summoned on behalf of her sister-in-law. It particularly annoyed her that it should be Letty, since the matter of the wedding invitation still rankled.

'Is Mary Louise around?'

Rose hesitated. She wasn't in a hurry to give any information about Mary Louise's whereabouts, feeling she needed time to think. At length she said:

'Your sister isn't.'

'Is that Rose? Or Matilda?'

'It's Rose Quarry speaking.'

'Would you ask Mary Louise if she'd phone me? Two four five.'

Rose thought she'd say yes and then omit to do so. But on an impulse she changed her mind. She said:

'We hardly ever lay eyes on your sister these days.'

'Is Mary Louise all right?'

'I'd say she wasn't. You could inform your parents things have progressed from bad to worse. We're beside ourselves, the state she's in.'

'State? What state, Rose?'

'You have to keep everything locked up. We have our hand-bags under lock and key the entire time. She broke into the safe in the office.'

To Rose's considerable satisfaction, there was a silence at the other end. It continued for several moments, before Letty said:

'What're you talking about, Rose?'

'We'd be obliged if you'd keep it in the family, Mrs Dennehy.'

With that, Rose returned the receiver to its hook. Elmer had specifically requested that the matter of the money taken from the safe should not be mentioned outside the house, but until the Dallons were aware of the extent of the girl's contrariness they apparently wouldn't act in any way whatsoever. Rose returned to the shop and reported the conversation to Matilda, who said she'd done the right thing.

Elmer shook his head. There weren't any rats in the house. A cat that hung about the yard saw to all that kind of thing. A few mice now and again that his sisters caught in traps were the height of any trouble.

'I sold her Rodenkil,' Renehan said. 'I believe she mentioned the attics.'

Elmer vaguely nodded, the gesture implying that he'd forgotten about the attics: privately he doubted that there were rats in the attics any more than anywhere else.

Renehan finished his drink and left Hogan's bar. Elmer was still on his own when Letty and her husband entered it a quarter of an hour later. Behind the bar Gerry was reading the *Evening Herald*. No one else was present.

'Elmer,' Letty said.

'I had a bit of business here,' he began.

'We want to talk about Mary Louise.'

Dennehy said he'd get the drinks. Letty led the way to a table in a corner. 'And whatever Mr Quarry's having,' Elmer heard Dennehy ordering. At the same time his sister-in-law said:

'We wanted to catch you on your own, Elmer. I've left messages for Mary Louise only she doesn't ring me back.'

'I'll tell her – '

'Rose said something about a safe.'

'That's a private matter, actually.'

'What's Rose talking about, Elmer?'

Elmer explained what had occurred was that Mary Louise, in a hurry for some money one day, had borrowed a sum from the safe in the accounting office. It was nothing, he said. A storm in a tea-cup.

'Rose said they have to keep their handbags under lock and key.

To Elmer's relief, Dennehy arrived at that moment with the drinks. 'Good luck!' Dennehy said, raising his glass and then occupying himself with the lighting of a cigarette.

'What's the matter with Mary Louise, Elmer?'

'Ah, she's all right. Mary Louise likes to be on her own, and it's a thing my sisters don't understand. She likes to go out on her bicycle, and then again she likes to have an area of her own in the house. That's all that's in it. No more than that.'

'Your sisters went out to Culleen a few months ago. They made certain statements about Mary Louise.'

'What kind of statements?'

'They said she was away in the head.'

Elmer gave a jump. He finished the liquid in his glass and signalled to Gerry to replenish it, as well as the two glasses of his companions. Noticing the gesture, Letty shook her head. Dennehy nodded.

'I didn't know that,' Elmer said.

'Didn't you know they went out to Culleen?'

'To tell you the truth, I didn't.'

'I haven't seen Mary Louise since our wedding. There wasn't much the matter with her then. Except, of course, she doesn't have a lot to say for herself any more.'

'We've all noticed that, Letty.'

'She was always talkative in the past.'

There were no rats in the attics. If there were rats in the attics you'd hear them scampering about above your head.

For all he knew, it was all over the town that she'd been buying rat poison.

'My parents wanted her to see Dr Cormican,' Letty said.

'It would do no harm. A check-up wouldn't hurt anyone.'

'She said she wouldn't.'

'Let me have a word with her, Letty.'

'I'm in every day. Tell her I'm waiting for her phone call.'

Abruptly, Letty stood up. She'd had only a sip or two of her drink. All the time they were talking, Elmer noticed, she hadn't stopped frowning, a small pucker of worry at the top of her forehead.

'I'll be seeing you,' he said loudly in case Gerry would think they weren't on terms.

'Come out to the house,' Dennehy invited, hastily finishing his drink. Letty didn't say anything.

Elmer returned to the bar and ordered a double measure of whiskey.

'God, isn't that shocking?' Gerry remarked as he handed back some change, and for a moment Elmer thought he was referring to some aspect of the conversation that had taken place in the bar. But Gerry, one eye still on the *Evening Herald*, was drawing his attention to the murder of King Feisal of Iraq.

Not interested in this far-off violence, Elmer nevertheless deplored the event. All it amounted to, he was thinking, was more of their outrageousness. There'd been no call to go visiting the Dallons, and definitely no call to say his wife was mentally affected or to mention the money borrowed from the safe. The truth was that Mary Louise had settled down the way she wanted to settle down, which was what he'd been endeavouring to explain to the sister. She slept up in the attic now, no reason why she shouldn't if that was what she wanted.

*

The chimney-sweep lit the first fire in the grate to make certain the chimney was drawing well. Mary Louise carried up coals and wood from the cellar. Her presence was unnecessary in the shop because customers were few; her serving there had been part of a general pretence, or so it seemed to her now. Days went by now during which she addressed neither her husband nor her sisters-in-law. Sleeping in the attic room, she no longer experienced feelings of shame when she first awoke in the mornings. In the kitchen she washed the dishes the household's food had been eaten from. She continued to perform the other household chores she'd been allocated, but always took her meals on her own. Whenever she felt like it she rode away from the town on her bicycle, going to the graveyard mostly, sometimes walking in the fields near her aunt's house. The house was empty now, though not yet sold.

Often she thought she would like to be more alone than she was. The voices of her sisters-in-law and of Elmer were tiresome. The tread of feet on the stairs was tiresome, the clatter of dishes, the rattle of the shop bell. To press away such sounds she played a game that reminded her of games played in her childhood: she closed her eyes and watched herself wandering from room to room, in and out of her sisters-in-law's bedrooms, opening the windows of the big front room, making the dining-room different. On the first-floor landing there was a glass chandelier in pink and scarlet. There was a smell of flowers and newly ironed table-linen. In the kitchen a cook moved her saucepans on the range; raw mutton waited on a table beside high piles of plates that rattled when the cabbage was chopped. In the yard chickens screamed, chased by someone intent upon wringing their necks.

Outside, blue shutters covered the windows of the shop; the entrance doors were locked and bolted. Somewhere, at the heart of everything, her cousin belonged, as delicately present as the confection of refurbished rooms. Everything was fragile:

only too easily it could all be broken, like porcelain falling on flagstones. Gently, fingers to their lips, she and her cousin laughed.

People no longer mentioned his wife to Elmer. In the town she was talked about less than she had been, accepted now as an eccentric person. She was seen regularly on her bicycle, wrapped up closely, a headscarf tied around her head. In January of the new year – 1959 – she visited her sister and admired the fittings in the kitchen, and listened while Letty told her what it was like to be pregnant. Her mother, in January also, called in at the shop again, only to be informed by Rose that Mary Louise no longer deigned to serve there. Mrs Dallon rang the bell at the halldoor of the house, but there was no reply. She returned to the shop and demanded to speak to Elmer, who shambled down the stairs from the accounting office, seeming to Mrs Dallon to be unsteady on his feet. He brought her upstairs to the house and asked her to wait in the front room, which Mary Louise entered a few minutes later. She smiled, and appeared to be normal except for her silence. 'You don't come to see us any more,' her mother gently chided her. Mary Louise promised to come the following Sunday, but she didn't arrive, on that Sunday or on subsequent ones.

Elmer himself still worried about the rat poison that had been bought. He didn't mention it to his sisters, nor to anyone else, but he questioned Mary Louise as casually as he could about the presence of rats in the attics where she spent so much time. 'I think I caught them,' she replied. 'They took the Rodenkil I put down.' He asked her what she had done with the poison that remained and she said she still had it in case the rats returned. Elmer shook his head: that wasn't a good idea, he suggested, in case she'd ever get the stuff on her hands or maybe someone else might pick it up, not knowing what it was. Now that she'd destroyed the rats it would be better to throw the poison out; if rats returned more could be bought. Mary Louise kept nodding. She'd wrap up what poison remained, she promised, and put it in the dustbin.

After Mary Louise's visit Letty's concern didn't lessen, but by now she was reconciled to the changes in her sister, accepting them because there was nothing else she could do. Then her baby was born and made demands on both her attention and her thoughts. She had expected that Mary Louise would ride out to see the infant, and felt aggrieved when she didn't. Kevin Aloysius the child was called, Aloysius being a Dennehy family name.

Rose and Matilda bided their time. They were pleased that Mary Louise no longer served in the shop; the dining-room without her was almost like old times. Yet there continued to be the irritation of what Matilda had once described as her 'smug face', the agreeableness that spread into it when you addressed her but which didn't last, being quickly replaced by a dead look, as though she couldn't be bothered listening to you for more than a minute at the most. There was the irritation of her presence in the lavatory or the bathroom when they wished to use one or the other, and her half-witted confining of herself in an attic. Above all, there was the appalling toll she was continuing to take of their brother. Sometimes in the mornings his eyes were so bloodshot you'd imagine he couldn't see properly. He had put on weight; his pallor was unhealthy; the next thing, he'd get the shakes in his hands, like old Crowe who came round with crab-apples every autumn. Not knowledgeable about the nature of addiction, the sisters believed that when the wife he'd erroneously married was either returned to her family or incarcerated in a suitable asylum, Elmer would revert to his normal self. He would call in at the YMCA billiard-room for the occasional game of billiards instead of spending his evenings in Hogan's Hotel. He would go out for summer walks the way he used to. His interest in business matters, having noticeably declined, would revive. That the shop would see the present generation out and pass to distant relatives in Athy mattered as little now as it had before the whole unfortunate episode of the marriage. It was only a pity Elmer hadn't been able to see that there was a natural threesome in the shop and in the house.

The sisters bided their time because they were certain that any day now there would be another occurrence similar to the theft of the money. On this occasion the culprit might not manage so easily to wriggle out of it. Both of them felt that since so much trouble had been caused it was only fair that matters should come to a head.

Mary Louise no longer broke down into fits of private weeping, as she had during the first weeks and months of her loss. It seemed to her that her own flesh and bones were so much lumber, real but without real interest.

'Of course I haven't,' she replied again when her cousin asked her if she'd fallen asleep. 'Of course not, Robert.'

Susan Emily, the moss-touched letters said, *wife of Charles. Safe now in Heaven's Arms. Peace, Perfect Peace.* The words were there beneath a net of other words, belonging with the drone of bees. When she closed her eyes in the graveyard, towers and pavilions were etched against the green of parkland. A tablecloth was spread beneath old limes. '*The coachman and a footman and a maid brought the baskets from the coach . . .*'

His voice continuing, and hers embracing it, was their act of love. There was a purity in it that delighted Mary Louise, now that she had moved herself away from her sisters-in-law and her husband. All she wished for was her cousin's watch to hang on her attic wall, on the nail that was already there, beside the fireplace. And if ever silence came in the house she would send out invitations – gold-edged, with her cousin's name on them also, giving a date and a time, with RSVP on the bottom left-hand corner.

Mrs Dallon was surprised, and pleased, when James came into the kitchen to say that he'd just seen Mary Louise from the high field, riding out in their direction. She pushed the kettle on to the hot ring of the range, and asked James to go and tell his father. In weary defeat she had come to accept part at least of the Quarry sisters' catalogue of accusations. There was nothing more that could be done, nothing more that could be said: everything would have been different, Mrs Dallon still believed, if a child had been born. Perhaps one day that would happen, but she felt more pessimistic than she had in the past.

'Sit down, pet. It's great to see you.'

Mary Louise took her coat off. In answer to her mother's questions, she replied that she was well. Mrs Dallon cut slices of brown bread and put butter and lemon curd on the table.

'The wanderer returns,' Mr Dallon said, pulling his wellington boots off at the door.

'Letty'd love to see you.' Mrs Dallon spoke with nervous haste, as though anxious to obliterate as soon as possible anything in her husband's levity that might have caused offence. In their bedroom she had repeatedly voiced her fear that some time in the past Mary Louise had taken offence. They had maybe seemed hesitant when Elmer Quarry proposed. Letty had been too outspoken. These attitudes had perhaps rankled and, combining with the attitudes of two trouble-making sisters-in-law, were the cause of Mary Louise's isolation. When Elmer began to drink the poor girl had felt she could turn to no one. Any girl would be ashamed when a husband took to drink.

'I hear it's quiet in there these days,' Mr Dallon remarked, referring to the town. He crossed the kitchen in his stockinged feet. He sat down and reached for a slice of bread.

'There's not much doing,' Mary Louise agreed.

He remembered her standing beside him in the yard when she was eleven or twelve, with some blackberries she'd picked into an old sweet tin. They'd give her a white coat when she went to work in the chemist's, she said. He didn't subscribe to the argument that she had taken offence. In his opinion this was – on his wife's part – a search for some consoling factor, any explanation being better than none at all. But when the argument had been put forward he hadn't dismissed it: if it gave some comfort, what harm was done?

'It's the times that are in it,' he pronounced. 'The people haven't the money.'

It disappointed him that Mary Louise didn't respond. In the yard that day she'd stood chattering for maybe a quarter of an hour, telling him about the window displays in the chemist's, the scents and powders and lipsticks, Coty, Pond's, Elizabeth Arden. A warm September evening, he recalled.

'George Eddery's gone to England,' Mrs Dallon said. 'Selling door-to-door apparently.'

This time Mary Louise did respond, slightly nodding, a shadowy smile altering the set of her features. A chemist's shop had represented all of town life for her, her father reflected. She'd always been attracted by the town, ever since her first day at Miss Mullover's. She'd always delighted in it, even when they drove through it on a Sunday and it was closed up and dead.

'Aunt Emmeline's not here?' she said.

'She's over at Letty's,' Mrs Dallon said. 'Your Aunt Emmeline's making a garden for Letty.'

'I wonder,' Mary Louise began, and paused. They watched her changing her mind, leaving the sentence she had begun unsaid, substituting another. 'I'd just like to look,' she said, 'at my room.'

Surprise flickered in both their faces. Mrs Dallon's bewilderment became a frown that only gradually disappeared. Cutting in half a slice of bread, her husband was arrested in the motion for an instant and then, more slowly, proceeded with it.

'Just for a minute,' Mary Louise went on, already opening the door that led to the stairs. They listened to the latch falling into place behind her. Mr Dallon pushed his cup towards the teapot. Mechanically, Mrs Dallon filled it. Was there something, after all, in the idea that Mary Louise should return to Culleen? Did she need looking after? Had she herself said as much to her sisters-in-law? Was that why she wanted to see her bedroom again?

'If she came back, where would Emmeline go?'

Mr Dallon didn't know what his wife was talking about. His thoughts had not followed the same course as hers. It struck Mr Dallon as very odd indeed that Mary Louise wished to visit a room, once shared with her sister, now occupied by her aunt. He could think of no rational explanation for this.

'It could be,' Mrs Dallon continued, 'she wants to leave him.'

'Elmer?'

'On account of he's drinking. And would you blame her, with those two women to put up with on top of everything else?'

'But she'd say it if that was the case. She'd say it out, wouldn't she, instead of going up to Emmeline's room?'

'I think what she's after is to see would both of them fit in it. Like herself and Letty in the old days.'

'We couldn't ask Emmeline – '

'We could if we had to.'

They had been told by Emmeline that Mary Louise had taken to visiting her cousin; the fact had come out one evening when they were sitting by the range. 'Didn't you know that?

Didn't she ever tell you?' Emmeline had said, and they listened to her recounting of the Sunday visits. 'Kindness itself,' Emmeline stated firmly. The Dallons received the impression that it had somehow been known – though not to them – that Robert was nearing the end of his life and that their daughter's attentions had been an act of kindness. 'She was lonely too, of course,' Mrs Dallon said, but even so she felt proud that a child of hers should have acted so. Lonely or not, it couldn't have been much fun, keeping company with a sickly youth.

When Mary Louise returned to the kitchen she put on her coat immediately. She drew from one of its pockets a headscarf with blue and red squares on it and tied it round her head. James came in just then, but she had to go, she said. She was sorry she could not stay to talk to him.

In the attic she hung the watch and chain on the nail by the fireplace. Her cousin had said that the watch lost a minute a day. She would enjoy setting it right, every night before she got into bed.

27

She listens to them abusing him. Who's going to cook for her? Who's going to clean up after her? They don't intend to watch her eating. They'll none of them last a week at the mercy of a mad woman. All these years he paid money for her to exist in luxury: isn't that enough? Insult on top of injury. Scandalous what he's done. They don't intend to lift a finger, why should they? So how's he going to manage for an instant, the state he's in?

'She's my wife,' he says.

'And we're to go in trembling of her. Your own sisters at the end of their days, driven tormented with fear.'

'It's the way things are. They're closing all those places down.'

'You're doing it to spite us.'

He is a seedy figure now, cigarette-burns on his clothes, his shirt-collars frayed, portions of his jowl forgotten when he shaves. Guilt has made him take her in; guilt made him visit her and pay a little so that she wouldn't have to drink out of an enamel mug. He'd be ashamed of himself if he'd ever struck her.

'Robert was buried in the wrong graveyard,' she tells him when the moment seems right for saying it. 'Will you help me over that, Elmer?'

He doesn't reply, and she tells him she never hated him. She tells him she thought about him often during her long time in

Miss Foye's house. 'Include others in your prayers,' they used to urge, and she included him.

'I'm sorry I caused you trouble,' she says. 'I'm sorry I made things worse.'

28

Waking in the middle of one night, Elmer found himself thinking about Bridget asleep in Hogan's Hotel – just as, when a
boy, he'd imagined Mrs Fahy and the housekeeper at the
school in Wexford asleep. The hotel manageress's clothes were
on a chair in her bedroom, her stockings draped over the top
of them. Although Elmer had never said so to his sisters, or in
any way intimated it to his wife, he'd been relieved when
Mary Louise decided she wanted to sleep in the attic. There
was more room in the bed; you could pull the bed-clothes
round you when it was cold and not have to leave an area of
them for someone else. All in all, he liked it better.

Elmer, when he was a boy also, had often heard about the
wife of Hanlon the solicitor, who suffered from a fear of
going out. It was necessary for a priest to come to the house
to give her Mass, and for a hairdresser to come also. The nun
who ran the library at the convent brought books to the house
twice a week. 'The unfortunate woman can't so much as set
foot in her garden,' Elmer recalled his father saying in the
dining-room. 'Seemingly she'll spend an hour at the bottom of
the stairs, unable to approach the front door. You'd be sorry
for poor Hanlon.'

Passing the Hanlons' house, Elmer had often seen the solicitor's wife sitting in the bow window of a downstairs room,
looking at the robins in the flowerbeds. A scrawn of a woman,
his father had described her as, and from what he could see

this was correct. She had developed the affliction soon after her marriage, and Elmer wondered if Mary Louise wasn't suffering from something similar, not that Mary Louise had a fear of going out, far from it.

'No doctor could treat a condition like that,' his father had pronounced in the dining-room. 'A nervous complaint, I'd call it.' Mr Quarry, as square and bulkily-made as Elmer himself, liked to address his family on such topics of interest in the dining-room. Half your education, he used to say, you received in the home. Elmer knew his father would have designated Mary Louise as one suffering from a nervous complaint also, and he resolved to have the expression ready should he again be approached on the subject by her parents or by the snooty sister. He had been struck by the same misfortune as the solicitor. He had married in good faith, giving a penniless girl a home. You could have Dr Cormican coming and going every day of the week for all the good it would do. A medical man had never once entered the Hanlons' house, he recalled his father reporting in the dining-room. Money down the drain it would have been.

The despondency Elmer had experienced during the week of the seaside honeymoon, and its continuance after he and Mary Louise returned, had finally lost its bitter pain. It could be muddled away, he had discovered, and though occasionally it distressfully returned, all he had to do was to open the safe in the accounting office and reach behind the strong-box.

'My God, what's this?' Matilda screamed one evening in the dining-room, the first of the three of them to place a forkful of rissole in her mouth. She spat it out immediately. It tasted dreadful, she screamed.

Rose, who had made the rissoles, bridled. There was nothing wrong with them, she maintained. They'd had them yesterday at dinnertime: what they were eating now were those that were left over, heated up. She tasted what was already on her own fork, then spat it out too.

'They've gone bad,' Matilda said.

'How could they have gone bad? Weather like this, how could they?'

Elmer pushed his plate away. If the rissoles were bad he had no intention of being foolhardy. Sometimes meat which Rose re-cooked for the second or third time didn't taste of anything at all.

'They were perfect yesterday,' Rose repeated.

Elmer said he would spread cheese on his bread if there was cheese available.

'Was the sirloin all right when it came in?' Matilda inquired, and Rose snappishly replied that of course it was. The same sirloin, with an undercut, arrived from the butcher every Friday, was roasted on Sunday, eaten cold on Monday, chopped up for rissoles on Tuesday. What remained of the rissoles appeared on the table again every Wednesday evening. All their lives this had been so; all their lives the Quarrys had consumed the Wednesday-evening rissoles without mishap.

'Are there maggots in them?' Matilda pressed apart the mush of potato and meat with her fork. 'I think something moved in my mouth.'

Rose told her to have sense. There were no maggots in the rissoles. They had been made as they always were, the meat and potato bound together with half a cup of milk, a beaten egg yolk fixing the breadcrumbs around each one of them.

The sisters continued to examine the food on their plates, poking with their forks and peering at the chopped meat and the crisp covering of egg and breadcrumbs. Gingerly, Rose lifted a fragment of this crispness to her lips. It tasted all right, she said.

Since neither sister had heeded Elmer's request for cheese, he rose and crossed to the sideboard. In the big centre drawer he found a round packet of Galtee spreadable triangles. He returned to the table with two of them and eased away the silver-paper wrapping.

'Look at this green stuff.' Matilda's voice had risen again. 'For God's sake, what's this stuff, Rose?'

She held her plate out. Rose investigated her own rissole further, then cut in half the two on Elmer's plate. A virulent shade of green tinged the centre of each.

'Food mildew,' Matilda said. 'How long did you keep the potatoes?'

Rose didn't answer. She'd never heard the expression 'food mildew' before and guessed that Matilda had made it up. If the rissoles had gone bad it wasn't her fault. She cut a slice of bread in half and buttered it. Two rissoles had been kept back in the kitchen by Her Ladyship, as two always were on a Wednesday evening. Rose wondered if she'd eaten them. It would be like her not to notice the taste or the colour they'd gone.

'You can get poisoned from food mildew,' Matilda said.

Afterwards, in Hogan's, those words echoed unpleasantly as Elmer listened to Gerry telling him about a victory achieved by a greyhound that was said to be the fastest animal since Master McGrath. In his mind's eye he saw again the halved rissoles on the plate in the dining-room. 'I sold her Rodenkil,' Renehan's voice echoed also.

If there were rats in the attics you'd know about it, not a shadow of doubt. She was all over the place due to the nervous complaint. She'd maybe put some of the Rodenkil into a cup and left it around by mistake. It wouldn't be difficult for Rose, if she was rushed or the light was bad, to get the cup muddled up with another one. Elmer pushed his glass across the bar. There'd be the mother and father of a commotion if he so much as opened his mouth.

'It's the way he has of crouching in the trap,' Gerry said. 'Off like a bomb he is.'

There was another woman Elmer remembered his father talking about in the dining-room, some woman whose name he couldn't remember, who lived out in the hills somewhere. She used to hoard fire-lighters. For no rational purpose she had the house filled to the brim with wax fire-lighters. If you'd put a match to the place, his father used to say, it wouldn't last longer than a minute.

That night Elmer didn't linger in the hall of the hotel, but hurried back after he'd had one more drink. He waited until he heard his sisters ascending the stairs to their rooms and then made his way to the kitchen. He searched in the cupboards, and then in the adjoining scullery, in the safe and the refrigerator. He lifted plates off bowls and jars, he examined packets and unlabelled paper-bags. In the waste-bin he found the contaminated rissoles, but nowhere was there a supply of the green substance, carelessly left about.

Moving cautiously so as not to rouse his sisters, Elmer descended the stairs again, entered the shop and mounted the brief stairway to the accounting office. He opened the safe and poured himself a measure of whiskey. He sat for a while, then as cautiously as before made his way through the house to the attics.

Mary Louise, not yet asleep, heard a fumbling at the door. The handle was turned. 'Mary Louise,' her husband's voice whispered.

The noise interrupted a pleasant recollection. A boy in a striped smock was standing in the snow, the landlady and her daughter were huddled on the doorstep. It was the moment of parting: a sleigh stood waiting.

'Mary Louise,' the whisper repeated. 'Mary Louise, are you awake?'

Knuckles rapped the panels of the door, not noisily as they had the last time Elmer had come to the attic, but surreptitiously, as though some secret existed between them.

Mary Louise didn't move from her chair by the embers of

the fire. Eventually she heard him creeping away. The recollection that had possessed her would not return, try as she would to induce it. This was usually so when there was an interruption, when other people poked themselves in. She remained by the fire for another twenty minutes, but all there was to think about was going to school with Letty and James, and spreading their schoolbooks out on the kitchen table, and the recitation of poetry that had been set.

'Listen,' Elmer said, drawing Renehan aside in the ironmongery. 'Don't sell Mary Louise any more Rodenkil.' His wife had become a bit forgetful he said: she had a way of leaving things about. He'd be worried in case someone would pick up the Rodenkil and maybe omit to read the warning on the packet.

'I know what you mean,' Renehan said. He'd been attaching price tags to saucepans when Elmer asked if he could have a private word with him. He still held a saucepan in his hand.

'Good man yourself,' Elmer said.

That evening it was said in the town that Elmer Quarry's wife had tried to poison herself.

Having had a night to mull over the mystery of the rissoles, Rose and Matilda reached the same conclusion: the rissoles had been interfered with. If rissoles had been cooked in the house in precisely the same manner for more than a lifetime and nothing had ever gone bad in them before, why should something go bad in them now? In the night they had both recalled an episode in the past, during the time when the Quarrys still employed a maid. Kitty this one had been called, 'a lump of a girl' their mother referred to her as, who was once caught licking the sugar in the sugar-bowl when she was setting the table. Any sweets that were left about she helped herself to, until Mrs Quarry decided to put a stop to that by coating a few toffees with soap. Not a word was said, but a sweet was never taken again.

'Her Ladyship,' Rose said. 'What's she to do all day except think up devilment to annoy us?'

This view confirmed the thought that had occurred to Matilda also: that Mary Louise, with time on her hands, sought to irritate her husband and her sisters-in-law by introducing some unpleasant-tasting substance into their food. In Matilda's view, and in Rose's, there was other evidence of the desire to vex: tea-towels hung sopping wet in the scullery when they should be hung on the line over the stove, forks put back in the wrong section of the cutlery drawer, the blue milk-jug put on a shelf instead of hung up, the potato-masher not hung up either, coal and sticks carted up to the attic, footsteps above their heads, ages spent washing herself, the sight of her trailing round the town on a bicycle so that people would begin to talk.

'She fried an egg for herself,' Rose remembered. 'She knew not to touch the rissoles.'

They put these conclusions to their brother, leaving the shop unattended, which before Mary Louise's arrival in the household they would have never done. Definitely something had been introduced into the rissoles, Rose said. Maybe some kind of cascara, anything that would cause embarrassment and distress. Matilda reminded Elmer of the maid who'd helped herself to the sweets: measures had had to be taken and where was the difference in this case? The maid was guilty of stealing and had to be stopped. Measures should be taken now.

'Beyond a shadow of a doubt,' Rose said.

'The rissoles were in a soup-plate in the fridge, Elmer, covered over with another plate. She cut them open and put something inside.'

They watched his face. His jaw slackened; the tip of his

tongue moistened his lips, passing slowly from one corner of his mouth to the other. He had taken off his jacket, as he sometimes did in the accounting office. The waistcoat beneath was fully buttoned, a pencil and a ballpoint pen clipped into one of the upper pockets.

'There's people that live and breathe only wanting to be a nuisance,' Rose said.

The tea-towels were mentioned, and the forks in the cutlery drawer, the potato-masher and the blue milk-jug. Elmer unsuccessfully attempted to interrupt. They couldn't hold their heads up, Matilda said. They couldn't walk into a shop in the town without a silence falling.

'I'll speak to Mary Louise,' Elmer promised.

'What good does it do?' Matilda's tone was dangerously sarcastic. 'If you've spoken to her once, haven't you spoken to her a thousand times?'

Elmer's shirt felt sticky on his back. He'd begun to sweat as soon as they'd started on about something being deliberately introduced into their food. He'd raised a hand to wipe away the beads of perspiration he could feel gathering on his forehead, hoping they wouldn't notice what he was doing. He could feel the sweat, damply warm, on his legs and in his armpits. He had changed the combination of the safe after the incident concerning the money. He hadn't told them that, in case they'd ask what the new sequence of numbers was. He kept the Jameson bottle on its side so that it couldn't easily be seen behind the strong-box, but even so it was better that no one should have access to the safe. If ever the Jameson was mentioned again he had it ready to say that the bottle had been in the safe since their father's day, kept there in case anyone fainted in the shop.

'Will I get her to come down here?' Rose offered. 'Will I go up and tell her you want her?'

Elmer began to undo the buttons of his waistcoat. He stopped because he could feel his fingers trembling and knew they'd notice. If nerve trouble had caused a solicitor's wife to be frightened of approaching her front door it wasn't outside the bounds of possibility that a person could imagine a plate of rissoles would be attacked by rats that didn't exist. But how on earth could he even begin to explain that to them?

'Leave her in peace,' he said.

'In peace!' Rose's eyes widened. 'In *peace*!'

'There's been no peace in this house, Elmer, since the night you took that girl to the pictures.'

'Will I tell her you want her?' Rose pressed her offer again.

'I'll go up myself,' Elmer said.

But there was no response when he rattled the handle of the attic door, when he rapped loudly and banged with his fist. It wasn't normal not to answer, there was no getting away from that. But then he looked in the yard and discovered that her bicycle wasn't there. In the shop he imparted that information to his sisters. If they heard her returning, he asked them to tell him.

The gondola was silent on the water, the stone of the buildings dank and slimily green. Later there was the ebb and flow of the dull blue sea, the shells and seaweed left on the sand when it receded. You looked back and saw the fat domes of the churches, the statues high in the sky . . .

She dipped about the pages, opening the books at random. She loved doing that. She watched while Yelena Nikolayevna, sleepless all night, kept clasping her knees with her hands and resting her head on them. She watched while Yelena Nikolayevna crossed to the window and held her aching forehead against the panes to cool it.

'. . . *The rain that began as a spatter became a sheet of water, glistening as it fell from a sky as black as night. Yelena Nikolayevna sheltered in a ruined chapel. A beggarwoman waited . . .*'

Among the gravestones she tidied her hair and smeared a little lipstick on to her lips, smiling at her reflection in the glass of her compact.

At Culleen the watch wasn't missed for some time. Drawers were searched, furniture was pulled out in case it had fallen down behind something. The general belief was that it would eventually turn up.

In fact it didn't, and one afternoon when Mrs Dallon was washing eggs at the sink she remembered the feeling of surprise when Mary Louise had said she'd like to see her old room again. The statements that had been made by Rose and Matilda returned to startle her and suddenly, an egg held in the palm of her hand, Mrs Dallon felt sick. Waves of nausea passed through her stomach. She felt weak in her legs and for a moment as she stood there she thought she might faint.

'I've come to see Mary Louise,' she announced in Quarry's an hour later.

Rose's response was to glance along the counter to where Matilda was re-rolling a bolt of satin.

'I rang the bell on the front door,' Mrs Dallon said. 'Only there wasn't an answer.'

'Your daughter could be out on her bicycle, Mrs Dallon. Then again I doubt your daughter can hear the doorbell up in the attic.'

Through the panes of the accounting-office window Mrs Dallon could see the square head of her son-in-law bent over the desk where he did his work. By now she knew the way through the shop into the house.

'I'll go up and see if she's in,' she said.

Neither Rose nor Matilda tried to stop her. Let her see for herself, both simultaneously thought. Let her climb up the stairs and not be answered when she knocks on the door.

But Mrs Dallon was answered. As soon as she spoke, the

key turned in the lock and the door was opened. Mary Louise was tidily dressed, in a navy-blue skirt and blouse, with a brooch that Mrs Dallon had once given her at her throat.

'Hullo, Mary Louise.'

'We'll go downstairs.'

The key was taken from the lock, and the door locked on the outside. In the front room Mary Louise asked her mother if she'd like a cup of tea.

'No, no, pet. Nothing at all.'

'Are you well at Culleen?'

'We are, Mary Louise. We're all well.'

'That's good so.'

Mrs Dallon hesitated. She felt uncomfortable, sitting on the edge of a tightly-stuffed armchair; and was made more so by Mary Louise's unruffled manner, her air of being calmly in command of herself.

'That day you came out to Culleen, Mary Louise? A while ago?'

Mary Louise nodded.

'You went up to your aunt's room.'

Mary Louise frowned. She shook her head. Then the frown cleared as swiftly as it had come. She made a gesture with her hands, indicating that she couldn't remember going into her aunt's room. It hardly mattered, the gesture implied also.

'It's only we've been hunting high and low for a watch she had there. A watch that used to be Robert's.'

Mary Louise nodded sympathetically.

'You didn't see it that day, pet? A watch on a chain?'

'He'd have wanted me to have it. If he'd known he was going to die he'd have given it to me.'

The same sickness she had experienced while washing the eggs again afflicted Mrs Dallon. A prickly discomfort affected areas of her body. She was glad she was sitting down.

'Did you take the watch, pet?'

Mary Louise said she'd looked for the watch and eventually had opened a drawer in the bedside table and there it was.

'That watch isn't yours, Mary Louise. It belongs to Aunt Emmeline.'

'Actually it belonged to Robert's father. It was the only thing of value he left behind. You can hardly count the soldiers.'

Since neither Mrs Dallon nor her sister had attended the auction they were unaware of the purchases Mary Louise had made. When her mother now displayed bewilderment over her reference to soldiers Mary Louise explained immediately. She had bought the soldiers, she said, and the furniture from her cousin's bedroom. She didn't mention buying the clothes from the unemployed man's wife because for the moment that didn't seem relevant.

'Oh, Mary Louise! Oh, my dear child!'

Unsteadily, Mrs Dallon rose and crossed to where Mary Louise was standing, between the windows. She put her arms around her daughter. She stroked her hair. She had to blink back tears, and was surprised to find – having stepped back a few paces and blown her nose – that Mary Louise herself was still quite composed, was in fact smiling, as though amused.

'You're not well, child.'

Mary Louise denied that. She repeated that her cousin would have given her the watch had he known he was going to die that night. They'd often spoken about his father. They'd often wondered what exactly his father had been like.

'Oh, Mary Louise!'

Mrs Dallon sat down again. I am never going to leave this room, she thought. I cannot leave her. I cannot walk away. The prickles of discomfort had gone from her shoulders. She no longer felt sick in her stomach, but all over her body she was aware of a coldness, like ice in her bloodstream.

'They're funny names,' Mary Louise said. 'Funny names for Letty to choose. Kevin Aloysius.'

'We weren't talking about that, dear.'
'Well, there you are.'

Afterwards Mrs Dallon repeated to her sister and her husband every statement Mary Louise had made. She recalled the inflections in her speech, her smiles, the way she had remained standing between the two windows of the big front room, the way she had not appeared to notice the disjointed wildness of the conversation. The bad news was not shared with James, since it was considered that at present no one was capable of breaking it to him as gently as his youth deserved. That night neither of the Dallons slept. They lay in silence in their bedroom, the room in which all other family worries had been discussed over the years. Mrs Dallon could still hear the sound of traffic in the street below while her daughter went on so, saying she was all right and commenting on the names chosen for Letty's baby.

'I'm worried, Mrs Dallon,' Elmer said, arriving at Culleen in Kilkelly's car during the afternoon of the next day. 'A terrible thing's after happening.'

He meant the poisoning of the rissoles; and the Dallons, who had imagined that nothing worse could occur than the filching of the watch, realized within a minute that they were wrong. In order to avoid worrying them further, Letty had passed on nothing of the accusation that a safe had been broken into. They heard about this now. They heard about the furniture arriving in the house.

'They can exaggerate,' Elmer conceded. 'Rose and Matilda can. They can be extravagant in what they say. So that at first you wouldn't believe them, but then you'd have to.'

A nightmare of understanding formed in the kitchen. Isolated fragments connected, like jigsaw pieces transformed into a picture.

'For God's sake, what caused it?' Mr Dallon muttered.

The question was too complicated for Elmer to answer. He wanted to say that he had married Mary Louise in good faith, that he was the last person who'd go about making inquiries about a prospective wife. Instead, he said nothing.

'But why,' Mrs Dallon whispered, 'why would she do that with the rat poison?'

'Any more, why would she buy furniture when the house is full of it, Mrs Dallon? You have to ask that, too.'

The watch was not mentioned. The feeling was that the watch was a Dallon matter, that knowledge of it was not yet a son-in-law's concern.

'My sisters don't know about what I told you,' Elmer said. 'They know about the money but not the other. I don't think they'd stop in the house if they knew.'

'We had a word with Dr Cormican after your sisters came out here a while back,' Mr Dallon said.

'I heard they came out here.'

'They came out and told us things.'

Elmer softly sighed. He said:

'There'll be steps I'll have to take.'

'What steps?' Mrs Dallon cried, suddenly shrill.

'They guessed it was Mary Louise who interfered with the rissoles. Only they don't know what she put in them. It isn't safe in the house the way things are.'

'What steps will you take?' Mrs Dallon repeated, calming a little.

Elmer didn't reply. 'What did Dr Cormican say when you saw him, Mrs Dallon?'

'He said if Mary Louise was sick he'd be sent for.'

'That's what I'll do then.'

When Kilkelly's car reached the outskirts of the town Elmer asked the driver to stop. He paid him off and entered the first public house he came to, a place he'd never been in before. It was dingy and cheerless, empty except for himself, but it suited his mood. He didn't want to have to talk to anyone, nor be addressed by name.

At Culleen, when James came into the kitchen after his day's work, he found his father and mother and his Aunt Emmeline sitting around the kitchen table. It surprised him that they should all be there at this particular time of day, not busy with their usual tasks. They were conversing very quietly when he entered the kitchen, their voices hardly raised above a whisper. They ceased immediately.

'What's up?' James asked, turning on both taps at the sink and working soap into his hands under the running water.

'Mary Louise isn't well, James,' his father said.

'Has she the 'flu?'

'Mary Louise has been doing funny things, boy. We're worried for her.'

'What kind of funny things?' James turned from the sink, the taps still running behind him, his hands dripping water on to the flagged floor. It was then that he saw his mother had been crying. His Aunt Emmeline looked as if she might have been crying also. His father's mouth was pulled down at the corners.

'What kind of funny things?'

They told him then, first asking him to sit down. That evening Mr Dallon drove over to tell Letty.

Alone in her bungalow, Miss Mullover found herself recalling Mary Louise's childhood fascination with Joan of Arc. Had she been wrong, she wondered now, not to find more significance in it than she had? When Mary Louise had confessed at her sister's wedding party that she and her cousin had been in love at the time of his death Miss Mullover had wondered if the confession, so abruptly offered to her, somehow belonged in that same realm of the imagination. More than once she had wondered so since, ending always with bewilderment. What she felt certain of was that the marriage of convenience that had taken place between a young girl and a draper could now be spoken of in the same breath as certain other marriages in the town – that of the couple who communicated through their pet, that of the wife who'd danced secretly in the Dixie dancehall, of the bread deliverer who'd run away with a tinker girl by mistake. Marriages collapsed for all sorts of reasons, but presumably you never really knew why unless you were involved in one. Not that it mattered if other people knew or not, Miss Mullover supposed, but still could not prevent herself from wondering about the future of Elmer Quarry and Mary Louise.

'That's a terrible thing to do, Mary Louise.'

'Terrible?'

'You poisoned the food with rat poison,' Elmer said.

She smiled. *I must not be mischievous* she had written a hundred times after the episode of the worms in Possy Luke's desk. Downstrokes heavy, perfect loops, otherwise it would all have to be done again. Tessa Enright hadn't owned up.

'You could have killed us stone dead,' he said.

'Yes.'

He had made up his mind: she could tell from the look in his eyes. Everything was there in his eyes, even – for a moment – something like distress.

'Yes,' she said again. 'Yes.' She thought of asking him if they'd let her bring her things with her, but she didn't. She was sure they would; the watch and the clothes at least, the books and the collar-stud.

29

'I am back in the town.'

'You're back because you're better these days, dear. Because of the medicine. All the old stuff is over and done with.'

'I'm back because of the grave.'

'You can't touch a grave. You have to leave a grave alone.'

'You can change things if you want to.'

His hand is on the doorknob. More than anything else, Elmer requires a drink. His want is a need; he has scarcely the strength to stand; he came up with her tray and she smiled at him, delaying him by speaking of a graveyard, a subject she has raised before. 'Let her back into the attics if she asks for it,' Miss Foye advised, and duly he made the arrangements, putting sheets on the bed himself.

'I must go now,' he says.

'You can open a grave. You can move the remains. Isn't it funny, that expression, Elmer – remains? To refer to a human person as remains?'

'Sure, what would be the point of it, dear?'

The first time he visited her in the asylum she said someone whose name he couldn't catch had stopped keeping a diary. A thick black line had been drawn and that was that. He asked her if it was herself, nervous about any diaries left lying about, but she didn't reply.

'Robert and I loved one another,' she says.

'Eat up that plateful before it's cold. And take the pills

when you've had it. Put the tray outside and I'll get it later on.'

'I don't need to take pills, Elmer.'

'Ah sure, you have to take them. Aren't they keeping you cured?'

'All it is is moving the remains from one graveyard to another. I want to be buried with him, Elmer.'

They maintained they wouldn't set foot on the attic stairs. They refused to so much as butter a slice of bread for her. They said if she came within ten yards of the pantry or the kitchen they'd walk out of the house. 'I'll see to her food,' he interrupted, and since her return he has done so, carrying her up anything that is left over, frying bacon and eggs for her if that is necessary.

'I have business down in the town,' he says. 'I can't be delaying.'

'All I want is to be buried with him.'

'I'll organize that. Only take your pills now.'

'Will you drive me out and I'll show you where the grave-yard is?'

'The first minute I have to spare we'll go out there. Myself and yourself.'

'It's the place where the Attridges are buried. The Attridge family.'

'I know it well.'

The desire to be away, to be in the bar at Hogan's, has developed into a soreness that spreads all over his body. That first time, the first occasion he visited her, he said: 'Well now, and how are you, dear?' She shook her head, referring to some beggarwoman with second sight. On later visits he told her the news from the town, how Foley's had been converted into a self-service, with wire baskets, how Sarsfield's in Lower Bridge Street was the first bar to have the television installed.

'I really want it,' she begs. 'It's the only thing I want.'

'No problem about the grave, dear.'

*

Once she was locked away it would be as though she had died. Her advent had been a destruction, and they imagined a fresh beginning for the three of them. But within ten months he was listening at last to Kilkenny's sales talk at the garage, and then he bought a car purely so that three or four times a year he could visit her. Not once have they sat in that car; not once have they seen, even in the distance, the house she went to. 'Come over for the drive,' he used to offer, but neither cared to reply.

They sit in the big front room, its grey wallpaper unchanged in their lifetime, a room their brother has not entered for almost thirty years. They manage their outrage at their sister-in-law's presence as best they can; they're too old now for the vigour of such feelings, Rose seventy-four, Matilda seventy-three. 'You damn fool,' Rose said when first he told them she was to all intents and purposes cured due to wonder drugs. He repeated words that had been used to him, 'caring', and 'commitment' and 'community'. Ridiculous, it sounded, all that coming out of a grown man. He was finished years ago; until then they had used their energy protesting, in an endeavour to conserve what remained. What does it matter now? The shop has gone and with it their standing in the town. Often he does not wear a tie. They have seen him pass out of the halldoor in his old felt slippers. As if he's feeding a dog, he gathers up the remains and carries the tray up the attic stairs, or carelessly breaks the egg yolk when he fries it, not noticing the splinters of shell that fall into the fat.

'You damn fool,' Rose says again, coldly stating the fact, her tone without the emotion that years ago would have made it shrill. She says it often.

'She has a brother and a sister,' Matilda reminds him, often also. 'It isn't here she belongs. Who says it's here?'

'She is my wife.'

These exchanges, and other passages of conversation, are recalled in the grey front room, but are not dwelt upon in further conversation, are not mulled over aloud. Memories possess the two old women, further souring their bitterness. There are echoes of a time that might so easily and so naturally have continued: he'd been the person in their lives when it seemed clear that no one else was waiting to transform their lives. Making cakes for him, roasting meat, darning and mending, changing his sheets, the presents given and received on Christmas Day, he in the accounting office, they receiving in the shop: once, like a promise, there was the perpetuity of all that. Modest enough, God knows; not much to ask.

James at Culleen would like to hand the farm on to any of his sons but none of them wants it. James married Angela Eddery, and both are disappointed about this family rejection but do not let it show. There isn't a living at Culleen, each of their sons has said, which bewilders James because there always was before. 'Well, at least it'll see us out,' Angela reminds him, and they agree that that's a blessing to be grateful for.

Soon after Mary Louise's return Angela reports in the kitchen at Culleen that she has seen her in Bridge Street. She recognized her after an initial hesitation and would have spoken to her if there hadn't been that moment of doubt. By the time she gathered herself together her sister-in-law had passed on.

'I suppose she'll have to come out here.' James sounds more grudging than he feels, the words too carelessly chosen.

'Of course she must, James! As often as she likes.'

Over the years Angela has had her ups and downs at Culleen. Often, when feeling low, she has thought of Mary Louise and seen her own life in perspective: she has been grateful for that. Once she and James visited his sister, but afterwards he

said he didn't want to go again. James has always been embarrassed by his sister's misfortune, and Angela is aware that this
has probably been sensed by Mary Louise. She won't come
out to Culleen, Angela intuitively guesses, and feels she could
confidently reassure James on that score. She chooses not to.

When Dennehy inherited the premises at Ennistane crossroads
he ceased to practise as a vet. He and Letty sold the house
they'd had rebuilt at the time of their marriage and moved
their family to the public house. Tired of being called out in
the middle of the night to attend ailing animals, Dennehy took
contentedly to the life of a publican and Letty enjoyed the
more substantial income that the change brought with it.

'She should live with us,' she remarked when her sister's
emergence from her sanctuary was first mooted. Dennehy
raised no objection. The house was large, the bars busy: no
matter how odd she was, another woman wouldn't be noticed
about the place.

'She should have come here,' Letty repeats when Mary
Louise has been back a while, and two days later she calls to
see her sister in order, again, to put the proposition to her.
'There'll be a home with us,' she has earlier assured Miss Foye
on her visits, and assured Mary Louise also. The big, noisy
public house with all that coming and going, and a family of
nephews and nieces, is surely more like it than the company of
Elmer Quarry. Years ago Letty came to a private conclusion,
shared only with her husband: Mary Louise had been
maddened by the gross presence of Elmer Quarry in her bed,
his demands had frightened and repelled her to a degree that
in the end affected her mind. She could understand it, Letty
maintained: you had only to imagine Elmer Quarry standing
naked in your bedroom and you'd want to close your eyes for
ever. Mary Louise has always been too innocent, too trusting
and unworldly, to cope with any of that. Hair sprouted out of

Elmer Quarry's ears, and out of his nostrils, black bristly hair that would sicken you when it came close. The sides of his face had a way of becoming damp with sweat, and that sweat would touch you. He took to drink because when it came down to it Mary Louise couldn't disguise her revulsion.

'Oh, I belong here,' Mary Louise insists. 'I'll visit you often.'

Like Angela, Letty knows she won't.

How could you have a grave up? How could you disturb the bones of the dead and for no good reason convey them five miles across the countryside to a graveyard that went out of business years ago? In the bar of Hogan's Hotel Elmer asks himself these questions, cogitating on their source. The cousin she spoke of had been an unfortunate with a delicate heart or lungs, never expected to live. A week ago she'd dragged her way through the long grass and pointed at a corner in the old graveyard where she and the cousin could go. She had it in her head that there'd been something between them.

'Replenish that, like a good man.' Elmer pushes his glass across the familiar surface of the bar, and Gerry receives it in an equally familiar grasp. He has a way of holding glasses these days, the fingers bent like claws due to arthritis.

'It's a fact what I was telling you, Mr Quarry. We have a one-way system threatened.'

'Are you serious?'

'Oh, I am, sir. They have the plans drawn up.'

'It'll damage trade.'

'Of course it will. Sure, you can't watch them.'

Elmer nods. The town is congested, no doubt about it, but a one-way traffic system will do more harm than good. He nods again, lending emphasis.

'Has she settled, sir?' the barman tentatively inquires a moment later.

'She has, Gerry. She's settled well.'

When he brings the trays up he talks to him about Russians. She has all the names off pat, no telling where she picked them up. A fortune it would cost, taking up remains, a whole long battle with the powers that be. Set stuff like that in motion and you wouldn't know where you'd end up. He was caught once through doing the decent thing; he was caught when they put it to him about the efficacy of the drugs, but if a woman who talks about Russians and opening up graves is back to normal it's a queer thing. The truth of it is they want them out of those places for economic reasons. He should have known that in the final analysis there's nothing that doesn't come down to pounds, shillings and pence.

'I saw her out walking a week back,' the barman chattily continues. 'Fit as a fiddle she looked.'

'Oh, game ball, Gerry, game ball.'

In mutual, unspoken agreement neither Elmer nor the Dallons have ever revealed the true facts about the purchasing of the rat poison. In the town it is generally believed that Elmer Quarry's wife was taken to the asylum because she couldn't be managed any more, which is true enough. At the time it went about the town that she played with toys and imagined rats were going to attack her. On several occasions she had attempted to administer poison to herself. She'd bought clothes from the poor when there was a shopful of clothes underneath where she lived.

'Well, that's great, sir.'

'It is of course, Gerry.'

He'd drive her out again tomorrow and get the bottoms of his trousers soaking wet in the grass. It annoys them to see him driving her out, especially since they don't know where the drive is heading. It's enjoyable sometimes to annoy them. 'Did you find out about a single gravestone?' she asked this morning, and he promised that the matter was well in hand.

When Elmer leaves the bar he does so by the door that opens on to the street, no longer passing through the hall of the hotel, as once he used to. Bridget retired several years ago, but even before that Elmer hadn't bothered with loitering in the hall any more.

30

Again she is the only one, a slight figure in the corner of the pew. Two colours – black and brown – are arranged, stylishly, in her coat, its fur collar turned up for warmth. They are repeated in her soft suede shoes. The first wrinkles of old age creep around her eyes and the corners of her mouth, but the beauty that only her cousin ever remarked upon has not yet deserted her. A madonna look, her cousin said to himself the night he died while dreaming of her.

'Amen,' she murmurs, thin fingers splayed on her forehead, eyes closed.

The clergyman who stands at the altar is tall, a young man still unmarried, not long the inheritor of five far-flung parishes. Every Sunday, from eight o'clock till nightfall, he makes the rounds of his sparse attendances, spreading the Gospel over many miles, among the few. Often now this woman, until recently accounted mad, is the only occupant of these pews.

'*Lighten our darkness* ...' he softly pleads. Shades of green and crimson, of blue and yellow, glow dully in the window behind him, scrolls looping, basketwork and swaddling clothes. No hymns are sung when she is the only one, the psalm is not intoned. Instead of a sermon the two converse. '*The peace of God, which passeth all understanding* ...'

She remembers how in childhood, and when she was a girl, church services constituted an outing, how after her marriage they provided an opportunity to meet her family. She began to enjoy them for themselves during the years she was away.

'That was very nice,' she compliments the clergyman. 'Beautifully conducted.'

'It's good of you to come so often.'

'I was thinking of Miss Mullover during our *Te Deum*. I don't know why.'

The schoolteacher was long before his time, but often on these Sunday occasions her name crops up. In a schoolroom two children glance at one another with curiosity, mildly anticipating the love there is to be: again that picture forms in his mind.

'It has always surprised me that she didn't guess. That she didn't know we belonged to each other.'

He nods, not signifying understanding, only making the gesture because a response is necessary.

'Robert and I belonged to one another before we could breathe, certainly before either of us knew the other existed.'

'You've told me.'

'Is that how love starts, belonging without knowing it? When you look back it seems so.'

Again he nods, acknowledging her greater experience. Beneath his surplice there is a shrugging motion also, honestly reflecting his uncertainty.

'God gives permission: is that it, d'you think?'

'Possibly.'

'And perhaps it's not allowed, either, that someone else may guess?'

'Perhaps not.' He lifts the surplice over his head. Her company is like a child's. Saying at once what occurs to her may have to do with her incarceration, a habit she picked up from her companions. Having not known her before that time, he cannot easily guess.

'He bought a motor-car so that he could visit me. It's

asking less that he should see to the graves. Is it still too much?'

He drapes the surplice over his left arm, smoothing the creases and watching them return. She has told him about reading the novels of Turgenev among the tombstones. She has told him that for eight years she has flushed the prescribed drugs down the lavatory, that she does not take them now because they are not necessary. As she stands in the pew, smiling up at him, her life seems as mysterious as an act of God, her innocence and her boundless love arbitrarily there, her last modest wish destined to go ungranted. The distress engendered in him by these thoughts turns into a familiar apprehension: contemplation of this woman's life could tease away his faith more surely than all his empty churches.

'May I take communion?'

It will make him late, but he does not demur. The surplice is replaced, the bread and wine unlocked, and measured out and offered. '*Do this,*' he mutters, '*in remembrance of me . . .*'

She remembers her cousin reading the bit that likened death to a fisherman. She remembers her husband bringing the bars of chocolate on his visits, Crunchie and Caramel Crisp. She remembers his saying that he'd had the front woodwork of the shop repainted blue. Best to stick with blue, he explained, you knew where you were with blue. 'I hear your sister's in a certain condition again,' he said as well. He'd bought the chocolate bars in Foley's.

There is a final prayer, a whispering sound that reminds her of a breeze. If he feels inclined, the fisherman keeps the caught fish in the water, still swimming although it's netted.

'I must go now,' the clergyman says, but listens while she tells him about Turgenev's fisherman. Inviting her into the world of a novelist had been her cousin's courtship, all he could manage, as much as she could accept. Yet passion came, like consummation in the end. For thirty-one years she'd clung to a refuge in which her love affair could spread itself, a safe house offering sanctuary. For thirty-one years she passed as mad and was at peace.

'I dress for him,' she says. 'I make my face up in our graveyard. It is nice I can dress for him again.'

He smiles, recalling how she giggled when she told him that she had never opened the Rodenkil. Still giggling, she said she once had written *I must not be mischievous* a hundred times. She bought the Rodenkil from her husband's friend on purpose. She stained the rissoles green with the Stephens' ink she'd taken from her cousin's bedroom. 'People think the worst of you,' she added when she'd said all that, and added further that you could hardly blame them.

'I'm sorry I delayed you,' she apologises before she turns to go. 'I'm a dreadful old nuisance.'

He watches as she walks away. Prosperous, she strikes him as just for a moment, her pretty shoes, her brown and black coat, a fragile figure, yet prosperous in her love. Does she tell Elmer Quarry that she dresses for her cousin? Does he pay for her clothes without question, because he doesn't want to think about any of it? Does love like hers frighten everyone just a little?

'Goodbye,' the clergyman calls after her, and she turns and waves, and then is gone.

Alone in the cold church he sees her again for an instant, the child in the schoolroom, glancing across the desks at her delicate cousin. In the bedroom she touches the collar-stud with her lips and takes from the dressing-table drawer the bottle of Stephens' ink. Warmed by sunlight, her finger traces the letters on an Attridge gravestone; in the blue-washed cottage she bargains for her cousin's clothes. She arranges the soldiers in a battle she does not understand; she hangs the watch on the nail by the fireplace. Their voices join, entangled, reading about Russians.

She'll outlive the Quarrys, the clergyman reflects, and sees her differently: old and alone, moving about from room to room in the house above the shop. 'I have arranged it,' his own voice promises, the least he can surely do.

There is the funeral, and then the lovers lie together.

MY HOUSE IN
UMBRIA

1

It is not easy to introduce myself. Gloria Grey, Janine Ann Johns, Cora Lamore: there is a choice, and there have been other names as well. Names hardly matter, I think; it is perhaps enough to say I like Emily Delahunty best. 'Mrs Delahunty,' people say, although strictly speaking I have never been married. I am offered the title out of respect to a woman of my appearance and my years; and Quinty – who addresses me more than anyone else – once said when I questioned him on the issue: '"Miss Delahunty" doesn't suit you.'

I make no bones about it, I am not a woman of the world; I am not an educated woman; what I know I have taught myself. Rumour and speculation – even downright lies – have abounded since I was sixteen years old. In any person's life that side of things is unavoidable, but I believe I have suffered more than most, and take this opportunity to set the record straight. Firstly, my presence on the S.S. *Hamburg* in my less affluent days was as a stewardess, nothing more. Secondly, it is a mischievous fabrication that at the time of the Oleander Avenue scandal I accepted money in return for silence. Thirdly, Mrs Chubbs was dead, indeed already buried, before I met her husband. On the other hand I do not deny that men have offered me gifts, probably all of which I have accepted. Nor do I deny that my years in Africa are marked, in my memory, with personal regret. Unhappiness breeds confusion and misunderstanding. I was far from happy in Ombubu, at the Café Rose.

In the summer of which I now write I had reached my fifty-
sixth year – a woman carefully made up, eyes a greenish-blue.
Then, as now, my hair was as pale as sand, as smooth as a
seashell, the unfussy style reflecting the roundness of my face.
My mouth is a full rosebud, my nose classical; my complexion
has always been admired. Naturally, there were laughter lines
that summer, but my skin, though no longer the skin of a girl,
had worn well and my voice had not yet acquired the husky
depths that steal away femininity. In Italy men who were
strangers to me still gave me a second look, although naturally
not with the same excitement as once men did in other places
where I've lived. I had, in truth, become more than a little
plump, and though perhaps I should have dressed with such a
consideration in mind this is something I have never been able
to bring myself to do: I cannot resist just a hint of drama in
my clothes – though not bright colours, which I abhor. 'I
never knew a girl dress herself up so prettily,' a man who sat
on the board of a carpet business used to say, and my tendency
to put on a pound or two has not been without admirers. A
bag of bones Mrs Chubbs was, according to her husband,
which is why – so I've always suspected – he took to me in the
first place.

Having read so far, you'll probably be surprised to learn
that I'm a woman who prays. When I was a child I went to
Sunday school and had a picture of Jesus on a donkey above
my bed. In the Café Rose in Ombubu I interested Poor Boy
Abraham in praying also, the only person I have ever influenced in this way. 'He's retarded, that boy,' Quinty used to
say in his joky way, careless as to whether or not the boy was
within earshot. Quinty's like that, as you'll discover.

I am the author of a series of fictional romances, composed
in my middle age after my arrival in this house. I am no
longer active in that field, and did not ever presume to intrude
myself into the world of literature – though, in fairness to

veracity, I must allow that my modest works dissect with some success the tangled emotions of which they treat. That they have given pleasure I am assured by those kind enough to write in appreciation. They have helped; they have whiled away the time. I can honestly state that I intended no more, and I believe you'll find I am an honest woman.

But to begin at the beginning. I was born on the upper stairway of a lodging-house in an English seaside resort. My father owned a Wall of Death; my mother, travelling the country with him, participated in the entertainment by standing upright on the pillion of his motor-cycle while he raced it round the rickety enclosure. I never knew either of them. According to the only account I have – that of Mrs Trice, who had it from the lodging-house keeper – my mother was on her way to the first-floor lavatory when she was taken with child, if you'll forgive that way of putting it. Within minutes an infant's cries were heard on the stairway. 'That was a setback,' Mrs Trice explained, and further revealed that in her opinion my father and mother had counted on my mother's continuing performance on the motor-cycle pillion to 'do the trick'. By this she meant I would be stillborn, since efforts at aborting had failed. It was because I wasn't that the arrangement was made with Mr and Mrs Trice, of 21 Prince Albert Street, in that same seaside town.

They were a childless couple who had long ago abandoned hope of parenthood: they paid for the infant that was not wanted, the bargain being that all rights were thereby relinquished and that no visit to 21 Prince Albert Street would ever be attempted by the natural parents. Although nobody understands more than I the necessity that caused those people of a Wall of Death to act as they did, to this day I fear abandonment, and have instinctively avoided it as a fictional subject. The girls of my romances were never left by lovers who took from them what they would. Mothers did not turn

their backs on little children. Wives did not pitifully plead or
in bitterness cuckold their husbands. The sombre side of things
did not appeal to me; in my works I dealt in happiness ever
after.

Quinty is familiar with my origins, for nothing can be kept
from him. In Africa he knew I had accumulated money,
probably how much. In 1978, when we had known one another
for some time in Ombubu, it was he who suggested that I
should buy a property in Umbria, which he would run for me
as an informal hotel – quite different from the Café Rose.
Repeatedly he pressed the notion upon me, tiring me with the
steel of his gaze. Enough money had been made; there was no
need for either of us to linger where we were. That was the
statement in his eyes. We could both trade silence for silence
in another kind of house. Half a child and half a rogue he is.

Quinty was born in the town of Skibbereen, in Ireland,
approximately forty-two years ago. He is a lean man, with a
light footstep, gaunt about the features. From the outer corner
of each eye two long wrinkles run down his cheeks, like
threads. When first I knew him in Ombubu he was shifty and
unhealthy-looking. 'There's a sick man here,' Poor Boy Abraham cried, excited because a stranger had arrived at the
café. I never knew where it was that Quinty had come from in
Africa, or what had brought him to the continent in the first
place. But I later heard, the way one does in an outpost like
Ombubu, that several years before he'd tricked into marriage
the daughter of a well-to-do Italian family, whom he had come
across when she was an au pair girl in London. She ran away
from him when she discovered that he was *not* the manager of
a meat-extract factory, as he had claimed, and that he
stole his clothes from D. H. Evans. He followed her to
Modena, bothering her and threatening, until one night her
father and two of her brothers drove him a little way towards
Parma, pushed him out on to a grass verge and left him there.

He did not attempt to return, but that was how he came to be in Italy and learned the language. When first he mentioned Umbria to me I'd no idea where it was; I doubt I'd even heard of it. 'Let me have just a little money,' he begged in Ombubu one damply oppressive afternoon. 'Enough for the journey and then to look about.' Africa had gone stale for me, he said, which was a delicate way of putting it; the regulars at the Café Rose had not changed for years. In other words, the place had become a bore for both of us.

He sang the praises of Italy; I listened to descriptions of Umbrian landscape and hill-towns, of seasons bringing their variation of food and wine. Quinty can be persuasive, and I was happy enough to agree that a time of my life had come to an end. He'd played a certain role during most of that time, I have to say in fairness, and I have to give him credit for it. When he raised the subject of Italy I did the simplest thing: I gave him the money, believing I'd never see him again. But he returned a fortnight later and spread out photographs of Umbria and of villas that might be purchased. 'No one would care to die in the Café Rose,' he pointed out, a sentiment with which I could not but concur. One house in particular he was keen on.

Imagine a yellowish building at the end of a track that is in places like a riverbed. White with dust unless rain has darkened it, this track is two hundred metres long, curving through a landscape of olive trees and cypresses. In summer, broom and laburnum daub the clover slopes, poppies and geraniums sprinkle the meadows. Behind the house the hill continues to rise gently, and there's a field of sunflowers. The great lake of Trasimeno is on our doorstep; only thirty kilometres to the south there's a railway junction at Chiusi, which is convenient; and in the same area there's a health spa at Chianciano. In Quinty's photographs of the house there were out-buildings, and machinery that had rusted, but all that has changed since.

Of the house itself, the window shutters are a faded green, and the entrance doors — always open in the daytime — are green also. Further doors — glass decoratively framed with metal — separate the outside hall from the inner, and the floors of both, and of the dining-room and drawing-room — called by Quinty the *salotto* — are tiled, a shade of pale terracotta. Upstairs, on either side of two long, cool corridors, the bedrooms are small and simple, like convent cells. All are cream-distempered, with inside shutters instead of curtains, each with a dressing-table, a wardrobe and a bed, and a reproduction of a different Annunciation above each wash-stand. What luxury there is in my house belongs to the antique furniture of the downstairs rooms and the inner hall: embroidered sofas, pale chairs and tables, inlaid writing-desks, footstools, glass-fronted bookcases, the dining-room's chandelier.

When the tourists come to my house they pull the bell-chain and the sound echoes from the outer hall. Then Quinty, in his trim white jacket, answers the summons. 'Well?' he says in English, for one of his quirks is not immediately to speak Italian to strangers. 'How can I help you?' And the tourists cobble together what English they can, if it happens not to be their native tongue.

A handful of travellers is all Quinty ever makes welcome at a time, people who have spilled over from the hotels of the town that lies five kilometres away. A small, middle-aged woman called Signora Bardini, dressed always and entirely in black, is employed to cook. And Quinty found Rosa Crevelli, a long-legged, dark-skinned maid, to assist him in the dining-room. He presents us to our visitors as a private household, not at all in a commercial line of business. From the outset my house was known neither as an *albergo* nor a *pensione*, nor a restaurant with rooms, nor an hotel. 'This is what suits?' he suggested.

Being profitable, it was what suited Quinty, but for other

reasons it suited me also. Once, somewhere, I have seen a painted frieze continuing around the inside walls of a church – people processing in old-fashioned dress, proceeding on their way to Heaven or to Hell, I'm not sure which. Over the years the tourists who have come to my house have lingered in my memory like that. I see their faces, and even sometimes still hear their voices: tall Dutch people, the stylish French, Germans who brought with them jars of breakfast food, Americans delighting in simple things as much as children do, English couples suffering from digestive troubles. Chapters of books have been read, postcards written, bridge played in the evenings, even pictures painted, on the terrace. I have suffered no bad debts, nor have there ever been complaints about the bedrooms or the food. Quinty gave Rosa Crevelli English lessons and took up something else with her in private, but I asked no questions. Instead, within a month of settling in this house, I taught myself to type.

All this began nine years before the summer of which I write – the nine years in which I left the past behind, as title succeeded title: *Precious September*, *Flight to Enchantment*, *For Ever More*, *Behold My Heart!* and many others. My savings had bought the house; now – though after difficult beginnings – there was wealth. One day it would be Quinty who woke up rich, yet he could not possibly have predicted what would happen here: that I would sit down in my private room and compose romances. As far as Quinty knew, there was nothing in my history to suggest such a development; I was not that kind of woman. To tell the truth, I'd hardly have guessed it myself. As a villa hostess in an idyllic setting, I would make a living for both of us out of a passing tourist trade, as I had made one in a different role in Africa. That's how Quinty saw the future and as far as it went he was right, of course. He's cute as a fox when it comes to matters of gain, that being his life really.

Besides the tourists, our visitors are rare: a functionary from the tax office, or would-be thieves arriving with some excuse to look the place over, a traveller in fertilizers seeking directions to a nearby farm. Ever since the summer of 1987, which I think of to this day as the summer of the General and Otmar and the child, and which I remember most vividly of all the seasons of my life, nothing has been quite the same. That summer and for a few summers after it no tourists were received. Yet had you, for some other reason, gained admission during that summer Quinty would have led you through the outer hall and through the inner one and into the *salotto*, to wait there for me. Depending upon the time of day, the General would probably have been reading his English newspaper in the cool of the shadows, the child engrossed in one of her drawings, Otmar soundlessly tapping a surface with his remaining fingers. Many times that summer I imagined a voice saying: 'I have come for Otmar,' or: 'I understand you are keeping an old Englishman here,' or: 'Gather up the child's belongings.' Many times I imagined the car that had drawn up, and the dust its wheels had raised. I imagined a little knot of official people outside our entrance doors, one of them lighting a cigarette to pass the time, the butt later thrown down on the gravel. In fact, it wasn't like that in the least. All that happened was that Thomas Riversmith came.

That summer the child was eight years old, Otmar twenty-seven, the General elderly. They were three people on their own, and so was I. 'Heart's companion' is an expression I used to some effect in *Two on a Sunbeam*, and the fact that it lingers still in my mind, so long after the last paragraph of that work was completed, is perhaps significant, personally. I have always been the first to admit that in this world we are eternal beggars – yet it is also true that alms are not withheld for ever. When I was in the care of Mr and Mrs Trice I longed for a cowboy to step down from the screen of the old Gaiety

Cinema and snatch me on to his saddle, spiriting me away from 21 Prince Albert Street. When I was a girl, serving clerks in a public-house dining-room, I longed for a young man of good family to draw his car up beside me on the street. When I was a woman I longed for a different kind of stranger to appear in the Café Rose. That summer, in Umbria, I had long ago abandoned hope. In my fifty-sixth year I had come to terms with stuff like that. My stories were a help, no point in denying it.

The winter and the spring that preceded that summer had been quiet. From time to time bundles of fan mail had arrived, forwarded by the English publishers. There had been invitations to attend get-togethers of one kind or another – I remember in particular a title that struck me, a 'Festival of Romance', in some Iron Curtain country. I have never gone in for that kind of thing, and politely declined. A man wrote from New Zealand, pointing out that he enjoyed the same surname as one of my characters – an unusual name, he suggested, which indeed it was: I imagined I had invented it. A schoolgirl in Stockton-on-Tees poured out her heart, as schoolgirls often do. An elderly person chided me for some historical carelessness or other, too slight to signify.

In January a pet died. Years ago a lame Siamese cat had wandered into the grounds one day, a pathetic creature, all skin and bone. Signora Bardini befriended her. She called the creature Tata and attached a little bell on a chain around her neck so that a gentle tinkling became a feature of my house. We watched her health recovering, her coat becoming silky again, contentment returning. But Tata was never young and never sprightly: we knew from the beginning that all she could give us was what remained of a mostly spent life. She grew old gracefully, which is nice, I think, for any creature, human or otherwise. Signora Bardini put a little wooden board up, that being her way.

Signora Bardini is a widow to whom no children were born. When her husband, a carpenter by trade, died in 1975 she apparently took some time to come to terms with her solitude. Although she speaks no English, I believe she was not happy again until she came to work in my house. Her life might have been perfect here were it not for Quinty, towards whom from the first she displayed an undemonstrative antipathy. Clearly she does not care for his relationship with Rosa Crevelli, nor his cheese-paring in household matters. But Signora Bardini is not, and never was, a woman to raise any kind of fuss.

That, then, was how things were at the beginning of the summer I write of. The house smelt faintly of paint, for some redecoration had recently been completed. 'We must have a garden,' I had repeatedly said that winter and spring, saying it mainly to myself. 'It is ridiculous that a house like this does not have a garden to it.' That was a little on my mind, as it had been for years. One April, passing through a railway station here in Italy, I noticed a great display of azaleas in pots. I did not then know what that flower is called, but later described it to Quinty, who found out for me. Ever since I had longed for an azalea garden, and for the lawns that I remember in England, and for little flowerbeds edged with pinks.

You may consider I was fortunate to lack only a garden and a particular friend, and of course you are right. I was, and am, immensely fortunate. Not many of us acquire the means necessary to occupy a place such as this, to choose as I may choose, rarely to count the cost. Not many pass a winter and spring with only the death of a lame cat to grieve over. In the eyes of the tourists who came here I was a comfortably-off Englishwoman, well looked after by my servants. Quinty no doubt struck them as eccentric, if not bizarre. For one thing he has a way of arbitrarily allocating to other people a particular obsession in order to hold forth on it himself. From encyclopaedias and newspapers he has acquired a wealth of chatty information on many subjects – royal families, the Iron Age, sewerage systems, land speed records, the initiation practices of blind Amazon tribes. A score of times I have heard him supplying some unfortunate tourist with the history of the Japanese railways or the nature of the jackal. 'Giuseppe Garibaldi gave his name to a biscuit,' he has confided in my hall; 'the city of Bath to another. Hard tack the first biscuit of all was called, and had to be broken with a hammer.' Jauntily gregarious, he endlessly leant against a pillar in the *salotto* that summer to conduct with the General a one-sided conversation about sport. When Mr Riversmith arrived he was imbued with an interest in holy women, although it could hardly have been clearer that Mr Riversmith's subject was ants.

In other ways Quinty can be dubious to a degree that makes him untrustworthy. One day in the April of that year Rosa Crevelli was rude to me in Italian, scornfully curling down her beautiful lower lip as she muttered something. Quinty observed this, but did not reprimand her. For the first time, I realized, he must have broken the unspoken agreement that had existed between us ever since we'd left the Café Rose: he had told this girl about the past.

Later I taxed him with this treachery. He laughed at first, but then he turned away and his cheeks were damp with tears when again he faced me. 'How can you make such an accusation?' he whispered in a broken voice, and went on for so long – professing loyalty and faithfulness, uttering statements to the effect that he and the girl would lay down their lives for me, and protesting their desire to be nowhere else on earth but in my house – that I forgave him. 'I've poured you a nice g and t,' he said with a smile, coming to find me that evening in the *salotto*. When I met her next Rosa Crevelli curtsied.

Of course I could not be certain: maybe they sniggered, who can say? That I have a tendency to give the benefit of the doubt is either a weakness or a strength, but whichever it is I certainly don't claim it as a virtue. In fact, for very good reasons, I claim very little for myself: there's not much to me, and I'm the first to confess it. Nor do I claim anything mystical for that particular summer, no angels making their presence felt in my house, no voices heard. The child was an ordinary child, and I believe the others were ordinary too. Yet I don't think anyone would deny that it was a singular summer, and constituted an experience not given to everyone.

On 5 May, in the morning, wearing a suit of narrow black-and-white stripes, handbag and shoes to match, I left my house to travel to Milan. Quinty drove me to the railway junction and gave me my ticket on the platform. I can manage to travel very well on my own, despite my limited understanding of the Italian language. I recognize the familiar phrase when the ticket collector demands to see my ticket. In Rinascente and all the other stores I shop successfully, and in the Grand Hotel Duomo, where I always stay, excellent English is spoken. I look forward to shopping for clothes and shoes, taking my time over their choosing, going away to think things over, returning twice or three times: all that I love.

No one was staying in my house that day; no tourists had been sent on by the hotels since the end of last year's season, and we didn't expect any until the middle of June at least. Not that it is ever necessary for me to be there when visitors do arrive, but even so I like to welcome them. In the dining-room we sit at one round table and if English is spoken we talk of this and that, of places that have been visited, of experiences while travelling. If English is difficult for my guests, they speak in whatever language their own is, and I am not offended. There are never more than five in my dining-room or at the table on the terrace when we choose to dine outside.

In the train I imagined Quinty driving from the railway

junction and shopping in the town, the large, grey, open-hooded car parked in the shade of the chestnut trees by the church. He would call in for a coffee and then return to the house, where he and Signora Bardini and Rosa Crevelli would have lunch in the kitchen. I imagined them there, the three of them around the table, Quinty repeating new English words and phrases for Rosa Crevelli. I wondered if Signora Bardini, too, had also been told about the past. Determinedly I pushed all that away, and then my mind became occupied by a title that had occurred to me at the railway junction. *Ceaseless Tears.* So far, that was all I had. A heroine had not come to me: I could not even faintly glimpse a hero. Yet that title insisted itself upon my consciousness, and I knew that when a title was insistent I must persevere.

The train was a Rome express; it had come through Orvieto before I boarded it; Arezzo and Florence lay ahead. Imagine the stylish interior of a First Class *rapido*, the pleasant Pullman atmosphere, the frilled white antimacassars, the comfortable roominess. Diagonally across from where I sat were a young man and a girl: you could tell from their faces that they were lovers. An older couple travelled with the father of the woman: you could tell that was the relationship from their conversation. This threesome spoke in English, the lovers in German. A mother and a father travelled with their two children, a boy and a girl: I could not hear what they said, but everything about them suggested Americans. A woman who might have been in the fashion world was on her own. Italian businessmen in lightweight suits occupied the other seats.

I watched the lovers. He stroked her bare arm; you could tell how much she was in love with him, though he wasn't exactly handsome or even prepossessing. Did the older couple find the father a tiresome addition to their relationship? If they did, their politeness allowed not a single intimation of it to show; but, oddly, that politeness worried me. The Americans

were stylish, the children arguing a little as spirited children
do, the parents softly conversing, sometimes laughing. The
mother was a particularly appealing young woman, fair-haired
and freckled, with dimples in both cheeks and a flash of
humour in her eyes.

Increasingly, I liked the title that had come to me, yet could
still find no meaning in it, no indication of this direction or
that. I recalled Ernestine French-Wyn, who had caused Adam
to weep so in *Behold My Heart!* But one story rarely prompts
the secrets of another and to avoid the nagging of my frustra-
tion I forced myself to observe again my fellow-travellers. The
heads of the lovers were now bent over a scrap of paper on
which the girl – she had a look of Lilli Palmer in her earliest
films – was making a calculation. The daughter and son-in-
law read; the old man had taken his watch off and was
meticulously re-setting it. The little American boy was being
reprimanded by his mother; the little girl changed places with
him and took her father's hand. Somewhere in my mind's
vision a description of this scene appeared: darkly-typed lines
on the green typing paper I always use. I had no idea why that
was.

The train moved swiftly, flashing through small railway
stations and landscape still verdant after the rains of spring.
The ticket collector appeared. Then the restaurant-car con-
ductor hurried by, tinkling his midday bell. The businessmen
went to lunch, so did the fashion woman. Out of nowhere,
words came: *In the garden the geraniums were in flower.
Through scented twilight the girl in the white dress walked
with a step as light as a morning cobweb. That evening she
hadn't a care in the world.*

It would go on. I would sit down at my little black Olympia
and paragraph would obediently follow paragraph, one scene
flowing into the next, conversations occurring naturally. I
turned the pages of *Oggi*, but soon lost interest. Where would

I be, I found myself thinking, if late in my life I had not discovered my modest gift? At my age there were women who still served clerks their plates of food in public-house dining-rooms. There were women who sold shoes – as I have also done – or swabbed out cabins on ferry-steamers. It had never seemed like good fortune that I'd found myself in the Café Rose, but in fairness to fate I have to say it was. I ran the place in the end – everyone's friend, as they used to say there. I was fortunate, I must record again, because without the Café Rose I don't believe I'd ever have put pen to paper.

I must have slept, for in a dream Ernie Chubbs approached me outside the Al Fresco Club and exclaimed, just as he had in reality, 'Hi, sugar!' He told me he loved me in the Al Fresco Club; he wanted to sit with me all night, he whispered. Ernie went on buying drinks, the way they liked you to in the Al Fresco, and when another man came up and bought drinks also Ernie was furious, and told him to go away. Then, as abruptly as it always is in dreams, I was shopping in Milan, trying on long suede coats in different colours – next season's cut, the assistant said. I liked the wrap-around style and was saying so when my eyes were wrenched open by a burst of noise. There was glass in the air, and the face of the American woman was upside down. There was screaming, and pain, before the darkness came.

2

'It's Quinty come to see you,' Quinty said. 'You're all right. You're OK.'

He tried to smile. The lines on his cheeks had wrinkled into zigzags, but the smile itself would not properly come.

'Is it Good Friday?' I asked, confused, because Good Friday did not come into any of it. I heard myself talking about the Café Rose, how one particular Good Friday the Austrian ivory cutter had been high on the stuff he took, and Poor Boy Abraham had been upset on account of anyone being high on the day when Jesus suffered on the Cross.

There were hours of shadows then – they might have been years for all I knew – and through them moved the white uniforms of the nurses, one nurse in particular, with thinning black hair. 'You've had a bang,' Quinty said, 'but thanks be to God you're progressing well.' He sniffed the way he sometimes does, a casual, careless sound, disguising something else.

'What happened?' I asked, but Quinty's reply – if he made one at all – eluded me, and when I looked he was no longer there. I didn't want to think; I allowed my mind to wander where it would, gliding over the past, swooping into it here and there, no effort made on my part, no exhaustion. 'Have they paid?' Mrs Trice asked her husband. She was always asking him that, he being a collector of insurance money. 'You're weak with them,' she accused him. 'Weak as old water.' As a child, I lived for eight years at 21 Prince Albert

Street before I realized that my presence there was the result of a monetary transaction. I'd always addressed the Trices as though they were my mother and father, not knowing about the people of the Wall of Death until Mrs Trice told me in the kitchen one Saturday morning. 'They were paid a sum by Mr Trice,' was how she put it. 'They weren't people you'd care for.'

Between sleep and consciousness the honest black face of Poor Boy Abraham edged out the Trices, his negroid features intent as he swept the veranda floor at the Café Rose, while the fans whirred and rattled. The four Englishmen played poker at the corner table. 'Where would I be if I did not come with my woes to you?' the Austrian ivory cutter asked and, as always, drew the conversation round to his hopeless coveting of some black man's wife. The aviator who was a regular in the café had been a skywriter, advertising a brand of beer mainly.

I dropped into sleep and dreamed, as I had on the train. 'Feeling better, girlie?' Ernie Chubbs was solicitous in Idaho. 'Fancy a chow mein sent up?'

A nurse spoke kindly in Italian. I could tell she was being kind from her expression. She rearranged my pillows and for a moment held my hand. I think I must have called out in my sleep. When I seemed calm again she went away.

When Ernie Chubbs suggested accompanying him to Idaho I did so because I wanted to see the Old West. To this day, the Old West fascinates me: Claire Trevor in her cowgirl clothes, Marlene Dietrich singing in the saloon. To this day, I close my eyes when a wheel of the stagecoach works itself loose; I'm still not quick enough to see a sheriff draw his gun. Mr Trice took me to the Gaiety Cinema on Sunday afternoons and we would watch the comedy short – Leon Errol or Laurel and Hardy, or Charlie Chase – and then the Gaumont News and the serial episode, and whatever else there was besides the main feature. Sometimes the main feature was a gangster thriller, or an ice-skating drama or a musical, and that was always a disappointment. I longed for the canyons and the ranches, for the sound of a posse's hooves, the saddles that became pillows beneath the stars.

Idaho was a disappointment too. Ernie Chubbs, who said he knew the region well, assured me it was where the Old West still was; but needless to say that wasn't true. A lifetime's dream was shattered – not that I expected to find the winding trails just as they had been shown to me, but at least there might have been something reminiscent of them, at least there might have been a smell of leather. 'You're simple, Emily,' the big doctor who came to the Café Rose used to say. And yes, I suppose I am: I cannot help myself. I'm simple and I'm sentimental.

'How long is it?' I asked. 'How long have I lain here?'

But the Italian nurses only smiled and rearranged my pillows. I worried about how long it was; yet a moment later – or perhaps it wasn't a moment – that didn't matter in the least. The Idaho of Ernie Chubbs – his going out on business, the waiting in the motel room – must have made me moan, because the nurses comforted me again. When they did, the Old West filled my thoughts, driving everything else away. In the Gaiety Cinema there were no curtains to the screen. On to the bare, pale expanse came the holsters and the sweat-bands of the huge-brimmed hats, the feathered Indians falling one by one, the rough and tumble of the fist fights. I was seven, and eight, and nine, when Dietrich sang. *'See what the boys in the back room will have,'* she commanded in her peremptory manner, *'And tell them I'll have the same.'* In my sedated tranquillity I heard that song again; and the Idaho of Ernie Chubbs seemed gone for ever. Young men I have myself given life to whispered lines of love to happy girls. The Wedding March played, bouquets were thrown by brides. The Café Rose might not have existed either.

*

'Quinty.'

'Rest yourself, now.'

'There were other people. A young man and his girl who talked in German. Americans. Italians in dark suits. A woman in the fashion business. Three English people. Are they here too, Quinty?'

'They are of course.'

'Quinty, will you find out? Find out and tell me. Please.'

'Don't upset yourself with that type of thing.'

'Are they dead, Quinty?'

'I'll ask.'

But he didn't move away from my bedside. He visited me to see if there were grounds for hope, promise of a relapse. His eyes were like two black gimlets; I closed my own. Little Bonny Maye was employed in Toupe's Better Value Store, attaching prices to the shelved goods with a price-gun. Small discs of adhesive paper, each marked with an appropriate figure, were punched on to the surface of cans and packets. At certain hours of the day she worked a till.

Little Bonny Maye was taken up by Dorothy, an older girl from the table-tennis club. Dorothy was secretary to a financier and had been privately educated. Her voice was beautiful, and so was Dorothy herself. Bonny couldn't think why she'd been taken up, and even if Dorothy had a way of asking her to do things for her rather a lot Bonny still appreciated the friendship more than any she had known. She was only too grateful: all the time with Dorothy that was what Bonny thought. Her single anxiety was that some silliness on her part would ruin everything.

'Did you ever read that story of mine, Quinty? *Little Bonny Maye*?' I was surprised to hear myself asking Quinty that. It wasn't our usual kind of conversation. He said:

'It's great you have your stories.'

'I thought about them in the Café Rose.'

'You told me that.'

'I don't remember telling you.'

'You had a drink or two in, the time you told me.'

The three words of the title were blue on the amber of the book-jacket, the two girls illustrated below. I must have said so because Quinty nodded. Soon afterwards he went away. He might even have guessed I had begun to hear the girls' voices.

'Dear, there is an "h" in "house", you know.' Dorothy could bring out Bonny's blushes, hardly making an effort. When they went on holiday together, while Bonny fetched and carried for the older girl, Dorothy drew up a list of words that Bonny should take special care with. 'Our fork belongs on our plate, not in the air. I had a nanny who said that.'

When I dozed, the pain in my face sometimes dulled to a tightness and for the first time, probably, I tried to smile. The two girls were on holiday in Menton, and when Blane came into their lives he naturally took Dorothy out, leaving poor Bonny to mooch about on her own, since it wouldn't have been right for her to tag along. 'Of course I don't mind. Of course not.' She tried to keep her spirits up by eating ice-cream or going to look at the yachts.

I was aware of making no effort whatsoever. I controlled nothing. Faces and words and voices flowed over me. 'Such an unhappy thing!' Blane exclaimed. 'Such rotten luck!' Dorothy had developed appendicitis. An ambulance had come. 'You need a cognac,' Blane insisted. 'Or a Cointreau. No, Bonny, I absolutely insist. Poor girl, how wretched for you too!' Dorothy's holiday was a write-off. Every morning Blane called for Bonny in his Peugeot and drove her to the bedside of her friend, who usually had made a list of things she wanted. Afterwards Blane and Bonny lunched together in the Petit Escargot.

Three months ago Blane had inherited Mara Hall, a great house in its own park in Shropshire. But as soon as he had done so he left England, being fearful of the house even though he loved it.

'My mother died when I was one and a half. There was always just my father and myself.'

'No brothers or sisters, Blane?'

'No brothers or sisters.'

Bonny thought how lonely that must have been: a boy growing up in a great house with only his father and the servants for company. His father was severe, expecting a lot of his heir.

'I'm a coward, I dare say. I'd give the world to take everything in my stride. I'm running away. I know that, Bonny.'

'Was your father – '

'My father did things perfectly. He was a strong man. He married the woman he loved and never looked at another. The servants and his tenants adored him.'

There was a head gardener at Mara Hall, and several under-gardeners. There was a butler and a cook and old retainers in the way of maids, all of whom had been there as long as Blane could remember. Once there'd been footmen, but that was ages ago.

Mara Hall was more vivid than the shadows of nurses whose speech I did not understand, and the odour of anaesthetic: the lawns and the tea roses, the mellow brick of the house itself and of the kitchen-garden walls, the old ornamental ironwork. I felt as Bonny felt – overawed with wonder. Bonny had not been abandoned in a bleak seaside town by a couple who rode a Wall of Death; but something like it was in Bonny's past, even if it did not come out in the story. I felt that strongly now; I never had before.

'It sounds so lovely, Blane. Your home.'

'Yes, it's lovely.'

They walked in the evenings on the promenade. He would marry Dorothy, Bonny thought, and take her to Mara Hall.

Dorothy was capable as well as beautiful. Dorothy would gently lead him back to his responsibilities. He would become as strong as his father; he would do things as perfectly.

'Dear Bonny,' he said, in a tone that made her hold her breath. She could not speak. The sea was a sheet of glass, reflecting the tranquil azure of the sky. 'Dear Bonny,' he said again.

The doctors who attended me conferred. One spoke in English, smiling, telling me I had made progress, saying they were pleased.

'I'm glad you're pleased,' I replied.

'You have been courageous, signora,' the same doctor said. 'And patient, signora.'

They passed on, both nodding a satisfied farewell at me. Blane took the modest creature's arm; she trembled at the touch because no man had ever taken Bonny Maye's arm before. No man had ever called her dear. She'd never known a heart's companion.

'Much better,' Dorothy said, but it was their last day in Menton. She'd left her dark glasses on her bedside table and Bonny went to fetch them. Blane drove her to Bordighera and Bonny miserably ate an ice-cream on the front. She wrote the postcards she should have written before, to the other girls in Toupe's Better Value Store. She'd be back before they received them.

Once only the story was interrupted by the ravenous features of Ernie Chubbs, his eyes seeking mine from the shadows of the Al Fresco Club, his fingers undoing my zips in the motel room. There was an old mangle in the motel room, and a tin bath in which kindling was kept. I knew all that was wrong. 'It wouldn't do to tell,' Ernie Chubbs said. 'Good girls don't tell, Emily.' That was wrong also. It wasn't Ernie who'd ever said good girls don't tell, and Ernie Chubbs hadn't been ravenous in that particular way.

The chill fag-end of a nightmare, darkly colourless, something like a rat in a drawing-room, went as quickly as it had arrived, crushed out of existence by a warmer potency. 'Well, really!' Dorothy was a little cross when they returned from Bordighera. She lay down to rest and complained that the bedroom was too hot and then, when the window was opened, that the draught was uncomfortable. She wanted Vichy water but they brought her Evian. Impatiently she stubbed out a cigarette she had not yet placed between her lips.

'Bonny,' he said, leaning on the open door of the little Peugeot. 'Oh, Bonny, if I could only make you happy!'

He is the kindest person I have ever known, she thought. He knows I love him; he knows I have been unable to help myself. This is kindness now, to speak of my happiness when it is his and Dorothy's that is at stake. They have had a little tiff this afternoon, but soon they will make it up. Tonight he will ask Dorothy to marry him, and after tomorrow I shall never in my life see either of them again. Dorothy'll be too busy and too full of happiness ever to return to the table-tennis club. There'll be the wedding preparations and then the honeymoon and then the return to Mara Hall.

'Look, Bonny,' he said, and in the sunlight sapphires sparkled. He had snapped open a little box; the slender band of gold that held the jewels lay on a tiny cushion. 'I bought it for her,' he said, 'three days after we met.'

'It's beautiful.' The words choked out of her. Tears misted her vision. She tried to smile but could not.

'I have to tell you that, Bonny. I have to tell you I bought it for Dorothy.'

She nodded bleakly.

'I might have offered it to Dorothy this afternoon. I could not, Bonny.'

Again she nodded, not understanding, trying to pretend she did.

'I can only love you, Bonny. I know that, if I know nothing
else in this world.'

'Me? *Me?*'

'Yes. Oh yes, my dear.'

His face was smiling down at her bewilderment. His lips
were parted. She heard herself saying she was nothing much,
while knowing she should not say that. She heard him laugh.

'Oh, but of course you are, my dear. You are everything in
this world to me. Darling, you are the sun and the stars, you
are the scent of summer jasmine. Can you understand that?'

She flushed and looked away, thinking of Dorothy and
feeling treacherous, and more confused than ever. She wanted
to laugh and cry all at once.

'Darling Bonny, you have the lips of an angel.'

His own touched the lips he spoke of. The gentle pressure
was like fire between them.

'Oh Blane, Blane,' she murmured.

'Say nothing, darling,' he whispered back, and in some
secret moment the sapphire ring found her engagement finger.

I would like to have married and had children. But Ernie
Chubbs, swearing to me that he took precautions, never did
so. In my association with him I had no fewer than four
abortions, the last of them in Idaho. I would not have children
now, they told me then. 'Sorry, girlie,' Ernie Chubbs said.
'Fancy a chilli con carne sent up?'

Crimson spread on denim. A hand that was crimson also
bounced back from the ceiling, dangled for an instant in the
air, fingers splayed. A screeching of terror was different from
the screams of pain. Even while it was happening you could
hear the difference.

'Twenty pound,' Mrs Trice said. 'That's what he give. He
likes a child, Mr Trice does. He got the dog for nothing.'
Rough type of people she said, to profit from a baby. 'You

bloody give it back,' I said to him, 'but they was gone by then. Fifty they ask, twenty he give.' Rum and Coca-Cola, Ernie asked for in the Al Fresco, a fiver a time. 'Easy money,' Mrs Trice said, lifting a slice of Dundee to her lips. 'Travelling people's always after easy money.'

'Lightning,' I said myself. 'The train was struck by lightning.'

The strength of the drugs was daily reduced; tranquillity receded little by little. At 21 Prince Albert Street I stirred milk in a saucepan, and Mrs Trice was furious because the milk burnt and milk cannot burn, apparently, while it is stirred. It was in the back-yard shed at 21 Prince Albert Street that the mangle was, and the kindling in the bath. It was in the back-yard shed that the man I took to be my father wept and said we mustn't tell, that good girls didn't. It was his face that was ravenous, not Ernie Chubbs's. Ernie loved me was what I thought.

Mr Trice possessed a smooth-haired fox terrier, a black and white dog of inordinate stupidity. With the chopping of kindling, washing up, and frying the breakfast, a task when I was nine was to exercise this animal, which refused to leave the confined space of the Trices' back-yard of its own accord. It would amble reluctantly behind me down Prince Albert Street and on the damp sand of the seashore. Seagulls would sniff it when I sat with my back against a breakwater and it stood obediently on the sand. They sometimes even poked at it with their beaks, but the dog displayed signs neither of alarm nor pleasure, seeming almost to be unaware of the seagulls' attention. When other dogs ran snarling up to it Mr Trice's pet stolidly sat there, unimpressed also by this display of hostility. If actually attacked, it would cringe unemotionally, tightly pressed to the ground, eyes closed, hackles undisturbed. 'A gentle creature,' Mr Trice would say if he had chosen to accompany me, which now and again, to my dismay, he did.

We would walk by the edge of the sea and Mr Trice would attempt to entice his pet towards the grey waves. But it always stubbornly resisted the temptation of the stones that were thrown and the whistles of encouragement that emanated from Mr Trice. 'It's a sign of intelligence,' he would remark in defeat. 'There's many a dog doesn't spot cold water before he's in it.' Mr Trice and I sat down by the breakwater and he always glanced over his shoulder before he put his arm around me to cuddle me. 'Tell your Daddy you love him,' he would urge, and I did as I was bidden, thinking it would be unobliging not to. Mr Trice would glance about him again. He would hold my hand and kiss the side of my forehead while the dog stood beside us, not seeming to know it would be restful to sit down also. The cuddles and the kisses were all Mr Trice ever went in for on the seashore. In the back-yard shed he took me on to his knee, and in the darkness of the Gaiety Cinema he kept a hand on my leg for all the time we were there, all the way through *Destry Rides Again* and *Stagecoach War*. It wasn't until later, when I was eleven, that Mr Trice took me into the bedroom when Mrs Trice was out at the laundry where she worked. He gave me a penny and I promised. People got the wrong end of the stick, he said.

Lying in that Italian hospital, I had no wish to dwell upon the uglier parts of my life yet could not prevent myself from doing so. In my fifty-sixth year, I had my beautiful house, and as I lay there that was where I endeavoured to see myself. But again my thoughts betrayed me. Wholly against my will, I was snagged in another kind of ugliness, keeping company with the tourists who over the years had gathered at my table. The mother and the nervous son, the homosexuals with Aids, the *ménage à trois* and all the others: so many tell-tale signs there were, in gesture or intonation. Long ago the mother had instilled fear in her son in order to keep him by her. The younger of the homosexuals had been unfaithful but was forgiven; both soon would die. The women who shared a lover had each settled for second best. In my dining-room or on the terrace Rosa Crevelli filled the tourists' wineglasses and offered them fruit or *dolce*. Wearily I rose from my table, drained by such human tragedy.

How joyfully then, how warmly, I kept company with pert Polly Darling or Annette St Claire! From pretty lips, or lips a little moist, poured whispers and murmurs and cries of simple delight. Dark hair framed another oval face, eyes were as blue as early-summer cornflowers. Often it was half-past three or four before I replaced the cover of my black Olympia. New light streaked the sky when I smoked, on the terrace, the last of the night's cigarettes. A lovely tiredness cried out for sleep.

They dabbed at my forehead. They bound the blood-pressure thing around my arm. They stuck in a thermometer. Their tweezers pulled out stitches.

'No harm in secrets,' Mr Trice said. 'No harm, eh?'

'No.'

After the third time he'd given me a penny I put the chair against my bedroom door, but it didn't do any good. So on the day before my sixteenth birthday I packed a brown card-board suitcase, and left five shillings in its place because the suitcase was Mrs Trice's and we'd been taught not to take things at Sunday school.

'Let's have a look at you,' the woman in the public house said. 'Have you served at table before?'

I never had, so they put me in the kitchen first, washing up the dishes. 'Gawky,' the woman said. 'God, you're a gawky girl.' My hair was frizzy, I couldn't keep my weight down, my clothes were bought in second-hand places mostly. Yet not much time went by before other men besides Mr Trice desired me and gave me presents.

*

'A timed device,' Quinty said.

'I thought it was lightning.'

'It was a timed device.'

'Where was it, Quinty? Near where I was?'

'It was close all right. The rest of the train was OK.'

'Is that why the police came?'

'That would be it.'

Early on in my hospital sojourn the *carabinieri* had been clustered round my bed. Their presence had interfered with my dreams and the confusion of my thoughts. Their dark blue uniforms trimmed with red and white, revolvers in black holsters, the grizzled head of one of them: all this remained with me after they had left my bedside, slipping in and out of my crowded fantasies. If conversation took place I do not recall it.

Later, in ordinary suits, detectives came with an interpreter. There were several visits, but soon it became clear from the detectives' demeanour they did not consider it likely that I, in particular, had been the target of the outrage, though they listened intently to their interpreter's rendering of my replies. A hundred times, it seems like now, they asked me if I had noticed anything unusual, either as I stepped on to the train or after I occupied my seat. Repeatedly I shook my head. I could recall no one skulking, no sudden turning away of a head, no hiding of a face. Each time, the detectives were patient and polite.

'*Buongiorno, signora. Grazie.*'

'Good day, lady,' the interpreter each time translated. 'Thank you.'

Carrozza 219 our carriage had been. I remembered the number on the ticket. Seat 11. In my mind's vision the faces of the people who'd been near me lingered: the American family, the lovers, the couple and their elderly relative. The fashion lady and the businessmen in lightweight suits had gone to lunch.

'They are here,' Quinty said, and glanced at me, and added: 'Some of them.'

Of the three English people, only the old man was alive. Of the German couple, only the boy. In the hospital they called the little American girl Aimée: the family passport had been found. She was the sole survivor of that family, and there was difficulty in locating someone in America to take re-sponsibility. It even seemed, so Quinty said at first, that such a person did not exist. The information that filtered through the *carabinieri* and the hospital staff appeared to indicate that there were grandparents somewhere, later that there was an aunt. Then we learnt that the child's grandfather suffered a heart condition and could not be told of the loss of his son, his daughter-in-law and a grandchild; the grandmother could not be told because she would not be able to hide her grief from him. Lying there, I approved of that: it was right that these people should be left in peace; it was only humane that elderly people should be permitted to drift out of life without this final nightmare to torment them.

'They're having difficulty in tracking down the aunt they're after,' Quinty reported. 'It seems she's travelling herself.'

She was in Germany or England, it was said, but the next day Quinty contradicted that. It was someone else who was travelling, a friend of the family who'd been assumed to be this relation. The aunt had been located.

'Unfortunately she can't look after a child.'

'Why not, Quinty?'

'It isn't said why not. Maybe she's delicate. Maybe she has work that keeps her on the go all over the place.'

I thought about this after he'd gone. I wondered what kind of a woman this could be, who, for whatever reason, could be so harsh.

'They got it all wrong again,' Quinty said on a later

occasion. 'That woman's the aunt of someone else. The same
story with those grandparents.'

I wouldn't have known any of this if Quinty hadn't been
interested in questioning the *carabinieri* on the matter. From
what I could gather, the policemen did not themselves appear
to know what was happening in the search – so far away – for
possible relatives or family friends. The hospital authorities
were worried because the child would not, or could not,
speak.

Apart from the victims of Carrozza 219 no one on the train
had been injured, and no one of political importance had been
on the train in any case. The old man's son-in-law had had
something to do with a merchant bank apparently; the American father had been a paediatrician. Yet a bomb had been
planted, deliberately to take life, ingeniously and callously
placed where those who by chance had been allocated certain
seats would be killed or maimed.

What would one see, I wondered, in the perpetrators' eyes?
What monstrous nature did such human beings seek to
disguise? There'd been crime, often more than petty, on the
S.S. *Hamburg*. Living human embryos had been scraped out
of my body and dropped into waste-disposal buckets. Seedy
confessions had surfaced in the Café Rose. An ugly guilt had
skittered about in the shifty eyes of Ernie Chubbs. Yet no
crime could rank with what had happened on the train I'd
caught at 11.45 on the morning of 5 May 1987. In search of
consolation, I wrote down the few lines I had composed in
Carrozza 219, the beginning of the work which had come to
me through its title. *In the garden the geraniums were in
flower. Through scented twilight the girl in the white dress
walked with a step as light as a morning cobweb. That evening
she hadn't a care in the world.* But I found it difficult to
continue and did my best, instead, simply to recover.

The old man and I suffered from shock. I'd had splinters of glass taken from the left side of my face; he from his legs and body. The German boy, called Otmar, had lost an arm. The old man was a general.

'An irony,' he murmured in the corridor where he learned to walk again. 'It was I who'd reached the end of things.'

He made the statement without emotion. I remembered his daughter as a pretty woman in a gentle, English kind of way, quiet and rather slight, a little faded. Aries probably.

'We are fortunate to be alive, General.'

He turned away his head, half shaking it as he did so. I told him about the child called Aimée, about the search for relatives in America. I hoped to involve him in the pathos of the child's predicament and perhaps to make him realize that someone else had lost even more than he had. He did his best to respond, later even to smile. With military stoicism he appeared to be resigned to what had occurred, his vocation no doubt demanding that. A sense of melancholy did not come from him, only one of weariness. I left him soldiering on, precisely obeying the nurses' strictures, marching with the aid of a metal stick, back and forth between his bed and a cur-tained balcony at the corridor's end.

'I'm sorry, Otmar,' I commiserated, and in a soft whisper, speaking quite good English, the German boy accepted the sympathy: that it was offered because of the loss of his sweet-heart or a limb was barely relevant. In the train he had been wearing a red and yellow lumberjack shirt and rather large glasses, which were shattered in the blast. He wore other spectacles now, wire-rimmed, and jeans and a plain grey shirt. His features were sallow, the eyes behind the magnifying lenses still terrified. Unlike the General, he did not attempt to smile. There was a cornered look about Otmar, as if the horror he had woken up to was too much for him.

'We must hope, Otmar. What there is left to us is hope.'

Every time I returned to my own room, and to the ward when I was a little better, I endeavoured to proceed with my new work, but still I found it difficult to continue. This had never happened before: with reason, I had been confident on the train as soon as the girl appeared in my mind's vision. Yet now it seemed as though a film had halted within seconds of its commencement. The fluttering of the girl's dress was frozen, her carefree mood arrested in a random instant. Was there some companion of whom my broken cinematograph held the secret, some figure waiting to step from the garden's shadows? Would the carefree mood become ecstatic? Would a gardenia nestle in the long fair hair? I did not know. I knew neither what joy nor sorrow there was; my girl was nameless, without detail in her life, vague as to parentage, born beneath a choice of all the stars. The title *Ceaseless Tears* appeared so naturally to belong to the suffering on the train that greater bewilderment, and blankness, was engendered. I was aware of a sensation that caused me to shiver in dismay, as though all that had been given to me had been snatched away. Then one day Quinty said:

'They could stay a while in the house, you know.'

A week ago the General had murmured that he would find the return to England difficult, and wished he did not have to face it immediately. 'The struggle back and forth,' he said. 'The bed, the corridor, the holy statue in the wall, the balcony. The faces of the patients, the smell of ether. You feel that's where you belong.'

Quinty was clearly out to profit from misfortune, but even so I saw nothing to object to in his suggestion. 'You would find it peaceful,' I told the old man. 'My house is high enough to be cool. Sometimes a breeze blows over the water of Lake Trasimeno.'

He nodded, and then he thanked me. When he sought me out two days later I explained that we were used to catering for strangers, that for many years we had taken in passing tourists when the hotels of the neighbourhood were full.

'I would insist on paying,' he gently laid down. 'I told the man I would insist on paying whatever rates you normally charge.'

'It is he who sees to all that.'

I'd known army officers of lower rank before; never a general. He had the look of one, sparely made, his hair the colour of iron, great firmness about the mouth, a grey moustache. He was a man of presence, but of course he was not young: touching seventy, I guessed.

'A week or two,' he agreed with unemphatic graciousness. 'That would be nice. But are you certain, Mrs Delahunty? I don't want to be a nuisance at a time like this.'

'Indeed I'm certain.'

Otmar refused at first. Poor boy, with every day that passed he seemed more wretchedly unhappy and I sensed that, even more than the General, he did not know how to return to the world he was familiar with.

'You are most good.' His voice echoed the distortion in his eyes. Often, in speaking to him, I found myself obliged to turn my head away. 'But it should not be. I have not money to pay this.'

Quinty cannot have known that, and I resolved, if necessary, to pay for Otmar's stay myself. I said the money didn't matter. Some time in the future, when everything had calmed for him, he could pay a little. 'If you would care to, Otmar, the house is there.'

The doctor who looked after the American child was a Dr Innocenti, a small, brown-complexioned man with gold in his teeth. He was the English-speaking one among the doctors and the nurses, and had often acted as interpreter for the specialists who were more directly concerned with the General and Otmar and myself. When he heard that hospitality had been offered in my house he came to see me and to thank me.

'It will do some good,' he said. 'I would prescribe it.'

He wore a pale brown suit and a silk tie, striped red and green. When I said the child also would be welcome in my house he doubtfully shook his head. The *carabinieri* would have to be consulted, he explained, since the child – being at present without a guardian – was in their charge. 'In Italy we must always be patient,' he said. 'But truly I would wish the little girl removed from the hospital ambience.'

'Is she recovering, doctor?'

In reply the little shoulders were raised within the well-cut suit. The hands gesticulated, the nut-brown head sloped this way and then that.

'Slowly?' I prompted.

Too slowly, a contortion of the neat features indicated: it was not easy. At present the prognosis was not good.

'The child is more than welcome if you believe it would be a help.'

'So Signor Quinty explain to me. There is nowhere else, you comprehend.' He spoke gently. His jet-black eyes were as soft as a kitten's. Piscean, I guessed. 'I will speak with the officers of the *carabinieri*. Red tape may be cut, after all. To be surrounded by people whose language she understands will be advantageous for Aimée.'

Later I learnt he'd been successful in persuading the *carabinieri* to agree to his wishes. They would visit us two or three times a week to satisfy themselves that the child remained safely in our care, and report their satisfaction to the American authorities. Dr Innocenti himself would also visit us regularly; if there were signs of deterioration in the child she would be at once returned to the hospital. But he believed that the clinical surroundings were keeping the tragedy fresh in her mind and preventing her from coming to terms with it.

'You are generous, signora. I have explained to Signor Quinty the expenses will be paid when the person they seek in

America is found. My friends of the *carabinieri* have reason to believe that this is not a poor family.'

We were all discharged on the same afternoon and the first night in my house we sat around the tiled table on the terrace, the General on my right, Otmar on my other side. The child was already sleeping in her bed.

Rosa Crevelli brought us lasagne, and lamb with rosemary, and the Vino Nobile of Montepulciano, and peaches. A stranger would have been surprised to see us, with our bandages and plaster, the walking wounded at table. I was the only one who had not lost a loved one, having none to lose. As I dwelt upon that, the title that had come to me floated through my consciousness, golden letters on a stark black ground. I saw again a girl in white passing through a garden, and again the image froze.

3

Miss Alzapiedi, our Sunday-school teacher, was excessively tall and lanky, with hair that was a nuisance to her, and other disadvantages too. It was she who gave me the picture of Jesus on a donkey to hang above my bed; it was she who taught me how to pray, pointing out that some people are drawn to prayer, some are not. 'Pray for love,' Miss Alzapiedi adjured. 'Pray for protection.'

So before I ran away from 21 Prince Albert Street I prayed for protection because I knew I'd need it. I prayed for protection when I worked in the public-house dining-room and the shoe shop and on the S.S. *Hamburg*, and when Ernie Chubbs took me to Idaho, and later when he abandoned me in Ombubu. Even though I was trying to be a sophisticate it didn't embarrass me to get down on my knees the way Miss Alzapiedi had taught us, even if there was a visitor in the room. To be honest, I don't get down on my knees any more. I pray standing up now, or sitting, and I don't whisper either; I do it in my mind.

At the end of my first year in this house I finished *Precious September*. I wrote it just for fun, to pass the time. When it was complete I put it in a drawer and began another story, which this time I called *Flight to Enchantment*. Then glancing one day through the belongings of a tourist who was staying here, I came across a romance that seemed no better than my own. I noted the publisher's address and later wrapped

Precious September up and posted it to England. So many months passed without a response that I imagined the parcel had gone astray or that the publisher was no longer in business. Then, when I had given up all hope of ever seeing my manuscript again, it was returned. *We have no use for material of this nature*, a printed note brusquely declared. I knew of no other publisher, so I continued with *Flight to Enchantment* and after a month or so dispatched it in the same direction. This elicited a note to the effect that the work would only be returned to me if I forwarded a money order to cover the postage. When that wound had healed I completed another story quite quickly and although it, too, was similarly rejected I did not lose heart. There was, after all, consolation to be found in the tapestries I so very privately stitched. They came out of nothing, literally out of emptiness. Even then I marvelled over that.

We are interested in your novelette. I found it hard to believe that I was reading this simple typewritten statement, that I was not asleep and dreaming. The letter, which was brief, was signed *J. A. Makers*, and I at once responded, impatient to receive what this Makers called 'our reader's suggestions for introducing a little more thrust into the plot'. These arrived within a fortnight, a long page of ideas, all of which I most willingly incorporated. Eventually I received from J. A. Makers an effusively complimentary letter. By now many others among his employees had read the work; all, without exception, were overwhelmed. *We foretell a profitable relationship,* Mr Makers concluded, foretelling correctly. But when I received, after I'd submitted the next title, a list of 'our reader's suggestions' I tore it up and have never been bothered in that way since. That story was *Behold My Heart!* Its predecessors, so disdainfully rejected once, were published in rapid succession.

Something of all this, in order to keep a conversation going,

I passed on to the General. I knew that conversation was what he needed; otherwise I would have been happy to leave him in peace. I wanted to create a little introduction, as it were, so that I might ask him to tell me about his own life.

'If you would like to,' I gently added.

He did not at once reply. His gnarled grey head had fallen low between his shoulders. The *Daily Telegraph* which Quinty had bought for him was open on his knees. My eye caught gruesome headlines. A baby had been taken from its pram outside a shop and buried in nearby woods. A dentist had taken advantage of his women patients. A bishop was in some other trouble.

'It sometimes helps to talk a bit.'

'Eh?'

'Only if you'd like to.'

Again there was a silence. I imagined him in his heyday, leading his men in battle. I calculated that the Second World War would have been his time. I saw him in the desert, a young fox who was now an old one.

'You're on your own, General?'

'Since my wife died.'

His eyes passed over the unpleasant headlines in the newspaper. There was something about a handful of jam thrown at the prime minister.

'Things were to change when we returned,' he said.

I smiled encouragingly. I did not say a word.

'I was to live with my daughter and her husband in Hampshire.'

He was away then, and I could feel it doing him good. Only one child had been born to him, the daughter he spoke of, that faded prettiness on the train. 'Don't go spoiling her,' his wife had pleaded, and he told me of a day when his daughter, at six or seven, had fallen out of a tree. He'd lifted her himself into the dining-room and covered her with a rug on the sofa.

She'd been no weight at all. 'This is Digby,' she introduced years later while they stood, all four of them drinking gin and French, beneath that very same tree.

'I couldn't like him,' he confessed, his voice gruff beneath the shame induced by death. I remembered the trio's politeness on the train, the feeling of constraint, of something hidden. I waited patiently while he rummaged among his thoughts and when he spoke again the gruffness was still there. If the outrage hadn't occurred he would have continued to keep his own counsel concerning the man his daughter had married: you could tell that easily.

He spoke fondly of his wife. When she died there'd been a feeling of relief because the pain was over for her. Her departure from him was part of his existence now, a fact like an appendix scar. When I looked away, and banished from my mind the spare old body that carried in it somewhere an elusive chip of shrapnel, I saw, in sunshine on a shorn lawn, a medal pinned on a young man's tunic and a girl's arms around a soldier's neck. 'Oh, yes! Oh, yes!' she eagerly agreed when marriage was proposed, her tears of happiness staining the leather of a shoulder strap. You could search for ever for a nicer man, she privately reflected: I guessed that easily also.

'No, I never liked him and my wife was cross with me for that. She was a better mother than I ever was a father.'

Again the silence. Had he perished in the outrage he would have rated an obituary of reasonable length in the English newspapers. His wife, no doubt, had passed on without a trace of such attention; his daughter and his son-in-law too.

'I doubted if I could live with him. But I kept that to myself.'

'A trial run, your holiday? Was that it?'

'Perhaps so.'

I smiled and did not press him. Jealousy, he supposed it was. More than ever on this holiday he had noticed it – in *pensiones* and churches and art galleries, permeating every conversation. No children had been born to his daughter, he revealed; his wife had regretted that, he hadn't himself.

'Have you finished with the *Telegraph*, sir?' Quinty hovered, not wishing to pick up the newspaper from the old man's knees. Rosa Crevelli set out the contents of a tea-tray.

'Yes, I've finished with it.'

'Then I'll take it to the kitchen, sir, if I may. There's nothing I like better than an hour with the *Telegraph* in the cool of the evening. When the dinner's all been and done with, the *Telegraph* goes down a treat.'

A glass of lemon tea, on a saucer, was placed on a table within the General's reach. Rosa Crevelli picked up her tray. Quinty still hovered. Nothing could stop him now.

'I mention it, sir, so that if you require the paper you would know where it is.'

The General acknowledged this. Quinty softly coughed. He inquired:

'Do you follow the cricket at all, sir?'

The General shook his head. But noticing that Quinty waited expectantly for a verbal response, he courteously added that cricket had never greatly interested him.

'Myself, I follow all sport, sir. There is no sport I do not take an interest in. Ice-hockey. Baseball. Lacrosse, both men's and women's. I have watched the racing of canoes.'

The General sipped his tea. There were little biscuits, *ricciarelli*, on a plate. Quinty offered them. He mentioned the game of *boules*, and again the racing of canoes. I made a sign at him, endeavouring to communicate that his playfulness, though harmless, was out of place in an atmosphere of mourning. He took no notice of my gesture.

'To tell you the truth, sir, I'm an armchair observer myself. I never played a ball-game. Cards was as far as I got.'

Quinty's smile is a twisted little thing, and he was smiling now. Was he aware that the reference to cards would trigger a memory – the Englishmen, and he himself, playing poker at the corner table of the Café Rose? Impossible to tell.

'I'm afraid he's a law unto himself,' I explained as lightly as I could when he had left the room. A tourist had once asked me if Quinty had a screw loose, and for all I knew the General was wondering the same thing, too polite to put it into words. By way of further explanation I might have touched upon Quinty's unfortunate life, how he had passed himself off as the manager of a meat-extract factory in order to impress an au pair girl. I might have told how he'd been left on the roadside a few kilometres outside the town of Modena, how later he'd turned up in Ombubu. I might even have confessed that I'd once felt so sorry for Quinty I'd taken him into my arms and stroked his head.

'It's just his way,' I said instead, and in a moment Quinty returned and asked me if he should pour me a g and t, keeping his voice low, as if some naughtiness were afoot. He didn't wait for my response but poured the drink as he stood there. Half a child and half a rogue, as I have said before.

Deep within what seemed like plumage, a mass of creatures darted. Their heads were the heads of human beings, their hands and feet misshapen. There was frenzy in their movement, as though they struggled against the landscape they belonged to, that forest of pale quills and silky foliage.

For a week I watched with trepidation while the child created this world that was her own. Signora Bardini had bought her crayons when we noticed she'd begun to draw, and then, with colour, everything came startlingly alive. Mouths retched. Eyes stared distractedly. Cats, as thin as razors, scavenged among human entrails; the flesh was plucked from dogs and horses. Birds lay in their own blood; rabbits were devoured by maggots.

Sometimes the child looked up from her task, and even slightly smiled, as though the unease belonged to her pictures, not to her. Her silence continued.

In her lifetime Otmar's mother had made lace. He told me about that, his remaining fingers forever caressing whatever surface there was. His mother had found it a restful occupation, her concentration lost in the intricacies of a pattern. He spoke a lot about his mother. He described a dimly lit house in a German suburb, where the furniture loomed heavily and there was waxen fruit on a sideboard dish. Listening to his awkward voice, I heard as well the clock ticking in the curtained dining-room, the clock itself flanked by two bronze horsemen. Schweinsbrust was served, and good wine of the Rhine. '*Guten Appetit!*' Otmar's father exclaimed. How I, at Otmar's age, would have loved the house and the family he spoke of, apfelstrudel by a winter fireside!

'Madeleine,' Otmar said, speaking now of the girl who had died in the outrage. I told him she had reminded me of a famous actress, Lilli Palmer, perhaps before his time. I recollected, as I spoke, the scratchy copy of *Beware of Pity* that had arrived in Ombubu in the 1960s, the film seeming dated and old-fashioned by then.

'Madeleine, too, was Jewish,' Otmar said, and I realized I'd been wrong to assume the film actress was not known to him.

They'd been on their way from Orvieto to Milan. Otmar was to continue by train to Germany, Madeleine to fly from Linata Airport to Israel, where her parents were. For weeks they'd talked about that, about whether or not she should seek her father's permission to marry. If he gave it he might also give them money to help them on their way, even though Otmar was not Jewish himself, which would be a disappointment. 'When the day comes you wish to marry you must seek his permission,' her mother had warned Madeleine years ago. 'Otherwise he will be harsh.' Her father had left Germany for Jerusalèm five years ago, offering his wealth and his business acumen to the land he regarded as his spiritual home. Madeleine had never been there, but when she wrote to say she wished to visit her family her father sent a banker's draft, its generosity reflecting his pleasure. 'So we afford the expensive train,' Otmar explained. 'Otherwise it would be to hitchhike.'

I did not say anything. I did not say that surely it would have been more sensible to travel to Rome to catch a plane, since Rome is closer to Orvieto than Milan is. I was reminded of the General revealing to me that he and his daughter and son-in-law had originally intended to travel the day before, and of the businessmen and the fashion woman going to the dining-car. Otmar went on talking, about the girl and the days before the outrage, the waiting for the banker's draft and its arrival. In August they would have married.

'The kraut hasn't any money,' Quinty said in his joky way. 'He's having us on.'

'He told me he hadn't any money. I'll pay what's owing.'

'You're not running a charity, don't forget.'

'I'm sorry for these people.'

I might have reminded Quinty that once I'd been sorry for him too. I might have reminded him that I had been sorry for Rosa Crevelli when first she came to my house, ill-nourished and thin as fuse-wire, her fingernails all broken. I'd been sorry for the cat that came wandering in.

'You'll get your reward in heaven,' Quinty said.

That summer I opened my eyes at a quarter past five every morning and wished there were birds to listen to, but the summer was too far advanced. Dawn is bleak without the chittering of birds; and perhaps because of it I began, at that particular time, to wonder again about the perpetrators. No political group had claimed responsibility, and the police were considering a theory that we had possibly been the victims of a lunatic. Naturally I endeavoured to imagine this wretched individual, protected now by a mother who had always believed that one day he would commit an unthinkable crime, or even by a wife who could not turn her back on him. What kind of lunatic, or devil? I wondered. What form of mental sickness, or malignancy, orders the death of strangers on a train? In the early morning I took my pick of murderers – the crazed, the cruel, the embittered, the tormented, the despised, the vengeful. Was it already a joke somewhere that six were dead and four maimed, that a child had been left an orphan, her own self taken from her too? The cuts on my face and body would heal and scarcely leave a scar: I'd been assured of that, and did not doubt it. But in other ways neither I nor any of the others had recovered and I wondered if we ever would. The ceaseless tears of my title mocked me now; still understanding nothing, I felt defeated.

We were in a nowhere land in my house: there was a sense of waiting without knowing in the least what we were waiting for. Grief, pain, distress, long silences, the still shadows of death, our private nightmares: all that was what we shared without words, without sharing's consolation. Ghosts you might have called us had you visited my house in Umbria that summer.

The police came regularly. Two *carabinieri* remained outside by the police car while the detectives asked their questions and showed us photographs of suspects. Signora Bardini carried out iced tea to the uniformed men. Every day Dr Innocenti spent some time with the child, his presence so quiet in the house that often we didn't notice he was there. Time, he always said – we must have faith in time.

In my private room I opened the glass-faced cabinet where my titles are arranged, and displayed for Aimée the pleasantly colourful jackets in the hope that they'd influence the hours she spent with her crayons. Obediently she examined the illustrations and even nodded over them. She opened one or two of the books themselves, and appeared briefly to read what was written. But still she did not speak, and when she returned to her room it was to complete a picture full of horrors even more arresting than the previous ones. 'The appetite is good,' Dr Innocenti soothingly pointed out, and appeared to take some heart from that.

One night there was at least a development. A telephone call came from the American official who had several times visited the hospital in connection with the child's orphaning. He informed Quinty that a brother of Aimée's mother had been located in America. This time there was no mistake. Dr Innocenti had already spoken to the man.

'Isn't that good news?' I remarked to the General the following morning while we were breakfasting on the terrace.

'News? I beg your pardon?'

'They've found Aimée's uncle.'

'Oh.'

'Riversmith the name is.'

'There was a Riversmith at school.'

'This one's an American.'

The General was fond of the child; I had watched him becoming so. But he had difficulty in concentrating on the discovery of an uncle, and with hindsight I can see he didn't even want to think about this man. The conversation drifted about, edging away from the subject I had raised. He spoke of the Cotswold village near the boarding-school he'd mentioned, the warm brown stones, the little flower gardens. He and his friends could walk to the outskirts of the village, where a woman – a Mrs Patch – would give them tea in her small dining-room, charging sixpence for a table which seated four. Mrs Patch made lettuce sandwiches, and honey sandwiches, and sardine sandwiches; and there were hot currant scones on which the butter melted, and banana cake with chocolate filling, and as much tea as you wanted. It was a tradition, the walk to the village, the small dining-room of the cottage, the sixpenny piece placed on the tablecloth, and Mrs Patch saying she had sons of her own, now grown up. If you paid more – a shilling for a table for four – and if you gave her warning well in advance, Mrs Patch would cook fish.

These memories of time past were delivered in a tone that did not vary much. Jobson played the organ in the chapel. He played the voluntary while everyone stood in long pews, parallel to the aisle, waiting for the masters to process to their places behind the choir. Handel or Bach would thunder to a climax and then there'd be a fidgeting silence before the headmaster led the way. Sometimes, afterwards, Jobson revealed the errors he had made, but no one had noticed because Jobson was skilful at disguising his errors even as he made them. Jobson and the General had been friends from the moment they met, their first night in the Junior Dormitory.

Odd, I reflected as I listened, how an old man's memory operates in distress! Odd, the flotsam that has been caught and surfaces to assist him: the mustiness of Mrs Patch's dining-room, a prefect's voice, a mug dipped into a communal pail of milk. Housemasters – six older men – sprawled in splendour in the Chapel, a chin held in a hand, an arm thrown back, black gowns draping their crossed legs. While he spoke, the old man's gaze remained fixed on the distant hills. Remembered bells had different sounds: the Chapel bell, the School bell, the night-time bell. A conjuror came once and performed with rabbits and with birds. Boys smoked behind a gymnasium. Rules were broken, but no one stole. Owning up was taken for granted, and if you were caught you did not lie. At that school, modestly set in undemanding landscape, he said he'd learned what honour was. Again there was his effort at a smile, more successful now than in the hospital.

'Crewe and McMichael are being a nuisance,' he confided a little later, and for a moment I imagined the two he spoke of were boys, like Jobson, at the school. In all four of us bewilderment easily became confusion.

In fact, he referred to solicitors. Crewe and McMichael were his: Johnston Johnson his son-in-law's. Both firms had written to him. Having offered their commiserations, they turned now to wills and property, to affairs being tidied up, legalities of one kind or another. Soothingly, I said:

'They see it as their duty, I suppose.'

He nodded, half resigned to that, half questioning such duty. He spoke of the empty house in Hampshire and of his daughter's effects: he was the inheritor of both. He did not say so but I knew he dreaded going from room to room, opening drawers and cabinets. Pieces of jewellery had been named, to be given to the children of friends. A letter from one of the solicitors stated in a pernickety way that there might well be doubt as to which article was which. There were the son-in-law's belongings also, his collection of Chinese postage stamps, his photographs. There were the clothes of both of them, and books and records. *Articles of a personal nature,* the same solicitor had written. *We shall in the fullness of time need to take instruction regarding all these matters.*

'A friend of your daughter would sort the stuff out, you know.'

He said he didn't want to shirk what was expected of him. And yet I knew – for it was there in his face – that his soldier's courage faltered, probably for the first time in his life. He could not bear to see those clothes again, nor the house in Hampshire where he might now be living with his daughter and the man he hadn't cared for. How petty that small aversion seemed to him in retrospect! How petty not to have come to terms with a foible! His gaze slipped from the far-off hills; tired eyes, expressionless, were directed toward mine. Had his heart been full of that dislike as he fiddled with his watch in Carrozza 219? Had it nagged at him even while death occurred?

'Oh, my God,' he whispered, without emotion.

Tears were repressed, lost somewhere in that sudden exclamation. His grasp on consolation weakened, the Memory Lane of boyhood was useless dust. I reached for his hand, took it in both of mine, and held it. In that moment I would have given him whatever he asked of me.

'No one can help disliking a person.' I whispered also. 'Don't dwell on it.'

'All these years she must have guessed. All these years I hurt her.'

'Your daughter looked far too sensible to be hurt when it wasn't meant.'

'I couldn't stand his laugh.'

I imagined his wife standing up for their son-in-law, saying he wasn't bad, saying what was important was their daughter's happiness. How could it possibly matter that a laugh was irritating? 'Now, you behave yourself': her reprimand was firm, though never coming crossly from her. She managed people well.

'No, it wasn't meant,' he said. He slipped his hand away, but I knew he had experienced the comfort I intended. His voice had calmed. He was less huddled; even sitting down, his military bearing had returned.

'I wish they'd just dispose of everything,' he said with greater spirit.

'Well, perhaps they will.'

I smiled at him again. He needed an excuse, a cover for what he saw as cowardice. 'When in distress, pretend, my dear,' Lady Daysmith pronounces in *Precious September*, and I pretended now, suggesting that his reluctance to return to England was perhaps because England was so very different from the country it had been in his Cotswold days. Tourists I'd talked to complained of violence in the streets, and derelict cities, and greed. Jack-booted policemen scowled from motor-cycles. In television advertisements there was a fashion for coarsely-spoken people, often appearing to be mentally afflicted. The back windows of motor-cars were decorated with snappy obscenities.

'I never noticed.' His interest was only momentarily held. He rarely watched the television, he confessed.

'Oh, I've been assured. Not once but many times. Corner-boys rule the roost in England's green and pleasant land. The Royals sell cheese for profit.'

Pursuing the diversion, I threw in that Ernie Chubbs had managed to get the royal warrant on the sanitary-ware he sold, that there'd been a bit of a fuss when it was discovered he was using it without authority. The General nodded, but I knew I'd lost him: in their grey offices the solicitors were already droning at him through pursed solicitors' lips. He stood forlorn among old books and box-files and sealed documents in out-trays. A lifetime's bravery oozed finally away to nothing.

'General, you're welcome to remain here for as long as you feel like it. You're not alone in this, you know.'

'That's a great kindness, Mrs Delahunty.' The beaten head was raised; again, blank eyes stared deeply into mine. 'Thank you so much,' the General said.

A conversation with Otmar was similar in a way. In the *salotto* I had just lit a cigarette when he entered and in his self-effacing way slipped into an armchair by the tall, wide-open french windows. I smiled at him. 'An uncle of Aimée's has been found,' I said. 'Isn't that good news at last?'

'Oh, *ja.*'

He nodded several times.

'*Ja,*' he said again.

I didn't press; I didn't try to draw enthusiasm from him. But the fact was that someone would love Aimée now; and in time Aimée herself would love. I didn't say to Otmar that there has to be love in a person's life, that no one can do without either receiving it or giving it. I didn't say that love, as much as a daughter and a girlfriend, had been taken away. I didn't say that love expired for me on a Wall of Death. 'They killed themselves in the end,' Mrs Trice callously replied when I asked. 'Stands to reason with a dangerous game like that.' A thousand times I have mourned the passing of the people who abandoned me, the motor-cycle skittering over the edge, smashing through the inadequate protection of a wooden rail. To this day, the woman's arm is still triumphantly raised in a salute. A red handkerchief still flies from her mouth, and the machine races on to nowhere.

'Where did you learn your English, Otmar?' I asked the question when I had poured the boy his coffee. I watched him awkwardly breaking a brioche.

'I learn in school. I was never in England or America.'

A finger ran back and forth on the edge of the saucer beneath his coffee cup. Once Madeleine had been in England, he said, working in some relation's business in Bournemouth. 'Silk scarves. At first she is in the factory, then later in the selling.'

For a moment it seemed he made an effort, as the General had, to contain his tears: his eyes evaded mine when he spoke of Madeleine. He dipped his brioche into his coffee and I watched him eating it. In answer to another question he said he'd had hopes of becoming a journalist. It was in this connection that he and Madeleine made the journey to Italy – because he'd heard so much about the murderer of lovers who was known in Florence as the Beast. The murders took place at night when couples made love in parked cars. Otmar had a theory about it and wanted to write an article in the hope that a Munich newspaper would print it. Following a lead, they travelled down to Orvieto and it was there they'd decided to get married, even though Otmar was penniless. It was in Orvieto that Madeleine had telephoned her father in Jerusalem.

'A cigarette?'

He took one and politely thanked me. It was the right arm that was gone. The coffee cup in his left hand, now placed on the table, was still unnatural. I smiled to make him feel a little more at ease. I lit my own cigarette and his, and as I did so my fingers brushed the back of his hand. I said:

'How did you meet her?'

'In a supermarket.'

She'd been reaching for a packet of herbs and had upset some jars of mustard. He had helped her to replace them, and later at the checkout they found themselves together again. 'Come and have a coffee,' he invited, and they walked through the car park and across a street to a café. I was reminded of the encounter in *Petals of a Summer*, but naturally I kept that to myself.

'These are good cigarettes,' Otmar remarked, rising as he spoke. 'I must walk now,' he said, and left me to my thoughts.

Such a romance had never occurred in Madeleine's life before. I imagined her saying that to herself as they strolled together to the café, he politely carrying the plastic bag that contained her supermarket groceries. In the café he confessed he'd seen her on previous occasions, that he had often seen her. He had bided his time, he confessed, and spoke with passion of her pretty features – how they had come into his dreams, how he had wondered about her voice. 'Oh, I'm not pretty in the very least,' she protested, but he took no notice. He said he was in love with her, using the word that had so endlessly been on the lips of the Austrian ivory cutter. '*Liebe,*'

Otmar repeated as they passed again through the car park. '*Liebe.*'

Madeleine could not sleep that night. She tossed and turned until the dawn. If there could be a pretence about her prettiness there could be none about his. He was not handsome, even a little ugly, she considered. Yet none of it mattered. Never before had she experienced such intense protestations, not just of love, but of adoration.

'*O Otmar, ich liebe dich,*' Madeleine said exactly a month later.

When Dr Innocenti came the next time he complimented Aimée on her latest drawings and then drew me aside. He spoke of her uncle, a professor of some kind apparently. Their conversation on the telephone had been a lengthy one.

'I have urged *il professore* that this tranquillity in your house should be maintained for a while longer. That she should not yet be returned to the United States.'

'Of course.'

'For the moment I oppose so long a journey for the child.' He paused. 'For you, signora, is inconvenient?'

'Aimée is more than welcome here.'

'You are generous, signora.'

'Doctor, what do you believe happened?'

'How, signora?'

'What was the reason for this crime? The police still come here.'

He shrugged in his expressive way, eyebrows and lips moving with his shoulders, his palms spread in a question mark.

'They still come because still they do not know.' The shrug went on. 'No one takes the blame.'

'There must be a reason for such an act. Somewhere there must be.'

'Signora, it is on all occasions the policy of our *carabinieri* to preserve a silence. They have the intention to entice forward some amateur tormented by their game.'

'Or a lunatic. I've heard that mentioned.'

'A clever lunatic, signora. A package that belongs to no one among the passengers placed on to a luggage rack. Terrorists, not lunatics, I think we guess.'

'But which one of us were they seeking to kill? These are just ordinary people.'

'Signora, which one did they seek to kill at Bologna? Angela Fresu, aged three?'

4

For the first time since the outrage I walked again in the early morning, on the roads that now and again turn into dusty-white tracks, among the olive shrubs and the broom. The line of the hills in the distance was softened by a haze that drained the sky of colour. Tiny clouds, like skilful touches in a painting, stayed motionless above the umbrella pines and cypresses that claim this landscape for Umbria.

I wondered about the American professor. As a name, River-smith had a ring to it, but it told me nothing else. Its bearer was the brother of the dimpled, fair-haired woman on the train, which suggested a man in his thirties. When I thought about him, his face became like hers.

'*Buongiorno, signora!*' an old woman with a stack of wood on her back greeted me. Further on, her husband was cutting the grass of the verge with a hook. You don't meet many on the white roads; sometimes a young man rides by on an auto-cycle; in autumn the harvesters come for the grapes, in November for the olives. It was pleasant to walk there again.

'*Buongiorno, signora!*' I called back. Once I made a terrible mistake in Sunday school when giving an answer to a question, saying that Joseph was God. Someone began to titter and I could feel myself going red with embarrassment, but Miss Alzapiedi said no, that was an error anyone could make. Miss Alzapiedi's long chest was as flat as a table-top. Summer or winter, she never wore stockings, her white, bony ankles exposed to all weathers. It seemed a natural confusion to say that Joseph was God, Joseph being Jesus's father and God being the Father also. 'Of course.' Miss Alzapiedi nodded, and the tittering ceased.

I dare say remembering Sunday school was much the same as the General having tea in Mrs Patch's cottage and Otmar recalling the comfort of his parents' house. It was a way of coming to terms, of finding something to cling to in the muddle; I dare say it's natural that people would. In all my time at Miss Alzapiedi's Sunday school there was only that one uneasy moment, before Miss Alzapiedi stepped in with kindness. Otmar similarly recalled being reprimanded because he'd over-turned a tin of paint when the decorators came to paint the staircase wall and the hall, and again when he stole a pear from the sideboard dish. There was a moment of embarrass-ment in the dormitory the old man had spoken of, with its rows of blue-blanketed beds and little boys in pyjamas. But these instances, dreadful at the time, were pleasant memories now.

'And they spread out palms before the donkey's feet,' Miss Alzapiedi said, and while she spoke you could easily see the figure of Jesus in his robes, with his long hair and his beard. The donkey was a sacred animal. 'You have only to note the cross on every donkey's back,' Miss Alzapiedi said. 'All your lives please note the black cross on that holy creature.'

The General had led his men to the battle-fronts of the world but always he'd returned to the girl he'd proposed to on a sunlit lawn, whose tears of joy had stained the leather of his uniform. He had not looked at other women. Amid the banter and camaraderie of the barracks his desires had never wandered, not even once, not even in the heat of the desert with the promise of desert women only a day or two away. His happy marriage was written in the geography of the old man's face, a simple statement: that for nearly a lifetime two people had been as one.

'Isn't that much better?' Otmar's mother said the first time

he wore spectacles, when a world of blurred objects and drifting colours acquired precision. In the oculist's room he
couldn't read the letters on the charts. The oculist had spectacles, too, and little red marks on the fat of his face, the
left-hand side, close to the nose. When Otmar asked his mother
if he'd always have to wear the spectacles now she nodded,
and the oculist nodded also. When the oculist smiled his white
teeth glistened. The mother's coat was made of fur.

It was Mary who began the business about donkeys, riding
on one all the way to the stable of the inn. Joseph walked
beside her, guiding the donkey's head, thinking about car-
pentry matters. Mary understood the conversation of angels.
Joseph sawed wood and planed it smooth. He made doors
and boxes and undertook repairs. To this day I can see
Joseph's sandals and Jesus's bare feet, and the women washing
them. To this day I can see Jesus on the holy donkey in the
picture above my bed.

'Fragments make up a life, my dear,' Lady Daysmith says in
Precious September. For the General, bodies lie where they
have fallen on the sand, sunburnt flesh stiffening, soldiers
from Rochester and Somerset. For the General, there are those
gentle Cotswold bells, the organ booming, evening hymns.
There is the beauty of virginity specially kept, to be given on a
wedding night; and drinks beneath that tree the child fell out
of. 'Darling,' the well-loved wife returns his love. 'Darling,
you are so sweet to me.'

For me, there is the stolid dog, the dampness of the beach,
the seagulls coming nearer. There are the searchlights of
Twentieth-Century Fox, the soft roar of the lion, Western Electric Sound. In a room a man removes an artificial leg and
pauses to massage the stump. Across a street a neon sign
flashes red, then green, all through a half-forgotten night. First
thing of all, there's a broken floor-tile, brownish, smooth.

Why is there fear left over in Otmar's eyes, behind the

spectacles? Does some greater ordeal continue, some private awfulness? In the supermarket the girl's hand reaches again into the shelves. The adoration in the car park and the café is an ecstasy in its first bright moment. *Liebe! Liebe!* Eyes close, fingers touch. But something is missing in all this; there is some mystery.

Years after her time as a Sunday-school teacher Miss Alzapiedi becomes Lady Daysmith – shortened to a reasonable height, supplied with hair that isn't a nuisance, given a bosom. Lady Daysmith is old of course, Miss Alzapiedi was scarcely twenty in the Sunday school. But a plain girl can grow old gracefully, why ever not? 'The peepshow of memory is what I mean by fragments': I hadn't been in my house more than a month before I caused the woman who had been the Sunday-school girl to utter so.

In the soft warmth of that early morning I paused on the track that led to the heights behind my house. I looked back at the house itself, in that moment acutely aware of how the malignancy of the act had reached out into us, draining so much from the old man, rooting itself in Otmar, leaving sickness with the child. Then I pushed all that away from me and tried once more, though without success, to find a beginning for *Ceaseless Tears*. I strolled on a little way before finally turning back.

'I have always wanted a garden here,' I remarked to Otmar on the terrace less than an hour later. We smoked together. I asked him if there'd been a garden at his parents' house and he said yes, a small back garden, shady in summertime, a place to take a book to. You could tell from the way he spoke that his mother and father were no longer alive. I don't know why I wondered if this fact was somehow related to the fear that haunted him. I did so none the less.

*

'Where is this?' the child asked, suddenly, a week after my first walk on the white roads. She had been engrossed in one of her pictures, stretched out on the floor. The blinds were drawn a little down for coolness, but there was light enough in the *salotto*.

'Where is this?' Aimée asked again.

The General was sitting with his newspaper, near the windows. Otmar had just entered the room. Neither of them spoke. Eventually I said:

'You are in my house, Aimée. I am Mrs Delahunty.'

She did not directly reply, but said that her mother was cross because there'd been a quarrel in the yard. Girls couldn't be robbers, her brother Richard insisted, because he wanted to be the robber himself. As if speaking to herself, the child explained that she was to be the old woman who hadn't the strength to get up from her sun chair when the robber walked in and asked where the safe was. But she was always the old woman; all you did was lie there. She continued to draw the foreleg of a dog that did not seem to be alive. She shaded its hollow stomach. She and her brother had tried to guess, on the train-station platform, what two Italians were saying to one another. The woman of the pair was angry. The man had forgotten to lock the windows of their house, Aimée guessed.

'I should think that was so,' I said.

'That woman was mad at him.'

It was difficult to know if she spoke in response to what I'd said or not. A frown gathered on her freckled forehead. Her flaxen hair, so like her mother's, trailed smoothly down her back. Her eyes, lit for the while she spoke, went dead again.

'Your uncle's coming, Aimée. Mr Riversmith.'

But she was colouring now, lightly passing the crayons over the misshapen limbs and bodies. The tip of her tongue protruded slightly, in concentration.

'Mr Riversmith,' I said again.

Still there was no response. Otmar left the room, and I guessed he had gone to ask Quinty to summon Dr Innocenti.

'Your uncle,' the General said.

Aimée spoke again, about another game she and her brother had played, and then, with the same abruptness, she ceased. She said nothing more, but those few moments of communication had more than a slight effect on both the General and Otmar, and in a sense on me. This spark had kindled something in us; the brief transformation fluttered life into a hope that had not been there before. At last there was something good, happening in the present. At last we could reach out from our preoccupation with ourselves alone.

The General smiled at Aimée, while she sat there on the floor, lost to us again. Aimée was a lovely name, I said, not knowing what else to say. 'Thank God for this,' the General murmured, to me directly.

'Yes, thank God.'

Otmar returned to the room and sat with us in silence, and in time we heard Dr Innocenti's car approaching. We didn't break the silence, but listened to the hum of the engine as it came closer, until eventually the tyres scrunched on the gravel outside.

'*Coraggio!*' Dr Innocenti said, speaking softly from the doorway, not coming quite into the room. '*Va meglio, vero.*'

Later he predicted that Aimée would make progress now, but warned us that on the way to recovery there might be disturbances. It was as well to expect this since often the return to reality could be alarming for a child: you had only to consider what this reality was, he pointed out. His hope was that Aimée would not be too badly affected. He charged us with vigilance.

The days and weeks that followed were happy. Diffidently, I put it to Dr Innocenti that the child was the surviving fledgling in a rifled nest, her bright face the exorcist of our pain. The beauty that was promised her, and already gathering in those features, was surely to be set against the torn limbs in Carrozza 219, against the blood still dripping from the broken glass, the severed hand like an ornament in the air? Her chatter challenged the old man's guilt and was listened to, as wisdom might be, by Otmar. '*Si. Si,*' Dr Innocenti several times repeated, hearing me out and appearing to be moved.

Local people, learning that some victims of the outrage were in my house, sent gifts – flowers and wine, fruit, *panettone*. The *carabinieri* came less often now, once in a while to ensure that Aimée was still being looked after, then not at all, instead making their inquiries of Dr Innocenti. Once I walked into the kitchen to find Signora Bardini weeping, and thought at first she suffered some distress, but when she lifted her head I saw that her streaming eyes gleamed with joy. Naturally no such display of emotion could be expected of Quinty, though Rosa Crevelli was affected, of that I'm certain. 'Aimée! Aimée!' she called about the house.

Perhaps for the General Aimée became a daughter with whom he might begin again. Perhaps for Otmar she was the girl who had died on the train. I do not know; I am not qualified to say; I never asked them. But for my own part I can claim without reservation that I became as devoted to the child during that time as any mother could be. It was enough to see her sprawled on the floor with her crayons, or making a little edifice out of stones near where the car was kept, or drinking Signora Bardini's iced tea. Aimée shuffled in and out of a darkness, remaining with us for longer periods as these weeks went by. Sometimes she would sit close to me on the terrace, and in the cool of the evening I would stroke her fine, beautiful hair.

5

The telephone in my house rings quietly, but never goes un-heard because there is a receiver in the hall and in the kitchen, as well as in my writing-room. It was I myself, in my private room, who answered it when eventually Aimée's uncle rang.

'Mrs Delahunty?'

'Yes.'

'Mrs Delahunty, this is Thomas Riversmith.'

'How d'you do, Mr Riversmith.'

'May I inquire how Aimée is?' He sounded as if grit had got into his vocal cords – a tight, unfriendly voice, unusual in an American.

'Aimée is beginning to return to us.'

'She speaks now every day?'

'Since the afternoon she spoke she has continued.'

'I've talked with your doctor many times.' There was a pause and then, with undisguised difficulty: 'I want to say, Mrs Delahunty, that I appreciate what you have done for my niece.'

'I have not done much.'

'May I ask you to tell me what the child says when she speaks to you?'

'In the first place she asked where she was. Several times she has mentioned her brother by name. And has spoken of being scolded by her mother.'

'Scolded?'

'As any child might be.'

'I see.'

'If Aimée wakes in the night, if there is a nightmare, anything like that, a cry of distress would be heard at once.
Otmar sleeps with his door open. In the daytime there is
always someone near at hand.'

At first there was no response. Then: 'Who is it that sleeps
with a door open?'

'Otmar. A German victim of the outrage. Also in my house
is an English general, similarly a victim.'

'I see.'

'It's strange for all of us.'

That observation was ignored. There was another pause, so
long I thought we'd been cut off. But in time the gritty voice
went on:

'The doctor seems anxious that the child should make more
progress before I come to take her home.'

'Aimée is welcome to remain as long as is necessary.'

'I'm sorry. I did not catch that.'

I repeated what I'd said. Then formally, the tone still not
giving an inch, socially or otherwise:

'Our authorities here have informed yours that I will
naturally pay all that is owing. Not only the hospital fees, but
also what is owing to yourself.'

This sounded like a speech, as though many people were
being addressed. I did not explain that that was Quinty's
department. I did not say anything at all. A woman's voice
murmured in the background, and Mr Riversmith – having
first questioned some remark made – asked if I, myself, was
quite recovered from the ordeal. The background prompt was
repeated; the man obediently commiserated. It had been a
dreadful shock for him, he confessed. He'd read about these
things, but had never believed that he himself could be brought
so close to one. You could hear the effort in every word he

spoke, as if he resented having to share a sentiment, as if anything as personal as a telephone conversation – even between strangers – was anathema to him.

'That is true, Mr Riversmith.'

The solemnity and the seriousness made me jittery. He was a man without a word of small talk. I knew he hadn't smiled during all this conversation. I could tell that smiling didn't interest him. Again I reflected that he wasn't at all like an American.

'If I may, I'll call again, Mrs Delahunty. And perhaps we might arrange a date that's convenient to both of us.'

He left a number in case of any emergency, not asking if I had a pencil handy. He had no children of his own: Dr Innocenti hadn't told me that, but I guessed it easily.

'Goodbye, Mr Riversmith.'

I imagined him replacing the receiver in its cradle and turning to the woman who had shadowed the encounter for him. In the lives of such men there is always such a woman, covering their small inadequacies.

'Not an easy person,' I remarked later to the General and Otmar – which I considered was a fair observation to make. I repeated as much of the conversation as I could recall, and described Thomas Riversmith's brusqueness. Neither of them said much by way of response, but I sensed immediately their concern that a man whom it was clearly hard to take to should be charged with the care of a tragically orphaned child. Already all three of us knew that that felt wrong.

The General walked with the assistance of a cane and always would now. But he walked more easily than he had at first. My neck and my left cheek had healed, and what they'd said was right: make-up effortlessly obscured the tiny fissures. By now Otmar could light his own cigarettes, gripping the matchbox between his knees. He had difficulty with meat, and one

of us always cut it up for him. He'd have to learn to type
again, but cleverly he managed to play patience. 'Solo?' Aimée
would say when a game had been resolved, and after they'd
played a few hands she would arrange the draughts on the
draughts-board. There was another game, some German game
I didn't understand, with torn-up pieces of paper.

The old man told her stories, not about his schooldays but
concerning the adventures he'd had as a soldier. They sat
together in the inner hall, he in a ladder-backed chair, she on
one of my peacock-embroidered stools. He murmured through
the quiet of an afternoon while the household rested, a faint
scent of floor polish on the air. They chose the inner hall
because it's always cool.

As for me, on all those days I stared at the only words I had
typed on my green paper since the outrage. I counted them –
thirty-six, thirty-eight with the title. Everything that should
have followed I was deprived of, and I knew by now that this
was the loss I must put beside the greater loss of a girlfriend,
and of a daughter, and of a father, a mother and a brother.

The private room set aside for my writing is a brown-shadowed
cubicle with heavy curtains that keep both heat and light out, the
ornate ivy of its wallpaper simulating a further coolness. Besides
the glass-faced cabinet that contains my titles, there is my desk,
surfaced in green leather, and a matching chair. Here I sat during
those days of June, the cover lifted from my black Olympia, my
typing paper mostly blank. I could not glimpse my heroine's
face, nor even find her name. Esmeralda? Deborah? I could not
find the barest hint of a relationship or the suggestion, however
foggy, of a story. There was still only the swish of a white dress,
a single moment before that flimsy ghost was gone again.

'Apparently, a scholarly gentleman, this Mr Riversmith,'
Quinty remarked one evening after dinner, interrupting my
weary efforts by placing a glass of gin and tonic on the desk
beside me. 'I don't think I ever met a professor before.'

I hadn't either. I sipped the drink, hoping he'd go away. But Quinty never does what you want him to do.

'The doctor tells me Mr Riversmith's never so much as laid an eye on young Aimée. Did he say the same to you? A rift between the late sister and himself?'

I shook my head. Briskly, I thanked him for bringing me the drink. I hadn't asked him to. One of Quinty's many assumptions is that in such matters he invariably knows best.

'What I'm thinking is, how will the wife welcome a kid she's never so much as laid an eye on either?'

Again I indicated that I did not know. It naturally would not be easy for Mrs Riversmith, I suggested. I didn't imagine she was expecting it to be.

'Interesting type of gentleman,' Quinty remarked. 'Interesting to meet a guy like that.'

He stood there, still tiresome, fiddling with objects on my desk. They'd never find the culprits now, he said; you could forget all that. As soon as Riversmith came for the child the old man and the German would go. That stood to reason; they couldn't stay for ever; the whole thing would be over then. 'You'll pay the German's bill, eh?'

'I said I would.'

He laughed the way he does. 'You'll get your reward in heaven,' he repeated for the umpteenth time in our relationship. A kind of catch-phrase this is with him: he doesn't believe it. What he knows – though it's never spoken between us – is that the house will be his and Rosa Crevelli's when I die. My own reward has nothing to do with anything.

'Roast in hell, the rest of us,' he said before he went away.

Mr Riversmith telephoned again; we had a similar conversation. I reported on his niece's continuing progress, what she had done that day, what she had said. When there was nothing left to say the conversation ended. There was a pause, a cough, the woman's voice in the background, a dismissive word of farewell.

A few days later he telephoned a third time. He'd had further conversations with Dr Innocenti, he said; he suggested a date – a week hence – for his arrival in my house. There was the usual prickly atmosphere, the same empty pause before he brought himself to say goodbye. I poured myself a drink and walked out to the terrace with it. The awkward conversation echoed; I watched the fireflies twinkling in the gloom. How indeed would that woman react to the advent of a child who was totally strange to her? What was the woman like? With someone less cold, the subject of what it was going to be like for both of them might even have been brought up on the telephone. Thomas Riversmith sounded a lot older than his sister. Capricorn, I'd guessed after our first conversation. You often get an uptight Capricorn.

On the terrace I lit a cigarette. Then, quite without warning, monstrously shattering the peaceful evening, the screaming of the child began, the most awful sound I've ever heard.

6

Dr Innocenti came at once. He was calm, and calmly soothed our anxiety. He placed Aimée under temporary sedation, warning us that its effects would not last long. He maintained from the first that there was no need to take her into hospital again, that nothing would be gained. His strength and his tranquillity allowed me to accompany him to the bedside; afterwards he sat with me in the *salotto*, sipping a glass of mineral water. He wished to be within earshot when Aimée emerged from her sleep, since each time she did so she would find herself deeper in what seemed like a nightmare.

'You comprehend, signora? Reversal of waking from bad dreams. For this child such dreams begin then.'

Together we returned to the bedside when the screaming started again, but Dr Innocenti did not administer the drug immediately. Aimée sobbed when the screams had exhausted her, and while she threw her head about on the pillow a dreadful shivering seeming to wrench her small body asunder. I begged him to put a stop to it.

'We understand, Aimée,' he murmured instead, in unhurried tones. 'Here are your friends.'

The child ignored the sympathy. Her eyes stared wide, like those of a creature demented. More sedation was given at last.

'She will sleep till morning now,' the doctor promised, 'and then be drowsy for a little time. I will be here before another crisis.'

From the hall he telephoned Thomas Riversmith to inform

him of the development. 'May I urge you to delay your journey, signore?' I heard him say. 'Three weeks maybe? Four?
Not easy now to calculate.'

It was impossible not to have confidence in Dr Innocenti.
All his predictions came naturally about, as if he and nature
shared some knowledge. There was compassion in the cut of
his features, and even in the way he moved, yet it never
hindered him. Pity can be an enemy, I know that well.

His presence in my house that night was a marvel. It affected
Otmar and the General: without speaking a word, as though
anxious only to be co-operative, they went to their rooms and
closed their doors. I alone bade the doctor good-night and
watched the little red tail-light of his car creeping away into
the darkness, still glowing long after the sound of the engine
had died.

'Very presentable, the doctor,' Quinty remarked in the hall,
even in these wretched circumstances attempting to be jokey or
whatever it was he would have called it.

'Yes, very.'

'A different kettle of fish from a certain medical party who
had better stay nameless, eh?'

He referred to the doctor who'd been a regular in the Café
Rose, a man whose weight was said to be twenty-four stone,
whose stomach hung hugely out above the band of his trousers,
whose chest was like a woman's. Great sandalled feet shuffled
and thumped; like florid blubber, thick lips were loosely open;
eyes, piglike, peered. 'We could make a go of it,' was the
suggestion he once made to me, and I have no doubt that
Quinty knew about this. I have no doubt that the offer was
later guffawed over at the card-table.

'I'll say good-night so,' Quinty went on. 'I think it'll be best
for all of us when Uncle comes.'

'Good-night, Quinty.'

*

I could not sleep. I could not even close my eyes. I tried not
to recall the sound of those screams, that stark, high-pitched
shrieking that had chilled me to my very bones. Instead I
made myself think about the obese doctor whom Quinty had
so conveniently dredged up. You'd never have guessed he was
a medical man, more like someone who drilled holes in the
street. Yet when an elderly farmer sustained a heart attack in
an upstairs room at the café he appeared to know what to do,
and there was talk of cures among the natives.

In my continued determination not to dwell on the more
immediate past I again saw vividly, as I had on my early-
morning walk, the hand of Otmar's girlfriend reaching for the
herbs in the supermarket; I saw the General and his well-loved
wife. 'I'll get Sergeant Beeds on to you,' Mrs Trice shouted the
day she came back early from the laundry. 'Lay another finger
on her and you'll find yourself in handcuffs.' The man I'd
once taken to be my father blustered and then pleaded, a kind
of gibberish coming out of him.

All through that night my mind filled with memories and
dreams, a jumble that went on and on, imaginings and reality.
'Please,' Madeleine begged, and Otmar moved his belongings
into her flat. When she was out at work he drank a great deal
of coffee, and smoked, and typed the articles he submitted to
newspapers. Madeleine cooked him moussaka and chicken
stew, and once they went to Belgium because he'd heard of an
incident which he was convinced would make a newspaper
story: how a young man had ingeniously taken the place of a
Belgian couple's son after a period of army service.

'So's you can't see up her skirts,' a boy who had something
wrong with him said, but no one believed that that was why
Miss Alzapiedi wore long dresses. Miss Alzapiedi didn't even
know about people looking up skirts. 'If you close your eyes
you can *feel* the love of Jesus,' Miss Alzapiedi said. 'Promise
me now. Wherever you are, in all your lives, find time to feel

the love of Jesus.' Nobody liked the boy who had something wrong with him. When he grinned inanely you had to avert your gaze. The girls pulled his hair whenever he made his rude noise, if Miss Alzapiedi wasn't looking.

'Ah, how d'you do?' the General greeted his would-be son-in-law beneath the tree I'd heard about. The drinks were on a white table among the deck-chairs, Martini already mixed, with ice and lemon, in a tall glass jug. 'So very pleased,' his wife said, and he watched the face of his daughter's fiancé, the features crinkling in a polite acknowledgement, the lips half open. The intimacy of kissing, he thought, damp and sensual. His stomach heaved; he turned away. 'So *very* pleased,' he heard again.

The aviator who wrote messages in the sky wanted to marry me before the obese doctor did. He had retired from the sky-writing business when I knew him, but often he spoke of it in the Café Rose, repeating the message he had a thousand times looped and dotted high above Africa: *Drink Bailey's Beer*. A condition of the inner ear had dictated his retirement, but one day he risked his life and flew again. 'Look, missy!' Poor Boy Abraham cried excitedly, pulling me out of the café on to the dirt expanse where the trucks parked. 'Look! Look!' And there, in the sky, like shaving foam, was my name and an intended compliment. A tiny aircraft, soundless from where we stood, formed the last few letters and then smeared a zigzag flourish. 'Oh, that is *beautiful!*' Poor Boy Abraham cried as we watched. 'Oh, *my*, it's beautiful!' Fortunately Poor Boy Abraham could not read.

'He forgot to lock the windows,' Aimée repeated firmly at the railway station. The Italian woman was angry and almost stamped her foot; the man was smaller than she was, with oiled black hair brushed straight back. 'More likely he left something turned on,' Aimée's brother suggested. 'Maybe the stove.' Aimée disagreed, but then the train came in and they had to find their way to Carrozza 219. When the train moved again Aimée gazed out at the fields of sunflowers, at the green vine shoots in orderly rows and the hot little railway stations. She stared at the pale sky, all the blue bleached out of it. Some of the fields were being sprayed with water that gushed from a jet going round and round. In the far distance there were hills with clumps of trees on them. 'Cypresses,' her father said as the bell of the restaurant attendant tinkled and the businessmen and the fashion woman rose. The woman would have turned off the stove herself, Aimée whispered, and her brother turned grumpily away from her. 'Stop that silly arguing,' their mother reprimanded.

'No, of course I don't mind,' Madeleine said when Otmar asked if his friends might come to the flat when she was out. His friends were intense young men, students or unemployed, one of them a girl whom Madeleine was jealous of. When Otmar and Madeleine were in Italy two of them came up while they were sitting in the sun outside a café. They gave Otmar the name of a cheap restaurant, but afterwards he lost the piece of paper he'd written it down on. 'Look, there're your friends,' Madeleine said a few days later, pointing to where they sat at a café table with two other men, but Otmar didn't want to join them, although they could have given him the name of the restaurant again.

'Rum and Coke,' Ernie Chubbs ordered in the Al Fresco Club, and the Eastern girl brought it quickly, flashy with him as she always was with the customers. They didn't put any rum in mine although Ernie paid for it. They never did in the Al Fresco, saying a girl could end up anywhere if she didn't stay sober. 'Now then, my pretty maid,' Ernie Chubbs said in our corner. I couldn't see his face, I didn't know what it looked like because it was shadowy where we sat and I'd only caught a glimpse of it on the street. 'Often come here, darling?' he chattily questioned me.

Best White Tits in Africa! the writing said in the sky, but in

my dream it was different. *Angela Fresu, aged three*, it said, as
it does in marble at Bologna.

When I awoke next there was a dusky light in the room. I
reached out for a cigarette and lit it, and closed my eyes. 'I
shall love you,' Jason says in *For Ever More*, 'till the scent has
gone from the flowers and the salt from the seas.' But Jason
and Maggie are different from the people I'd kept company
with in the night. You can play around with Jason and Maggie,
you can change what you wish to change, you can make them
do what they're told.

I must digress here. To compose a romance it is necessary
to have a set of circumstances and within those circumstances
a cast of people. As the main protagonists of a cast, you have,
for instance, Jason and Maggie and Maggie's self-centred sister,
and Jason's well-to-do Uncle Cedric. The circumstances are
that Jason and Maggie want to start a riding stables, but they
have very little money. Maggie's sister wants Jason for herself,
and Jason's Uncle Cedric will allow the pair a handsome
income if Jason agrees to go into the family business, manufac-
turing girder-rivets. You must also supply places of interest –
in this instance the old mill that would make an ideal stables,
the little hills over which horses can be exercised, and far
away – darkly unprepossessing – the family foundry. You
need dramatic incident: the discovery of the machinations of
Maggie's sister, the angry family quarrel when Jason refuses to
toe his Uncle Cedric's line. None of it's any good if the people
aren't real to you as you compose.

In the early morning after that unsettled night it seemed to
me that the only story I was being offered was the story of the
summer that was slipping by. The circumstances were those
that followed a tragedy, the people were those who had
crowded my night, the places you can guess. *Ceaseless Tears*
was a working title only, and that morning I abandoned it. All

I had dreamed was the chaos from which order was to be drawn, one way or another. Everything in storytelling, romantic or otherwise, is hit and miss, and the fact that reality was involved didn't appear to make much difference.

I prayed, and then I finished my cigarette and soon afterwards rose. I walked about my house in the cool of the morning, relishing its tranquillity and the almost eerie feeling that possessed me: inspiration, or whatever you care to call it, had never before struck me in so strange a manner. I poured myself some tonic water and added just a trace of the other to pep it up. It seemed like obtuseness that I hadn't realized the girl in the white dress was Aimée.

7

Aimée was calm when she awoke, but during the days that followed there were further setbacks, though thankfully none was as alarming as the first one. Her uncle's departure from America was again delayed to allow her further time to make a recovery. But even so Dr Innocenti was optimistic.

We ourselves – the General, Otmar and I – were naturally apprehensive and each day that ended without incident seemed like a victory of a kind. And for me there was another small source of pleasure, a bolt from the blue as agreeable as any I have experienced. As I recall it now I am reminded, by way of introduction, that overheard conversations do not always throw up welcome truths. 'Pass on, my dear, for you'll hear no good,' Lady Daysmith advises in *Precious September*, but of course it is not always so. Pausing by the door of the *salotto* one evening, I overheard Otmar and the General tentatively conversing.

'Yes, she has mentioned that,' the old man was saying, and this was when I paused, for I sensed it was I who was referred to, and who can resist a moment's listening in such circumstances?

'I would take the chance,' Otmar said, 'to pay my debt to her.'

His wife had been quite expert, the old man said next, especially where the cultivation of fritillaries was concerned. Otmar didn't understand the term; an explanation followed, the plant described. The name came from the Latin: *fritillus* meant a dice-box. 'She was always interested in a horticultural derivation. She read Dr Linnaeus.'

Otmar professing ignorance again, there came an explanation. I heard that this Linnaeus, a Swedish person apparently – Linné as he'd been born – had sorted out a whole array of flowers and plants, giving them names or finding Latin roots for existing names, orderliness and Latin being his forte.

'She wants a garden,' Otmar said, not interrupting but by the sound of it repeating what he had said already, in an effort to bring the conversation down to earth.

'Then we must make her one.'

How could they make me a garden? One was too old, the other had but a single arm left! Yet how sweet it was to hear them! As I stood there I felt a throb of warmth within my body, as though a man had said when I was still a girl: 'I love you . . .'

'He's not the sort of person,' the old man was observing when next I paid attention. 'He's not the sort to be a help or even be much interested.'

I guessed they spoke of Quinty, and certainly what was deduced was true.

'A machine is there?' Otmar asked then. 'An implement to break the earth?'

'There's a thing in England called a Merry Tiller. A motorized plough.'

I imagine Otmar nodded. The General said:

'Heaven knows what grows best in such dry conditions. Precious little, probably. We'd have to read all that up.'

'I do not know seeds.'

Fuchsias grew in the garden of his parents, Otmar went on. He was not good about the names of plants, but he remembered fuchsias in pots – double headed, scarlet and cream. The geranium family should do well, the General said, and brooms. To my delight he mentioned azaleas. Shade would be important, and would somehow have to be supplied. The azaleas would have to be grown in urns, and moved inside in winter.

'With one arm,' Otmar reminded him, 'I could not dig.'

'It is remarkable what can be done, you know. Once you settle to it.'

I moved away because I heard them get to their feet. A few minutes later I saw them at the back of my house, gesturing to one another beside the ruined out-buildings. Their voices drifted to where I watched from; the old man pointed. Here there'd be a flight of steps, leading to a lower level, here four flowerbeds formally in a semi-circle, here a marble figure perhaps. A few days later, when they revealed their secret to me, they showed me the plans they had drawn on several sheets of paper in the meantime. The General promised a herb bed, with thyme and basil and tarragon and rosemary. There would be solitary yew trees or local pines, whichever were advised. They'd try for box hedges and cotoneaster and olean-der. There'd be a smoke tree and a handkerchief tree, and roses and peach trees, whatever they could induce to thrive.

'When I'm grown up I'd like to tell stories too.'

Aimée had *Flight to Enchantment* in her hand. She had asked me and I had related its contents, while effortlessly she listened.

'I like being here in the hills,' she said.

8

On 14 July Thomas Riversmith arrived. Telephoning a few
evenings before, he insisted that he did not wish to be met;
that he wished to cause the minimum of inconvenience. So he
took a taxi from Pisa, which is an extremely long journey, and
then there was difficulty finding my house. From an upstairs
window I watched him paying his driver in one-hundred-
thousand-lire notes. He had black Mandarina Duck bags. I
went downstairs, to welcome him in the inner hall.

He was a tall, thickset man, rather heavy about the face,
not at all like the young woman on the train. His eyes, between
beetle-black brows, were opaque – green or blue, it wasn't
apparent which; his crinkly hair was greyish. Mr Riversmith
was indeed as serious and as solemn as he had seemed on the
telephone: the surprise was that, in his way, he was a handsome man. He wore a dark suit, which had become creased on
his air flight and creased again due to his sitting in a hired car
for so long. His wife would have bought him the Mandarina
luggage; it didn't match the rest of him in any way whatsoever.

'I'm Mrs Delahunty.'

He nodded, not saying who he was because no doubt he
assumed that no one else was expected just then. He stood
there, not seeming interested in anything, waiting for me to
say something else. It was a little after six in the evening; the
cocktail hour, as the Americans call it. A certain weariness

about his features intimated that Mr Riversmith could do with a drink.

'Drink?' he repeated when I suggested this. He shook his head. He had better wash, he said. He had a way of looking at you intently when he spoke, while giving the impression that he didn't see you. Beneath the scrutiny I felt foolish, the way you do with some people.

'Quinty'll take you up, Mr Riversmith.'

'After that I should see my niece.'

'Of course. Simply when you're ready, Mr Riversmith, please join us in the *salotto*.'

He followed Quinty upstairs. I made my way to my private room. Earlier in the day an accumulation of fan mail had come, forwarded from the publisher's offices in London. After that brief encounter with Mr Riversmith I found it something of an antidote. People endeavour to explain how much a story means to them, or how they identify. *I quite felt I was Rosalind. Years ago, of course. I'm in my eighties now.* Occasionally a small gift is enclosed, a papier mâché puzzle from Japan, a pressed flower, inexpensive jewellery. *Was Lucinda really furious or just pretending? Will Mark forgive her, utterly and completely? Oh, I do so hope he can!* Little adhesive labels come, for autographs. *I have all your stories, but dare not trust them to the post. Return postage enclosed.* I do my best to reply, aptly, but sometimes become exhausted, faced with so much. *What a lovely birthday party Ms Penny Court had! It reminded me so much of my own when I was twenty-one and Dad made a key out of plaster of Paris and silver paint! I'm forty now, with kiddies of my own and Alec (husband) is no longer here so I do my best on my own. I always think of her as Ms Penny Court, I don't know why. I envy her her independence. Dad and I were close, that's why he made the key for my twenty-first, you remember things like that. I'm fond of the kiddies of course, it goes without saying, and they wouldn't be here if I hadn't married Alec. He went off two years ago, a woman security officer.* Often the letters go on for many pages, the ink changing colour more than once, the writing-paper acquiring stains. When gifts of food are sent I am naturally touched, but I throw the food away, having been warned that this is advisable.

Dear Ron, I wrote on the evening of Thomas Riversmith's arrival, addressing my correspondent so familiarly because I'd been supplied with that name only. *Thank you for your nice letter. I am glad you enjoyed 'More than the Brave.' It is interesting what you say about Annabella and Roger being acquainted in a previous life. I quite accept this may be so, and I am interested in what you tell me about your pets. I do not believe your wife would be in the least aggrieved to know you find Fred a comfort. In fact, I'm sure she's delighted.* I added another sentence about the ferret, Fred, then placed the letter in an envelope and sealed it. I never supply strangers with my address, having been warned that this is inadvisable also. And some correspondents I really do have to ignore. Correspondence with the disturbed is not a good idea.

Mr Riversmith was standing in silence in the *salotto* when I entered.

'Would I mix you a drink, sir?' Quinty offered.

'A drink?'

'Would you care for a refreshment after your journey, sir?'

Mr Riversmith requested an Old Fashioned, then noticed my presence and addressed me. He remarked that his niece was pretty.

'Yes, indeed.' But I added that Aimée was still mentally fragile. I said that Dr Innocenti would visit us in the morning. He would explain about that.

'I greatly appreciate what Dr Innocenti has done for my niece.' Mr Riversmith paused. 'And I appreciate your looking after her in her convalescence, Mrs Delahunty.'

I explained about the tourists who stayed in my house when the hotels were full. It was no trouble was how I put it; we were used to visitors.

'You'll let me have an account?' Mr Riversmith went on, as if anxious to deal with all the formalities at once. 'I would wish to have that in order before we leave.'

I said that was Quinty's department, and Quinty nodded as he handed Mr Riversmith his glass. 'G and t would it be tonight?' he murmured. He rolls that 'g and t' off his tongue in a twinkling manner, appearing to take pleasure in the sound, heaven knows why.

'Thank you, Quinty,' I said, and as I spoke the General entered the room.

I introduced the two men, revealing in lowered tones that the General had been only a couple of seats away from Aimée on the train. I mentioned Otmar in case Mr Riversmith had forgotten what I'd said on the telephone. Lowering my voice further, I mentioned the old man's daughter and son-in-law, and Madeleine. In the circumstances I considered that necessary.

'You've come for the child,' the General said.

'Yes, I have.'

There was a silence. Quinty poured the General some whisky, and noted the drinks in the little red notebook he keeps by the tray of bottles. The old man nodded, acknowledging what had been said. In order to ease a certain stickiness that had developed I asked a question to which I knew the answer. 'You do not know Aimée well?' I remarked to Mr Riversmith.

'I met my niece for the first time in my life half an hour ago.'

'What?' The General frowned. 'What?' he said again.

'I never knew either of my sister's children.' He appeared not to wish to say anything more, to leave the matter there.

But then, unexpectedly, he added what I knew also: that there'd been a family quarrel.

'So the child's a stranger to you?' the General persisted. 'And you to her?'

'That is so.'

His wife would have accompanied him, Mr Riversmith continued, apropos of another question the General asked, but unfortunately it had been impossible for her to get away. He referred to his wife as Francine, a name new to me. In answer to a question of my own he supplied the information that his wife was in the academic world also.

'We should be calling you professor,' I put in. 'We weren't entirely certain.'

He replied that he didn't much use the title. Academic distinctions were unimportant, he said. The General asked him what his line of scholarship was, and Mr Riversmith replied – his tone unchanged – that the bark-ant was his subject. He spoke of this insect as if it were a creature as familiar to us as the horse or the dog.

The General shook his head. He did not know the bark-ant, he confessed. Mr Riversmith made a very slight, scarcely perceptible shrugging motion. The interdependency of bark-ant colonies in acacia trees, he stated, revealed behaviour that was similar to human beings'. It was an esoteric area of research where the layman was concerned, he admitted in the end, and changed the subject.

'My niece will not forget the time she's spent here.'

'No, she'll hardly do that,' the General agreed.

Otmar came in, his hand grasping one of Aimée's. I introduced him to Mr Riversmith, and I thought for a moment that he might click his heels, for Otmar's manner can be formal on occasion. But he only bowed. Quinty, still hovering near the drinks' tray, poured Aimée a Coca-Cola and Otmar a Stella Artois. He made the entries in the notebook and then sloped away.

'Those are interesting pictures you drew,' Aimée's uncle said.

'Which pictures?'

'The ones on your walls.'

'I didn't draw them.'

'I drew the pictures,' Otmar said.

'Otmar drew them,' Aimée said.

For the first time Mr Riversmith was taken aback. I knew that Dr Innocenti would already have spoken to him on the telephone about the pictures. I watched him wondering if he'd misunderstood what he'd been told. He opened his mouth to speak, but Aimée interrupted.

'When are you taking me away?'

'We'll see what Dr Innocenti says when he comes tomorrow.'

'I'm better.'

'Of course you are.'

'Really better.'

Aimée, in a plain red dress that she and Signora Bardini had bought together, took up a position in the centre of the room. Otmar leaned against the pillar of an archway. The fear was still in his eyes, but it had calmed a little.

'Feel like that long journey soon?' Mr Riversmith was asking Aimée in the artificial voice some people put on for children. 'Tiring, you know, being up in the air like that.'

'You want to rest?' She stumbled slightly over the words, and then repeated them. 'You want to rest, Uncle?'

'It's just that we mustn't hurry your uncle,' I quietly interjected. 'He needs a little breathing space before turning round to go all that way back again.'

The conversation became ordinary then, the General in his courteous way continuing to ask our visitor the conventional questions that such an occasion calls for: where it was he lived in the United States, if he had children of his own? You'd

never have guessed from the way he kept the chat going with
Mr Riversmith that the General's courage had deserted him,
that he could not bring himself to visit an empty house or
even to expose himself to the talk of solicitors.

'Virginsville,' Mr Riversmith responded, giving the name of
the town where he resided. 'Pennsylvania.'

He supplied the name of the nearby university where he
conducted his research with the creatures he'd mentioned. I
was right in my surmise that no children had been born to
Francine and himself.

'Nor to my daughter,' the General said.

In response to further politeness, Mr Riversmith revealed
that his wife had children, now grown up, by a previous
marriage. I asked if he'd been married before himself, and he
said he had. Then he went silent again, and the General saved
the situation by telling him about the garden that was planned.
In a corner Otmar and Aimée were whispering together, playing their game with torn-up pieces of paper. The General
mentioned the names of various plants – moss phlox, I remember, and *magnolia campbellii*. He wondered if tree peonies,
another favourite of his wife's, would thrive in Umbrian soil.
Trial and error he supposed it would have to be. Enthusiasti-
cally, he added that Quinty had discovered a motorized plough
could be hired locally, with a man to operate it.

'I have little knowledge of horticultural matters,' Mr Riversmith stated.

As he spoke, for some reason I imagined 5 May in Virginsville, Pennsylvania. I imagined Mr Riversmith entering his
residence, and Francine saying: 'One of those bomb attacks in
Italy.' Easily, still, I visualize that scene. She is drinking orange
juice. On the television screen there is a wrecked train. 'How
was your day?' she asks when he has embraced her, as mechanically as he always does when he returns from his day's
research. 'Oh, it was adequate,' he replies. (I'm certain he

chose that word.) 'They're colonizing quite remarkably at the moment.' *Her* day has been exhausting, Francine says. She had difficulty with the hood of the Toyota, which jammed again, the way it has been doing lately. No terrorist group claimed responsibility, the television newscaster is saying.

'Does your wife research into ants too, Mr Riversmith?' I asked because another lull hung heavily and because, just then, I felt curious.

Before he replied he drew his lips together – stifling a sigh, it might have been, or some kind of nervous twitch. 'My wife shares my discipline,' he managed eventually. 'Yes, that is so.'

Weeks later, it would have been the local police in Virginsville who supplied the information that those television pictures concerned him more than either he or Francine had thought. That scene came clearly to me also, still does: the officers declining to sit down, sunlight glittering on their metal badges. 'Italy?' The staccato tightness of Thomas Riversmith's voice seems strained to the policemen, and even to himself. 'The little girl's out of hospital, sir,' one of the men informs him. 'She's being looked after in a local house.' Still numbed, Mr Riversmith mumbles questions. Why had the explosion occurred? Had it in any way to do with Americans being on the train? Had those responsible been apprehended? 'My God!' Francine exclaims, entering the room just then. 'My *God!*'

We had dinner on the terrace. Mr Riversmith stirred himself and with an effort admired the view.

The next morning Dr Innocenti went through for Mr Riversmith his lengthy account of Aimée's progress. From the doctor's tone and from Mr Riversmith's responses, it was clear that much of what had already been said on the telephone was being repeated. Patiently, Dr Innocenti confirmed and elucidated, expanding when he considered it necessary. In the end he said he saw no reason why the return journey should not be made as soon as Mr Riversmith felt ready for it. He himself had done all he could for the child. Making what for him was quite a little speech, Mr Riversmith thanked him.

'One thing I'd like to raise, doctor. Aimée insists she didn't paint those pictures.'

'She doesn't know she did, signore.'

'The German – '

'It's good that Otmar helps.'

'Aimée and Otmar have become friends,' I said.

Mr Riversmith frowned. Impatience flitted through his features. It was that, I realized then, that made him seem cross from time to time. Impatience was his problem, not nerves. He held his seriousness to him, as though protectively, as though to cover his impatience. But sometimes it was not up to the task and a kind of irritated fustiness resulted.

'*Non importa, signore,*' Dr Innocenti assured him. 'The pictures are only pictures. Colour on paper.'

'Mr Riversmith does not perhaps understand,' I suggested, 'because he has not observed his niece's recovery.'

'Yes,' Dr Innocenti agreed. For once uncharacteristically vague, he added: 'We must hope.'

That afternoon Mr Riversmith wrote the necessary cheques, for the hospital and for Dr Innocenti. He made arrangements for a gravestone, and paid for it in advance.

Then there was an unexpected development. In one of his many conversations with Aimée Dr Innocenti had described to her the city of Siena, of which he is a native. He had called it the proudest of all Italian cities, full of mysterious corners, sombre and startling in turn: before she returned to America she must certainly visit it. 'You haven't yet?' he'd chided her in mock disappointment that morning. 'Won't you please your old friend, Aimée?'

Later Otmar brought the subject up in the *salotto*. Aimée

had promised Dr Innocenti, he reported, but was too shy to ask.

'Siena?' her uncle said.

It wasn't far, I explained. An excursion could easily be arranged. 'It's a pity not to visit Siena.'

Quinty would drive us. The General would accompany us in the hope of purchasing some gardening books that Quinty might translate for him.

'Would you object to an early start,' I questioned Mr Riversmith, 'in order to avoid the worst of the heat?'

He agreed quite readily to that, though briefly, without elaborating on his sleeping habits as another person might. I couldn't help wondering if Francine was like that too.

'Quinty'll wake you with a cup of tea at half-past six.' I lowered my voice and glanced about me, for this was something I didn't wish the others to overhear. It would be the first time we had all done something together, I confided. 'Since the outrage we haven't had the confidence for much.'

I don't know whether Mr Riversmith heard or not. He simply looked at me, and again I had the impression that he stifled a sigh. It surprised me that Francine, or his previous wife, hadn't ever told him that this habit of his seemed rude.

9

Soon after seven the next morning I observed the General pointing out to Mr Riversmith the features of the motor-car that Quinty has a habit of referring to as his, although, of course, it belongs to me. The old man drew attention to the huge headlights, the chromium fastenings of the luggage-box and of the canvas hood, now folded down. I heard him say that motor-cars were no longer manufactured with such panache and pride. Mr Riversmith no doubt considered it antique. He said something I did not catch.

I had chosen for our excursion a wide-brimmed white hat and a plain white dress, with black and white high-heeled shoes, black belt and handbag. On the gravel expanse in front of my house I greeted the two men, and in a moment Otmar and Aimée appeared, Aimée in the red dress she'd been wearing the evening her uncle arrived. To my amazement, Rosa Crevelli came out of the house also, clearly attired for the outing, in a flowered green outfit with lacy green stockings to match.

'Look here,' I began, drawing Quinty aside, but he interrupted before I'd even mentioned the girl's name.

'You agreed it was OK,' he said. 'When we asked you last night you said the more the merrier.'

'I said no such thing, Quinty.'

'You did, you know. I remarked it would make an outing for the girl. I remarked she was looking peaky these days.'

I firmly shook my head. No such conversation had taken place.

'You had a drink in at the time, signora.'

'Quinty – '

'I'm sorry.'

He hung his head the way only Quinty can do. He protested that neither he nor the girl would offend me for the world; he'd maybe misheard when he thought I'd said the more the merrier.

'You're coming with us in order to drive the car,' I pointed out. 'It's different altogether for a maid to tag along. There's neither rhyme nor reason in it.'

'It's only I promised her when you said that last night. She said you were kindness itself.'

This spoiled everything. I'd so much wanted things to go nicely. I'd wanted it to be a pleasant day for Aimée and her uncle; I'd wanted to get to know Mr Riversmith better; I'd wanted the General and Otmar to go on pulling themselves together, benefiting from the diversion; I'd wanted everyone to begin to be happy again.

'It's peculiar, Quinty, for a maid to mix with house-guests.'

'I know. I know. We're servant class. All I'm saying is, since the misunderstanding is there let it stay. It would be a terrible disappointment for the poor creature. She was ironing her clothes till the small hours.'

So in the end I gave in, even though I felt acutely embarrassed. I resolved to apologize to our guests – well, at least to Mr Riversmith and the General – when a suitable moment arrived. I am servant class myself, as Quinty well knows, but with everyone waiting I didn't want to explain that naturally there was a difference.

'Sorry,' he said again.

I did no more than shake my head at him. Rosa Crevelli had been watching us, gauging the content of our exchanges. I saw him glance at her, and the pout that was just beginning to disturb her sallow features turned into a smile. I approached the others and quietly suggested that Aimée and the maid should occupy the two rear seats, which are a feature of the car, the long middle one folding forward to allow access. Otmar, Mr Riversmith and I occupied this centre section, the General sat with Quinty in the front.

'*Andiamo!*' Quinty exclaimed as he engaged the gears, his sombre mood of a moment ago quite vanished. 'We're on the off!'

The sky was empty of clouds. The morning air was cool and fresh. As we drove, I pointed out distant hill-towns and avenues of cypresses for Mr Riversmith's benefit. Sometimes I indicated a church or, if none loomed near, a roadside café or a petrol station, knowing that for the stranger everything is of interest. Mr Riversmith nodded an acknowledgement from time to time, appearing otherwise to be mulling over matters he did not share. 'Magnificent, this car,' I heard the General say. Now and again Otmar turned round to exchange a word with Aimée.

'You may find it strange,' I remarked to Mr Riversmith, for what I had touched upon the day before had been on my mind in the night, 'that we should be going out on a jaunt while still in the grip of the horror that has torn our lives asunder.'

He shook his head. In a conventional manner he said it was a sign of healing and recovery.

'We long to escape our brooding, Mr Riversmith. We stitch together any kind of surface. But when we look into our hearts we see only a grief that is unbearable.'

I chose those words carefully, and did not add that the loss I'd suffered myself had been far less than that of the others because I'd had far less to lose. I didn't go into detail because it wasn't the time to do so. All I wished to make clear was that when, today, he observed his niece and Otmar and the old Englishman he was observing a skin drawn over human debris. Mr Riversmith said he wouldn't put it quite like that, but didn't offer an alternative form of words.

'I just thought I'd mention it,' I said, and left it at that. The debris of our times, I might have added, but I did not do so.

When we reached Siena, Quinty parked just inside the city gates, positioning the car beneath a tree to keep it cool. When he had raised the canvas roof and locked it into place we set off to walk to the café in the Piazza del Campo, where we were to breakfast. It was quite chilly in the narrow streets we passed through.

'I must apologize,' I murmured in a private moment to Mr Riversmith.

'I beg your pardon?'

I smiled, indicating Rosa Crevelli's presence with a sideways glance. There is something of the gypsy in Rosa Crevelli, which was considerably emphasized by the vivid green of her dress and her lacy stockings.

'I beg your pardon?' Mr Riversmith repeated.

I said it didn't matter because the moment had passed and we could now be overheard. He said yes when I asked him if his wife would care for this city, if the grey alleys in which its natives moved like early-morning ghosts would impress her. When finally we reached our destination the contrast was startling: a bright blaze of sunshine was already baking the paving-stones and terracotta of the elegant, shell-shaped con-cavity that is the city's centre. Would that, I wondered, impress Mrs Riversmith also?

He didn't reply directly. In fact, strictly speaking, he didn't reply to my question at all. 'Dr Innocenti gave my niece this guide-book,' was what he said, and handed the volume to me, unopened.

The great tower of the city-hall rises imperiously to claim a dominance against the plain serenity of the sky. I glanced through the guide-book when we'd settled ourselves at a table in the shade of the café's awning. Chattering in Italian, Quinty and Rosa Crevelli shook the waiter's hand. Noisily they ordered coffee and brioches. 'The journey's perked her up,' Quinty whispered when he saw me looking at them.

'This is very pleasant,' the General said.

'Yes, indeed,' Mr Riversmith agreed, somewhat to my surprise since he had been so taciturn on the walk from the car.

When the coffee came I drew his attention to an entry in the guide-book about the Palio – the horse-race that takes place each summer through the streets of Siena and around the slopes of the Campo where we now sat. I read the entry aloud: that the race was an occasion coloured by feuds and sharp practice, by the vested interests of other cities and the jealousies of local families, that it was wild and dangerous.

'You'll notice the decorated lamp standards,' Quinty interrupted. 'Tarted up for the big day.'

I wore my dark glasses, and from behind their protection I observed my companions while Quinty continued for a moment about the lamp standards, prompted in what he was saying by the maid. I observed the nervous movement of Otmar's fingers and the twitch of anxiety that caused him often to glance over his shoulder, as if he distrusted his surroundings. The old man's masking of his anguish remained meticulously intact. Aimée examined the pictures on the little sachets of sugar that had come with our coffee.

'The Sienese are renowned for the macaroons they bake,' I remarked to Mr Riversmith. 'Those *ricciarelli* we have at tea-time.'

'Yes,' he said.

Later, on the way to the cathedral, we called in at a travel agency, where he confirmed with the clerk the details of the flight back to Pennsylvania. The booking was made for four days' time, I myself gently pressing that Mr Riversmith should allow his jet-lag to ease before rushing off. 'I expect you've thought about how Aimée'll settle with you,' I said when these formalities were completed and we were on the street again. 'You and your wife.'

Again there was the tightening of the lips, the sharp, swift nod, another silence.

'Tell me about your sister,' I invited, tentatively, as we moved on.

Before I'd finished speaking Mr Riversmith stopped in his walk. He turned to me in a deliberate way and said that every time he looked at Aimée he was reminded of his sister. Aimée had Phyl's hair and her eyes and her freckles. I said yes, I knew, but the observation was ignored. Then, to my astonishment, while still standing on the street, the others now far ahead of us in their climb to the cathedral, Mr Riversmith related the history of the family trouble there had been. His sister had been particularly fond of his first wife. His second, the one called Francine, had somehow discovered this, had even learnt of Phyl's repeated endeavours to bring the two together again. A couple of months after he married Francine she and Phyl quarrelled so violently that they had avoided speaking to one another since. He had taken Francine's side and Phyl hadn't forgiven him. The ugly breach that followed accounted for the fact that her children were unknown to him; he remembered his brother-in-law Jack only from the single occasion he'd met him. A dozen times Mr Riversmith had apparently been on the point of writing to Phyl to see if amends might be made. But he had never done so.

'Naturally, I was apprehensive, coming out here,' Mr Riversmith confessed. 'I'd never even seen a photograph of my niece.'

All the fustiness had gone from him. For the first time he appeared to be a normal human person, endeavouring to contribute to a conversation. He was not a loquacious man; no circumstances in the world would ever alter that. Yet this moving little account of family troubles had tumbled out of him in the most natural way – hesitantly and awkwardly, it's true, but none the less naturally. I was aware of a pleasant

sensation in my head, like faint pins-and-needles, and a pleasant warmth in my body. My first concern was to throw the
ball back.

'Aimée didn't know she had an uncle,' I pointed out. 'So if
you and Francine imagine you were condemned in her eyes by
your sister that wouldn't be correct.'

He appeared to be taken aback by that. He even gave a
little jump.

'Of course you weren't condemned,' I repeated. 'Your sister
had a generous face.'

He didn't comment on the observation. I asked when he'd
last seen his sister and he said at their mother's funeral.

'A long time ago?'

'1975.'

'And your father? Yours and Phyl's?'

Again there was surprise. The father had died when Phyl
was an infant, and I imagined the household that was left, he
taking the father's place, much older than the sister. I imagined
him mending things about the house the way his father had,
cultivating lettuces and eggplant. I wondered if Phyl had
thought the world of him, as younger sisters in such circumstances often do.

'Don't feel guilty,' I begged, and told him how the General
hadn't been able to respect his son-in-law and could not find
the courage to walk into an empty house or even to cope with
solicitors – he whom courage had so characterized. I mentioned Otmar's Madeleine.

While I was speaking I recalled a dream I'd had the night
before. At once I wished to recount it, the way one does, but
Mr Riversmith being the man he was, I found myself unable
to do so. As you've probably deduced by now, dreams have a
fascination for me. The Austrian ivory cutter – and, come to
that, Poor Boy Abraham – used regularly to seek me out in
order to retail a dream, and occasionally I would pass on

what I'd dreamed myself. This one, in fact, concerned Mr
Riversmith and might indeed have interested him, but still I
felt inhibited. In it he was a younger man, little more than a
boy. He was repairing a kitchen drawer that had fallen to
pieces in Phyl's hands, the sides dropping away from one
another as if the glue that held them had become defective. He
scraped away a kind of fungus from the joints and placed the
drawer in clamps, with fresh glue replacing the old. 'You're
clever to do that,' Phyl said, and the wooden slat of the
kitchen blind tapped the window-frame, the way it did in even
the slightest breeze when the window was half open. I longed
to ask him about that as we climbed the hill to the cathedral,
but still I held my peace.

The others were by now out of sight. We found them
waiting for us on the cathedral steps, and with Dr Innocenti's
guide-book open the General led the way into the wasp-like
building, reading aloud about the floor and the carved pulpit.
When we had exhausted the marvels of this most impressive
place and had visited the little museum near by, we made for
the picture gallery proper. To my considerable relief, Quinty
and Rosa Crevelli had disappeared.

In the quiet of the gallery I would have liked to pursue my
conversation with Mr Riversmith, but as we made the rounds
of the pictures he fell into step with Otmar and the General,
leaving me for the moment on my own. Aimée had wandered
on ahead.

'Look at this!' I heard her cry in another room, and a
moment later we were all congregated around the painting
that excited her.

It was called *Annuncio ai pastori*, and depicted two shepherds and a rat-like dog crouched by a fire that had been
kindled beside carefully penned sheep. The hills around about
were the hills of Italy turned into a brown desert, the sky an
Italian sky, and the buildings in the background and the

foreground were of Italian architecture. But an angel, holding
out a sprig of something, was floating in a glow of yellow
light, and didn't, to my untutored eye, seem quite to belong.

'I've never seen a picture as beautiful,' Aimée said.

It occurred to me, as she spoke, that had the outrage not
happened, she would probably have come to this city with her
parents and her brother. They would probably have stood in
front of this very picture. I looked at her, but her face was
radiant. I edged closer to Mr Riversmith, hoping to share this
thought with him in a quiet whisper, but unfortunately just as
I did so he moved away.

'Look at how the sheep are fenced,' she said. 'Like with a
net.'

'*Sano di Pietro was born in Siena in 1406 and died in 1481,*'
the General read from Dr Innocenti's guide-book, and then
explained that this was the person who had painted the picture.

'More than five hundred years ago,' I pointed out to Aimée,
thinking that would interest her.

'Eight trees,' she counted. 'Eight and a half you *could* say.
Nineteen sheep maybe. Or twenty, I guess. It's hard to make
them out.'

'More like twenty,' the General estimated.

It was difficult to count them because the shapes ran into
one another when two sheep of the same colour were close
together. The guide-book, so the General said, suggested that
the dog had noticed the angel before the shepherds had. To
me that seemed somewhat fanciful, but I didn't say so.

'I love the dog,' Aimée said. 'I *love* it.'

Otmar, who had wandered off to examine other pictures,
rejoined us now. Aimée took his hand and pointed out all
the features she'd enthused over already. '*Especially* the dog,'
she added.

I was quite glad when eventually we descended the stairs

again. Pictures of angels and saints, and the Virgin with the baby Jesus, are very pretty and are of course to be delighted in, but one after another can be too much of a good thing. I wondered if Mr Riversmith's wife would have agreed and, since I very much wanted to establish what this woman was like, I raised the subject with him. I said I had counted more than thirty Virgins.

'The cathedral would perhaps be more Francine's kind of thing?'

But Mr Riversmith was buying a postcard at the time and didn't hear. It was interesting that he'd been married twice. I wondered about that, too.

'Otmar says you can climb up the town-hall tower,' Aimée said in the postcards place. 'We're going to.'

On the way back to the Piazza del Campo I noticed Quinty and Rosa Crevelli loitering in a doorway. They were smoking and leafing through a photographic magazine, giggling as Quinty turned the pages. I was glad they didn't see us and that no one happened to be looking in their direction as we went by. You could tell by the cover the kind of magazine it was.

'Why didn't I ever see you?' I heard Aimée ask her uncle. 'I didn't even know I *had* an uncle.'

I didn't catch his reply, something about the distance between Virginsville, Pennsylvania, and wherever it was she and her family had lived. Clearly he didn't want to go into it all, but as we turned into the piazza she still persisted, appearing to know something of the truth.

'Didn't you like her?'

'I liked her very much.'

'Did you have a fight?'

He hesitated. Then he said:

'A silly disagreement.'

The old man remarked that he would not ascend the tower but instead would search for his gardening manuals. We made an arrangement to meet in an hour's time at the restaurant next to the café where we'd had breakfast, Il Campo. I went off on my own, to look in the shoe shops.

I was after a pair of tan mid-heels, but I wasn't successful in my search so I slipped into a bar near that square with all the banks in it. '*Ecco, signora!*' the waiter jollily exclaimed, bringing me what I ordered. It was pleasant sitting there, watching the people. A smartly dressed couple sat near me, the woman subtly made up, her companion elegant in a linen suit, with a blue silk tie. A lone man, bearded, read *La Stampa*. Two pretty girls, like twins, gossiped. '*Ecco, signora!*' the waiter said again. It was extraordinary, the dream I'd had about Mr Riversmith, and I kept wondering how on earth I could have come to have such knowledge of anything as private as that, and in such telling detail. I kept hearing his voice telling me about the family dispute, and I rejoiced that we had at last conversed.

'*Bellissima!*' a salesgirl enthused a little later. I held between my hands a brightly coloured hen. I had noticed it in a window full of paper goods, side by side with a strikingly coiled serpent and a crocodile. Each was a mass of swirling, jagged colours on what from a distance I took to be papier mâché. But when I handled the animals I discovered they were of carved wood, with paper pressed over the surface instead of paint.

I bought the hen because it was the most amusing. It was wrapped for me in black tissue paper and placed in a carrier-bag with a design of footprints on it. Did he love Francine? I wondered, and again I tried to visualize her – inspecting insects through a microscope, driving her Toyota. But I did not succeed.

Instead, as I left the shop, I saw Mr Riversmith himself. He was turning a corner and disappeared from view while I watched. I paused for a moment, but in the end I hurried after him.

'Mr Riversmith!'

He turned and, when he saw who it was, waited. The street we were in was no more than an alley, sunless and dank. If we turned left at the end of it, Mr Riversmith said, we would soon find ourselves in the Campo again.

'Let's not,' I suggested, perhaps a little daringly.

I had noticed, through a courtyard, a small, pretty hotel with creeper growing all over it. I drew Mr Riversmith towards it.

'This is what we're after.' I guided him through the entrance and into a pleasant bar.

'Are the others coming here? I thought we arranged – '

'Let's just sit down, shall we?'

Imagine a faintly gloomy interior, light obscured by the creeper that trails around the windows. The table-tops are green, chairs and wall-coverings red. The two barmen look like brothers, young and slight, with dark moustaches. Only a sprinkling of other customers occupy tables. There are flowers in vases.

'Are they coming here?' Mr Riversmith asked again.

'A little peace for you,' I replied, smiling friendlily. 'I think you'd welcome a bit of peace and quiet, eh? Now, I insist on standing you a cocktail.'

He shook his head. He said something about not drinking in the middle of the day, but recognizing that this was a polite reluctance to accept more hospitality I ignored it. I ordered him an Old Fashioned, since in my house that had been established as his drink.

'It's awfully pleasant here,' I remarked, smiling again in an effort to make him feel at ease. I said there was no reason why he and I shouldn't be a little late for lunch. If tongues wagged it would be nonsense.

He frowned, as if bewildered by this vernacular expression. I shook my head, indicating that it didn't matter, that nothing of any import had been said. The barman brought our drinks. I said:

'I wonder what sort of a person Sano di Pietro was.'

'Who?'

'The artist who painted the picture the child was so taken with. Incidentally, I thought it was a bit extravagant, that remark in the guide-book about the dog noticing the angel first.'

He appeared to nod, but the movement was so slight I might have been mistaken.

'You thought so too? You noticed that?'

'Well, no, I really can't say I did.'

The place filled up. I drew Mr Riversmith's attention to an elderly man with tiny rimless spectacles in the company of a young girl. Lowering my voice, I asked him what he thought the relationship was. He replied, blankly, that he didn't know.

I asked him about other couples, about a group of men who clearly had some business interest in common. I was reminded of the men in Carrozza 219, but I considered it inappropriate to mention this. One of the group repeatedly took small objects from one of his pockets and placed them for a few moments on the table. I thought they might be buttons. I wondered if the men were in the button business.

'Buttons?' Mr Riversmith said.

'Just a notion,' I said, and then a Japanese party entered the bar and I said that there was one most noticeable thing about the Japanese – you could never guess a thing about them.

'Yes,' Mr Riversmith said.

I kept wanting to reach across the table and touch the back of his hand to reassure him, but naturally I didn't. 'What's the matter?' I wanted to ask him, simply, without being fussy with the question. He didn't offer to buy a drink, which was a pity, because for a man like Mr Riversmith the second drink can be a great loosener. All that sense of communication there'd been when he'd talked about his sister a couple of hours ago had gone.

'I really think we should join the others, Mrs Delahunty.'

Although I'd said it was to be my treat, he had already placed a note on the table and within a few minutes we were back on the street again. I had to hurry to keep up with him.

'I just thought,' I said, a little breathless, 'a few minutes' rest might be nice for you, Mr Riversmith.'

Although he in no way showed it, I believe he may possibly have appreciated that. I believe his vanity may have been flattered. He slowed his stride, and we stepped together into the bright sunlight of the Campo. The others were seated round an outside table beneath a striped blue and white awning. To my horror, Quinty and the maid were there also. Quinty was boring the General with details of the Tour de France.

'I see Jean-François has taken the Yellow,' he was saying as we approached them, and the old man nodded agreeably. He showed me a book of flowers he'd bought, the text in Italian but with meticulously detailed illustrations of azaleas. 'Mollis and Knaphill,' he said, a forefinger following the outline of the species. 'Kurume and Glenn Dale. We shall *make* them grow.'

Otmar and Aimée were looking through their postcards. Rosa Crevelli had opened a powder compact and was applying lipstick. Having given up his effort to interest the General in bicycle-racing, Quinty was smiling his lopsided smile, his head on one side, admiring her.

'I've bought a really gorgeous hen,' I said.

I carefully unwrapped my prize. Aimée gasped when the pretty thing emerged from its black tissue paper.

'They have crocodiles and serpents as well, Aimée, but I thought the hen the best.'

'Wow, it's fantastic!'

'"Who'll help me grind my corn?" D'you know about the little red hen, Aimée?'

She shook her head.

'"I won't," said the dog. "I won't," said the cat.' I told the tale in full, as Mrs Trice had related it to me so very long ago, when I was younger than Aimée.

'Well, I never heard that one,' Quinty said. '*Capisci?*' he asked Rosa Crevelli. 'Signora's on about a farmyard fowl. *Una gallina.*'

I leaned toward Mr Riversmith, next to whom I was seated, and said I had hoped Quinty and the girl would have lunch on their own. 'I must apologize for your having to sit down with servants.'

He shook his head as if to say it didn't matter. But it *did* matter. It was presumptuous and distressing. I attracted a waiter's attention and indicated that Mr Riversmith would be grateful for an Old Fashioned and that I'd like a gin and tonic myself. I did so quietly; but Quinty has an ear for everything.

'G and t!' he shouted down the table at the waiter, who repeated the abbreviation, appearing to be amused by it. 'You like g.t.?' he offered everyone in turn. 'I like,' Rosa Crevelli said. Mr Riversmith said he didn't want an Old Fashioned.

'It wasn't arranged, she invited herself. They're lame ducks, as you might say.'

Quinty had been down and out, I went on; the girl was of gypsy stock. As I spoke, the waiter returned with my gin and tonic, and one for Rosa Crevelli as well. '*Due* g.t.!' he shouted, affecting to find the whole episode comic. When taking our orders for lunch he clowned about, striking attitudes and rolling his eyes. All this had been started off by Quinty and the maid. I drew Mr Riversmith's attention to the fact, but added that they meant no harm.

'It can be hurtful,' I said, 'but there you are.'

The General had put his horticultural manual aside and was describing to Otmar the purpose of different kinds of spades. Quinty joined in the conversation, saying something about a local firm that would supply fertilizer at a good price. When labour was required he advised the General to get estimates. In Italy nothing was done without an estimate. There was a babble of Italian from Rosa Crevelli and everyone had to wait while it was translated. It didn't amount to much, something to do with where urns for the azaleas might be obtained.

'A most extraordinary thing,' I remarked to Mr Riversmith, unable any longer to resist telling him about the dream. While I was speaking the waiter came with bottles of wine and mineral water. He joked again, pouring me two glasses of wine and then, in mock confusion, a third one. Aimée enjoyed his nonsense, and I suppose it was innocent enough.

'No more than a boy you were,' I said. 'Fifteen or so.'

But Mr Riversmith displayed no interest. I asked him if he had dreamed himself the night before and he insisted he hadn't. He rarely did, he said.

I suggested, though diffidently, that none of us can get through a night's sleep without the assistance of dreams. Sometimes we forget we dream. We remember briefly and then forget. Or do not remember at all.

'I am not familiar with the subject,' Mr Riversmith said.

Hoping to encourage him, I carefully retailed the details of the dream. I described the boy he'd been. I described the child his sister, Phyl, had been. I asked him if he remembered a Venetian blind that on occasion might have rattled, a slat tapping against the kitchen window-frame.

'No.'

The reply came too quickly. To remember, it is necessary to think for a moment, even for several minutes. But I didn't want to press any of this. I finished my drink and pushed away a plate of soup, not caring for the taste of it. It was disappointing that Mr Riversmith wasn't going to bother, but of course it couldn't be helped.

'I just thought I'd mention it,' I said.

I don't think he spoke again while we had lunch but afterwards, as we walked through the streets to where the car was, I noticed to my surprise that he attempted to engage Rosa Crevelli in conversation. Since her English scarcely exists, it must have been an extremely frustrating experience for him. It was all the more bewildering that he appeared to persevere.

I was a little upset by this and somewhat gloomily walked with the General, whose slow pace suited me. The day before I'd noticed further letters from the two firms of solicitors, so I raised the subject as we made our way together.

'I've written to say I am creating a garden.'

'Good for you, General!'

'I've been meaning to say, actually: you've no objection to Otmar and myself delaying our departure a while, have you?'

'Of course I haven't.'

'He's nervous to mention it to you, but he's wondering if the garden could be his way of paying for his board and lodging?'

'Of course it could be.'

'From me, it's a gift, you understand? I shall continue to pay my weekly whack.'

'That's as you like, General.'

Since we were passing various small cafés and bars I suggested that he might rest for a few minutes and have another cup of coffee. He readily agreed, and when we found somewhere agreeable I decided not to have more coffee but ordered a glass of grappa instead.

'A garden can't make up for anything.' The old man, quite suddenly, returned to the subject, perhaps feeling that this was the time to say it, now that he had me on my own for a few minutes. 'But at least it will mark our recovery in your house.'

'Stay as long as you like.' I replied softly, knowing that that, really, was what we were talking about.

'You're kind,' he said.

We made a detour on our journey back to my house, turning off the main road and winding our way up to a Benedictine monastery. It was cool and leafy, with a coloured sculpture high up in an archway, and another in the same position on the other side: this is the abbey of Monte Oliveto Maggiore, as close to heaven on earth as you will ever find. With the exception of the General, we all descended several flights of steps, through a forest of trees, to the monks' church in a cool hollow below. Along the cloisters were murals of St Benedict's life. Doves cooed at one another, occasionally breaking into flight. In the monks' shop mementoes were laid out tastefully.

'Gosh!' Aimée exclaimed, as delighted as she'd been by the picture of the shepherds and by the hen I'd bought. 'Otmar, isn't it fantastic?'

Otmar was always there, unobtrusively behind her. His devotion was remarkable, and constantly she turned to him, to share a detail that had caught her imagination or to tell him something she'd thought of, or just to smile.

'It is fantastic,' he said.

'What's "fantastic" in German, Otmar?'

'*Phantastisch.*'

'*Phantastisch.*'

'That is good, Aimée.'

'Would a German understand me?'

'*Ja. Ja.*'

'Tell me another word. Tell me the name of a bird.'

'*Taube* is for dove. *Möwe* is for seagull.'

'How do you say "beautiful"?'

'*Schön* is for beautiful.'

'*Schön.*'

'That is good.'

'*Möwe.*'

'That is good too.'

Mr Riversmith bought her a little red and green box with drawers in it, and then we climbed back to where the General awaited us. He had found a tea-room and was reading about flowers again.

'It's really beautiful down there,' Aimée told him. 'A monk patted my head.'

As we moved towards the car I managed to draw Otmar aside, to reassure him that his proposal for paying what was owing was quite acceptable, and to repeat that he, too, was welcome to remain in my house for as long as he wished.

'I have no skills for the work. I bring no knowledge.'

I reassured him on this point also, and for some reason as I did so a vivid picture came into my mind: of his buying the railway tickets to Milan on 5 May and counting the notes he received in change. 'Shall we have a cappuccino?' Madeleine suggested. 'There's time.' I might have placed a hand on the shoulder from which his arm had been cut away, but somehow I could not bring myself to do so. I might have said he must not blame himself. Without knowing anything, I might have said it was all right.

'It is possible,' I said instead. 'A life you did not think of when you lay in that hospital is possible, Otmar.'

For a second the eyes behind the large spectacles fearfully met mine. I remembered his fingers interlaced with Madeleine's, and the old man as straight as a ramrod beside his daughter. I remembered the two children arguing in whispers, and a workman with a shovel, standing by the railway line.

'She is going back to America,' Otmar said, and there our conversation ended.

In the car Quinty regaled Mr Riversmith with information

he'd picked up somewhere about St Mary of Egypt. 'Singer
and actress she used to be,' his voice drifted back to where I
was sitting, and he went on about how scavenging dogs
wouldn't touch the remains of St Bibiana, and how the Blessed
Lucy endured a loss of blood through her stigmata every
Wednesday and Friday for three years. I was unable to hear
how Mr Riversmith responded and didn't particularly try to,
because that Quinty was having a field day didn't matter
any more. What mattered was that Mr Riversmith was an
ambitious man: that hadn't occurred to me before. He was
ambitious and Francine was ambitious for him, and for herself.
There were other professors with microscopes, watching other
colonies of ants in other trees. He and Francine had to keep
ahead. They had to get there first. What time could they
devote to a child who had so tiresomely come out of the blue?
Would serious ambition be interrupted in Virginsville,
Pennsylvania? That's what I wondered as Quinty continued
to be silly and Mr Riversmith, poor man, was obliged to
listen.

When we returned I lay down for an hour; it was almost seven
when I appeared downstairs again. Aimée was in bed, the
General said, and wished to say good-night to her uncle and
myself. He and I went together to her room, where the shutters
had been latched to create an evening twilight. When Mr
Riversmith spoke her name she answered at once. I sat on the
edge of the bed. He stood.

'Aimée, I would like you to have the hen I bought. It's a
present for you.'

To my surprise, she seemed bewildered. Her face puckered, as
if what I'd said made no sense. Then she turned to her uncle.

'I didn't ever know there was a quarrel.'

'It wasn't important.'

'But it *happened*.'

'Yes, it happened.'

Since that seemed inadequate, I added:

'Disagreements don't much matter, Aimée.' And deliberately changing the subject, I added: 'Remember the picture of the shepherds?'

'Shepherds?'

'The shepherds with their dog.'

'And a *hen*?'

'No, no. The hen was what I bought for you.'

'What else was in the picture?'

'Well, sheep in a pen.'

'What else?'

'There were hills and houses,' Mr Riversmith said, and although I wasn't looking at him I guessed that that familiar frown was gathering on his brow.

'And eight trees,' I added. 'Don't you remember, we counted them?'

Through the gloom I watched her shaking her head. Her uncle said:

'I guess you remember the angel in the sky, Aimée?'

'Have you come to say good-night? I'm sleepy now.'

I mentioned the visit to the monastery, but the entire day except for that reference to a quarrel appeared to have been erased from Aimée's memory. Her breathing deepened while we remained with her. I could tell she was asleep.

'This isn't good,' her uncle said.

Of course the man was upset; in the circumstances anyone would be. He asked if he might telephone Dr Innocenti, and did so from the hall. I listened on the extension in my private room, feeling the matter concerned me.

'Yes, there will be this,' Dr Innocenti said.

'The child's suffering from periodic amnesia, doctor.'

'So might you be, signore, if you had experienced what your niece has.'

'But this came on so suddenly. Was it the excitement today, the visit to Siena?'

'I would not say so, signore.'

Mr Riversmith said he had arranged to return to Penn-sylvania with Aimée in four days' time. He wondered if he'd been hasty. He wondered if his niece should be taken back to the hospital for observation.

'The journey will not harm your niece, signore.'

'All day she seemed fine.'

'I can assure you, signore, she has recovered more of herself than we once had hopes of in the hospital. What remains must be left to passing time. And perhaps a little to good fortune. Do not be melancholy, signore.'

Naturally, in all honesty, Dr Innocenti had had to say that the journey would not be harmful. It was not the journey we had to dwell upon but the destination. And this was not something Dr Innocenti could presume to mention. There were further reassurances, but clearly Mr Riversmith remained far from relieved. No sooner had the conversation with Dr Inno-centi come to an end than he made a call to his wife in Virginsville. I guessed he would, and again picked up the receiver in my room. She was not surprised, the woman said. In a case like this nothing could be expected to be straight-forward. Her voice was hoarse, deep as a man's, and because I'd heard it I at last pictured without difficulty the woman to whom it belonged: a skinny, weather-beaten face, myopic eyes beneath a lank fringe, eyebrows left unplucked.

'What you need's a good stiff drink,' I said a little later, when Mr Riversmith appeared in the *salotto*. He looked shaken. For all I knew, she'd given him gip after I'd put the receiver down. For all I knew, this weather-beaten woman blamed him for the mess they'd got into – having to give a home to a child who by the sound of things was as nutty as a fruitcake. Added to which, the heat in Siena might well have adversely affected the poor man's jet-lag. I poured him some whisky, since whisky's best for shock.

10

After I'd had my bath that evening I happened to catch a glimpse of myself, as yet unclothed, in my long bedroom mirror. My skin was still mottled from the warm water, the wounds of 5 May healed into vivid scars. A dark splotch of stomach hair emphasized the fleshiness that was everywhere repeated – in cheeks and thighs, breasts, arms and shoulders. To tell you the truth, I think it suits me particularly well in my middle age. I'd feel uneasy scrawny.

I chose that evening a yellow and jade outfit, a pattern of ferns on a pale, cool ground. I added jewellery – simple gold discs as earrings, necklace to match, rings and a bangle. Not hurrying, I made my face up, and applied fresh varnish to my fingernails. My shoes, high-heeled and strapped, matched the jade of my dress.

'You're putting us to shame tonight,' the General remarked as we sat to dinner on the terrace, and you could see that Otmar was impressed as well. But Mr Riversmith reacted in no way whatsoever. All during dinner you could tell that he was worried about the child.

'You mustn't be,' I said when we were alone. A local man who hired machines for ploughing had arrived, and the General and Otmar had gone to talk to him at the back of the house.

'She's suffering from a form of amnesia,' Mr Riversmith said. 'She draws the pictures and then forgets she's done them. She's forgotten a whole day.'

'We're lucky to have Dr Innocenti here.'

'Why did the German say he'd drawn the pictures?'

'I suppose because there must be an explanation for the pictures' existence. It would be worrying for Aimée otherwise.'

'It isn't true. It causes a confusion.'

Because of his distress he was as forthcoming as he'd been when he'd felt guilty about his sister. Distress brings talk with it. I've noticed that. In fairness you couldn't have called him ambitious now.

'Look at it this way, Mr Riversmith: an event such as we've shared draws people together. It could be that survivors understand one another.'

His dark brows came closer together, his lips pursed, then tightened and then relaxed. I watched him thinking about what I'd said. He neither nodded nor shook his head, and it was then that it occurred to me he bore a very faint resemblance to Joseph Cotten. I didn't remark on it, but made the point that all four of us would not, ordinarily, have discovered a common ground.

'D'you happen to know if they've given up on the case?' he asked, not responding to what I'd said.

I didn't know the answer to this question. Since the detectives had ceased to come to my house we'd been a little out of touch with that side of things. The last I'd heard was that they considered their best hope to be the establishing of a connection between the events of 5 May and some other outrage, even one that hadn't yet occurred. I repeated all that, and Mr Riversmith drily observed:

'As detective-work goes, I guess that's hardly reassuring.'

I sipped my drink, not saying anything. It was Joseph Cotten's style, rather than a resemblance. A pipe would not have seemed amiss, clenched between his strong-seeming teeth. You didn't often see those teeth because he so rarely smiled. Increasingly that seemed a pity.

'There are mysteries in this world,' I said as lightly as I could. 'There are mysteries that are beyond the realm of detectives.'

He didn't deny that, but he didn't agree either. If he'd had a pipe he would have relit it now. He would have pressed the tobacco into the cherrywood bowl and drawn on it to make it glow again. I was sorry he was troubled, even though it made it easier to converse with him. Around us the fireflies were beginning.

'I've been trying to get to know you, Mr Riversmith.'

Perhaps it was a trick of the twilight but for a moment I thought I saw his face crinkling, and the bright flash of his healthy teeth. I tapped out a cigarette from a packet of MS and held the packet toward him. He hadn't smoked so far and he didn't now. I asked him if he minded the smell of a cigarette.

'Go right ahead.'

'You brought up mysteries, Mr Riversmith.' I went on to tell him about the feeling I continued to experience – of a story developing around us, of small, daily details apparently imbued with a significance that was as yet mysterious. I spoke of pieces of a jigsaw jumbled together on a table, hoping to make him see that higgledy-piggledy mass of jagged shapes.

'I don't entirely grasp this,' he said.

'Survival's a complicated business.'

From the back of the house the voice of the Italian with the motorized ploughs came to us, a halting line or two of broken English, and then the General's reply. As soon as possible, the old man urged. It would do no harm to turn the earth over several times, now and in the autumn and the spring. The Italian said there would have to be a water line, a trench dug for a pipe from the well. There would be enough stone in the ruined stables, no need to have more cut. Dates were mentioned, argued about, and then agreed.

'It's been a long day.'

As he spoke, Mr Riversmith stood up. I begged him, just for a moment longer, to remain. I poured a little wine into his glass, and a little into mine. Because of his American background, I told him how I'd found myself in Idaho. I mentioned my childhood fascination with the Old West, first encountered in the Gaiety Cinema. I even mentioned Claire Trevor and Marlene Dietrich.

'Idaho is hardly the Wild West.'

'I was misled. I was no more than a foolish child.'

I told him how Ernie Chubbs had been going to Idaho in search of orders for sanitary-ware and had taken me with him on expenses; I told him how he'd taken me with him to Africa and then had disappeared. In the Café Rose they said they expected I'd met Mrs Chubbs, and it was clear what they were hinting at. 'A healthy woman,' they used to say. 'Chubbs's wife was always healthy.' All I knew myself was that every time Ernie Chubbs referred to his wife he had to cough.

I described Ernie Chubbs because it was relevant, his glasses, and tidy black hair kept down with scented oil. I explained that he didn't travel with the sanitary-ware itself, just brochures full of photographs. In order to illustrate a point, I was obliged to refer again to the Café Rose, explaining that he took an order there but when the thing arrived eight or so months later it had a crack in it. 'The place was unfortunate in that respect. "I Speak Your Weight", a weighing-machine said in the general toilet, but when you put your coin in nothing happened. Chubbs sold them that too. He used to be in weighing-machines.'

'I see.'

There was another line Chubbs had, what he called the 'joke flush'. When you pulled the chain, a voice called out, 'Ha! ha!' You kept pulling it and it kept saying, 'Ha! ha!' What was meant to happen was you'd give up in desperation;

then you'd open the door to go out and the thing would flush on its own. But what actually happened was that when people installed the joke flush the voice said, 'Ha! ha!' and they couldn't make it stop, and the flush didn't work no matter what they did. Another thing was, when the light was turned on in the toilet, music was meant to play but it hardly ever did.

'In the end the defective goods people caught up with Ernie Chubbs.'

'I really think I must get along to bed now.'

Women were Ernie Chubbs's weakness: he was Aries on the cusp with Taurus, a very mixed-up region for a man of his sensual disposition. Before my time he took someone else round with him on expenses, but when she wanted to marry him he couldn't afford to because of the alimony. It was then that Mrs Chubbs conveniently turned up her toes, and after that the other lady wouldn't touch him with a pole. Maybe she got scared, I wouldn't know. I was eighteen years old when I first met Ernie Chubbs, green as a pea. 'All very different from your ants,' I said.

The engine of a motor-car started. *'Buonanotte!'* the old man called out, and then Otmar wished their visitor goodnight also. There was a flash of headlights as the car turned on the gravel before it was driven off.

Again Mr Riversmith stood up and this time I did so too. I led him from the terrace into the house, and to my private room. I switched the desk-light on and pointed at my titles in the glass-faced bookcase. I watched him perusing them, bending slightly.

'You're an author, Mrs Delahunty?'

I explained that the collected works of Shakespeare had been part of the furniture at the Café Rose, together with the collected works of Alfred Lord Tennyson. That was my education when it came to writing English. I knew 'The Lady of

Shalott' by heart, and the part of Lady Macbeth and 'Shall I
compare thee to a summer's day?' I said:

'You might like to call me Emily.'

There was something about his forehead that I liked. And
to tell the truth I liked the way, so unaffectedly, he'd said he
didn't grasp what I was endeavouring to relate to him. There
was reassurance in his sombre coolness. He kept coming and
going, emerging when he was troubled, hiding because of
nerviness when he wasn't. Clever men probably always need
drawing out.

'You're Capricorn,' I said, making yet another effort to put
him at ease. 'The moment I heard your voice on the phone I
guessed Capricorn.'

He turned the first few pages of *Bloom of Love*. There was
a flicker of astonishment in the eyes that had been so ex-
pressionlessly opaque a moment before. He picked up *Waltz
Me to Paradise*, then returned both volumes to where he'd
taken them from.

'Most interesting,' he said.

'Your ants are interesting too, Tom.'

Perhaps it was ridiculous to think that a professor of en-
tomology in his middle years would ask if he might take *Little
Bonny Maye* or *Two on a Sunbeam* to bed with him, but even
so it was a disappointment when he didn't. We stood without
saying anything for a moment, listening to the sound of one
another's breathing. I kept seeing his ants, running all over the
place, a few carrying others on their backs, all of them intent
upon some business or other.

'I would listen if you told me, Tom. About your ants.'

He shook his head. His research was of academic interest
only, and was complex. An explanation of it did not belong in
everyday conversation.

'What was it you didn't grasp, Tom?'

'What?'

I smiled encouragingly, wanting to say that if he smiled more himself everything would be easier for both of us, that it was a pity to possess such strong teeth and not ever to display them. I asked him to pick out *Precious September*. By Janine Ann Johns, I said, and watched him while he did so.

'Open it, Tom.'

I asked him to look for Lady Daysmith, and to read me a single sentence concerning her. There was an initial hesitation, a shifting of the jaw, the familiar tightening of the lips. I sensed a reminder to himself of the care, and love, that had so cosseted his sister's child in this house.

'*Lady Daysmith knelt,*' he read eventually. '*She closed her eyes and her whisper was heard in the empty room, beseeching mercy.*'

He replaced the volume on its shelf and closed the glass-paned door on it.

'Sit down, Tom. Have a glass of grappa with me.'

He rejected this, but I begged him and in the end he did as I wished because I said it was important. I poured us each a glass of grappa. I said:

'Lady Daysmith had her origins in a Sunday-school teacher.' I described the humility of Miss Alzapiedi, her gangling height, the hair that should have been her crowning glory. 'Flat as a table up front. I turned her into an attractive woman, Tom.'

'I see.'

'All her life she never wore stockings. Her skirts came down to her shoes.'

He began to rise, his drink untouched.

'Drink your grappa, Tom. I've poured it for you.'

He sipped a little. I told him that that was how it was done: you turned Miss Alzapiedi into elegant Lady Daysmith. I told him how Miss Alzapiedi had come to my assistance when I mixed up God with Joseph. I didn't claim that making her Lady Daysmith was a reward. It was just something that had occurred.

'But it's nice, Tom. And it's nice that an old man who's had the stuffing knocked out of him can still find his last reserves in order to create an English garden in the heat of Umbria.'

'Yes, indeed.'

Illusion came into it, of course it did. Illusion and mystery and pretence: dismiss that trinity of wonders and what's left, after all? A stick of an old creature in misery as he walks up and down a hospital corridor with a holy statue in it. The suffering in the heart of a Sunday-school teacher who wears her dresses long. Dismiss it and you're face to face with a violent salesman of sanitary-ware, free-wheeling about with young girls on expenses. Dismiss the conventions of my house in Umbria and Quinty, for one, would be back where he started.

'If I gave Quinty his marching orders, Tom, he'd take his gypsy with him and they'd end up on a wasteland. They'd make a shack out of flattened oil-drums. They'd thieve from people on the streets.'

'Mrs Delahunty – '

'I've seen the tourists here looking askance at Quinty, and who on earth can blame them? You must have thought you'd come to a madhouse when he began his talk about holy women. Yet eccentric conversation's better than being a near criminal. Or so I'd have thought.'

Politely he said he found Quinty not uninteresting on the subject of hagiology. I smiled at him: once again he was doing his best. I remembered him walking beside Rosa Crevelli after we'd had lunch, making an effort to converse with her. He'd had a glass or two of wine, and I wondered if he'd thought to himself that she had an easy look to her. No reason why a reticent man shouldn't have a fancy, shouldn't go for that sallow skin and gypsy eyes, a different ball-game from Francine. But this wasn't the time to wonder for long about any of that.

Perhaps in the morning, I suggested, we might look for a bark-ant together so that he could show me his side of things, since I'd been going on so about my own. For a start, I'd no idea if a bark-ant looked different from the kind of ant that lives beneath a stone. I asked him about that, pouring just a thimbleful more grappa into my glass. I said it was fascinating what he'd said about bark-ants behaving like human beings. I asked him how they came by their name. He didn't answer, and when I looked up I discovered he was no longer in the room.

11

The old man showed me what he intended, passing on to me the gist of the deliberations that had taken place the evening before, how the Italian had pointed out that in order to create the different levels a mechanical digger rather than a ploughing machine was necessary. This, too, he could supply and operate himself. The General showed me where the terracing and the flights of steps would be. Part of the garden would be walled: the Italian had machinery for demolishing the half-ruined stables and moving the stone to where it could be attractively put to use.

The General repeated that the garden was a gift. But he did not feel he could make such drastic alterations without my agreement. He showed me where a fountain would be, and where the shade trees would be planted.

'It'll be beautiful, General.'

'A garden should have little gardens tucked away inside it. It should have alcoves and secret places, and paths that make you want to take them even though they don't lead anywhere. What grows well, you cherish. What doesn't, you throw out.'

The digger would bite into the slope beside the sunflower field. As well as terraces, there would be sunken areas. The Italian who'd come was a man of imagination; he'd entered into the spirit of the challenge. A separate well for the garden might be necessary, rather than the pipeline he'd first suggested. The old cypress tree beside the stables would remain.

'This'll be costly, General. Are you sure – '

'Yes, I'm sure.'

Then, for the last time in my presence, the old man mentioned his daughter. We stood among the rank growth of that wasted area, to which the dilapidated old buildings and rusty wheels and axles lent a dismal air. The General stared down at the ground of which he expected so much. In his daughter's lifetime he had resented the fact that what wealth he left behind would be shared with her husband. 'I would happily give all the days remaining to me if it might be now,' he murmured, and said no more.

So it was left. I had accepted gifts from men before, but never one like this, and never without strings that tied some grisly package. I was moved afresh by what was happening, by faith being kept in so many directions at once, by frailty turned into strength. The timbers of these useless buildings and the discoloured iron that had sunk into the ground would be scooped away, the fallen walls given an unexpected lease of life; an old man's dream would spread on the hill beside the sunflower slope. He knew, as I did, that he would not live to see his garden's heyday. But he knew it didn't matter.

That day was hotter, even, than the days that had preceded it. At half-past ten Aimée and her uncle went for a walk, advised to do so before the day became oppressive. There is a selection of straw hats in the outer hall, kept for the tourists, since people who come here always want to walk about the hillsides no matter what the temperature. I insisted that Aimée should wear one, and her uncle also; I warned them to keep to the roads and tracks for fear of snakes. For a few moments I watched their slow progress through the clumps of broom and laburnum, Aimée in a light-blue dress, her wide-brimmed panama too big for her, he in shirtsleeves and fawn cotton trousers, and a hat with a brown band. When they passed from sight I hurried into the house and made my way to his bedroom.

I'd hoped to find a photograph of Francine that would confirm the picture I had formed, but there wasn't one. His clothes hung neatly in the simple wardrobe, a tie was draped over the back of a chair. A sponge-bag contained an electric razor, toothbrush and toothpaste, aspirin and deodorant. Airline tickets and cufflinks were on the dressing-table; soiled laundry had been folded and placed at the bottom of one of the black Mandarina Duck bags. On the bedside table there was a grey-jacketed volume entitled *The Case for Differentia*. I opened it, but could not understand a word. Convoluted sentences trailed sluggishly down the page. Words were brandished threateningly, and repeated for good measure: *empirical, behavioural, delimit, cognitive, validation, determinism, re-endorsement. Can this be designated an urban environment?* a question posed, followed by the statement that *a quarter of the 'given population' are first-generation immigrants.* From what I could gather these were ants, not human beings. I closed the volume hastily.

Beneath it there was a blue notebook full of jottings in what I took to be the handwriting of Mr Riversmith. The script was more than a little difficult to read, pinched and without any attempt at an attractive effect. *?Is evidence, co-operation economic activities, exchange goods, service. ?Trade, familial lines. Pilsfer's recreation theory shaky. Recurrent exchange gifts cannot be taken recreational. ?Sanctions on miscreant. No evidence Pilsfer's sleep motive. Seasonal migration dubious. No evidence P's hospital theory. This surely invalid.*

I turned the pages. There were diagrams that looked like family trees without names, but with all the lines joined together, suggesting an electrical circuit of unusual elaboration and complexity. There were further references to recreation and to Pilsfer, who didn't at all appear to know what he was up to. A particular observation caught my eye, since it was heavily underscored. *Maeslink's theory exploded, premises no*

validity now: 3 April '87. Impossible extrapolate. By its nature,
sensation indefinable. The last entry, marked *Italy July '87,*
was: *Sleeping-bag theory ignores monoist structure.* In what
I'd read the word *theory* occurred four times.

All this was what occupied him. All this was what fuelled
his ambition. All this was what made him reticent. I knew a
man once who was scarcely able to address a word to anyone,
but that reserve was as brittle as the ice it seemed like, and
when it cracked there was a flow I couldn't stop: there was
little evidence to suggest that Mr Riversmith was like that,
even if he *was* more voluble when upset. He was eminent and
distinguished and looked up to. There were people who would
listen, intrigued, when he explained the world in terms of ants
who bred in bark: you could tell all that by his manner. He
was not aware of ordinary matters, as the Italian who was
bulldozing out my garden was; in fact, he had so far displayed
no signs of awareness whatsoever. His cleverness was there as
a substitute and it could hardly be worthless. That's what I
thought as I left his room that morning, 24 July 1987, a date I
have never forgotten.

I have not forgotten it because what happened on the afternoon of that day was that I received one of the most unpleasant
shocks of my life. Mr Riversmith asked permission to make
yet another telephone call to Pennsylvania; I said of course,
and went to my room. He was remarking, when I lifted the
receiver, that he had never before encountered a romantic
novelist. Then, distressing me considerably, he referred to as
'trash' what last night he had called most interesting. He
referred to the grappa we'd enjoyed together as an unpleasant
drink. The word 'grotesque' was used in a sentence I couldn't
catch. The brief, and private, revelations I had made – in
particular the death of Mrs Chubbs – were described as 'a
drunken fantasy'. He said I'd gone to Idaho thinking I'd find
the Wild West there, which had he listened he would have

realized wasn't so. 'Some honey!' the hoarse voice at the other end more than once interrupted.

I couldn't understand it. In good faith I'd shown him my titles. I'd gone to a great deal of trouble to arrange an outing to Siena. I'd given him drink after drink and had not even considered entering them in Quinty's book. 'Her imagination has consumed her,' he said. From his tone, he could have been referring to an ant.

I replaced the receiver and simply sat there, feeling weak, as though I had been bludgeoned. He hadn't even become familiar with the books' contents: all he had done was to read a few lines because I asked him to, and to glance at the illustrations on the jackets. I smoked, and drank a little, hardly anything really. Quinty knocked on my door and said there was tea downstairs; I thanked him but did not go down. He knocked again at dinner-time, but again I chose to remain on my own. I watched the dusk gathering and welcomed it, and welcomed darkness even more. When I slept I dreamed a terrible dream:

It was Otmar who brought the thing on to the train. Long before they'd met in the supermarket he and his friends had picked the girl out. They knew all about her. She was suitable for their purpose.

In my dream I saw Otmar as a child, in the dining-room with his mother and father, Schweinsbrust on the table. There is a sudden crash, the battering down of the outside door; then four men enter the dining-room and greet the diners softly. The tears of Otmar's mother drop on to the meat and potatoes and little stewed tomatoes. His father stands up; he knows his time has come. For a moment the only sound is the ticking of the clock on the mantelpiece, between the two bronze horsemen. Otmar's mother does not cry out; she does not attempt to fling herself between the men and their prisoner. A long time ago she endeavoured to accept her husband's fate in anticipation; she, too, knew the men would one day come.

For crimes committed in Hitler's war he is the four men's prey, and the clock still ticks when they have taken him away. It ticks even though there will be no trial; the execution will be discreet. It ticks as sportingly as ever, while the tears of Otmar's mother fall on to the little stewed tomatoes, while she decides she does not wish to live herself. It ticks when she stands up and goes away, and when Otmar finds her, tied up to a light fixture in another room.

'Otmar it is,' an unhurried voice states, the children of the fathers locked in another turn of the wheel, a fresh fraternity of vengeance. Broken matchsticks are cast as lots. 'Otmar is the chosen one.'

In Carrozza 219 he strokes her arm. She'll carry the vengeance through Linata Airport, on to the plane that's bound for Tel Aviv. The victim, as Otmar's father was, is occupied now with other matters; the past is past. In the fields the sunflowers are brilliant against the pale sky. Is it Madeleine's hand that is like an ornament in the air, the same hand that dislodged the stack of mustard jars?

When I pushed the shutters back from my window the next morning the first person I saw was Mr Riversmith. He was bending over a tiny apricot shoot I knew well, no more than five inches of growth, which Signora Bardini had marked with a bamboo cane. Signora Bardini suspected it had sprouted from a stone of the fruit, either thrown down or possibly dropped by a large bird. Clover rather than grass thrived in this area at the side of my house. Two circular beds had been dug by Signora Bardini, but nothing grew in them. Only the day before the General had noticed these beds and said he intended to plant roses in them.

Although it was early I poured myself a little something on my way through the *salotto*. I sat down for a moment, bracing myself. The memory of the telephone conversation was sharper than ever in my consciousness. I wanted to dull it just a little before I spoke, again, to Mr Riversmith. I poured myself a second glass, mostly tonic really, and felt much better when I'd drunk it. I lit a cigarette and put on my sunglasses.

Mr Riversmith had moved from the apricot shoot when I reached him, and was shading his eyes with a hand in order to admire the view of the hills. Naturally I wanted to say I'd been hurt by what had been said. I wanted to refer to it in order to clear the air immediately. I felt that, somehow, there might have been an explanation. But I knew it was far better to wait.

'What a lovely morning, Mr Riversmith!'

'Yes, indeed, it is.'

'I love this time of day.'

He nodded so pleasantly in agreement that I wondered if I could possibly have misheard a thing or two on the telephone. It sometimes isn't easy when you can't see a person's face. But his face was there now, and it seemed more disarming than I remembered it, certainly more relaxed than it had been in my private room. Perhaps he had indeed been suffering from jet-lag and was now recovered. I said what I had planned to say.

'I'm afraid I was a nuisance to you when we talked on the terrace two evenings ago, Mr Riversmith.'

'No, not at all.'

'When I'm nervous I have a way of going round in circles. I'm sorry, it must have been disagreeable for you.'

He shook his head. I didn't speak at once in case he wished to comment. When he didn't I said:

'Jet-lag can be horrid.'

'Jet-lag?'

We had moved a little further away from the apricot shoot by now.

'They keep searching for a pill to take, but I believe they haven't had much success.'

He indicated his understanding by slightly inclining his head. He did not speak, and I permitted the silence to lengthen before I did so again myself.

'You were tired and I delayed you. I offended you by presuming to address you by your Christian name. I'm truly sorry.'

'It's perfectly all right.'

'You were not offended?'

'No.'

'It's friendlier to call you Tom.'

'By all means do so.'

'Professor makes you sound ancient.'

It had occurred to me that in spite of his protests to the contrary on his first evening in my house, he might have been offended that this title was never used. I said the apricot plant had grown from a stone, dropped possibly by a bird, and again wanted to mention the telephone conversation. I wanted to get it out of the way, to be told I had misheard and then to leave the subject, not ever to think about it again. But I knew it was not yet the moment. I knew there would be embarrassment and awkwardness.

'Let me show you where the garden'll be,' I said instead, and led him to the back of the house. In Italy you long for lawns, I said; in Africa too. I described all that the General and Otmar and their friend the Italian intended. I pointed to where the herb beds would be. The azaleas would be dotted everywhere, in their massive urns.

'Should be impressive,' he said. Would later he say to Francine that it was all an illusion? Would he say it was trash and only wishful thinking that an old Englishman intended to make a gift of a garden? Was he wondering now if the experience on the train had taken a greater toll of me than had been at first apparent? He looked away, and I thought it might be in case his expression revealed what he was thinking.

'Let's walk a little way, shall we?'

I led him along the dusty road I was so familiar with, by slopes of olive trees and vines. Endeavouring to keep the conversation ordinary, I was about to apologize for Quinty's conversation in the car on the way back from Siena, but then I remembered I had already made an effort to do so.

'I hope you find it peaceful here,' I said.

'Yes, indeed.'

'There's an Italian expression, professor – *far niente*. D'you know it?'

'I don't speak Italian, Mrs Delahunty.'

'No more do I. *Far niente* means doing nothing. *Dolce far niente*. It's nice to do nothing.'

'*Far niente,*' he repeated.

'You'd say it about sitting in a café. As we did in Siena. Or doing as we're doing now, ambling aimlessly. Enjoying the peace.'

'I see.'

That brought another subject to an end. Nothing was said for a while: then remembering that my companion had revealed he'd been married twice, I asked something about that, whether he considered that divorce was like death in a marriage.

'As great a sadness?' I hinted.

'Yes.'

'It cut you up, Tom?'

'Yes, it was painful.'

I dragged from him the name of his first wife: Celeste Adele. Sometimes there is not the slightest difficulty in visualizing a person spoken of, perhaps because of the intonation or expression that accompanies the reference. This was so now: the woman who appeared in my mind was kittenish and petite, dark-haired, much prettier than Francine.

'When was your first wife's birthday, Tom?'

'Adele's?' He had to think. Then: 'May twenty-nine.'

I stopped. 'No wonder it didn't work out, Tom.'

'I don't imagine our break-up had to do with her birthday!'

This opinion was delivered lightly, possibly intended as a joke. If it was, it was the first time he had endeavoured to make one since his arrival in my house.

'What's Francine's birth sign, Tom?'

'I'm afraid I'm not aware of it.'

'When's her birthday?'

'August eighteen.'

'Oh, Tom!'

He frowned, appearing to be genuinely bewildered. When I explained he said:

'I'm afraid I can't accept that individual characteristics have much to do with when a person's born.'

I didn't contradict that. I didn't argue. We walked on again. In a companionable way I slipped my arm through his. The truth was that when I'd picked up the receiver and overheard that unpleasant conversation I'd already had a drink or two, though not much by any means. Sometimes things aren't as crystal clear as they might be when you've had a drink. On top of that the line to Pennsylvania had not been all that good. He'd said something about what he called a 'little-girl voice', and that, of course, might well have been a compliment. I couldn't help thinking that it was nice to have your voice likened to a young girl's. For some reason my thoughts kept harping on that, and while they did so I kept wanting to tell him about the couple in the travelling entertainment business who'd perished when their motor-cycle soared towards heaven over the top of a Wall of Death. It was ludicrous of course, but I wanted to tell him – of all people – about taking that dog for a walk by the sea, and about the person I'd assumed to be my father importuning me in a cinema and in a shed and finally in a bedroom. I even wanted to tell him about the Oleander Avenue scandal. But he was cautious himself in what he said and in time I caught caution from him.

'Was it a hell with Adele, Tom?'

'We were unsuited.'

'She left you in the end?'

'No.'

'Geminis often do the leaving. I only wondered. Did Adele have children later on?'

He replied, rather curtly, that Adele was forty-three when they parted and had not had children, though in fact she had re-married. I said I was sorry it had been a hell with her.

We paused and looked back. I pointed out a hill-town in the misty distance, and a few more landmarks, a tower that two Swedish women had begun to renovate and then had given up, a rock formation that looked like human figures. As we walked on again I said:

'Why did they dislike one another, Tom? Your sister and your wife?'

He was reluctant to supply this information. His eyes had a faraway look and I remembered the jottings in the notebook at his bedside. No doubt he was among those jottings now, no doubt castigating Pilsfer for some fresh inadequacy. I pressed him, very gently. He said:

'They didn't dislike one another. It was simply that my sister wanted me to try again with Adele.'

'But it was your life, eh?'

'She didn't seem to appreciate that it was.'

Time had passed, they hadn't made it up: there was more to all this than the bald explanation I'd been offered. Perhaps he didn't know: men sometimes don't. But I sensed that his sister had recognized Francine for what she was and made it clear to her at the time of the divorce. 'It won't last, Tom': he didn't confess his sister – less outspoken and quieter in his presence – had said that, but I guessed she had. I also guessed that the wound this opinion left behind was deep.

'There's another very good Italian word, Tom. *Colpa*.'

'What's it mean?'

Again I was careful not to alarm him. *Colpa* meant guilt, I explained. The General experienced guilt because of his daughter. Otmar experienced it because he was responsible for Madeleine's presence in Italy. 'And you quarrelled with your sister instead of standing up to Francine.'

He said something I didn't catch. We turned off the road on to a path that wound up a hill where umbrella pines grow in clumps. Here we must keep a special eye out for sleepy vipers, I warned. Better to have worn rubber boots, but Quinty's would be too small for him, and it was only after we'd begun our walk that I realized there was something on that particular hill I wanted him to see.

'This is a beautiful country, Tom. There are beautiful moments hidden away in corners. I have seen, near the Scala in Milan, a stout little opera singer practising as he strolled to a café. I have seen a wedding in the cathedral at Orvieto, when the great doors were thrown wide open and the bride and groom walked out into the sunshine. Something choked in my throat, Tom.'

I believe he nodded. Sometimes his gestures were so slight it was hard to make them out. There was the tranquillity of my house, I went on; in time there would be the garden. Where there had been only rusted iron and tumbled-down buildings before, birds would nest. Bees would search for honey among the flowers.

'It is as though, Tom, we are all inside a story that is being composed as each day passes. Does that explain it better?'

'I guess I don't entirely grasp what you're suggesting. And about my sister – '

'All right, Tom, all right.' I pressed his arm a little closer. He was on the way to becoming agitated, and really there was no need for that. Why should not Aimée be healed, I asked him, as the scratches on my face had healed already, as Otmar's stump would heal, and the General's leg?

'That is what we hope for.'

'She is happy here, you know. Or as happy as she can be at the moment.'

'My wife and I are extremely grateful to you – '

'Is there not a sacrifice you would make, Tom? After years of keeping your young sister at arm's length, through no fault of hers? Do you not owe something to her memory? As the old man does to his daughter's and Otmar to Madeleine's?'

'I've come here to bring my sister's child home.' He spoke flatly; stolidly, I thought. For the first time he sounded a little stupid, although I knew that was ridiculous. 'I am taking in my sister's child,' he said.

Again I was aware of the jottings in the notebook, the darting swiftness of a mind reflected in that impatient scribbling. He knew about the brains of ants. He knew about the nature of their energy. His own brain contained the details of their thought processes or whatever he liked to call them. Of course he could not be stupid.

'Could it be, Tom, that you had to come here to know you should go back alone?'

'Mrs Delahunty – '

'Look,' I interrupted, feeling it was necessary to do so. 'That's the grave of an American soldier.'

I pointed at an iron cross in the grass beside the path. I explained why there was no inscription.

'It is in memory of one man, but it also stands for many. The soldiers of the official enemy gave food and cigarettes to the peasants when the peasants were near starving. One man in particular gave all he had; they didn't even know his name. He died here in some pointless skirmish, but long afterwards they didn't forget him. What a gesture, Tom, to give away your food because you can go without and strangers cannot! And what a gesture, in return, to put a cross up to a nameless benefactor! It can't have been much food, or many cigarettes.'

I stepped forward when I'd finished and tore away grass and weeds from the base of the cross. Then we turned and retraced our steps. He had made no comment whatsoever on the soldier's grave. I took his arm again.

'They thought it was a miracle, Tom, that a soldier should do that. They put a cross up to a miracle.'

My sandals were covered with dust. So were his shoes. The paint on my toenails had temporarily been deprived of its gleam. Against the softness of my breast I could feel a tightening in the muscles of his arm.

'May I tell you something, Tom? Will you listen?'

'I have been listening.'

'Two men in love came to my house, dying a little more each day. In my house a son was terrified of his mother because fear was what she'd instilled in him since his birth, because she couldn't bear to let him go. In my house the women of a *ménage à trois* were cynically used. Pity made me gasp for breath, for there was no escape for any of them. It's different now, Tom.'

There had been a terrible evil was how I put it to him, but in this little corner of Italy there was, again, a miracle. No one could simply walk back into the world after the horror of Carrozza 219. Three survivors out of all the world's survivors had found a place in my house. One to another they were a source of strength. Again I referred to the garden. I quoted the lines that had come to me, only to bewilder me until the General spoke so extraordinarily of a gift.

'Dare we turn our backs on a miracle, Tom?'

I sought his fingers, the way one does when one speaks like that, but roughly he disengaged himself. Suddenly he was cross and I thought he was going to shout, as other men have in my presence. But he didn't. He simply looked at me, not saying anything at all, not speaking again, not answering questions when I asked them. I offered him a drink when we arrived back at the house, but he said he didn't want a drink at nine o'clock in the morning.

12

After that morning's walk I knew what Francine was.

Francine was a disruptive; she couldn't help herself. Francine had seen him and had desired him. Francine considered Celeste Adele a nobody, with her too-sweet manner and her looks and her bird-brain. 'I want Tom Riversmith,' Francine said aloud, although there was no one in the room except herself. 'God damn that silly bitch to hell!' Francine had lost her own husband because he'd been playing around. Fourteen years of marriage, three children conceived and born, and still he came home with someone else's smell. A girl in a panty-hose department – one o'clock in the morning, he'd confessed to that. Francine didn't ask him how he'd come across a panty-hose employee. She only wondered if it was true or if he was getting at her by making her second best to such a person. She'd stopped caring years ago.

That was why she was alone when she discovered she was on a wavelength with Tom Riversmith. Celeste Adele gave itsy little cocktail parties because she liked to play at being a hostess. She handed round Japanese crackers shaped like sea-shells; she made Tom cut slivers of lemon and use a shaker. He did his best among the real-estate people she invited, the lawyers and art-gallery people, all of them off-campus, not his type at all.

'Now *join* us,' Celeste Adele would welcome in a sugary gush as soon as you stepped into the room, where the chatter was already like a tumult. She loved noise. Later, when the party really got going, she put on Big Band music. 'Having a good time', she called it.

Francine had been taken to the first such occasion by a man who'd once invited her to the movies, and once to the Four Seasons for dinner. She knew that nothing was going to come of the relationship. Over ribs at the Four Seasons he'd talked about a wife he'd left and how he regretted that now. 'It's always a gas at the Riversmiths',' he promised, adding that Celeste Adele Riversmith loved to see new faces. On the way, driving with the radio on, he extolled the virtues of his ex-wife, so tediously that Francine moved away from him as soon as they reached their destination. 'I'm Tom Riversmith,' her host introduced himself, finding her alone.

Vaguely recognizing her from the campus, he was interested in her presence at a party of his wife's. (Later Francine learnt that Celeste Adele never invited university people to her parties because she considered it did her husband good to mix what she called 'the real world'.) Francine was working on the newly discovered Kristo papers at the time and he was fascinated: four years of Kristo's research, thought to be lost in the swamps of Cambodia, had come to light in the safe of a New York hotel.

'You're fortunate.' He sounded envious. For more than eleven years, since Kristo's death, there'd been the mystery of the missing notes, with nothing to indicate where they might possibly be. Kristo, who'd trusted no one, had been notorious for jealously guarding every detail of the evidence he turned up.

'Yes, I have been fortunate.'

She liked his reticence. She couldn't imagine him blustering like the man she'd married and had spent so long with, a campus flop if ever there was one. She couldn't imagine him lying, or being caught with a girl in the back of a sedan. He'd be grizzled when he was older – grey and grizzled, and that would suit him.

'I will always despise you for this,' his sister said when several months had passed.

She stood there, a woman Francine had never seen before, a woman who'd travelled three thousand miles to make that statement. Tom *needed* Celeste Adele, their marriage was a perfectly satisfactory one. Tom and Celeste Adele were opposites, but as often as not opposites belonged together, and they did in this case.

'You've smashed your way in,' his sister bitterly accused. 'You're taking what you can get. You're only thinking of yourself.'

There were tears then, but they weren't Francine's. They ran, unchecked, on the other woman's cheeks. Francine didn't attempt to argue.

'She's done so much for you,' his sister pleaded with Tom. 'You couldn't give her children. You used up her best years. Please, Tom, you mustn't turn around and tell her she doesn't matter.'

He shook his head. He hadn't told Adele that.

'What you're doing says it.'

She begged him, while Francine watched and listened. He'd never been like this, his sister said, and then repeated it. He'd always had a heart before.

'It's best,' he quietly muttered.

Hopelessly now, she disagreed. More spurts of tears came, but then she calmed. She blew her nose and wiped at her cheeks. Francine thought that with all this guff out of her system she'd accept the inevitable, would realize she'd gone too far and say so. There was a moment for an apology, for a mumbled effort to repair unnecessary damage. But no apology came.

'You foul bitch,' his sister snapped, like ice cracking. Then she went.

13

The old man lolled in the ladder-backed chair, Aimée was perched on one of the peacock stools. Looking down from the top of the stairs, I couldn't hear what he was murmuring but I was aware of her pleasure in his tenderness.

'I'd love to see England.' Just for a moment, Aimée's voice floated to me, and again the old man murmured.

'The last day.' Otmar had quietly joined me and was looking down also. Through the mist of my tears he seemed even more sombre than he'd been of late: a face I can only describe as defeated was turned in my direction when he spoke, as though the prospect of the child's going left him bereft. Our eyes held, and locked, and the dream I'd had about him took vivid form again. For a moment it seemed like a shaft of truth, coming to complete the story of that summer, illuminating everything. I saw the matchsticks broken, some long, some short. I watched the choice being made. 'Otmar is the chosen one,' the unhurried voice said, and I must have swayed, for he put his hand out to assist me.

At dinner that evening we were quiet. Aimée's clothes, all of which had been bought while she was in the hospital, were already packed into the bag Mr Riversmith had brought specially from America, matching the black Mandarina Duck luggage Francine had chosen for him.

The General hardly opened his mouth; nor did Otmar; nor

I, come to that. Mr Riversmith must have found it restful. He passed a remark or two and afterwards went off for a stroll on his own. I kept reminding myself that if we'd asked him he would have held forth eloquently about the digestive tracts of his chosen creature: an understanding of the human condition didn't come into it. For all I knew, he privately considered that people damaged in an outrage were best forgotten, delegated to a rubbish tip, as the broken metal and bloodstained glass had been.

I listened for his return and, when I heard him passing through the hall, I considered going to wish him good-night, but I did not feel entirely up to it. In the kitchen I poured boiling water on to a tea-bag and dropped a slice of lemon into the glass. I fished the tea-bag out immediately, just as the water changed colour. I added a measure of grappa as I always do when I take tea as late as this, for on its own it keeps me awake. I carried the glass on to the terrace. The sky was clear and full of stars. I could hear the whirring of mosquitoes, but the fireflies all had gone. It was as warm as day.

'Madeleine.' Otmar's voice echoed, repeating the girl's name, nothing more. As I sipped my tea, I heard as well the voice of Miss Alzapiedi telling us about the devil cast out of the Syrophoenician woman's daughter. When evil was made good it was as though the evil had never existed. The greatest wonder of all, Miss Alzapiedi said.

In the kitchen I threw away the remains of my tea. I arranged two glasses and the grappa bottle on a tray. I was wearing an Indian silk dressing-gown, in shades of orange, and slippers that matched it, with gold stitching. I spent a moment in my room, applying a little make-up to my lips and eyes, a little powder, and eau-de-Cologne. I ran a comb through my hair.

When I knocked softly on his door there was no answering murmur. I had hoped he might be awake, thinking about things, but clearly he wasn't. I pushed open the door and for a moment stood there, framed against the dim light of the corridor, before I moved towards his bedside table. I put the tray down and switched the light on. The notebook and the grey-jacketed volume had not yet been packed. I crossed the room again to close the door.

'Once I sold shoes, Tom.' I said that to myself, even though I spoke his name and glazed at his sleeping face. I stood leaning against the door, not immediately wishing to be closer to him or to wake him. I was still aware of the stockinged feet of women, of old shoes cast aside while I knelt and fitted whatever it was the women desired. As hot as ovens, the feet odorously perspired. 'Swollen from walking, dear. Blown up beyond their size.' They always bought shoes that were too small. The narrower fit, dear. Easily take the narrower.' They stared down at the flesh that overlapped the straps and at the little fancy buckles. 'Yes, I'd say they suit, dear.'

Quietly I moved to where he slept. His mouth was drawn down a little as if in some private despair, but I knew this was not the reason. In sleep his forehead wasn't wrinkled, his closed eyes were tranquil. The lips' expression was only a rictus of the night.

'Mr Riversmith,' I whispered. 'Mr Riversmith.'

He stirred, though only slightly, one limb or another changing position beneath the sheet that covered him. I turned away, feeling I should not be too close when he awoke in case he was alarmed. I sat on the room's single chair, half obscured by shadows in a corner.

Again my thoughts were interrupted by moments from my past. In the dining-room of the public house the clerks roughly called out their orders. In the Café Rose I opened a leathery old volume and was lost in another world: *Only reapers, reaping early, in among the bearded barley, hear a song that echoes cheerly* ... 'Two shepherd's pie 'n' chips. A toad-'n-the-hole. A plaice 'n' peas.' You had to repeat the orders so that the clerks could hear; you had to catch their attention, otherwise you'd bring the wrong plateful and then they'd jeer at you, asking you how long you'd been at it. 'Nice pair of nylons, them.' Quick as a flash the clerks would get a hand on you. On the S.S. *Hamburg* I was in love.

'Oh,' Mr Riversmith said.

'It's all right, Mr Riversmith.'

He pushed himself up, leaning on an elbow. He was looking straight at the grappa bottle. He didn't quite know what was what. My voice might have belonged to the sleep he'd come from. He didn't see me in the shadows.

'Nothing's wrong, Mr Riversmith.'

I remembered how, time and time again, I had lain there in the heat of Africa, waiting for whichever man had money that day. Afterwards, downstairs, I would make coffee and cook. The men played cards, I smoked and drank a lemonade. People who didn't exist – not the people of the books I'd found but people of my own – flitted in from somewhere: as I've said before, I'd never have written a word if I hadn't known the hell that was the Café Rose.

'What time is it?'

'Three, I think.'

'Is something – '

'No, nothing's wrong.'

I rose, smiling at him, offering further reassurance. I poured some grappa, for him and for myself. I offered him a glass.

'Look, I don't think I can drink just now.'

'Tomorrow you'll be gone. Take just a sip.'

I returned to the chair in the corner. Tomorrow they'd both be gone.

'I was fast asleep,' he said, the way people who've been roused do.

'I wanted to say I'm sorry.'

'Sorry?'

'For this morning.'

'That doesn't matter.'

'It matters to me, Mr Riversmith.'

Even now, he wasn't quite awake yet. In an effort to shake off his drowsiness he closed his eyes tightly and opened them again. He sighed, no doubt in a further effort to combat that lingering sleep.

'I was almost dreaming myself,' I confessed, 'even though no one could be more wide awake.'

He hadn't taken a sip of his grappa yet. I thought the hand that held the glass might have been shaking due to his not being properly awake; I wasn't sure.

'Phyl didn't care for Francine, and Francine is to be Aimée's second mother. That's all I'm saying, Tom.'

Still the glass was not lifted to his lips.

'You can't blame Francine for hating Phyl, Tom. If you're hated you hate back. It would be straining any woman's humanity not to.'

'My sister is dead. I'd prefer not to discuss this.'

'I was there when her death occurred, Tom,' I gently reminded him.

'My sister's child will be looked after by my wife and myself. To suggest otherwise is ridiculous.'

'I know, Tom, I know. You will take Aimée back to Pennsylvania, and Francine will make efforts — an extra cut of lemon meringue pie, another chocolate cookie. And you will say, when things get dodgy, let's go to the movies or let's drive to Colorado to see the Rockies. You'll buy Aimée a kitten; you'll make excuses for the weakness of her high-school grades; you'll say how pretty she is. But underneath it all Francine's resentment smoulders. Francine is jealous of the attention you have to lavish on your sister's child because of all that's happened. Francine tries, but your sister spoke to her like that. Why should she be reminded of it now, day after day?'

For the second time I witnessed his anger. Crossly, he said I knew nothing whatsoever about the woman he was married to and very little about him. How could I possibly predict Aimée's grades at high school?

I listened. I felt indulgent towards him, protective almost; he hadn't experienced much, he hadn't been much around; he didn't understand how one woman can guess accurately about another. At the Café Rose men had insisted that I appeared to know only too well the women they told me about. 'What must I do?' the ivory cutter demanded. 'Emily, tell me how I may have her.' But when I told him, when I was frank and explained that any woman could see it coming that his violence would land him in gaol, he turned sullen and disagreeable.

'I liked the look of Phyl, Tom.'

'What you liked or didn't like about my sister is without relevance.'

'It's just an observation. I only thought you'd care to know.'

'You saw my sister on a train. In no way whatsoever were you acquainted with her. Yet you speak as if you knew her well.'

Again I paused before responding. Then I told him about the meeting in the supermarket, the jars of mustard that had fallen when Madeleine reached for the herbs, the first cup of coffee she'd had with Otmar. I watched his face as I spoke; I watched his eyes, and was prepared to repeat what I was saying if they momentarily closed.

'There is nothing left of Otmar now. No will, no zest. Otmar's done for. That's why he will remain here.'

'I must ask you to leave me now.'

'The old man's done for too.'

'Mrs Delahunty, I know you've been through a traumatic ordeal – '

'It's unkind to call me Mrs Delahunty, Tom. It's not even my name.'

The dark brows closed in on one another. The forehead wrinkled in a frown. His tongue damped his lips, preparatory to speech, I thought. But he did not speak.

'Is there not a chance you would take, Tom? That a woman such as I can have a vision?'

'The fact that my sister's child spent some time in your house after the tragedy does not entitle you to harass me. I am grateful. My wife is grateful. The child is grateful. May I pass that message on to you, Mrs Delahunty? And may I be permitted to go back to sleep now?'

I rose from the shadows and stood above him, my replenished glass in my hand. I spoke slowly and with emphatic clarity. I said I was unable to believe that he, a man of order and precision, an ambitious man, stubborn in his search for intellectual truth where insects were concerned, refused to accept the truth that had gathered all around him.

'I don't know what you're talking about, Mrs Delahunty.'

'It frightens you, as it frightens me. For weeks the German boy was like a blob of jelly. The General would willingly have put a bullet through his head. The child went into hiding. More had occurred than a visit to a dentist, you know.'

'Why are you pestering me in this way?'

'Because you're dishonest,' I snapped at him. I hadn't meant to, and as soon as I'd spoken I apologized. But his tetchiness continued.

'You've pestered me since I arrived here. You talk to me in a way I simply fail to comprehend. I have said so, yet you persist.'

'One day the child will know about that quarrel and what

was said. One day she'll reach up and scratch Francine's eyes
out.'

He made some kind of protest. I bent down, closer to him,
and emphasized that this wasn't a change of subject, though it
might possibly appear so. I described the scene in Otmar's
boyhood: the fat congealing on the Schweinsbrust, the bronze
horsemen on the mantelpiece. I told him how Otmar's father
was led away, and how Otmar and his mother had listened
to the dull ticking of the clock. I described the children of
the fathers locked, years later, in another turn of the wheel,
and Otmar choosing the shortest matchstick.

'What on earth are you talking about?'

What I'd said had caused him to sit up. His hair was
slightly tousled. I told him not to be silly, to take a little
grappa because he might feel the need of it. But he didn't heed
me. 'What *is* this?' he persisted.

'I'm talking about what happened,' I said. 'I'm talking about
people getting on to a train, and what happened next, and
Quinty taking in three victims of a tragedy because they were
conveniently there, because Quinty on all occasions is greedy
for profit.'

'You are insinuating about the German.'

I poured myself another drink. I lit a cigarette. Before I
could reply he spoke again.

'Are you suggesting the German had something to do with
what occurred on the train? Has he made some kind of confession to you? Are you saying that?'

'How can we know, Tom, the heart and mind of a murderer
when he wakes up among his victims? How can we know if
fear or remorse is the greater when he lies helpless among the
helpless? If my house is a sanctuary for Otmar it is his rack as
well. Any day, any hour, the *carabinieri* may walk from their
car, dropping their cigarettes carelessly on to the gravel.
Any day, any hour, they may seek him in my garden. Does

he choose this torment, Tom? We may never know that either.'

He was listening to me now. For the first time since he'd arrived in my house he had begun to listen to me. When I paused he said:

'What exactly are you saying?'

'I'd love it if you'd take a little grappa, Tom.'

'I don't want any grappa. Why do you keep pressing drink on me? At all hours of the day and night you seem to think I need drink. You make appalling accusations – '

'I'm only saying this might be so. Tom, no one can be certain about anything except the perpetrators – we both know that. No one but they can tell us if we're right when we guess it was a crime turned into an accident.'

'Have you or have you not grounds for making these statements about the German?'

I paused. I wanted him to be calm. I said:

'I had a dream, and when next I looked into those moist eyes behind the discs of his spectacles all of it was there. He lost his nerve. Or at the very last moment – perhaps at Orvieto railway station – he fell in love with her. In relief and happiness he stroked her arm in Carrozza 219, perhaps even whispering to himself a prayer of thanksgiving. Then came the irony: the accident occurred.'

'A *dream*?'

I explained that there was evidence, all around us, of what each and every one of us is capable of. There was the purchase of a female infant so that a man could later satisfy his base desires. A man who lavished affection on a pet could lay his vicious plans while an infant still suckled a bottle. Quinty scarred a young girl's life. In the Café Rose my flesh felt rotten with my loathing of it.

'The old man longed for unhappiness in his daughter's marriage. You rejected your young sister in favour of a predatory woman. If Otmar is guilty there is redemption in a child's forgiveness, and for Aimée a way back to herself in offering it. If Otmar is guilty the miracle may be as marvellous as the soldier giving away his food.' Ages ago it had struck me that there was something odd about Madeleine's journey. 'Flights from Rome full,' he would have lied.

'You're drunk, Mrs Delahunty. All the time I've been in your house you've been drunk. You wake me up at three o'clock in the morning with your garbled rigmaroles about executions and vengeance, expecting me to return to Pennsylvania without my niece just because you've had a dream. It's monstrous to suggest that my niece should continue to grow fond of a boy you claim might be the murderer of her family. It's preposterous to invent all this just in order to make a fantasy of the facts.'

In that same manner he went on speaking. He said it was inconceivable that an innocent girl had been stalked in the manner I described. It was inconceivable that a total stranger had caused her to fall so profoundly in love that a relationship had been formed which on his side was wholly deceitful. An incendiary device could not have been packed into her luggage without her knowledge. Such a device could not pass undetected through Linata Airport. No terrorist attack could possibly have been planned with such ineptitude. And terrorists did not go in for changes of heart.

'Please let me sleep,' he said.

Angrily I shouted at him then, all gentleness gone, not caring if I woke the household. I could feel the warmth of a flush beginning in my neck, and creeping slowly into my face.

'You're a man who always sleeps,' I snapped at him. 'You'll sleep your way to the grave, Mr Riversmith.'

I gulped at what remained of my drink and poured some more. His glass was still where he had placed it on the bedside table. I picked it up and forced it into his hand. A little of the liquid spilt on to his pyjama front. I didn't care.

'Hell is where men like you wake up, Mr Riversmith, with flames curling round their naked legs.'

He said nothing. He feared my wrath, as other men have. I calmed, and wiped the spilt drink from his pyjamas.

'You're extremely drunk,' he said.

It's always easy to maintain a person's drunk. It's an easy way for a man to turn his back. While I looked down at him in his bed a memory of the car-girls of 1950 came into my mind, I don't know why. A drizzle was falling as they sheltered in doorways, their faces yellow in the headlights of the cars. I didn't mention them because I couldn't see that they were relevant. I prayed instead that at last he would understand. 'Please, God,' I said in my mind.

I sat down on the edge of the bed and leaned in toward him, determined that he should visualize the picture I painted: the evening fireflies just beginning beyond the terrace, the General in a linen suit, Otmar among the shrubs of the garden, Aimée smiling. Survivors belonged together, no matter how eccentric it seemed. Normality had ceased for them: why should she not grow fond, and come to understand the bitterness there'd been? Why should she not?

'Don't come closer to me,' he warned unpleasantly. 'I've never given you this kind of encouragement.'

My Indian dressing-gown had accidentally parted. Hastily he looked away. I prayed that a blink of light would enter his expressionless eyes, but while I begged with mine his remained the same. I said:

'Among the few possessions that remained to Otmar after the incident I found a photograph of his mother.'

A newspaper item that told of her death was pasted to the back of it. If the pillow-talk of the Austrian ivory cutter had not always been in German I wouldn't have been able to comprehend a word. But I stumbled through it, and learnt to my astonishment that Otmar's mother had hanged herself from the electric light, exactly as in my dream.

But when I told him Mr Riversmith wasn't in the least astonished. He stared blankly back at me, even though I repeated what I'd said twice to ensure that the order of events had clearly registered. Speaking carefully and slowly, I described the scene: how I had stood among Otmar's last few belongings with the photograph in my right hand, how I had taken nearly ten minutes to comprehend the German, how I had entered the *salotto* fifteen minutes later and found Otmar and the child playing their game with torn-up pieces of paper. My dream had been a month earlier, I said.

The eyes of Thomas Riversmith didn't alter. I did not speak again.

If someone had had a camera there would be a record of the General with his hand held out and Mr Riversmith about to shake it. There would be an image of Signora Bardini still holding the sandwiches she had made for their journey, and Rosa Crevelli saying something to Quinty, and Aimée smiling up at Otmar. There would be one of me too, in a pale loose dress and sunglasses, still standing where Mr Riversmith had turned his back on me when I endeavoured to say goodbye.

I wish a photograph had been taken because just for a moment everything was of a piece and everyone was there. Ten figures stood on the gravel in front of my house, each shadowed by other people, although the camera would not have caught that subtlety. Francine was there, and Celeste Adele, and Phyl and her husband and Aimée's brother. The General's daughter, his son-in-law and his wife were there, and Madeleine, and the girl whom Quinty had wronged. All sorts were there with me.

'Mr Riversmith.' Quinty beckoned, and Mr Riversmith walked towards the car. Aimée carried the hen that was my gift to her.

The dust thrown up by the car wheels settled, and rose

again when the machines that were to make the garden came.
I watched them arrive, and watched while earth was turned,
in preparation for the planting in the autumn. Letters from
strangers also came that morning. *I thought Oberon would
never ask her. What a joyful outcome that was in the end!*
Mrs Edith Lumm of Basingstoke wrote that she and her husband, staying with her husband's sister in Shropshire, had
visited Mara Hall, although it was not called by that name
any more. Her husband and his sister had pooh-poohed the
idea that it was the house which featured in my story, but she
herself was certain because of details she'd noticed, the maze
for a start. Trimleigh Castle it was called now, being an hotel.

That day just happened, time ordinarily passed. It didn't
require much of an effort to know that in the car Quinty
chatted while Mr Riversmith considered the validity of a rule
structure, and said to himself that Pilsfer had got that wrong
also. On the plane the child slept, and a few notes were
scrawled in the blue notebook, important thoughts put down:
hierarchism was almost certainly the governing factor.

*My friend wonders if Derek ever turned up again, and
wonders how Rose fares in later life. My friend – Miss Jaci
Rakes – believes Rose's love for Rick may not be constant.* All
through the afternoon the engines clanked and rattled, moving
stone and earth, roughly laying out paths and flowerbeds. No
one said there was something wrong because the child had
gone, not Otmar certainly, not the old man.

Time was gained as it passed, hours added to Aimée's life.
That evening in Virginsville the untended skin of Francine's
cheek was rough to the touch in Aimée's first embrace. 'How
about scrambled eggs?' Francine suggested as they drove
through rain to the house. 'Will you help me make scrambled
eggs, Aimée, the first thing in your new home?' The child
was silent, staring at the rain on the windshield, the wipers
swishing back and forth.

'You would like something?' Quinty said, coming to my private room, not knocking, for he never does. He didn't in the Café Rose and the habit stuck.

'No, I'm all right, Quinty.'

He changed my ashtray. He placed a little ice-box we have on my desk, with a lemon he had sliced. He left me a fresh glass.

'I'm all right,' I said again.

Darkness came in Pennsylvania. The Riversmiths lay beneath a sheet, his pyjamas bundled away and Francine's lean body naked also. Strength passed from one to the other, now that they were together again. Nutty as a fruitcake that child was, but they'd manage somehow. They'd think of something, being in the thinking business, both of them.

14

By now that summer belongs to the shadows of the past.

I watch the videos of old Westerns with the outside shutters of the *salotto* drawn against the afternoon light. I smoke, and sip a little tonic water livened with just a taste of spirits. The stagecoach horses neigh and judder when they're pulled up with a jerk. Masked men twitch their guns, indicating how they want the passengers to hand over their valuables. One of the men is nervous, which makes it worse. He spews out chewed tobacco. Far away and unaware, the sheriff puts his feet up.

The old man died.

Two autumns later, when Dr Innocenti visited my house for the last time it was to tell us that in Virginsville they decided that expert care was no more than the child's due. Better for her own sake to be looked after by people who were skilled, in a place that contained others of her kind.

One day I looked down into the garden and saw that Otmar had gone, into whatever oblivion he had chosen.

Except to write about that summer I have never since sat down at my black Olympia, and never shall again. I haven't learned much, only that love is different among survivors. The caravan passed by because we hesitated, but that is how things are.

The tourists come again now. They talk of Lake Trasimeno and the attractions of the hill-towns, the cafés in the sun. They visit Siena and write their postcards, they play their bridge. In my house I am the presence you are familiar with, as you can see me now. I am as women of my professional past often are, made practical through bedroom dealings, made sentimental through fear. I know all that, I do not deny it. I do not care much for the woman I am, but there you are. None of us has a choice in that.

In my garden the shrubs are parched because Quinty's search for someone to tend them is half-hearted due to his desire to save money, even though the money's mine. The tourists upbraid me and sometimes become angry, a withered petal rubbed between finger and thumb, the shreds accusingly held out. The Germans shake their heads in disapproval, the French say it's typical, the English get the hose going and water the azalea urns. I explain to them that all this, too, is how things are. They politely listen, but afterwards they frown and mutter.

Perhaps I'll become old, perhaps not. Perhaps something else will happen in my life, but I doubt it. When the season's over I walk among the shrubs myself, making the most of the colours while they last and the fountain while it flows.

Printed in Canada